THE CELEBRITY DOCTOR'S PROPOSAL

BY
SARAH MORGAN

A MOTHER BY NATURE

BY
CAROLINE ANDERSON

**This month we are delighted to present a special
selection of six classic stories in four books
(two 2-in-1s and two singles) from your favourite
Mills & Boon® Medical™ Romance authors!**

This exclusive bestselling author
collection includes:

THE CELEBRITY DOCTOR'S PROPOSAL
by Sarah Morgan
with
A MOTHER BY NATURE
by Caroline Anderson

THE SURGEON'S GIFT
by Carol Marinelli
with
BUSHFIRE BRIDE
by Marion Lennox

EARTHQUAKE BABY by Amy Andrews

TWICE AS GOOD by Alison Roberts

Collect all four!

THE CELEBRITY DOCTOR'S PROPOSAL

BY
SARAH MORGAN

First published in Great Britain 2003. This edition 2013.
by Mills & Boon, an imprint of Harlequin (UK) Limited,
Eton House, 18-24 Paradise Road, Richmond, Surrey TW9 1SR

© Sarah Morgan 2003

ISBN: 978 0 263 90657 8
ebook ISBN: 978 1 472 01236 4

03-0613

Harlequin (UK) policy is to use papers that are natural, renewable and recyclable products and made from wood grown in sustainable forests. The logging and manufacturing processes conform to the legal environmental regulations of the country of origin.

Printed and bound in Spain
by Blackprint CPI, Barcelona

USA Today bestselling author **Sarah Morgan** writes lively, sexy stories for both Mills & Boon® Modern™ Romance and Medical™ Romance.

As a child Sarah dreamed of being a writer, and although she took a few interesting detours on the way she is now living that dream. With her writing career she has successfully combined business with pleasure, and she firmly believes that reading romance is one of the most satisfying and fat-free escapist pleasures available. Her stories are unashamedly optimistic, and she is always pleased when she receives letters from readers saying that her books have helped them through hard times.

Romantic Times has described her writing as 'action-packed and sexy', and nominated her books for their Reviewer's Choice Awards and their 'Top Pick' slot.

Sarah lives near London with her husband and two children, who innocently provide an endless supply of authentic dialogue. When she isn't writing or reading Sarah enjoys music, movies, and any activity that takes her outdoors.

Readers can find out more about Sarah and her books from her website: www.sarahmorgan.com She can also be found on Facebook and Twitter.

Recent titles by the same author:

AN INVITATION TO SIN *(Sicily's Corretti Dynasty)*
SOLD TO THE ENEMY
WOMAN IN A SHEIKH'S WORLD
(The Private Lives of Public Playboys)
A NIGHT OF NO RETURN
(The Private Lives of Public Playboys)
THE FORBIDDEN FERRARA

CHAPTER ONE

'I CAN manage without you just for the summer. I
want you to go off and breathe mountain air and
forget all about medicine and your patients.' Anna
turned off the motorway and followed the signs for
the airport. She was all brisk efficiency, mentally
ticking off things to be done when she got home.
There were lots of them. *Too many.* Her life was
manic, but she loved it that way. 'And when you
come back your lungs will be better and you'll be
totally refreshed and raring to go.'

At least she hoped he would be because she
couldn't keep this pace up for much longer.

David McKenna glanced across at her with a tired
smile. The smile said it all. 'We both know that that
isn't true. The truth is that you should be looking for
a new partner. I'm getting too old for this, Anna,' he
said gruffly. 'Your dad and I set up the practice almost thirty-five years ago. It's time for new blood.'

'That's right.' His wife, Elizabeth, nodded agree-
ment, a determined look in her clear blue eyes as she
leaned forward from the back seat to join in the conversation. 'It's time for us to enjoy retirement and
our grandchildren.'

Anna glanced in her rear-view mirror and laughed.
'You don't have any grandchildren.'

'Not yet,' Elizabeth agreed placidly as she settled back in her seat and adjusted her seat-belt. 'But it's going to happen shortly.'

Anna carefully fixed her eyes back on the road and clamped her jaw closed. Safer to do that than voice an opinion on *that* particular subject. The McKennas only had one son and he showed absolutely no inclination to settle down. He was far more interested in pursuing a glamorous career as a high-profile media doctor and dating everyone female.

And he drove her nuts. Always had done. Always would do.

Anna ground her teeth and tightened her grip on the steering-wheel. The mere thought of the man was enough to raise her blood pressure to dangerous levels. Every time she turned on the television, Sam McKenna was on the screen, giving his opinion on something medical. Dr Smooth. Dr Handsome. She doubted he even remembered what it was like to be a real doctor. He'd spent far too long in front of the cameras to remember how to diagnose anything other than an ingrowing toenail.

Reminding herself that dwelling on Sam McKenna wasn't good for her health, she turned her attention back to the present and braked neatly as a car cut in front of her. 'You can't possibly talk about retiring, David,' she said briskly, adjusting her speed to ensure a safe following distance. 'The patients love you and you're a brilliant doctor. And you know you enjoy it. You just need to get yourself well again.'

The practice needed him. The practice he and her

father had built from nothing. *She needed him.* She didn't want her life to change. She liked it just the way it was.

David looked at her thoughtfully. 'It will be interesting to see how you find working with the locum I've arranged,' he said idly. 'We both know you've been carrying the lion's share of work for months now. You might find you prefer a younger person who can share the load fairly.'

Anna shot him a quick glance, her brown eyes searching. There was something in his tone that wasn't quite right. But the look he gave her seemed completely innocent so she decided that she must have imagined it.

'I don't want younger,' she said firmly, flicking the indicator and turning towards the airport. 'I want *you.* With all your experience. Which reminds me— we've been so busy, you still haven't told me anything about this locum. You just arranged it all. I hope he knows something about medicine.'

But she wasn't really worried. She trusted David's judgement in everything. If David thought the locum would cope then she had no doubt that he would.

'Of course he does. And you've been far too busy to bother you with the details,' David said vaguely, glancing at his watch and casting a pointed glance at his wife. 'We don't have time for you to dither in the airport, dear.'

'I never dither,' Elizabeth protested with dignity, and her husband smiled.

'So why are we late?'

Anna glanced at them fondly as she pulled up outside the terminal building. Since her own parents had died, Elizabeth and David had stepped into the role. And why not? David had been at medical school with her father. They'd worked together for all those years and she'd taken over her father's role in the practice when he'd been forced to retire because of ill health. It was hardly surprising that the McKennas regarded her as a daughter.

Suddenly filled with an awful feeling that her whole life was about to change, and hating the thought, Anna switched off the engine and turned towards them. 'I want you to be careful,' she said urgently, undoing her seat-belt and reaching across to hug David. 'I want you to rest and take it easy. I couldn't bear it if anything—' She broke off, a lump in her throat, and David hugged her back, as understanding as ever.

'Nothing's going to happen to me, Anna, so stop worrying,' he said gruffly, stroking her long, dark hair with an affectionate hand. 'It was just a nasty dose of pneumonia brought on by mixing with too many ill patients! I'm recovering well and I'm intending to see my grandchildren grow up.'

Anna sniffed and then gave him a shove. 'You're definitely getting senile. I keep telling you, you haven't *got* any grandchildren.'

'Yet.' Over the top of her head, David winked at his wife. 'Gather your belongings, woman. Time to get this show on the road.'

Anna pulled away from him, feeling as though

something momentous was happening. Suddenly she really, really didn't want them to go. Which was utterly ridiculous, she told herself firmly, since this whole sabbatical idea had been her brainchild.

What was the matter with her?

She wasn't the sentimental sort. She was practical and efficient and she really tried not to let emotions get in the way. David and Elizabeth needed a break and it was great that they were finally having one. She should be delighted. It was just the last few months, she decided, stepping out of the car and walking round to retrieve the luggage from the boot. She'd been working too hard. Not having enough time off.

Suddenly she envied David, taking a long break.

She tugged one of the cases from the boot, the reality of her life looming large in her brain. 'David, you still haven't told me about this locum and I—'

'Oh, no!' David peered into the boot and pulled a face. 'Don't say we forgot the green case. Elizabeth, did you remember to bring the green case from the bedroom?'

'It's here.' Anna shifted the luggage. 'Under the blue one.'

She dragged it out and added it to the pile on the pavement.

'Thank goodness for that. It contains all my reading matter.' David rummaged in his pocket for his glasses. 'All right, now, have we got everything? Tickets, passports, money—'

Anna tried again. 'About this locum—'

'Surgery door keys? Did we give Anna the spare set?' Elizabeth fussed in her handbag and Anna realised with a mixture of frustration and affection that neither of them was taking the slightest bit of notice of her. They were already on holiday. Far away from life in a Cornish fishing village. Far away from her and the practice.

David patted his other pocket and smiled. 'I left the spares on the kitchen table. Now, we really need to dash.' He leaned forward and kissed Anna on the cheek. 'No need to come in with us. It was wonderful of you to bring us this far. I hate goodbyes and you have to get back to the needy.'

He waved a hand at a porter, who immediately brought a trolley and loaded the bags.

It was only after the glass doors of the terminal building had closed behind them that Anna realised that he'd left without answering her question about the locum.

She gave a sigh of exasperation and settled herself back in the car, ready for the long drive back to Cornwall. She knew nothing about the doctor David had appointed to cover his absence, except that it was a man. But perhaps it didn't matter. She didn't really need to know the details. Just that he was going to turn up.

Knowing that the summer holidays were almost upon them, Anna just hoped he liked hard work. Because he was going to get it in spades.

*   *   *

'Do you think she's guessed?' From inside the privacy of the terminal building, David watched Anna's little car pull away. 'She kept asking and I kept evading the question. Now she thinks I'm going senile.'

'She was joking. If she'd guessed then we wouldn't be standing here now,' Elizabeth said calmly. 'You know what our Anna is like when she loses her temper. We'd be lying in pieces on the pavement and the fire brigade would be on their way.'

David rubbed a hand over the back of his neck and cast her a dubious look. 'I hope we've done the right thing. Just because you and Anna's mother always had this thing about our children marrying each other…'

'You and Philip had the same dream,' Elizabeth reminded him firmly, 'and don't think Susan and I didn't know it. You wanted to hand the practice over to the two of them. You still do.'

Her husband shot her an impatient look. 'Well, of course I do. It would be perfect. The only thing that isn't perfect is that they can't stand the sight of one another. I have to admit that, much as I would like this whole plan to work, I can't see how it is going to.'

Elizabeth delved into her handbag for a mirror. 'They're both strong characters. Neither would want an insipid partner for the journey through life. They suit each other. It's just that they're both too stubborn and blind to see it themselves and that's just because they've never been forced to spend time together.

Hopefully, by the time we return, they'll have discovered that they can't live without each other.'

David pulled a face. 'They might kill each other first.'

'Possibly.' Elizabeth gave a womanly smile and checked her lipstick. 'But I don't think so. Now, that's our flight they're calling. Are you ready?'

David cast a glance through the window again but Anna's car was long gone. 'There are going to be fireworks in Cornwall tonight,' he muttered, and his wife clipped her bag shut and gave him a little push.

'Then it's just as well we'll be in Switzerland. Now, stop worrying. Everything is in place and we can do no more. We have to leave the rest up to fate and the chemistry that has always been there between those two. Oh…' She gave a smug smile. 'And then there's the whole of the village, of course. I'm sure they'll be only too happy to give fate a helping hand.'

Anna drove home, mentally listing all the urgent jobs that had to be done. *Too many jobs, not enough time.*

She just hoped the locum was a good swimmer because he was going to be thrown right in the deep end with no buoyancy aid.

The sun blazed down on the car, the sea sparkled and Anna turned up the volume on the radio. Cornwall in the summer might be a crazy place to work but it was a beautiful place and she'd never want to live anywhere else. She smiled and the smile lasted for the time it took for her to pull up outside the surgery.

She was met by a film crew and her smile went out like a light.

For a moment she just sat in her little car and stared at the big van and the cameras and then finally she opened the door and ventured outside.

'Are you Dr Riggs?' A man with a microphone scurried over to her and she nodded.

'Yes. Is there a problem? What's going on here?'

'Just hold it right there.' The man held up a hand to halt her movement and gestured to the cameraman. 'We want to get some footage of you greeting Dr McKenna. Wait just a moment…'

Footage? Of her greeting Dr McKenna?

To the best of her knowledge, she'd just waved Dr McKenna off at the airport and there was only one other Dr McKenna that she knew of, and he wasn't…

She glanced at the film crew again and shook her head in denial.

Oh, no. No. No. David wouldn't have done that to her. He couldn't…

Ignoring the man's plea for her to stay put while they prepared to shoot, she slammed her car door and stalked across the small car park towards the group of people gathered by the entrance, a suspicion growing inside her.

'McKenna?' She growled his name like a threat and the people moved to one side. But she had eyes only for one person.

Cool blue eyes swept over her and his mouth tilted slightly. 'Riggs. What an unexpected pleasure.'

He was as handsome as the devil and his arrogance drove her nuts.

'Unexpected?' She slammed her hands on her hips and glared at him. 'This is *my* surgery, McKenna, so how can my presence here be unexpected? What *is* unexpected is the fact that *you're* standing outside it. You'd better have a damn good reason for causing a disturbance.'

He lifted a dark eyebrow in that lazy, careless way that always drove her mad. 'Nice to see you haven't changed. I have to confess that I thought you'd leg it once my father told you that I was coming,' he drawled. 'Never thought you'd show up to greet me. I'm flattered, Riggs. And touched. I obviously mean more to you than I thought.'

'Greet you? I'm not greeting you, and you need to move yourself and that van…' she stabbed a finger towards the offending vehicle, her dark hair swinging over her shoulders as she turned her head '…from my car park before I have it towed away. I have a surgery starting in an hour and at the moment there is no room for my patients.'

'*Our* patients,' he corrected her mildly, not moving an inch, 'and you're going to have to learn not to swear while the cameras are here. You'd be amazed how little it takes to get complaints from viewers. They like their doctors wholesome and clean-living. No sex or swearing.'

She opened her mouth to make a sharp observation

about his reputation for the former and then stopped herself. It wasn't worth it. She really didn't care about his sex life. And anyway, something he'd said was jarring inside her head.

She stared at him, drew breath and finally mentally reran the last few sentences. 'Hold on.' She lifted a hand as if to ward him off. 'What did you mean when you said that your dad should have told me you were coming? Tell me he didn't know you were coming. Tell me this isn't what I think it is.'

Surely David wouldn't have done that to her.

He couldn't...

Sam leaned impossibly broad shoulders against the wall and looked at her, a trace of amusement lighting his blue eyes. 'He's been nagging me for more than three months, Riggs. Finally he resorted to emotional blackmail. ''I need this break, Sam, and if I can't find a decent locum I can't leave poor Anna.'''

His imitation of his father was so good that if she hadn't been so horrified, Anna would have laughed. Instead she gaped at him. 'Locum? *You're* the locum?' Her voice cracked and all her important bodily functions like breathing and staying upright suddenly seemed threatened. It had to be a joke. 'You have a sick sense of humour, McKenna.'

He shrugged. 'Better a sick sense of humour than no sense of humour at all.' He gave her a meaningful look. 'Now, enough chatting. You can thank me later.' He straightened and waved a hand to the cameraman who was still hovering. 'In the meantime, we have work to do.'

She clenched her fists in her palms. He was implying that she had no sense of humour. He'd always accused her of being too uptight. Of not knowing how to relax. Of planning every detail of her life.

'What I mean is, there is no way your dad would arrange for you to be the locum,' she said, her teeth gritted as she spoke. 'He knows we'd kill each other.'

'That possibility does exist,' Sam agreed, stifling a yawn and moving past her with a loose-limbed stride that betrayed absolutely no sense of urgency. 'However, I reckon that if you stay in your space and I stay in mine, we should just about manage to co-exist without significant injury.'

'Wait a minute.' She elbowed her way past the cameraman and planted herself in front of Sam again. Strands of dark hair trailed over her face and she brushed them back with an impatient hand. 'If you're really the locum, why are *they* here?' She glared at the film crew as if they were a disease and he muttered something incomprehensible under his breath.

'They're here because I have a job to do,' he said bluntly. 'Normally I'd be in London, filming a new series. It seems I'm spending the summer in Cornwall so we've had to make some changes to the programme. We've had to adapt. You ought to try it some time.'

At that point, the woman who had been hovering at a tactful distance stepped forward. 'It's going to be brilliant, Dr Riggs.' She reached out and shook Anna's hand. 'I'm Polly. I'm the producer of this series of *Medical Matters*. When Sam told us he was going to be working down here, we decided to do a whole series on summer health. It will be fantastic. We can look at taking care of yourself in the sun, first aid—everything families should know before they go on holiday.'

Warm and friendly, she listed her ideas with enthusiasm, and in normal circumstances Anna would have liked her immediately. But these weren't normal circumstances. And she couldn't like anyone who looked at Sam McKenna with such blatant adoration.

'This is a busy practice,' she said crisply. 'We work flat out to cater to the needs of the locals and at this time of year our numbers double because of the tourist population. We don't have time for film crews.'

'But that's the beauty of it,' Polly said cheerfully, 'Sam already knows the score. He's used to being filmed all the time. There'll be very little intrusion, I can assure you.'

'The patients won't like it.'

'The patients will love it,' Sam predicted dryly, lifting a hand and shielding his eyes from the sun. 'And if they don't, they don't have to take part. They always have the right to refuse to be filmed. But I can tell you now that they won't.'

'We're going to do a variety of different things,' Polly explained eagerly, 'a straightforward *Medical Matters* from the surgery, which is our usual format, but we're also going to film on location, do some first-aid stuff on the beach—that sort of thing.'

'It sounds as though you've got it all worked out,' Anna said frostily, her eyes on Sam who simply shrugged. 'We need to talk, McKenna. And we need to do it now.'

Polly glanced towards the cameraman who was still hovering. 'Perhaps we should film you discussing it—it might be interesting.'

'Well, unless you want to film something which needs a warning for bad language and violence, I suggest you switch off the camera and go and have a cream tea in the village,' Anna said sweetly, her eyes still blazing into Sam's. 'You and me. Inside. Now.'

Without waiting for the sharp comment that she knew would come, she turned and strode to the front door, unlocking it and letting herself in. Functioning on automatic, she switched off the alarm and picked up the post, aware that he was behind her.

'Don't you have a receptionist any more? What happened to Glenda?' He peered behind the empty reception area with a frown and she gritted her teeth.

She didn't need his comments on the way the surgery ran.

'Glenda is sometimes a bit late,' she muttered, dropping the post behind Reception, ready for Glenda to sort out when she arrived. 'She'll be here in a minute.'

'Late?' He frowned, his expression suddenly thoughtful. 'But she used to be the most punctual person in the world. Really dedicated. Why would Glenda be late?'

Anna bit her lip. She'd asked herself the same question a few times lately and she was steeling herself to address the matter with Glenda. But there was no way she was discussing this with Sam McKenna.

'It's really none of your business,' she said coldly, and he gave a dismissive shrug.

'Fair enough. Just didn't sound much like the Glenda I used to know, that's all.'

'Well, you haven't exactly been spending much time around here lately and people do change,' Anna said tartly.

He ran a hand over his jaw, his expression thoughtful. 'Have you tackled her?'

She gave an impatient sigh. 'No. No, actually, I haven't. If you must know, I haven't had time to breathe or eat in the last few months, let alone sit down and get cosy with the staff.'

His eyes narrowed and his gaze swept her face. 'That bad, huh?'

She gritted her teeth again and cursed herself for showing emotion in front of Sam. He would waste no time throwing it back at her. 'Not bad. Just busy. And if it's all right by you, I'd like to drop the subject now. When I need your advice, I'll ask for it.'

'No, you wouldn't.' He hooked his fingers into the pockets of his jeans and lounged against the reception desk. He had a lean, athletic physique, honed to perfection by his obsession with dangerous sports. 'You wouldn't ask my advice if you were hanging off a cliff by your fingernails. You're so crazily independent, Riggs, that you'd drown rather than ask someone to throw you a lifebelt.'

'Then it's a good job I'm not drowning,' she said coldly, walking through to the reception area and automatically picking up some scattered toys and returning them to the basket. 'And for your information, I'd take the lifebelt as long as you weren't the one throwing it. Now, are we going to sort this problem out?'

He shrugged and stifled a yawn. 'What's there to sort out? You need a locum. I'm here.'

She straightened one of the chairs. 'As far as I'm concerned, those two statements are not linked.'

He drew a breath and she lifted a hand to indicate that she hadn't finished. 'What I need, McKenna, is a serious doctor willing to do some serious work. What I *don't* need is some image-hungry film-star medic with an over-inflated ego which is going to get in my way every time I try and see a patient.'

To her surprise and immense irritation, he smiled. An all-male, sexy smile that tugged something deep in her pelvis.

Damn, he irritated her.

Completely aware of that fact, he straightened up and strolled towards her, a dangerous gleam in his blue eyes as they swept her face. 'Oh, boy, oh, boy, I really do unsettle you, don't I, Riggs? Why is that, I wonder?'

'Do you want a list?' She backed away, trying to maintain her personal space. 'And I can't imagine this is exactly your idea of heaven either. Why did you agree to it?'

His blue eyes glittered. 'I told you. Emotional blackmail on the part of my father. He was ill. He needed a holiday. He couldn't find anyone else. That kind of thing. Tugs at the heart.'

'You don't have a heart.'

He grinned. 'Ouch. Been reading my press cuttings again, Riggs?'

'Hardly.' Her glance was impatient. 'The way you run your love life—or should I say sex life—is your business. But the practice is my business. Your dad certainly never mentioned to me that he was having trouble finding anyone.'

Sam gave a careless shrug. 'Well, the fact is I'm here now. Make the most of me.'

She angled her head and lifted an eyebrow. 'Excuse me? I'm supposed to be honoured that you've graced us with your presence? Let me tell you something, Dr Charm, I'm not at all convinced you'll know a real patient when you see one. You see, here in real life surgery land, the problems aren't staged.'

His gaze didn't flicker. 'Is that so?'

'What happens when you deal with something that doesn't make good television? Are you going to pass them through to me? Or do you grab a textbook?'

He examined his fingernails thoughtfully. 'You really aren't going to make this easy, are you, Riggs?'

She bit her lip. Somehow he made her feel small, childish. 'It's just that this practice is busy,' she said wearily, sweeping her dark hair away from her face and risking eye contact. 'I need proper help. Heavy-duty help.'

Sharp blue eyes searched hers. 'My dad hasn't been pulling his weight, has he?'

She didn't trust herself not to give too much away so her own eyes slid from his, away from that penetrating gaze that saw too much. 'Your dad is a good doctor. The best.'

'But he hasn't got the stamina that he used to,' Sam said softly, running a hand over the back of his neck and giving a frustrated sigh. 'Damn. It's hard, watching your parents grow older. You have this vision of how they are and you never want it to change. I always knew this moment would come, but that doesn't make it any easier.'

She frowned. 'What moment?'

His hand dropped to his side and his glance was ironic. 'The moment when I have to decide whether to go into the family business.'

'You mean, take your father's place?' She stared at him in horror. 'You can't possibly be serious! You don't need me to remind you that you couldn't wait to leave Cornwall at the earliest opportunity. Even if we go along with your dad's plan, it's only short term. No one suggested it was for ever. He's coming back...'

Sam looked at her. 'And when he does, he'll retire and spend his days fishing.'

Anna shook her head. 'He won't retire.'

Sam gave a sigh and stabbed long fingers through his dark hair. 'He has to. We both know that. And you being stubborn about it isn't going to change that fact.' He paced over to the reception area. 'But while he's working out how to break the news to you that this is all too much for him and he doesn't want to do it any more, we'll get the place in order. And work out a plan. Things are going to have to change around here.'

Anna felt as though she'd been doused in cold water.

She didn't want things to change. She loved the way the practice was now. She loved working with David. They understood each other.

Was Sam right? Was David really planning to tell her that he was going to retire from the practice?

She sank onto the nearest chair, her legs suddenly wobbly. It was a moment before she realised that Sam was pressing a glass of water into her hand.

'Drink something,' he said roughly. 'You've obviously been working too hard. You look done in. You're pale and you've got black rings under your eyes. You always were too stubborn to ask for help. I'm going to get rid of the film crew for now and then come back and we can work out what's to be done.'

Anna took a sip of water and found her voice. 'Whatever's to be done,' she muttered, 'I really, *really* don't want to do it with you, McKenna.'

He was the last person in the world that she could imagine developing a good working relationship with.

He laughed and rose to his feet in a fluid movement. 'Likewise. But seeing as that is what fate has decreed, I'd say we're both in for an interesting summer. Looks like we're going to be meeting at dawn. Swords or pistols?'

SHE hadn't changed a bit.

Sam strode out of the reception area and paused in the foyer, trying to get his emotions back under control before he faced the camera crew. Anna Riggs always did that to him. Drove him so mad that he needed to pump iron for a week in order to burn off the frustration coursing around his body. Thanks to some nifty avoidance tactics on both their parts, they hadn't seen each other for a couple of years, but she was still the same hard-nosed, bossy control freak she'd always been. Not at all his kind of woman. He liked his women soft and gentle. Anna Riggs was about as soft as steel. And the fact that she had a pair of legs that stopped a man in his tracks didn't do anything to change his opinion of her.

And he'd allowed himself to be manipulated into spending the summer with her.

He smashed a fist against the wall and inhaled deeply. Damn, she was right. They were going to kill each other. What had his father been thinking of, arranging for them to work together when he knew that there was so much animosity between them? When he knew that they were just *so* different? It was all very well saying that they didn't need to see much of each other, but they were running a small practice. They were the only two doctors. How could they *not* see each other?

And how was he going to cope with Anna being confrontational and prickly with a camera stuck in his face all day?

He gritted his teeth and applied his brain to the problem.

The first thing was that the cameras certainly couldn't be allowed free access, otherwise they could find themselves filming bloodshed. He'd have to stage each shoot carefully, making sure that Anna wasn't within firing distance.

And the second thing was that he was going to work as independently as possible. Surely he could just see his patients and she could see hers? Did they really need to talk much?

And he wasn't going to involve himself in the practice. He was going to do the job and then see what happened. And if his father decided to retire, he'd find him the best possible replacement. And it wasn't going to be him. Hadn't his parents always accepted that this wasn't the practice for him? His life was in London. He'd chosen a different path. He didn't want to work here permanently any more than Anna wanted him to.

Satisfied that, given sufficient thought, it would be possible to minimise the contact between them, he finally pushed open the glass door of the surgery and walked into the car park.

*   *   *

Glenda turned up, breathless and apologetic, five minutes before surgery started. She dropped her bag behind the reception desk and smoothed her hair, clearly flustered.

'Are you OK?' Anna frowned in concern and Glenda gave a bright smile.

'I'm fine. Sorry I'm a bit late. I was caught up.'

Caught up with what? Anna wanted to ask, but now wasn't the time with a busy surgery about to start and Sam strolling across the reception area as if he'd worked here all his life.

How could he be so relaxed?

'Hi, Glenda.' He gave the receptionist a big hug and for some reason that she couldn't quite identify Anna felt her tension rise.

It was just her that he needled and goaded. With everyone else he was capable of being extremely civilised. Warm. People in the village had always adored Sam McKenna and now he was a major TV personality they never stopped talking about him.

Glenda's face softened. 'Oh— Dr McKenna. How lovely to see you.' She pulled away and tried to straighten her hair, her movements jerky and un-coordinated. 'I suppose you'll be helping our Anna. Good thing, too. She needs some help around here. She's been struggling for far too long.'

Anna's frown deepened. Glenda knew that she and Sam didn't see eye to eye on anything. Why would she think it was a good thing that he'd arrived? Had she known that David had appointed him as locum?

Or was it just that she wasn't concentrating because she had something else on her mind?

She hated to admit that Sam was right about anything, but suddenly Anna decided that a conversation with the receptionist was becoming a priority.

'Busy surgery.' Glenda flicked on the computer and checked the appointments, seeming more flustered than usual. 'Open those doors and let the battle commence.'

Resolving to tackle Glenda in private later, Anna turned to Sam. 'I know that this is throwing you in at the deep end, but can you take your father's surgery? I expect you'll know some of the patients anyway, and if you need to know anything that isn't in the notes you can buzz through to me. Press 4 on your phone. Or I'm just next door.'

Sam lifted an eyebrow, his expression mocking. 'Sure you don't want to sit in with me, just to be sure that I don't kill anyone?'

She gritted her teeth. 'I don't think you're about to kill anyone.'

'No.' His voice was dry. 'You just think my clinical skills are rustier than an old garden fork.'

'I'm just aware that it's probably a long time since you did a consultation that wasn't staged. The way our surgeries run at the moment, there's not a lot of time to look in a textbook between cases. And you only get the one take.' Anna sucked in a breath. 'I was *trying* to be helpful. Next time I won't bother.'

'Good idea. You worry about your own patients. I'll worry about mine.' Without giving her time to respond, Sam strode down the corridor towards his father's consulting room.

'I'm going to kill him.' For the first time since she was five years old, Anna found herself wanting to stamp her foot. With an enormous effort of will she managed to restrict herself to an inward growl of frustration. 'Well, at least we don't need to change the name on his door,' she muttered, and then turned to Glenda who was watching open-mouthed. 'Don't look like that.'

Glenda found her voice. 'Nice to see that neither of you have changed,' she said faintly, and Anna sighed.

'Oh, don't make me feel guilty. Maybe I shouldn't have spoken to him like that, but the guy drives me crazy. And whatever he says to the contrary, he hasn't seen a real patient for ages. Diseases that they stage for the camera aren't the same thing at all.'

Glenda frowned. 'Anna, I thought he'd—'

'He won't admit it, of course, because he's a man, and a man with a big ego,' Anna said, reaching forward to pick up a pile of results, 'but you'd better keep an eye on him, Glenda. If you think he's got a problem with someone, let me know because his pride won't let him do it himself and he certainly won't ask me.'

Glenda looked confused. 'But, Anna, I thought that Dr McKenna—'

'Oh, let's drop the subject for now,' Anna muttered, deciding that she'd had enough of talking about Sam McKenna. 'Just buzz me if you think there's a problem.'

With that, she walked through to her own surgery

and settled herself behind her desk. Instantly she felt calmer and more in control. This was her space, a place that she loved, and even having Sam next door couldn't spoil it.

She switched on her computer and pressed the buzzer for her first patient. Seconds later there was a tap on the door and a young mother entered, struggling with a wriggling toddler.

'Hello, Heather, how are things?' Anna had been in the year above Heather at school and the two of them were still friends.

That was the wonderful thing about general practice, she mused as she stood up and walked around her desk to admire the baby. You knew the patients. Not like Accident and Emergency where she'd spent six months during her GP rotational training. There the patients were little more than cases and numbers. In general practice the patients had lives. They were real. And the family doctor was part of all that. It was a job worth doing.

'It isn't me, Anna,' Heather murmured, settling herself in the chair and trying to persuade the whining toddler to sit still with her. 'It's Grace. She's had a personality change lately and, frankly, I'm ready to scream.'

Anna reached for her favourite puppet and slipped her hand inside. 'Hi, Grace,' she said cheerfully, waggling the furry fox at the toddler. 'Nice of you to visit me.'

The little girl stopped grizzling at once and stared

at the puppet, transfixed. Then she held out a hand to stroke its nose. 'Fox.'

'That's right.' Anna waggled the puppet. 'Fox.' While the little girl's attention was caught she questioned the mother. 'So what's been happening, Heather?'

'It's Grace. She just doesn't seem to listen to me any more,' the young mother said helplessly. 'She takes absolutely no notice of anything I say and she's so loud all of a sudden. She shouts all the time.'

Anna frowned. 'How long has it been going on for?'

'I don't know.' Heather shrugged. 'A couple of months, I suppose. We had a terrible winter with her as you know. We virtually lived in your surgery with colds.'

Anna tickled Grace's ear with the puppet and reached across her desk for some equipment. 'How's her speech?'

'Well, she was doing really well but if anything she's slipped back.' Heather gave a rueful smile and cuddled the little girl closer. 'Whoever said being a mother was easy? Do you think it's just her age? That she's just being naughty?'

'No, I don't. I suspect that she might have glue ear,' Anna said calmly, judging whether it was a good moment to abandon the fox in favour of a clinical examination. 'Heather, hold out your hand. I need you to take over acting duties while I take a look at her ears.'

Heather dutifully slipped her hand inside the puppet, leaving Anna to concentrate on the little girl.

'Grace, I'm just going to look inside the fox's ears,' she said cheerfully, 'and then I'm going to look inside yours.'

Grace watched with round eyes as Anna pretended to look inside the puppet's ears, then she sat still while Anna gently used the auriscope to examine her.

'I'm just checking that there's no wax or foreign bodies,' she murmured as she examined the eardrum. 'Oh, yes, there's the problem. I see it. The eardrum is very dull and looks indrawn. She definitely has glue ear.'

'Glue ear?' Heather frowned. 'What exactly is that?'

'It's a condition where the child has fluid deep in the ear,' Anna explained, 'but without signs of infection. It's called glue ear because the fluid tends to be like runny glue—thick, clear and sticky.'

Heather pulled a face. 'Sounds awful. But why does that make her shout?'

'Because I suspect it is affecting her hearing.' Anna reached for a pad and scribbled a simple diagram. 'People can hear because sound waves are transmitted via their eardrums and tiny bones inside the middle ear. The eardrum and bones vibrate.'

Heather stared at the diagram and pulled a face. 'I was always bottom in biology.'

Anna smiled and put the pencil down. 'Doesn't matter. All you need to know is that in glue ear the middle ear, which is usually full of air, becomes filled with a sticky fluid and that damps down the vibrations.'

'And stops the child from hearing?'

'It can do.' Anna stood up. 'It's very common in children so don't think Grace is the only one. Speech is affected because she isn't hearing well.'

'So what do we do about it?'

'Fortunately glue ear almost always settles down of its own accord but if Grace's hearing gets worse then we may need to look at referring her to an ENT specialist. But at the moment I don't think we should do that. I'm going to refer her to the audiology department for an assessment of her hearing and we'll take it from there.'

'So she doesn't need antibiotics or anything now?'

Anna shook her head. 'She doesn't have an infection so they won't work. I'm fairly confident that if we leave it alone it will go by itself, but we'll keep a close eye on it and if we're worried at any point then we can refer her.'

'I'm not wild about her having an operation,' Heather admitted, and Anna smiled sympathetically.

'I doubt it will be necessary so let's cross that bridge when we come to it. I'll refer her to Audiology today and you'll get a letter from them in the next month or so, inviting Grace to come for a test.'

'Thanks, Anna.' Heather stood up and brushed her curls away from her face, her cheeks slightly pink. 'I heard a rumour that our Sam's back. Is it true that he's going to be working here for the summer?'

Anna stiffened. Not if she could find a way out of it. 'Well, he's here at the moment, but he may not be able to stay for the whole summer.'

At least, not if she had anything to do with it.

'Oh, I hope he can,' Heather enthused, shifting the toddler more comfortably in her arms. 'I mean, it's so brilliant having him. I never miss him on the telly. He's so sympathetic, isn't he? So warm. Can't believe it's our Sam, really.'

Our Sam.

Anna clamped her jaws together and resisted the temptation to point out that Sam McKenna was a gifted actor and was warm when it suited him to appear that way. With her he was about as warm as the polar icepack.

Then she remembered that Heather had had a massive crush on Sam when they'd been at school. As had most of the girls. Except her.

Anna rolled her eyes. She and Sam had been thrown together a lot because of their parents' working relationship and at one time she knew that both sets of parents had harboured a fond hope that they might take over the practice. But that had never been an option for Sam. He hadn't been able to wait to get away.

And just as well, she thought briskly, otherwise there would have been bloodshed. She and Sam would *not* have made a good partnership. They clashed on just about everything.

Heather was still talking. 'Everyone thinks it would be great if he stayed permanently,' she gossiped happily. 'I mean, it used to be both your dads, then it was you and his dad and now it could be the two of you.'

'I don't think so.' Anna rose to her feet so rapidly she almost knocked the chair over. Aware that Heather was looking at her in surprise, Anna produced a smile. 'You're jumping the gun, Heather. This is temporary. Just temporary.'

And she certainly didn't want that sort of gossip and speculation spreading around the village.

'Well, you never really know how things are going to turn out, do you?' Heather said sagely, standing up and reaching for her bag. 'Thanks, Anna. See you soon.'

She left the surgery and Anna stared after her. Heather had said, *Everyone thinks*. So did that mean that everyone in the village were already aware that Sam was here? Did that mean that the whole village already thought that this might be a permanent arrangement?

No, no, no.

She covered her face with her hands and stifled a groan. If it turned out to be a permanent arrangement then she would have to leave. There was no *way* she could spend every day working alongside Sam. Her blood pressure wouldn't be able to stand it.

But he wouldn't stay, she consoled herself, applying logic to the situation. No way. Sam had chosen a very different life for himself. The City. Bright lights. Fame and fortune. He wouldn't last five minutes in a sleepy Cornish fishing village. In fact, she doubted he'd even last the summer. He'd already made it clear that there wasn't enough here to keep him entertained.

Cheered by that thought, she buzzed for her next patient and steadily worked her way through her afternoon list.

When she finally emerged from her surgery, she found Glenda deep in conversation with Sam who was perched on the desk, an intent expression on his handsome face.

Glenda coloured and broke off the moment she saw Anna, and Sam slid off the desk and walked towards her.

'So, how did your surgery go, Riggs? Nothing you needed to ask me about?'

She ignored his sarcastic tone and gave him a withering look. 'When I need help, I'll consult a textbook.'

'How boring,' he drawled, lifting a hand and tucking a strand of her long dark hair behind her ear. 'Better watch it, the country girl is trying to escape.'

Country girl.

It was what he'd always called her when she'd been little. He'd loved to tease her for being so at home in the outdoors. Unlike him, she'd never been comfortable with bright lights and hordes of people.

Aware that his fingers were still in her hair, she jerked her head away from him with a frosty glare, handed Glenda a pile of results for filing and stalked back to her room. For a moment she just stood there, sucking in deep breaths, and then she moved over to the wash-basin and opened the taps, splashing her face with cold water to cool her burning cheeks.

'Drowning yourself?'

She reached for the towel, dried her face and turned slowly. 'Just answer me that one question, McKenna. Why? Why did you come here? We both know that a GP practice in Cornwall isn't where you see your future. So why are you here? Or have they run out of women in London?'

He strolled into the room and leaned narrow hips against her desk, wickedly handsome and altogether too dangerous for words. 'You know the answer to that. I'm here because Dad asked me to come. And because Cornwall isn't a bad place in the summer.'

He was winding her up and she knew it. Even he couldn't fail to like Cornwall in the summer. Especially as being here would undoubtedly allow him to indulge in his favourite sports. She knew he'd be kite-surfing and windsurfing the moment he'd unpacked his suitcase.

'So this is a free holiday.' She ground her teeth. 'You could have said no. You *should* have said no.'

He raised a dark eyebrow. 'Why?'

'Because you know this isn't going to work, that's why.'

'I hate to disappoint you but saying no to a sick man, especially when that sick man is my father, isn't exactly my forte.' He gazed at one of the photographs on her wall and Anna bit her lip, hating the intrusion into her personal space. 'That's nice. Bedruthan steps. Do you remember that time we were almost cut off by the tide? You always loved that beach when we were kids.'

'Stop changing the subject. You could have pretended you couldn't get away. You could have encouraged him to arrange a locum.'

'He did arrange a locum. Me.' Sam ran a hand over the back of his neck and shot her an impatient look. 'All right, you tell me how I was supposed to say no. With Dad so ill and Mum so worried, how was I supposed to say no?'

'You've said no before, lots of times.'

'When he's asked me to join the practice, to be part of the family firm,' Sam agreed. 'This is different. This is an emergency. I don't say no to emergencies.'

'Just to commitment.' The words were out before she could stop them and even before she saw the narrowing of his eyes she regretted them. 'Forget I said that. The way you run your life is none of my business.'

'No, it isn't.' He folded his arms across his chest, his gaze fixed on hers. 'But the way I run my life clearly bothers you.'

Suddenly the room felt unusually warm. 'It doesn't bother me. What bothers me is that you're going to swan in here for a few weeks or until you get bored then leave us in the lurch.'

'No, that isn't what bothers you.' His gaze didn't shift. 'What really bothers you is the fact that you haven't planned this and we both know that you have to plan everything. You think you have your whole life sorted, don't you, Riggs?'

'There's nothing wrong with planning.' She wondered why she was defending herself to someone she didn't even like.

'Except that life has a way of throwing you surprises. And it's harder to cope with surprises if you're inflexible.'

'I'm not inflexible. And you're not a surprise, McKenna. You're a nightmare.'

'I promised my father I'd stay for the summer and that's what I intend to do.'

'Along with your film crew.'

He shrugged. 'Life goes on. When I return to London in the autumn I'll want to pick up where I left off. The film crew is part of my life.'

Anna shook her head. 'It isn't going to work, McKenna.'

'It'll work if you don't get all high and mighty on me. Why shouldn't it?' He was as direct as she was, hard and uncompromising in his approach to life. 'Because I'm the only person you can't control, Riggs? Because I don't fit your image of a doctor? Because I don't do things the way you do them?'

She tilted her head, her gaze cool. 'Because you drive me nuts.'

'Likewise.'

Their eyes locked in combat for endless minutes and then she gave a sigh. 'All right. Let's look at the facts here. I need help and I don't have time to look for a new locum. You're here. You can stay until I find a suitable replacement. But there are rules.'

'You amaze me.' He folded his arms across his broad chest. 'And there I was thinking you were such a relaxed, laid-back person. Always willing to go with the flow.'

She chose to ignore his sarcasm. 'No filming without my permission, and the patients' permission, and if it interferes with your workload then it stops.'

His eyes glittered dangerously. 'Anything else?'

'Yes, actually.' Her tone was businesslike with just a touch of frost around the edges. 'I'm the partner in this practice, you're the locum. You do things my way. If you disagree, we still do things my way.'

'What if my way's better?'

She gritted her teeth. He was doing it on purpose, of course. Annoying her. Irritating her. Winding her up so tightly that she was ready to explode. 'It won't be. You don't have any experience of primary care. And even if you did, why would you even care about changing things? We both know you won't be hanging around long enough to make an impact.'

He studied her carefully. 'Unfortunately, Riggs, your rules don't work for me. If I see something that I think needs changing I'm going to say so and we're going to talk about it. I may be the locum but I still have an opinion on how the practice is run and you're going to listen to it. Starting with Glenda.'

Anna stared at him. 'What about Glenda?'

'What do you know about her home life?'

Anna frowned, thrown by the sudden shift in the

conversation. 'Well, I know she lives with her elderly mother in a cottage down by the harbour. Her mother is your father's patient and to be honest I haven't seen much of her for the past few years so I can't honestly say I know her. She doesn't go out much. Why?'

'Because her mother is the reason Glenda was late this morning. She had her buttons done up in the wrong holes,' Sam said calmly. 'She hasn't told me much yet but she hinted that her mother isn't herself.'

'I didn't know that. Your father hasn't said anything.' Anna felt a twinge of guilt that she hadn't found the time to question Glenda's lateness herself. If she was honest, she'd found it more annoying than concerning. It hadn't occurred to her that something might be wrong. She bit her lip. She was the doctor, for goodness' sake. She should have noticed that Glenda was upset about something.

It annoyed her that Sam had spotted it first and it made her feel guilty.

Resolving to talk to the receptionist immediately, Anna poured herself a glass of water and took a few sips.

'This practice is stretched to the limit,' Sam said grimly, 'and we need efficient staff. If Glenda can't perform the role then we need to get someone in who can.'

Anna slammed the glass down on the table. 'And what are you proposing to do with Glenda?' Her eyes sparked into his. 'Fire her?'

'No, actually.' He stood in the centre of her consulting room, legs planted firmly apart, totally comfortable and maddeningly sure of himself. 'Support her. And expecting her to fulfil a full-time employment commitment with what I suspect is a major family problem brewing isn't support.'

Anna sagged slightly, her conscience pricking her. 'Oh, hell. You're right,' she muttered, rubbing her fingers across her temples to ease the ache. 'I should have noticed that something was wrong. She hasn't been herself for weeks now I come to think of it.'

'Don't blame yourself.' Sam's voice was deep and slightly roughened. It was the voice that turned millions of female viewers to jelly. 'I know you've had your work cut out covering for my father while he's been so ill. But now it's time to accept some help. You can't run the whole show by yourself, Riggs. No matter what you may think of yourself, you're not superwoman.'

She felt nothing like superwoman.

Anna's hand dropped into her lap. Suddenly she didn't have the energy to argue. 'All right.' Her voice was brisk and professional. 'We'll make the best of the situation. You take your father's surgeries but if you have any queries, you refer them to me.'

He arched an eyebrow. 'You think I can't cope?'

'I think it's been a long time since you've seen real patients. I'm not prepared for you to practise on mine.'

He would never admit he was wrong and she couldn't take that risk with people's lives.

'Fine. If I get stuck, I'll call.' His voice was a

drawl and she had a feeling he was mocking her. 'Anything else?'

'We share the clinics and the house calls. The deputising service does the on call and weekends.' She took a deep breath. 'And any filming or fancy stuff that you want to do takes place outside surgery time.'

He gave a wry smile. 'Thanks for the welcome, Riggs.'

She stiffened. What did he want? Applause? 'If you're expecting a red carpet and a cheering crowd, you're not going to get one here.'

'Evidently.'

'And I'll sort out Glenda.'

'Her mother is my patient.'

'Your father's patient.'

He shrugged. 'Same thing. As you just said, I'm taking my father's patients.' He gave a humourless laugh as he realised what he'd just said. 'Following the old man's dream.'

'But not your dream, thank goodness.'

He lifted an eyebrow. 'Why "thank goodness"?'

'Because if you decided to take over your father's half of the practice permanently, we'd really be in trouble.' Frowning, Anna studied him. 'We can make this work because it's temporary, McKenna. Let's both remember that. Temporary.'

'If you think I'd want to make this a permanent arrangement then you're even more deranged than I already think you are.' He stifled a yawn and strolled out of the room as if he had all the time in the world, leaving her ready to punch something.

CHAPTER THREE

'SUBSIDENCE.'

'Sorry?' Anna juggled several bags and her mobile phone as she tried to concentrate on what the surveyor was saying. She still had one more house call to make before she finished for the evening.

'This cottage that you're hoping to buy has subsidence.' The man stepped back and angled his head. 'Didn't you notice that the windows are crooked?'

Anna followed his gaze, squinting against the bright evening sunshine. 'It's one of the reasons I fell in love with it. Crooked windows add to the character, Mike. They're what makes it quaint.'

'They're what makes it dangerous and a complete no-no for your mortgage company.' The surveyor looked at her sympathetically. 'I hope you're better at diagnosing patients than you are buildings, Doc. If this was an animal and you were a vet, you'd be putting it down.'

Anna groaned and dropped two of her bags. 'Mike, no! I don't need this. Tell me you're joking. You have to be joking. This is my new home.'

Her dream.

Her cottage by the beach.

'Not joking.' He shook his head solemnly, stepping back to look at the cottage with a gloomy expression on his face. 'It's a bad lot, Anna, love. Let it go.'

'Let it go? No way.' Anna stuck out her chin at an angle that made the surveyor sigh.

'Determination and backbone isn't going to fix this one, I'm afraid. The only way this is going to be yours is if you put up all the cash yourself.'

Anna almost growled with frustration. 'You know I can't do that.'

'Or find a rich man.'

Anna kicked a stone at the mere thought. 'I don't attract rich men. Rich men want useless trophy wives who'll agree with everything they say.'

Mike laughed. 'Not much chance of that with you. In which case, I think you're looking at another house, Anna.'

Anna shook her head in denial and disbelief. 'But it's all going through. I've chosen the curtains…'

Mike shrugged. 'Hang them in your next house,' he advised, 'but you have to give this one a miss. It's a bundle of trouble.'

Anna closed her eyes and breathed deeply. Did nothing in her life ever go right any more?

'It isn't exactly that simple, is it? I sold my flat two weeks ago, Mike, on the strength of moving into this place. I've been lodging with the McKennas while I've been waiting for the sale to go through.'

And much as she loved their place, it wasn't the same as having somewhere of her own.

'And they're away for the summer so they'll be glad to have you in their house for the duration.'

'It was just temporary.' She ran her fingers through her dark hair in a gesture of frustration. 'Just a couple of weeks to tide me over.'

Anna looked at the little cottage that had been part of her dreams.

Subsidence.

For a moment she let the wild, romantic side of her that she rarely acknowledged enjoy a wonderful dream about somehow finding the money and moving in, despite the subsidence. Then the practical side took over. As it always did.

'OK.' Her voice was weary and resigned. 'So I'll tell the solicitors that it's all off. And I'll start house-hunting again. In the meantime, I'll have to find a place to rent.'

Damn, damn and double damn. With David away and her workload already ridiculously heavy, she didn't have time for house-hunting. And anyway, she didn't want any old house. She wanted this one. She'd coveted it for years.

'In the summer?' Mike snapped his briefcase shut and gave her a rueful smile. 'Forget it, love. No chance. Why not just stay on at the McKennas'?'

Because she wanted her own home.

And because Sam was there.

Anna bit her lip.

'I'll find a place to rent.' She lifted her chin in a gesture of pure determination that had Mike sighing.

Anyone who had known Anna Riggs as a child recognised that look, and it wasn't to be messed with.

'OK, well, good luck. And call me when you find your next place. I don't want you ripped off.'

Anna gave him a wan smile. 'Thanks, Mike. I think.'

It wasn't his fault he'd had to give her bad news and she knew he had her best interests at heart.

That was another benefit of living in a small community, she mused as she watched Mike walk back up the path towards his car. People looked out for each other. Cared. There was no way that would happen in a city. Where was the goodwill among strangers?

Acknowledging that all the goodwill in the world was unlikely to find her a place to rent at the peak of the tourist season, Anna carried her bags back to her car, made her last call and drove up the coast road to the McKennas'.

Their spectacular house sat on a curve in the bay, just steps from the beach. It was the best property for miles around and it had been the McKennas' home for ever. Usually she loved coming here. Just walking up the path and breathing in the sea air was enough to put her in a good mood.

Not today.

Today, Sam's low, black sports car was parked outside, a blatant statement of masculine self-indulgence that irritated her beyond belief. Why couldn't he just drive a normal family car?

Because Sam McKenna wasn't a normal family man.

He was a stallion on the loose. A lone male who

had no intention of attaching himself to anything or anybody. And he was undoubtedly *not* going to be pleased to discover that he'd just got himself a housemate. It would seriously cramp his style.

Anna almost smiled at the thought. If living here for a while was going to irritate Sam, maybe it wouldn't be such a bad thing after all.

Bracing herself for conflict, she let herself in and paused. The house was silent so she opened the French windows that led from the spacious sitting-room and walked onto the bleached wooden deck that overlooked the beach below. Squinting at the foaming waves, she could see several surfers and gave a short laugh. Undoubtedly one of them would be Sam. He obviously hadn't wasted any time in enjoying the benefits of Cornwall. For a wild moment she was tempted to join him and then she remembered the calls she had to make and the stack of medical journals that she was determined to at least scan before tomorrow.

Feeling uncomfortably sticky from her long working day and the warm weather, Anna showered quickly and washed her hair. Then she pulled on a pair of skimpy shorts, an equally skimpy top, poured herself a cold drink and walked onto the terrace to catch up on some reading.

'Nice to know you couldn't stay away from me, Riggs.'

She dropped the medical journal she was reading and registered the time with a twinge of shock. It was always like that with her. She became so absorbed in what she was reading that the world outside ceased to exist.

She glanced up at Sam, at the broad shoulders clearly outlined by the wet suit, at the growth of stubble on his hard jaw. He looked wickedly handsome and the long, leisurely look he gave her irritated her in the extreme.

No matter that they couldn't stand the sight of each other. If it was female, he still had to look. He just couldn't help himself.

'Stop staring, McKenna.' She gave him a frosty stare. 'I'm not one of your bimbos.'

He gave her a maddening grin, water dripping from his dark hair onto his wet suit. 'You've got good legs, Riggs. Always have had. But fortunately for both of us the rest of you is questionable so I'm able to resist you. I prefer my women gentle and cuddly.'

'You prefer your women brainless.'

He reached for a towel which he'd slung over the back of a chair in readiness for his return. ' "Soft" is the word I'd choose. Soft and yielding. You're more like a cactus. A man could get injured touching you.'

'If you touched me then you'd definitely be injured.' She angled her head and shot him a warning glance. 'And if being a cactus keeps you away, that's fine by me.' Feeling unaccountably warm under his lazy gaze, she glared at him. 'I suppose you're wondering why I'm here.'

He wandered back into the house and returned

with a cold beer. 'I know why you're here.' He lifted the bottle to his lips and drank deeply, the muscles in his throat working as he swallowed. 'You find me irresistible. Don't worry about it. Women often do. You'll learn to live with the feeling.'

Anna glanced down at the beach below them. 'Just how far is the drop from here?'

He gave an appreciative grin and set the beer down on the table. 'Far enough. Why?' He lifted an eyebrow. 'Do you want to give it a go?'

She gritted her teeth. 'Don't tempt me, McKenna. If you have any concern for your safety, you'll drink that beer somewhere else.'

His grin widened. 'Trouble is, this is *my* home, Riggs, and you're the one sitting on my deck.'

'It's your parents' deck. And, believe me, I wouldn't be here unless there was a crisis.'

'My parents love having you. You're like a daughter to them.' He reached for the beer again. 'So what's the crisis?'

She bit her lip. She hated even saying the words. Hadn't got used to the idea herself yet. 'My house purchase has fallen through.'

He frowned. 'You sold your flat? What was wrong with it?'

'I wanted something bigger. Somewhere nearer the sea.'

'Yeah. You always did dream about that. Living virtually on the sand. Another one of your plans.' His eyes narrowed and he glanced at the view from his parents' deck. 'And maybe I don't blame you for that. I have to admit, it doesn't get much better than this.'

'It's a perfect spot,' Anna agreed, 'so why are you in London?'

He lifted the beer to his lips. 'Because there's more to life than a good view and a swim in the surf, Riggs. So where was the house? The one that you were hoping to buy?'

'Tub's Creek.'

'Old Jack Lawson's place?'

Anna nodded. Of course Sam would remember. He'd been brought up here, just like her. 'He died six months ago. Had a massive heart attack just after Christmas.'

'Not surprised with all the smoking, eating and drinking he usually did.' Sam gave a rueful smile. 'I think we can safely say that he lived life to the full. What was wrong with the cottage? Subsidence?'

Anna's jaw fell. 'How do you know?'

He shrugged. 'Common sense. It was pretty old and the windows were wonky. Had to be something.'

Anna sighed. 'I thought wonky windows gave a place character.'

'And major structural problems,' Sam said dryly. 'So now you're homeless.'

'I completed on the flat two weeks ago. It was that or lose the sale. I was expecting to exchange and complete in two weeks. It never occurred to me that there'd be a problem that I couldn't cope with. I was ready to buy it regardless.'

Sam shrugged broad shoulders. 'So buy it.'

'With what?' Anna shot him an impatient look. 'I need a mortgage and unfortunately people don't lend you money on wrecks.'

'Find somewhere new. Somewhere with straight windows.'

'Given the fact your father has landed me with a dud locum, I won't have the time to trawl estate agents. I'll rent for now.'

He ignored the dig and lifted an eyebrow. 'Rent? You're kidding. How do you expect to find somewhere to rent at this time of year? Every inch of available bed space is already let out to tourists. You wouldn't even find a stable.'

'All right, well, I'll sleep in the surgery if I have to,' she said irritably, and he yawned.

'Why would you need to? You can sleep here as far as I'm concerned. With six bedrooms, the house is big enough for both of us. You'll just have to try and resist me.'

'Believe me, no house would ever be big enough for both of us. Your ego takes up too much space.'

'Don't push your luck.' He finished the beer. 'I'm trying to be generous and giving here. If you're going to argue, you can sleep on the damned beach.'

'Sorry.' Something that she couldn't identify made her suddenly need to apologise. She ran a hand through her hair which had dried sleek and straight. It fell past her shoulders, halfway down her back. 'I'm just disappointed about the house. Worried about your dad. Anxious about the practice.'

Unsettled.

'Scared about the future.' Sam's gaze fixed on hers. 'Safe Anna. Careful Anna. Anna the planner. So ballsy on the outside but on the inside you crave security.'

She bit her lip, hating the fact that he knew her so well.

'Spare me the amateur psychology. Anyway, what's wrong with planning? And what's wrong with enjoying life and wanting it to stay the same?'

'Nothing. But think what you could be missing.'

She frowned. 'There's nothing missing in my life.'

'Apart from a social life.'

'I have a perfectly satisfactory social life, thank you.'

He leaned against the balcony, the wet suit lovingly displaying every muscular curve of his body. 'Bingo on a Friday, lobster night at the Dog and Duck. The beach barbecue. Take-away seafood from Hilda's Kitchen. Wow.'

'Never underestimate Hilda's seafood.' Anna clamped her jaw shut to prevent herself from rising to the bait. It was true that her social life was pathetically limited but that was as much because she was exhausted all the time as to lack of opportunity. By the time she finished work all she had the energy for was a date with a good book. But that was fine for now. She was busy establishing herself as a GP. Time for the rest later. It was all part of her life plan.

She leaned back in her chair and pretended to enjoy the view. 'At least my social life doesn't make the newspapers. Face it, McKenna, you just can't settle down with one woman, can you?'

Every time she saw a picture of him, he had a different woman on his arm. Usually blonde. Usually extremely curvaceous. None of them looked like the marrying type.

'Why would I want to?'

'Your mother is waiting for grandchildren.'

He threw his head back and laughed, a rich masculine sound that triggered an answering feminine response deep inside her. 'I hope she's a slow knitter.'

Suddenly Anna found herself noticing the tiny creases around his eyes and the way his jaw flexed when he smiled.

Disturbed by such unusually intimate observations, she rose to her feet and walked towards the house. His voice stopped her in the doorway.

'So, what are we eating tonight, Riggs?'

She turned back to face him, one brow arched in question. 'How would I know?'

'Perhaps because you've been living here for a few weeks? Presumably you've filled the fridge? Planned a few meals? Surprise me.'

She smiled sweetly. 'You've been reading fairy tales again. I'm not Little Red Riding Hood and you're every bit as capable of making a meal as I am. Probably more. You know where the fridge is, McKenna. If you want to eat, eat. Don't involve me in it.'

She hated to cook, even for herself. There was no

way she'd be cooking for Sam. Unless she was aiming to poison him.

'Well, presumably you have to eat at some point, too.'

She leaned against the door-frame, her dark hair tumbling over her shoulders, her legs long and lightly tanned. 'I don't see why my eating habits are of any interest to you.'

'It's just that if you're cooking, it's as easy to cook for two as one.'

'If you're hoping I'm going to cook for you then you don't know me as well as I thought you did.'

Those blue eyes flashed a challenge. 'Eating is supposed to be an opportunity for social interaction between people.'

'People who like each other, McKenna. We don't. All the more reason for us to eat alone.'

He straightened up, his body lithe and powerful, stretching his shoulders to relieve the tension. 'All right. You never did quite have the woman thing sorted. So it looks as though I'm cooking.'

'Wait a minute.' Despite her vow not to rise to the bait, she couldn't stay silent. 'I've had enough of your digs for one night. What do you mean, I never did quite have the woman thing sorted?'

He hooked the empty beer bottle with his finger, his movements slow and casual. 'You just don't do woman stuff, do you? Never have.'

'Woman stuff? What woman stuff? You want me to dress in pink?'

He grinned. 'Can't see you in pink somehow.'

She made a mental note to buy something pink at the earliest opportunity. 'So what exactly do you mean?'

He shrugged. 'You don't cook. You don't play house. You just don't do girly stuff.'

Girly stuff?

Annoyed that he'd managed to make her feel inadequate, she glared at him. 'I have a full-time job, McKenna. And I eat perfectly healthy food—'

'Sandwiches.'

'I happen to like sandwiches. And I have a cleaner to do the house stuff. Or at least I did before I sold my flat. What you really mean is that you don't want a woman with an opinion.'

'*An* opinion?' He laughed. 'You've got so many opinions, honey, that talking to you is like negotiating an obstacle course.'

'Oh, for goodness' sake.' She frowned in irritation. 'It'll be a treat for you to hang around with someone who isn't a bimbo for a while. If you get really lucky I might talk to you from time to time about something other than facials and pedicures. And don't call me honey. It's completely demeaning and it winds me up.'

'That's why I do it.' He smiled smugly and strolled past her towards the kitchen. 'All right, this once I'll cook for you. But don't get used to it. If we're going to live together, you'll have to contribute. If you like, you can wash my socks.'

'Shame the camera isn't running,' Anna said tartly. 'I would have liked my response to that suggestion recorded for the nation's entertainment. And talking of cameras, if you're seriously going to stay and try and make this thing work, we need to talk.'

'More ground rules?'

'Just a few observations about the way things are going to be. I'll dump these journals in my room and I'll meet you in the kitchen. We can go through a few things.'

'Will you be wearing black leather and carrying a whip? I love it when you're dominating.' He unzipped the neck of his wet suit and Anna felt her breath catch and something slow and dangerous uncurl low in her pelvis.

Damn. Immediately she turned on her heel and strode out of the room, cursing her female hormones.

How could you react to a man that you didn't even like?

She of all people, who was so much more interested in the human mind than the human body.

She dumped the magazines on the bed with an impatient sigh. Unfortunately for her, Sam had an incredible body. And he knew it. But fortunately for her, she didn't like the man. So she was safe.

She sucked in a breath, gathered her thoughts back on track and mentally sketched out a few plans for how they could work together most efficiently. How they could work together with minimum contact.

When she marched into the kitchen fifteen minutes later she was armed with a notepad and determination not to let him unsettle her otherwise perfectly ordered life.

Despite the fact that she'd been quick, he'd already showered and changed and was dressed in a pair of cut-off jeans and a T-shirt which clung lovingly to the muscles of his broad shoulders. He was standing at the granite work surface, chopping vegetables with the speed and skill of a surgeon. For a moment she stood still, fascinated by those long, strong fingers and his sure touch.

Then she pulled herself together, dropped onto the nearest kitchen chair and blew a strand of hair out of her eyes. 'It's hot.'

'Yeah—stuffy. Good night for skinny-dipping.'

Anna sighed. 'Will you ever grow up?'

'If growing up means coming down here with a notepad and an official expression then I sincerely hope not.' He tossed slices of spring onion and ginger into a wok and waited while they sizzled. 'OK, Captain Riggs. Let's have it. Outline the plan of attack.'

Just being in the same room as him made her temper sizzle.

'You can mock all you like.' Her hair fell forward, brushing the table. 'But how do you think we're ever going to work together and deliver a reasonable standard of care for our patients if we don't do some planning?'

He added chicken to the wok. 'Do you plan with Dad?'

'We'd have meetings, yes.' She tapped her pen on the pad. 'But he and I have worked together for a long time. We know each other.'

Sam lowered the heat. 'We know each other, too, Riggs.'

'Too well.'

'Maybe.' He glanced towards her. 'Or maybe we'll both get some surprises. Life does that to you sometimes. Just when you think you've got it all worked out, the unexpected happens.'

He could say that again.

'You coming back to Cornwall is certainly unexpected,' she agreed, frowning as he handed her a glass. 'What's this?'

'An extremely good Sancerre. Excellent for hot weather and it will go well with my stir-fry. It might also soften your mood.'

'There's nothing wrong with my mood.'

He shot her a look. 'Just try it.'

She did and had to stop herself moaning out loud with sheer pleasure. It was cool and sharp and the alcohol oozed into her tired bones with immediate effect.

'It's good.'

'A lot of the things I do are good, Riggs. You ought to try a few more of them.'

She ignored the dig, set the glass down on the table and picked up the pen. 'I thought I could start by running you through some of the clinics that we do. You can tell me what you're comfortable with. I don't want you working outside your comfort zone.'

'You're questioning my abilities as a doctor again, Riggs.' He scraped the pan viciously to loosen the stir-fry. 'And it's only fair to tell you that it really ticks me off.'

She cursed men and their egos.

'You're being ridiculously sensitive,' she said stiffly. 'You haven't worked as a proper doctor for so long it's only natural that there are going to be areas that you're less experienced in. Obstetrics, for example. We have a ridiculous number of teenage pregnancies here. And emergencies. You know how far it is to the local hospital and how many accidents we get on the beach every day in the summer. Our surgeries are crammed with them.'

'You should run an emergency surgery for the tourists. It would save them traipsing miles to the hospital or filling up surgery time with minor accidents. I've suggested it to Dad before.'

So had she, on numerous occasions, but she wasn't going to let him know that.

'What we do now works perfectly well.'

He shrugged. 'Maybe. And maybe it would work even better if you designated some time to doing an emergency surgery. You should have done it ages ago.'

He was completely right. 'We'll end up encouraging the tourists to come and see us with every bump and bruise.'

'That's my father talking.' His gaze flickered to hers, challenging. 'You don't really believe that.'

It was completely true. She didn't believe that. She thought it was a great idea. Always had. 'We'll see. It's only the start of the summer.'

'Fine. But it's the best plan.'

Anna frowned and tapped her pen on the pad. 'Let's look at practicalities. What this job is going to mean for you. It must be a while since you stitched a patient.'

'I think if I rack my brains it will all come back to me. I don't need tuition.' He lifted the wok and divided the contents between two plates. 'Here. Stop organising for one minute and eat.'

'Organisation is what keeps this show running.' But Anna pushed the pad to one side and reached for her wine. 'So when did you learn to cook?'

He handed her a plate piled high with food and a fork. 'I learned to cook when I decided that I liked eating decent food.'

'I'm surprised you don't just call on one of your women to cook whenever you're hungry.' She picked up her fork and stabbed some chicken and vegetables. 'Isn't that what primitive caveman is supposed to do?'

'This particular caveman can find plenty of other occupations for his women.' His eyes glittered slightly as he surveyed her over the rim of his glass. 'I don't want them wasting their energy in the kitchen.'

'You're a complete Neanderthal.' She felt the colour rise in her face and hated herself for being so sensitive to his comments. Particularly as she knew they were designed to wind her up. 'And I still think you should brush up on your emergency medicine.'

He topped up his glass. 'If we ran an emergency

clinic it would make great television. The type of medical problems you're likely to encounter on your average beach holiday.'

'Oh, now I see why you're so keen to do it. Real-life casualties for your programme.' She twirled noodles around her fork. 'A bit of blood and gore will lift your image no end. Dr Handsome doesn't just know about ingrowing toenails—he can even save lives.'

He lounged back in his chair, his expression mocking. 'Never knew you thought me handsome, Riggs.'

She took a mouthful and shrugged carelessly. 'Well, fortunately for both of us, I'm not as shallow as the women you date. You look all right on the outside but it's what's on the inside that interests me and you just don't grab my attention, McKenna. Never have done. Never will do.'

He leaned forward, his gaze suddenly intent on her face. 'Is that a challenge?'

She looked at him, appalled. 'Of course it wasn't a challenge. Just the thought of you and I together is completely ludicrous.'

'That's right.' His fingers played with the glass. 'It is.'

'Exactly.' Something in his blue gaze was making her feel horribly uncomfortable. It was probably just the topic of conversation. 'All right, we'll do an emergency surgery from next week.'

'You're saying I'm right.'

'I'm saying we'll try it. Glenda can do a poster on the computer. We'll see how you get on.'

'Testing me?'

'Just looking out for my patients.'

He drained his glass. 'And when I prove to you that I'm perfectly competent, do I get an apology?'

'No, you get to see patients without me looking over your shoulder.'

'You certainly know how to deliver an incentive.' He put the empty glass down on the table. 'It's going to be a joy to work with you, Riggs.'

'Follow the rules, McKenna, and we just might survive.'

CHAPTER FOUR

THE first thing Sam saw when he walked into the surgery the next morning was a sensational pair of legs. Slim, brown and long enough to make a man forget what was in his head.

For a moment he just looked, and then he reminded himself of the price attached to admiring those particular legs.

Anna was leaning over the reception desk to grab a pen and the movement revealed enough of her to heat his blood.

'Good morning, Riggs. Nice skirt.'

He told himself that he could admire her legs without having to admire her as a person.

'You're late,' she snapped, straightening up so fast she almost lost her balance. It gave him some satisfaction to see that he'd flustered her.

'Not late.' He dragged his gaze away from those legs and glanced at the clock. 'On time. Punctual. And there's a queue at your door.'

'There's always a queue,' Anna said wearily, nodding at Glenda. 'OK, let's unlock the doors and get started.'

Sam took a good look at Glenda. Her hair wasn't combed and she hadn't bothered with lipstick. As long as he'd known her, Glenda had always worn lipstick. Something was definitely wrong. 'Polly, my producer, wants to come and look round and discuss some ideas over our lunch-break. Are you free, Riggs?'

Anna balanced a pile of papers under one arm and reached for her coffee with the other. Her black hair hung down her back, as glossy and shiny as silk. With her slanting brown eyes, she reminded him of a sleek cat. 'I don't have time for a lunch-break. And neither will you if you're intending to pull your weight.'

He ground his teeth and decided that even legs as good as those couldn't make up for the sharp tongue and the bossy nature. 'Not eating just shows poor time management.'

'I didn't say I didn't eat. Just that I don't take a lunch-break. That's a luxury we can't afford in the summer. If you want lunch-breaks, hang around until winter when the tourists leave.'

'I'm meeting Polly and we're starting filming this afternoon,' he said calmly, wondering whether the urge to strangle her had always been this powerful or whether it had just got a great deal worse. 'If you want to have some input, you might like to be there.'

She turned to face him, her head slightly tilted. 'This is why it is never going to work. Before you arrived I was struggling to cope with the workload and now, thanks to your perpetual need to have your ego stoked, I also have to cope with advising you on where to put your camera.'

He clamped his jaw to prevent himself saying that

he knew exactly where he wanted to put the camera at this precise moment.

'OK, Riggs.' He ran a hand along the back of his neck and exercised his temper control skills. 'First of all, I know you've been struggling to cope but that's because Dad has been limping along at half-pace for months. Now I'm here and I'm more than capable of picking up all his work and probably some of yours.'

'I don't need you to touch mine—'

'I'm merely pointing out that I have the capacity to do so. The second point is that once we know what we're doing, the filming is surprisingly unobtrusive. We're filming normal, everyday surgeries. Despite what you think, nothing is staged for the cameras.'

'It'll probably take several takes to get your stitches straight.'

He wondered how many stitches it would take to sew her mouth up. He took a deep breath. 'You think I'm going to undo a wound and do it up again?'

She shrugged. 'How do I know to what lengths you'd go to make yourself look good?'

'That's why I'm inviting you to join this meeting.' He kept his voice even. 'Then you'll know. You might even enjoy it.'

She looked at him and then nodded. 'All right. I'll listen in. But only because I don't want things going on in my surgery that I don't know about. And I have to do the house calls first.'

'Fine. We'll arrange some sandwiches for after that.'

'I carry my mobile,' she said crisply, 'so if you need to consult on anything, you can call.'

'I'll remember that.'

Damn, the man was annoying!

The emergency surgery was a good idea. She'd suggested it herself, months ago, but David had been resistant to changing their current set-up. In fact, he was pretty reluctant to institute any changes at all. He and her father had run the practice a certain way and since she'd joined him as his partner, David had expected her to fit in.

Anna frowned. To begin with that had been fine. She'd been finding her feet as a new GP and had been only too grateful to fall into a familiar structure. But as she gained confidence she'd seen things— things that needed to be changed. Things that would have improved the care for their patients.

But she'd learned to sneak changes in gradually, and the emergency surgery wasn't one that she'd tackled for a while. Unfortunately Sam was right about that one. She should have done it ages ago.

Then he wouldn't have had the satisfaction of thinking that it was his idea. She hated it when he was right about anything.

But one thing he wasn't right about was the filming, she told herself firmly. It would seriously disrupt the practice and make the patients feel uncomfortable.

She pondered the subject all the way through

morning surgery, all the way through her house calls and all the way back to the surgery.

By the time she walked into the bright, airy reception area, she'd made up her mind that the whole thing was a mistake.

And leaving Sam alone had been a mistake, too. She should never have allowed him to finish his surgery without her there. What if something had happened? Something that he wasn't qualified to handle? He was too arrogant to admit that he needed help and he'd probably got himself into serious difficulties. David had one or two tricky patients.

Preoccupied with these thoughts, it came as a serious surprise to her to find Sam laughing with Glenda as the receptionist tidied up from the morning.

He didn't look like a man who'd had a stressful morning.

Anna dropped her bag and looked at him expectantly. 'So how was your surgery?'

'Good. There were one or two cases that would have made interesting television.'

She shot him an impatient look. 'Do you think of everything in terms of camera angles?'

'Not everything, no.' He winked at her suggestively. 'Just my work.'

She chose to ignore that, just as she chose to ignore most of the things he said. 'See anything interesting?'

'Fiona Walker's dog has been on the rampage

again.' He rolled his eyes. 'One day she'll learn that it isn't the sweet little thing she thinks it is.'

Anna winced. 'That dog has kept her going since her Bill died last year.'

'I know that,' Sam said steadily, 'but it needs a muzzle. Fortunately the bite wasn't severe. They wanted to report it to the police but I promised that I'd talk to Mrs Walker.'

'You did?' Anna couldn't hide her surprise. 'Why would you do that?'

'Because, as you said, that dog is her life.'

'You don't know anything about her life.'

'I was brought up here, same as you and my mother writes to me,' Sam reminded her dryly. 'Endless gossip about harbour life. I know everything about everyone, not just Mrs Walker. I know that Doris in the gift shop had her gall-bladder out last winter, I know that her mother and grandmother have both had hip replacements and that the Stevensons are getting a divorce. I know that Hilda still gets eczema and Nicola Hunt is—'

'All right, all right.' Anna cut him off, hiding her surprise. 'I just didn't think those sort of details interested you.'

'All part of harbour life.'

'And you hate harbour life. That's why you choose to live in London.'

Sam gave an implacable smile. 'But I'm here now. And those are the details that you need as a family doctor. Those are the details that we're going to bring out in the programme. The way that we care for generations of the same family.'

'You mean that the way your father and I care for generations of the same family.'

Before he could answer the doors to the surgery crashed open and a man shouldered his way in, a child cradled in his arms, a frantic expression on his face. 'Quickly! I need a doctor. Someone help me—she's really struggling to breathe.'

'What happened, John?' Anna was beside him instantly, a brief examination of the child revealing that her lips were swollen and that she was wheezing badly.

'She's got a rash,' Sam murmured from next to her, his large hands lifting the child's T-shirt and exposing her abdomen. 'This is anaphylactic shock. I wonder what's caused it.'

'Let's get her into my consulting room.'

'I'll get the drugs.'

Acting as smoothly and efficiently as if they'd worked together all their lives, they swung into action.

'Do you know what happened, John? Any clues at all?' Anna questioned the father as she took the child and laid her on the examination couch, trying to obtain a history that might help them work out what had happened.

John was frantic, both hands locked in his hair as he watched helplessly. 'I don't know. God, I just don't know. We were on the beach, having a picnic—'

'What were you eating?' Anna took the oxygen mask from Sam and covered the child's mouth and nose while Sam adjusted the flow. 'Any food she hasn't eaten before? Nuts maybe? Strawberries?'

'No nuts. Hell— I don't know what she ate. All the usual stuff, I suppose.' He ran a hand over the back of his neck, his brow beaded with sweat. Then he glanced towards the door. 'Michelle will know. She's following with the baby. I came with Lucy because I can run faster.' He took several shallow breaths, fighting for control. Struggling to be strong in the face of a crisis. When he wasn't doing his job as a carpenter, John was the helmsman of the lifeboat and well used to dealing with emergencies. Just not in his own family. 'Crisps. She ate crisps. I remember that because Michelle was nagging her to eat a sandwich.'

Sam attached a pulse oximeter to Lucy's finger and checked the reading. 'Her oxygen saturation is 90 per cent.'

'Is that OK?' John glanced between them, anxious for information. 'Tell me that's OK. Tell me she's going to be OK.'

'We'd like it to be a little higher, but the oxygen will help,' Anna said calmly, holding the mask and stroking the little girl's head to try and calm her. 'Better give her some adrenaline and hydrocortisone, McKenna.'

'Ahead of you, Riggs.' Within seconds Sam had given the little girl an injection of adrenaline into her muscle. 'I'm going to put a line in. I have a feeling we might need it.'

Without question Anna handed him the necessary equipment and then examined the little girl's arm. 'This looks like a good vein.' She slipped on the tourniquet, tightened it and then shifted her position to allow Sam access.

In one swift movement he slipped the needle into the vein. No fumbling. No hesitation.

Anna hid her surprise. For someone who was out of practice, he hadn't seemed remotely hesitant. And he hadn't missed. She had to admit she was impressed. And relieved.

'Here…' She reached for some strapping to secure it. 'Don't want to lose that.'

'Right.' With a steady hand Sam gave the hydrocortisone and Anna checked the pulse oximeter again.

'Her sats are up to 94 per cent. Her breathing seems a little easier.'

'That's good. Let's see if this helps.' He gave the hydrocortisone and at that moment the door opened and Lucy's mother hurried in, white-faced and out of breath.

'Glenda's taken the baby for me. Is Lucy OK? What's wrong with her? She was fine one minute and then she just collapsed.' The questions tumbled out of her and, satisfied that Sam had Lucy under control, Anna hurried over to the distraught Michelle.

'She seems to have had an allergic reaction to something, but the drugs are helping. We need to know what caused it, Michelle. What were you doing when it happened?'

Michelle Craddock looked at her helplessly, her face shiny from the heat, her hair damp from running. 'Eating a picnic. Nothing exciting or dangerous. I just don't understand what could possibly have happened.'

'Could she have picked something up from the beach?' Sam dropped the empty syringe onto the trolley and glanced at Anna with a question in his eyes. 'Drugs?'

Her gaze held his. They both knew that during the summer months teenagers congregated on the beach in the evenings. The local police did their best to keep things under control but the odd broken bottle and syringe had been cleaned up the following morning by vigilant locals. Had the little girl picked something up from the sand?

Michelle was shaking her head. 'She didn't wander from the picnic rug. I would have noticed if she'd picked something up.'

'Her vital signs are improving and her sats are good,' Sam murmured, keeping a close eye on the child.

Anna was still questioning the mother. 'What was the very last thing she was doing before she collapsed, Michelle? Try and think. It could be very important.'

'Eating the picnic.' Michelle glanced at her husband for help. 'She was eating a ham sandwich, I think. No, it was crisps. Because I was nagging her about not touching the healthy stuff.'

John frowned. 'Actually, that's wrong, too.' His brow cleared. 'She was drinking, Miche. I remember now because her crisps fell onto the sand when she reached for her can.'

Sam glanced up. 'Can?'

'Fizzy drink.'

Sam's eyes narrowed. 'Had the can been open for a while?'

Michelle bit her lip. 'Not really. A few minutes, I suppose. She'd certainly had a few sips from it. Why?'

Anna picked up the questioning, following Sam's train of thought. 'And did she drink straight from the can?'

Michelle nodded, her expression anxious. 'Why? Why would that make her ill?'

'Because wasps crawl into cans of fizzy drink,' Sam said grimly, turning back to the child and checking her mouth and throat. 'Our guess is that she may have swallowed a wasp.'

'Oh, my God.' John's face was pale. 'You think she's been stung in her throat?'

'Possibly.'

John closed his eyes briefly and then looked at his wife and shook his head. 'We had no idea.'

'Lucky you brought her here as quickly as you did,' Sam said. 'Her breathing is improving and her heart rate is good. We'll get her transferred to the hospital and they'll keep her in overnight just to be sure.'

'Keep her in?' Michelle stroked Lucy's hair to keep her calm. 'But if she's better…?'

'There's a chance she might have a relapse,' Anna explained, glancing towards the window. 'I can hear the ambulance now. We'll transfer her to hospital and they can take a good look at her throat.'

'A wasp in the can. I can't believe I didn't think of that,' Michelle groaned, shaking her head in disbelief. 'And I think I'm such a careful mother.'

'Accidents still happen, Michelle, and you're a great mother,' Anna said quietly, walking towards the door as the paramedics hurried in, guided by Glenda. 'Hi, Todd. We need to get this little one to hospital quickly.'

She explained what had happened, gave him a summary of the care they'd given and then looked at Sam. 'One of us ought to go in the ambulance with her. You or me?'

'I'll go,' Sam said immediately. 'You might be needed here. I'll grab a lift back from someone.'

Now that the immediate danger to the child had passed, Anna swept her dark hair away from her face and gave a reluctant grin. 'Good work, McKenna. Maybe you're not as rusty as I thought.'

'If that's supposed to be a compliment then I'd say you need more practice.' He returned the smile and straightened. 'You didn't do badly yourself, Riggs. Good teamwork.'

Teamwork.

She frowned, slightly unsettled to realise that that was exactly what had happened. They'd worked as a team. A very effective team. And it wasn't at all what she would have expected. In the pressure of an emergency there had been no dissention between them—in fact, they'd hardly needed to speak. Each had worked smoothly alongside the other, instinctively anticipating each other's needs.

And then she noticed the camera. Her smile faded. 'You've been filming? You filmed what just happened?'

A girl with a clipboard murmured something in the producer's ear and Polly smiled. 'It will make fantastic television. But obviously only with the family's permission. And I agree that it was amazing teamwork.' The producer stepped forward, an awed expression on her face. 'The two of you were so slick. It was like watching a medical drama! Better, because it was real.'

Anna gritted her teeth and Sam drew in a breath, clearly anticipating a problem. 'Anna—'

'You shouldn't have filmed without the patient's permission.'

'We put a notice up saying that anyone not wishing to be filmed simply has to say so.'

Anna glanced at the wall, scanned the notice and scowled. 'Well, the Craddocks weren't exactly reading the notices on the wall when they came in here, were they? They wouldn't even have seen it!'

John Craddock rubbed the back of his neck and

cast a glance towards his daughter, who was now sitting on his wife's lap. 'Can't honestly say I mind if they show it, Dr Riggs. Not if it saves someone else. What do you think, Michelle?'

His wife gave a wavering smile. She was still very pale from the experience. 'To be honest, I'm only too pleased for other people to learn the risks of not drinking straight from cans in the summer. It had never even occurred to me. And I worry about everything when it comes to the kids!'

Anna released a breath, unable to argue with that. It was an important health education message, that was true, and something that people often overlooked in the summer months when the weather was hot and wasps were abundant. 'Well, I suppose if you don't mind…'

John grinned. 'Just tell me when it's going to be shown, so that I can tell everyone who knows me.'

'We'll certainly do that.' The producer smiled, standing to one side as the paramedics prepared to take Lucy to the hospital. 'It'll be part of our series on summer health.'

Sam picked up his bag, helped himself to a few extra pieces of equipment that he thought he might need and gave Anna a nod. 'I won't be long. I'll just hand over and then catch a lift back.'

'Fine. I've got paperwork to do anyway. We'll delay that lunch. If there's going to be a camera stuck in my face every time I turn round, I definitely want to be part of the discussion.'

*   *   *

In fact, they didn't need to delay lunch for long.

Sam was back within the hour and the news on Lucy was good. 'She's stable now but they're keeping her in overnight. Now, let's get on with the meeting before the sandwiches curl. Glenda, are you joining us for this?'

'Oh, Dr McKenna...' Slightly breathless, Glenda glanced at them nervously, her hand shaking slightly as she smoothed her hair. 'I was thinking of popping home in my lunch-break, if that's all right with you. But I could come if you'd rather...'

'Not at all,' Sam said easily, giving her a smile that made Glenda visibly relax. 'Have a nice lunch. See you later.'

Glenda vanished through the door so hastily that her bag tangled on the handle. With a murmured exclamation she tugged it free and hurried off without looking back, clearly in a hurry and very flustered.

Sam's smile faded. 'There goes a very stressed woman.'

Anna nodded, pacing over to the window and watching as Glenda virtually sprinted down the street towards the harbour. She knew that the receptionist would be home within five minutes. But why the hurry?

'You're right,' she said quietly. 'Something is very wrong and I feel very guilty that it took you to point it out.'

Sam strolled across the reception area and stood next to her. 'Just one of the advantages of having an injection of fresh blood in the practice.'

'Don't.' She glanced up at him, her expression troubled. For once she wasn't in the mood to argue with him. 'It worries me that I didn't notice.'

'Why should you have noticed? You're not super-woman.' He lifted a hand and brushed a strand of dark hair away from her face. The gesture was so unexpected that she jumped as though she'd received an electric shock.

'Just because we've managed to be civil to each other for the past half an hour, don't think you can take liberties, McKenna.' Thoroughly unsettled by the sudden wild increase in her pulse rate, she glared at him and he glared back.

'Just clearing your vision, Riggs. You need a hair-cut or you're going to trip on the stairs.'

She resisted the temptation to lift a hand to her hair. She always wore her hair long and he knew it.

'You know, it would make for riveting television if you let us film the two of you working together for the whole series.' The voice of Polly came from behind them and they both turned. 'There's a tre-mendous chemistry between you. The room just pulses with energy whenever you're together. And the best thing is that you two don't even seem aware of it.'

Chemistry?

Anna gaped at her. 'The sort of chemistry that causes an explosion,' she muttered darkly, and Sam grinned.

'I don't think our Anna sees herself as a film star, Polly.'

The producer looked thoughtful. 'Well, a lot of

people are resistant to the thought of being filmed but once they get used to it they usually find they forget about the cameras and just get on with the job. That's one of the reasons that these fly-on-the-wall documentaries are so successful. The viewers feel as though they're genuinely part of what's going on.' The producer tipped her head on one side and narrowed her eyes. 'Even without looking at what we just filmed, I can tell that you're going to look fabulous on camera. Gorgeous.'

Anna glared at both of them. 'I do not want to be filmed.'

'Fine by me.' Sam suppressed a yawn. 'Personally I think it would be pretty hard to find your good side anyway.'

The smooth working relationship was gone. Back was the constant needling.

'You are unbelievably shallow.'

Polly glanced between them and grinned. 'If you're both willing to suspend hostilities, the sandwiches are looking particularly tempting.'

'Yeah, we're ready.' Sam strolled across the reception area and made for the stairs that led to the staffroom.

Aware that the producer was still staring at them in fascination, Anna followed more self-consciously.

Chemistry.

It was utterly ridiculous to suggest that she and Sam shared any sort of chemistry. And as for looking good on the camera—the whole idea was totally ridiculous.

'It would be great if we could incorporate more of your accident and emergency skills, Sam,' Polly was saying as Anna grabbed a cup of coffee and took her seat at the table. 'I know we need the routine stuff, too, but a bit of that does get the adrenaline pumping.'

'What accident and emergency skills?' Anna helped herself to a sandwich. 'Since when did you have accident and emergency skills?' Then she remembered the calm, competent way he'd reacted to the crisis downstairs and something clicked in her brain. 'What jobs have you been doing in London, McKenna?'

Polly smiled. 'When he's not doing his usual surgery and working for us, he does nights at the A and E department of…' She named a busy London hospital and Anna put the sandwich back on her plate untouched, her eyes on Sam.

'You're working nights in an A and E department? Why?'

His eyes gleamed. 'So that my medical skills don't become as rusty as a garden fork, Riggs, that's why. We see a range of conditions in the London practice but there's nothing like nights in A and E to hone your skills.'

She stared at him. 'That explains why you were able to get that line into the child.'

'I've done it a few times, yes.'

She glared at him. 'You should have told me.'

'You shouldn't have assumed that I was useless.'

'Now, now, children.' Polly's expression was amused. 'It's always fun to watch the two of you in action, but we're already pushed for time so can we move on to the matter in hand? We need to discuss our plans for filming this summer.'

Anna bit hard into her sandwich and glared at Sam. But her anger with him for deliberately deceiving her was tinged with respect. The guy clearly knew what he was doing. And he was an impressive doctor.

It was just a shame that she wanted to strangle him.

That evening, despite the heat, Anna decided to go for a run on the beach. She always found exercise good for tension, and the tension in her life had rocketed ever since Sam had walked into her surgery.

Despite all their reassurances during the lunchtime meeting that the patients would love the idea of being 'on the telly', she still had serious reservations about filming. They'd agreed to seek permission from every patient but still Anna couldn't quite imagine that people would want their lives exposed on television. For herself, she couldn't think of anything worse. She liked her privacy too much and she never had been able to understand why some people craved public attention.

Despite the fact that it was past seven o'clock, the beach was still crowded with families and Anna jogged slowly down to the water's edge and then lengthened her stride, enjoying the cool breeze blowing off the sea.

This was a popular surfing beach and the water was still crowded with teenagers determined to make the most of the waves.

By the time she returned to the McKennas' house she was panting and uncomfortably hot. She ripped off her running gear and stepped straight under a cold shower, moaning with relief as the water cooled her heated flesh. Bliss. She was tempted to stay under the water all evening but her stomach was rumbling and she knew she had to eat something after such a long run.

She slipped on a short linen dress, padded down to the kitchen and opened the fridge.

'I cooked last night so I guess tonight has to be your turn.' Sam lounged in the doorway, a beer in his hand, watching her.

Anna turned. 'Has anyone ever told you that you look more like a beach bum than a doctor?'

His hair was slightly too long, his jaw rough with stubble and he wore a pair of long surf shorts and a loose T-shirt that clung to the powerful muscles of his shoulders.

He gave her a lopsided grin that made her heart kick uncomfortably against her chest. 'You want me to wear a suit and tie?'

'I don't care what you wear.' She yawned and turned back to the fridge. 'It isn't looking promising. The only thing I can cook is omelette and we're right out of eggs.'

Sam strolled over to her and peered over her shoulder. 'So you'd better buy me dinner.'

She wrinkled her nose and slammed the fridge shut, forcing him to step backwards or risk injury. 'Why should I buy you dinner?'

'Women fight to buy me dinner, Riggs.' He hooked his thumbs in the waistband of his shorts, his blue eyes mocking. 'This could be your lucky night. I'm making you an offer you shouldn't be able to refuse.'

Her heart kicked against her ribs and she wished he'd move away slightly. He was standing far too close.

'I have no trouble refusing.' But then her stomach rumbled and she remembered how hungry she was. And how empty the fridge was. 'On the other hand, I'm starving. What exactly did you have in mind?'

'That new place on the beach? Plates of seafood. Lashings of garlic butter. Chilled white wine.'

Anna felt her taste buds react with enthusiasm. 'I've heard good things about that place.' She tilted her head to one side and considered. 'And the only price is being civil to you for the duration?'

'Who said anything about being civil?' He lifted the bottle to his lips and drained the beer. 'Just be yourself.'

She glared at him. 'I'm civil with most people, McKenna. It's just you that drives me nuts.'

'And why is that, I wonder?' He put the bottle on the table and surveyed her, his eyes gleaming with speculation. 'Perhaps you're harbouring secret fantasies.'

'The heat must have gone to your brain.'

He lounged against the table, broad-shouldered and unreasonably handsome. 'Face it, Riggs. You have trouble resisting me. And that really annoys you.'

'You're the one who annoys me. And it's worse when I'm hungry. So let's get going before I commit bodily harm. You won't look so handsome with a black eye and no teeth.'

He reached for his car keys. 'In the interests of personal safety, I'll drive.'

She followed him to the curving gravel driveway and paused, a frown on her face as she looked at his sleek black car. 'You expect me to sit beside you in that sex machine?'

'Well, it's that or the boot, honey, because there's no room in the back. This is definitely a two-seater.'

She sighed and slid into the car, too hungry to argue. 'OK, but only because my stomach is more important to me than my reputation at this particular moment in time.'

She was starving.

He turned the key, started the engine and smiled. 'Don't you just love that sound?'

'It's an engine.'

He shot her a pitying look. 'No appreciation for the finer things in life, that's your problem.' He hit the accelerator, sending gravel flying. 'And what does sitting in my car have to do with your reputation?'

'If I'm seen with you then people will automatically think I'm a bimbo.' She scooped her hair out of her eyes and held it firmly at the back of her neck as he picked up speed and headed for the coast road. 'But to sample the lobster at that new restaurant, I'm willing to take the risk. And don't call me honey. I draw the line at that, even when I'm starving.'

The restaurant was heaving but the manager took one look at Sam and found them a secluded table overlooking the sea.

'Never miss one of your programmes. Love the way you make complicated medical stuff easy to understand. Pleasure to have you back, Sam.' The manager handed him a menu. 'And dining with our Dr Riggs. That's cosy.'

'Convenient, not cosy.' Anna shot him a pointed look and took the other menu. She didn't want gossip in the village. 'This is just business. We have things to talk about, we both have to eat and we both wanted to try your new place, Ken. It's that simple.'

'Well, the first drink is on the house. I'll treat you to a couple of glasses of champagne.' He snapped his fingers, gestured to a waiter and then turned back to the two of them. 'Been meaning to come and talk to your dad, actually, Sam. Something on my mind, to be honest.'

'Stop by any time,' Sam said easily, leaning back

in his chair and closing the menu. 'I'm covering all Dad's surgeries now. Be glad to catch up with you.'

Ken nodded. 'I think I'll do that. Thanks.' At that moment one of the waiters arrived with two brimming glasses of champagne and Ken stepped to one side, giving Anna a quick wink. 'Have a nice evening, both of you.'

Anna watched him go and then lifted her champagne. 'Why was he winking at me? Has he developed a problem with his eye? And why all this man-to-man stuff about seeing you in the surgery? He could have come to see me.'

'There are some things a man can't discuss with a woman.'

'That's rubbish.' She swallowed a mouthful of champagne and moaned with appreciation. 'Ooh, that's fantastic. And, McKenna, I can deal with everything you can deal with. Probably more.'

'You know as well as I do that there are some things a woman prefers a woman doctor for. It's the same for men.'

Anna took another sip and felt her head swim. She put the glass down on the table and decided to wait for the food before drinking any more. Otherwise she'd be tipsy and she needed her wits about her to cope with Sam. 'That's why I always end up with the women's problems. Because you guys avoid them like the plague.'

'That's nonsense.' His tone was calm and he broke off to deliver their order to the waiter. Anna stared at him as the waiter left to give their order to the kitchen.

'I'm perfectly capable of reading a menu and using my voice. And for your information, I don't have any trouble with decision-making. I can pick my own food. If I concentrate I can even use a knife and fork.'

'We both want to try the seafood.' He spoke with exaggerated patience. 'I ordered seafood. Relax, will you?'

Despite her resolve, Anna reached for the champagne again. She couldn't relax around Sam. It just wasn't possible. 'You were trying to pretend that you don't avoid women's problems.'

'I certainly don't. In fact, it's an area that we cover frequently on the programme, as you'd know if you ever bothered to watch it.'

'I get enough of you in real life.'

He leaned forward, his blue eyes fixed on her face. 'It's a fact that lots of women prefer to see a female doctor for some things, and it's the same with male patients. If Ken wants to see me, you shouldn't be defensive about that.'

'I'm not being defensive.'

Damn. She wished she hadn't drunk all that champagne so quickly. She definitely should have waited for the food.

Fortunately it arrived quickly, huge platefuls of seafood with hot garlic butter and baskets of freshly baked bread.

'Oh, this looks fantastic,' Anna muttered, reaching

for a langoustine and stripping it quickly. 'Great idea, McKenna. Beats omelette.'

'There were no eggs,' he reminded her. 'Omelette was never an option.'

'That's right.' She grabbed a napkin before the buttery juices could slide down her chin. 'No eggs. So someone needs to go shopping. I'll grab a few things tomorrow on my way home.'

He scooped another langoustine onto her plate. 'Are you offering to shop, Riggs? Something wrong?'

'I don't mind the shopping. It's the cooking I can't stand. And tonight I'm feeling mellow. Blame the alcohol and the food.'

'You really know how to make a guy feel good.'

'You don't need me to make you feel good. You already feel far too good about yourself. It would be much easier for the rest of us mortals if you'd let a little bit of self-doubt creep in. You need to lose some of those female fans and realise that you're human, like the rest of us.'

He looked at her thoughtfully. 'Do you suffer from self-doubt?'

She paused with a langoustine halfway to her mouth and then dropped it back on her plate. 'Yes. Of course I do. You try joining an established practice run by our respective parents. No matter how many times I prove myself, I'm still the child. I'm not capable of having an idea worth listening to.'

And it rankled. She knew she was a good doctor. She had ideas of her own. Ideas that she wanted to develop for the good of her patients. For the good of the whole practice.

Wondering why on earth she was telling him this when it wasn't something she ever voiced to anyone, she scowled and reached for her glass. Then she changed her mind and lifted her water instead. It was probably the alcohol that was making her so garrulous.

'Yes, I can imagine it must be hard. Dad hasn't let you make any changes, has he?' Sam wiped his fingers on a napkin. 'He can be a stubborn old guy when he wants to be. I'm amazed you haven't walked out before now. Spread your wings.'

'I feel a responsibility to give something back to this place. And I love your dad and I love the practice,' Anna said softly, turning her head and staring out across the sea. The sun had dipped behind the cliffs and streaks of scarlet shot across the sky, casting lights on the waves. On their table a candle flickered and a vase of sweet peas scented the air. For some reason Anna felt a lump building in her throat. 'And this is my home. I'd never want to work anywhere else. I don't know how you can bear London. Don't you miss it here?'

'Yes, of course I miss it.' His tone was equally soft and his eyes were locked on hers. 'It's my home every bit as much as it's your home. Yes, I miss it. But this place didn't give me what I needed.'

'And what was that?'

He stared into the candle, watching the breeze toy with the flame. 'Space to make my own discoveries.

Freedom to make my own mistakes.' He shrugged and reached for his glass. 'I didn't want to just move into something that my father had built. That was his dream and I suppose I needed to follow my own dream. I needed something different.'

'Bright lights and adulation.'

He looked at her thoughtfully over the rim of his glass. 'You really don't think what I do rates very highly, do you?'

'You truly want to know what I think?'

'Just this once, yes, I'll risk it.' He put the glass down and sat back in his chair, eyes narrowed. 'Tell me what you think, Riggs.'

She took a deep breath. 'I think you're an extremely talented doctor who's wasting those talents. You could be making a real difference to people's lives. Saving lives. You did it this morning. Don't you miss that, Sam? That feeling of having really helped someone?'

His gaze didn't shift from hers. 'You don't think I help people?'

She shrugged, wishing that he'd look at his plate or his food. There was something about those killer blue eyes that she found more than a little disconcerting. 'I can see the job is glamorous.'

He leaned forward. 'In the last six months we've had dozens of letters from people whose lives have been changed by things they've seen on the programme. My programme. Sometimes it's life-saving stuff, Riggs. First-aid tips that come in useful. People remember them if they've seen them on television.

And they use them. Sometimes it's something far less dramatic but no less important. We tackle subjects that some people find too embarrassing to discuss with their own doctors. And sometimes that gives them the courage to see their own doctors and sort out a problem that's limiting their lives. We make a difference.'

Anna stared at him. 'You're pretty passionate about it.'

'Very. I think it's a very useful method of patient education. These days patients want to be informed. They need to be informed.'

'That's all very well...' Anna picked at a piece of bread '...but from where I'm sitting there's nothing more irritating than a patient coming into the surgery clutching a magazine announcing the arrival of another wonder drug.'

'I'm not saying that all media reporting of health stories is good,' Sam said. 'I'm just saying that you shouldn't dismiss it. Watch my programme. Tell me that what we're doing in the surgery wouldn't make good summer viewing. There's a lot people could learn from us.'

'Well, I agree that the wasp message is a useful one,' Anna conceded, and Sam nodded.

'And what we need to do now is a piece talking about first aid for anaphylactic shock, how to recognise and deal with it. Remind people with known allergies to carry adrenaline.'

'I still think that the cameras will put patients off coming.'

'It won't put them off,' Sam predicted. 'It will attract them like magnets. Trust me on that one. You'd be amazed at the number of people who are only too delighted to air their health problems on national TV.'

He sat across from her, talking easily, making her laugh with outrageous stories, and when she finally looked at her watch she was astonished to find it was past midnight.

'Look at the time! I've got a pile of reading to do before I go to bed.'

He yawned and finished his coffee. 'Forget the reading for once. Have a night off.'

'I like to stay up to date and stuck down here in Cornwall in a two-man practice, I never get to conferences.'

He looked at her. 'Reading. Conferences. What about parties? Nights on the town? Don't you ever have doubts about devoting your life to medicine?'

She frowned and tilted her head to one side, her silken dark hair sliding over her shoulder and brushing the table. 'I'm not devoting my life. I'm twenty eight, not a hundred. This is just my focus for now. Not for ever.'

'Precisely. You're twenty-eight. You should have a sex life.'

She straightened her shoulders. 'My sex life is none of your business, McKenna, but just in case you haven't scrutinised the electoral role lately, I ought to warn you that there's a shortage of single, eligible men in this village. And I don't sleep with my patients.'

'Then spread your net wider.'

Her frown deepened. 'I'm quite happy as I am, for now. My plan is to carry on until I feel I've really grasped the job. Then maybe it'll be time for more personal stuff.'

'Anna the planner.' He lifted his glass and drained it, his eyes glittering slightly in the flickering candlelight. 'And what if fate intervenes? What if Mr Right arrives before you've scheduled him in to your life plan?'

She grinned airily. 'I'll probably be too busy reading my journals to notice him.' She waved a hand at Ken who was hovering at a nearby table, chatting to the diners. 'We're off, Ken. You'd better charge us for this feast while we're still sober enough to pay.'

Sam reached into his wallet for his credit card and Anna frowned. 'What's that for?'

'Well, unless you intend to spend the rest of the night in the kitchens, washing up, I was planning to pay.'

'You're not paying for me. We'll go halves.'

Sam yawned. 'For goodness' sake, Riggs. Can't you even let a guy buy you dinner?'

'I can buy my own dinner and this wasn't a date, McKenna. It was an alternative to omelette.'

Sam surveyed the pitiful remains of food on the table. 'It was a good alternative. Especially given that there were no eggs. And I'm paying.'

'That's just ridiculous.'

'No, that's just the way it is.' He handed his card to Ken. 'Fantastic food, Ken. Great evening. Make that appointment to see me any time.'

'Has anyone ever told you that you're stubborn and opinionated?' Anna rose to her feet and reached for her bag. 'Just for the record, your macho, he-man act doesn't work on me, McKenna. If you're expecting it to make my legs go weak, it's only fair to warn you that I'm still walking with no problems.'

'Really?' He pulled a face. 'Damn. I must be losing my touch. Need to lift a few more weights. Practise my walk. And for the record, you're more stubborn than me.'

They left the restaurant and walked back to the car.

'Now, this is when I love Cornwall.' Sam stopped and stared out across the darkened beach. The sea hissed as the waves hit the sand and behind them they could hear laughter from the restaurant. 'I love it when the tourists leave and the beach is ours again.'

Anna stood next to him. 'The trouble is nowadays the tourists never leave. Most of these beaches are as crowded at night as they are during the day. Once it gets dark the partying starts.'

They stared at a group of teenagers gathered at the water's edge and Sam frowned. 'The problem with this place is that the teenagers don't have anywhere to go. And there's no privacy. If one of them makes an appointment at the surgery, everyone knows.'

'What's wrong with that?'

'Well, if you're trying to be cool, or if you're trying to hide something from your parents, then making an appointment with us is like taking out an ad in the paper.'

Anna stared at him. 'You think that's why teenagers don't come?'

'One reason.' He looked at the group on the beach. 'We ought to start a teenage health group. Somewhere they can go, mingle and chat to a doctor if they want to.'

It was a great idea. 'No one would turn up.'

'They'd turn up if we made it cool.'

'And how would we do that?'

He turned and gave her a lopsided smile. 'I'd be the doctor.'

She grunted with exasperation. 'You are so arrogant.'

'What's the teenage pregnancy rate here?'

'It's high, as you well know.'

'Probably because if they go to the doctor, they broadcast the fact from the rooftops. If there was a clinic for teenagers, we could deal with all sorts of things. Drugs, eating disorders, contraception and the positive stuff, exercise, healthy eating.'

It was a fantastic idea. 'It would never work.'

'Let's try it. Send invitations to all the teenagers in the area.'

'I'll think about it.' She was definitely going to do it.

'You're afraid I'll be proved right.'

'You're never right, McKenna. And all our teen-agers want to do is party.'

'Talking of parties, when is the beach barbecue to raise money for the lifeboat? Must be soon.'

Anna laughed. 'The highlight of our social calendar. I'm amazed you remember it.'

'It was at the beach barbecue that I finally scored with Daisy Forest,' Sam said smugly. 'Not likely to forget that in a hurry. What a girl.'

'Well, it's probably only fair to warn you that Daisy Forest is now a happily married woman with three little girls and a doting husband whose shoulder measurements exceed even yours. You might want to rethink that attachment.'

Sam winced and gave a wry smile. 'Damn. There go my dreams.'

'Just for my own interest and research, what was it that wrecked them? The three little girls or the dimensions of her husband?'

'Both. I'm a man who hates competition. So when is it?'

'The beach barbecue? Three weeks on Saturday. Usual fund-raising stuff. Ken does the food, there's dancing, several people get drunk and make fools of themselves. We raise some money, we buy new equipment. You know the sort of thing.'

'Sounds too good to miss.' He stood next to her, broad-shouldered and handsome. Sexy.

Anna scooped her hair away from her face and frowned. Since when had she ever found Sam McKenna sexy?

Obviously since she'd drunk too much champagne on an empty stomach. She was hallucinating. Her judgement was failing. It was time to go home.

'Do you want to leave the car and walk?'

He turned. 'Unlike you, I didn't indulge. I'm fine to drive. And I'll need the car in the morning.'

She yawned as they walked to the car park. 'So tomorrow filming starts in earnest?'

'Polly has all sorts of plans, but often we just see what comes in. What looks interesting.'

He drove back slowly and Anna closed her eyes, loving the feel of the wind in her hair. 'All right, you win. This is bliss. Not the engine, just the lack of roof.'

'Glad I've finally pleased you. Remind me to give you champagne more often,' Sam said dryly. 'You become more human.'

'With most people I'm human,' she murmured. 'It's just you that brings out the worst in me. Always have done, McKenna. Always will do.'

'We've done all right tonight.' He pulled up outside the house and they walked inside. 'No bloodshed. No visible wounds.'

They made their way to the kitchen and both of them reached for the light switch. Their fingers touched and suddenly she realised how close they were. She could feel the warmth of his breath near her face, feel the brush of his powerful body against hers. The lights flickered on and his gaze slid slowly to hers. Suddenly they were eye to eye and awareness shot between them like a bolt of lightning.

The breath caught in her throat and her heart bumped against her chest. 'Do you…want coffee?' Her voice sounded strange. Totally unlike her own. And she found herself noticing things about his eyes that she'd never noticed before. Like the fact that in this light they looked an even deeper blue. And that his lashes were thick and sinfully dark. Lashes that should have looked feminine but somehow made him more male than ever.

'Coffee?' His gaze slid to her mouth as if he was trying to make sense of something extremely complicated. 'I thought you were keen to get back to those journals of yours.'

'That's right.' She fought the temptation to lift her fingers to her lips, but his gaze fixed on her mouth was making her tingle. 'Journals.'

'No coffee, then.' His eyes lifted to hers and locked. 'I'll see you in the morning.'

'Presumably.'

Their fingers were still tangled together, still on the light switch, and they both pulled away at the same time, their bodies bumping together as they turned for the door.

'Hell, Riggs…' He hauled her against him and brought his mouth down on hers hard, one hand sliding behind her neck and holding her fast.

She fell into his kiss, drowning in the heat and the fire, a dangerous thrill curling upwards from deep inside her. It was hot and frantic and totally out of character, but for a brief moment in time she didn't care. She didn't care about the future and she didn't care about the past. She just wanted now.

She grabbed the front of his shirt to press herself closer, and without lifting his head he backed her against the wall, his kiss impossibly intimate, his hands sliding with sensual purpose up the sides of her body until they rested on her breasts. She felt the cool wall against her back, felt the press of solid muscle and hard, sexy male and closed her eyes.

When he finally dragged his mouth from hers and slid hot kisses down her throat, she gasped for air and struggled to rescue the situation.

'We should stop this.' Her eyes stayed closed and a soft gasp escaped from her lips as he jerked the strap of her dress down and trailed kisses over the swell of her breast. 'McKenna...' She groaned his name. 'I said we should stop.'

'We probably should.'

Her head tilted back as his lips moved lower still. 'This isn't a good idea.'

'Feels pretty good from where I am,' he murmured hoarsely, straightening and returning his full attention to her swollen mouth. 'Never thought you'd taste this good, Riggs. Incredible.'

She dragged her eyes open and tried to summon up some of the old feelings of irritation and exasperation. But all she could feel was heat.

She was in big trouble.

'We really can't do this. We have to stop.'

'Good idea.' His tongue slid into her mouth and he kissed her again. Then he lifted his mouth just enough to speak. 'We'll stop. Any minute now, we're going to stop this. God, you smell good.' He rubbed his face over her cheek. 'Have you always smelt this good or have I just not breathed you in before?'

She was aware of every single masculine inch of him, pumped up and virile and so devastatingly sexy that it was almost impossible for her to breathe. The wanting was so powerful that she couldn't think straight.

'You're going to have to stop this, McKenna.'

His mouth played with hers. Teasing. Tantalising. 'Not sure I can. You taste as good as you smell.'

'Then we'll both do it. On three. You move away. I move away.' She felt his tongue coaxing hers and she groaned and curled her fingers into the hard muscle of his forearms. 'I said, on three. One, two, three.'

She gave him a shove and he stepped backwards. It gave her some satisfaction to see that his breathing was decidedly unsteady. Hers was, too. If she had a patient in this state she'd be considering medication.

'OK, well, that worked.' She lifted the strap of her dress with shaking fingers and raked her tangled hair out of her eyes. She dreaded to think what she looked like but, judging from the look burning in his eyes, she decided it was probably better not to know. 'I'll just go to bed…'

He inhaled deeply. 'Just so that there's no misunderstanding here—on your own, I presume?'

'Definitely on my own.' She backed towards the

door, her legs decidedly unsteady. 'And we're going to forget this happened.'

He raked long fingers through his already roughened hair. 'That easy, huh?'

'I didn't say it was going to be easy,' she said honestly, 'just that that is what we're going to do.'

'Unless we go with Plan B.'

'Which is?'

His eyes were on her mouth. 'We take this to its natural conclusion.'

The air stilled and her heart skipped a beat. 'I can't believe we're having this conversation. We drive each other crazy, McKenna.'

His eyes darkened. 'I think we've just proved that.'

'You know what I mean. We don't even like each other and I need to like a man before I take him to bed. It's the barest minimum requirement. And we can't even converse without annoying each other.'

'Riggs…' His voice was sexier than a man's voice had a right to be. 'At the moment, I'm not thinking about conversation. I'm just thinking about your body in my bed. And more of what we just sampled.'

His words made her stomach flip. Her body in his bed. *His body tangled with her body.*

His shirt was half undone where she'd dragged at the bottom and she saw the haze of dark hair on his chest. He was a man designed to tempt a woman from the straight and narrow.

And she was tempted. So tempted.

'We'd regret it in the morning.'

'I never regret anything I do. It's a waste of emotion.'

'Look…' She scooped her hair away from her face and licked her lips, struggling to be rational. 'Let's just admit this was a mistake. We had a nice evening and that's rare for us. We both drank a bit too much.'

'I'm stone-cold sober.'

'We're going to forget it happened.' She ignored his soft statement and backed through the door, holding onto the wall for support. Ever since he'd kissed her, her legs didn't seem to be working that well.

'Riggs.' His voice stopped her before she made it to the stairs. 'What if we can't forget it happened?'

She paused, her hand curled tightly round the banister for safety. 'We will.'

They had to.

Otherwise they were in big trouble.

CHAPTER FIVE

THE following morning the surgery was crowded with patients and Anna was relieved that there was no sign of Sam. She couldn't face him at the moment. Not until she'd managed to wipe out all memories of that incredible kiss.

Chemistry.

Damn. Who would have thought it? It just went to prove that the mind and the body were totally incomprehensible.

'Glenda rang.' Hannah, the other receptionist, looked at Anna searchingly, clearly wondering what was wrong with her usually sharp-minded boss. 'She's been caught up at home but she'll be in as soon as possible.'

Anna frowned. Caught up with what? 'Fine. Do you know what's wrong, Hannah? Did she say anything?'

Hannah shook her head. 'No.' The young girl looked thoughtful. 'But she didn't sound herself. And she hung up in a hurry.'

'OK. Any sign of Dr McKenna?'

'He phoned just before you arrived to say that he was making one call on his way in and to explain to his patients.'

'Oh.' For a moment Anna was annoyed that he

hadn't thought to call her on her mobile and tell her his plans. Then she remembered that she'd gone out of her way to avoid him that morning. She'd showered early, skipped breakfast and sneaked out of the house before she'd heard sounds from his bedroom. Presumably he'd taken the same approach and that was why he hadn't called her.

Which proved that her plan was the right one. Ignore the whole thing. Pretend it had never happened. They should never have indulged in that kiss and the sooner they both put it behind them and started to act normally again, the better for both of them.

'OK, Hannah, I'll get on with my surgery. Let me know when Dr McKenna arrives. If he's horribly delayed I'll tuck his patients in between mine.'

Her first patient was Katy, a seventeen-year-old who walked in with her mother. Anna took one look at the teenager's face and knew this was going to be a difficult consultation.

Sam was right. They needed a clinic for teenagers.

'Hello, Katy.' She offered the girl the seat closest to her and gave her mother a brief smile. 'Hello, Mrs Walker.'

'She doesn't want to be here,' Mrs Walker said briskly, 'but I've told her that if she doesn't come, I'll cut off her allowance.'

Anna winced mentally and glanced at Katy, gauging her reaction. The girl looked sullen and uncooperative but that was hardly surprising given the circumstances.

'She doesn't eat and she spends her life in the gym,' Mrs Walker began, her mouth tightening in disapproval as she looked at her daughter.

'At least I don't sit on the couch playing computer games,' Katy muttered, scowling at her mother. 'And there's nothing wrong with going to the gym. It's healthy.'

Anna thought for a moment and then smiled at Mrs Walker. 'Would you mind if I spoke to Katy alone?' She rose and walked to the door, leaving the mother no choice but to stand up and walk through it. 'If you take a seat in the waiting room, Katy and I will just have a chat and we'll be with you shortly.'

Anna closed the door firmly and then turned back to her patient. 'Would you have come if it hadn't been for your mother?'

'No.' The girl stared at her. 'There's nothing wrong with me. I'm perfectly healthy. Mum's just a nag.'

Anna sat back down and started to talk to Katy, asking questions about her eating history and questioning her on her attitude to her weight. 'How often do you go to the gym, Katy?'

The girl shrugged. 'Dunno. Most days, I suppose. For about two hours.'

Anna nodded. 'That's quite a lot. It's great to exercise, you're right about that, but we probably need to reduce it slightly and look at your eating patterns.'

She spent some time discussing normal eating, diet and exercise, as well as the physical consequences of an eating disorder.

'I want you to try and eat three meals a day, and would you keep a food diary for me and come and see me again?'

She knew that eating disorders could be extremely difficult to treat but she sensed that in Katy's case the problem was relatively new, which meant that she might be successful in preventing the problem becoming entrenched.

Katy shrugged. 'I suppose so. As long as Mum doesn't come, too. She thinks she understands me.' She rolled her eyes. 'It's tragic.'

Anna suppressed a smile. Far be it from adults to understand teenagers. A sudden inspiration struck. 'Katy, you know everyone in the village...'

The girl shrugged. 'I've lived here all my life,' she said gloomily, 'so I certainly should do.'

'Dr McKenna and I are thinking of setting up a clinic for teenagers, and some input from you as to what would work and what wouldn't would be really helpful.' Anna gave a small smile. 'We'd hate to be seen as "tragic".'

Katy stared at her and a ghost of a smile crossed her face. 'If Dr McKenna is involved, it might be cool.'

Anna ground her teeth. Great. The man was going to be proved right again. If she hadn't been so convinced that the teenage clinic was the right thing for the practice, she might have buried the idea.

As it was, her encounter with Katy made her determined to get the clinic off the ground.

She made a mental note to herself to sort it out

at the earliest opportunity and carried on with her surgery.

She'd just seen her third patient when there was a tap on her door and Sam entered.

Her heart skipped in her chest.

Annoyance and another emotion which she chose not to examine made her voice cooler than she'd intended. 'For future reference I'd like to know if you intend to be late for surgery.'

'I took an emergency call this morning. A fact I would have shared with you if you hadn't been so desperate to avoid me.'

'I wasn't desperate.'

He gave a humourless laugh and closed her door firmly behind him. 'Then you're the lucky one. I was so desperate after last night that my body refused to go to sleep.'

Her heart hit her ribcage. 'I don't want to talk about last night.'

'Fine. We'll try it your way to start with. Pretend it didn't happen. If that doesn't work then we'll try it my way. Agreed?'

She stared at him. 'What's your way?'

'We're trying it your way first. When that fails to work, I'll tell you mine.'

Her heat skipped a beat. 'You've got patients piling up outside your surgery, McKenna. You may want to do something about it.'

'In a moment. I'm just checking you're free at lunch-time.'

She glared at him. 'I've already told you, I don't

take a lunch-break. And I certainly don't go on dates at lunch-time.'

He strolled across the room, planted both hands on her desk and locked his gaze with hers. 'Firstly, I didn't mention taking a break and, secondly, I didn't say anything about a date.'

'But you—'

'I want to talk to you about Glenda. She has problems we need to help her with. Big problems.'

Anna stared at him. 'Tell me.'

He straightened. 'In case you've forgotten, we've got patients piling up outside the door, Riggs. Let's clear the decks and then we can concentrate on Glenda.'

'She called me this morning in a state.' Sam nursed a coffee, trying not to notice Anna's hair. He loved the sleekness of it. The smoothness. The darkness against her perfect white blouse. It was all he could do to keep his fingers out of it. And away from the rest of her. He just wanted to reach out, grab and help himself. Just as he had the night before.

Damn, he should never have touched her. Then he wouldn't have known that she tasted like a dream.

'A state about what?'

He struggled to keep his mind on the job. 'How much do you know about her mother?'

Anna sat back in her chair. 'Not much, I suppose. Just to say hello to her in passing. She's your father's patient. I don't think she's consulted me at all in the time that I've been here. I only know her as Glenda's mum. You think there's something wrong with her?'

'It would seem so. Glenda rang me this morning because she was afraid to leave her on her own in the house.' Sam ran a hand over his face, trying to keep his mind on the job in hand. Concentration had never been so difficult. 'Basically, she's been trying to ignore the problem. Pretend it isn't happening. But yesterday she lost her mother when they were out shopping.'

'She lost her?'

'She wandered off. Glenda panicked. Apparently that was the final straw that made her call me.'

Anna stared at him. 'You're suggesting that her mother has a form of dementia?'

'I think it's highly probable. We need to refer her to a specialist mental health service for assessment.'

'There's an excellent memory clinic at the hospital.' Anna closed her eyes and breathed out. 'Oh, help. Poor thing. And poor Glenda. What a thing to cope with. And she's an only child, isn't she? No other siblings to help?'

'That's right. And she's really been struggling. Afraid to leave her mother on her own for any length of time, desperate to do her job here and not let us down…'

'She needn't worry about the job,' Anna said immediately. 'We'll make whatever arrangements are necessary to cover her if she needs to be at home, but her job is here for as long as she wants it.'

Sam felt something shift inside him. The woman

might be tough on the outside but she was marsh-mallow on the inside. Loyal and giving. And maybe a part of him had always known that. After all, hadn't she been the one to stay and help his father while he'd chosen a different path? 'It won't be easy.'

'It's Glenda that matters, not the practice. Hannah can do extra time and I'll rack my brains to think of who might be able to help her.' Anna frowned and drummed her fingers on the desk, her neat fingernails tapping a rhythm while she thought. Her brow cleared. 'I know. We'll ask Fiona.'

'She retired a year ago.'

'But she was the most efficient receptionist we ever had and she taught Glenda everything she knew,' Anna reminded him, flicking through a box on her desk and pulling out a card. 'I've got her number here. Once we've spoken to Glenda, we can give her a ring if necessary. But the more important question is how to help Glenda and her mother.'

'I went round there this morning,' Sam told her, a drawn look on his face as he recalled the visit. 'Frankly, I can't begin to imagine how Glenda has coped without help up until now. It's no wonder she's been so stressed. I'm amazed she's been mak-ing it to work at all. Her mother was really agitated and aggressive. And she clearly forgets everything, which drives Glenda up the wall.'

Anna groaned. 'I just wish she'd said something sooner. This is all my fault.' She scooped her hair away from her face in a gesture that made him want to groan aloud. 'I should have noticed sooner that something was very wrong. She hasn't been herself for ages. And now I see why. And I see why she's always dashing off at lunch-time and arriving late in the mornings.'

With a determined effort Sam shifted his gaze away from her, trying to remind himself just how badly they clashed. 'She's been checking on her mother—afraid to leave her for too long,' he agreed, 'but don't blame yourself, Riggs. You've been propping up this place virtually single-handed for too long. And that brings us to another subject we're going to have to tackle. You should have told Dad he was no longer up to the job a long time ago.'

Anna bit her lip. 'That isn't true.'

'It's true,' Sam said heavily. 'You've been covering for him, picking up his workload. The sabbatical idea was genius. It enabled you to get some help without telling him outright he needed to retire. Hopefully he'll get the message himself when he's away.'

Her eyes slid away from his. 'Your dad is a brilliant doctor.'

'But his health has been getting worse and you need to be on full power for this job,' Sam said steadily, ignoring the ache inside him. 'It's hard to acknowledge that he's getting old, but that's the truth. There are things Dad should have been doing that he hasn't.'

'That reminds me.' She looked him straight in the eye. 'I want to talk to you about your ideas for that teenage clinic. I want to try it.'

He nodded. 'Good. What changed your mind?'

'I always thought it was a good idea.' Her mouth tilted slightly at the corners and she angled her head. 'It's just that I had to get my head round the fact that it came from you.'

He laughed with appreciation. 'Well, that's honest.'

'I had a girl in here this morning…'

He listened while she told him about Katy and about her plan to involve some of the teenagers in setting up the clinic. It was a great idea.

'I have to hand it to you, Riggs, when you go with an idea, you don't hang around.'

'Now's the time to get them,' she said briskly. 'Long, hot summer evenings are the time when they get carried away. A significant number of our teenage mothers give birth in March.'

'So let's get started. Set up your meeting. What's the problem?'

She breathed in and looked slightly pink. 'You have to be there. Apparently you're "cool".'

He grinned. 'And doesn't that just bug you, Riggs?'

'Actually, no.' She sat back in her chair and surveyed him with those amazing brown eyes. 'If you get the teenagers here, I don't care what tactics you employ. Use your movie-star status if it helps.'

He smiled. 'Any time you want my autograph, Riggs…'

'I'll try and survive without it. But let's get on with this clinic.'

'I thought you hated change.'

'Only when it's done for the sake of change. I can see the benefit of the clinic.'

'My father couldn't. It's one of the reasons I know he should retire. He's stopped seeing what his patients need.'

He saw her eyes cloud, saw the evidence of her very real affection for his father.

'I don't want him to retire.' Anna's chin lifted. 'Changing a few clinics won't matter to him. We can explain why we did it. Things are still the same in the practice.'

'Things never stay the same,' Sam said flatly, rising to his feet in a fluid movement. 'Time moves on and we need to move with it. Let's get through the summer and then we'll sort out what the practice needs, what Dad needs…' He hesitated. 'And what you need.'

He saw her stiffen defensively. 'What do you mean, what I need? I don't need anything.'

He gave a slow smile and watched with satisfaction while her colour rose. 'No? Then it must be just me. Catch you later, Riggs.'

He left the room, ignoring the throb in his loins and the kick of his heart. Who would have thought it? Usually he liked his women gentle and compliant. Everything that Anna wasn't. Anna was stubborn and had a tongue like a whiplash, but he respected her. And that respect was growing, the more he saw of her.

And the fact that the chemistry between them so clearly didn't fit into her plans made the situation even more interesting.

CHAPTER SIX

'MUM'S got an appointment at the memory clinic.' Glenda dropped her bag and removed her cardigan. 'I never thought it would be that quick.'

Aware that Sam had pulled several strings and had had several conversations with the consultant over the past week, Anna merely smiled. 'I'm pleased. When is it?'

'End of the week.' Glenda pulled a face and settled in her chair behind Reception. 'Do you mind if I take a few hours off in the afternoon to go with her?'

'Of course not.' Anna put down the pile of journals she was carrying. 'I wish you'd told me about your mum sooner, Glenda. I feel dreadful, knowing that you were struggling with that on your own.'

Glenda fiddled with her hair. 'Well, to be honest, I don't think I was willing to admit it even to myself.' She flicked on the computer and gave Anna a rueful smile. 'These things happen to other people, don't they? For ages I managed to convince myself she was just a bit forgetful, a bit crotchety. I didn't want to admit it might be anything worse. But lately she's been dreadful. Can't remember a thing.'

'There are things you can do that might help with that.' Anna sat down on the corner of the desk. 'Like keeping everything in the same place and having a routine. Put telephone numbers by the phone and label cupboards to help her remember where things live in the house. I've got a leaflet somewhere with practical tips—I'll look it out for you although I'm sure the clinic will be able to give you something, too.'

Glenda buried her face in her hands. 'I just don't want her to have to go into a home. But I know that I can't carry on like this either, and that makes me feel so selfish.'

'You're not selfish, Glenda,' Anna said quietly, 'and it's about finding a compromise that works for both of you. Why don't you stop worrying about it until after the appointment? The consultant will be able to assess your mother properly and give you some idea of the future and the options available.'

Glenda nodded and breathed out heavily. 'I suppose that's good advice. It's just that your mind keeps running forward. What if she just can't manage at home any more? What if she isn't safe? To be honest, every morning when I leave the house I wonder whether she's going to have burned it down by the time I come home. It's a nightmare.'

'Well, there are definitely practical things you can do to at least help in that department,' Anna reminded her. 'You can get safety devices installed—gas detectors, smoke alarms, that sort of thing.'

Glenda nodded. 'I know.' She sighed. 'I suppose admitting there's a problem is the first step to doing something about it. At least now it's out in the open.'

She looked at Anna and her eyes filled. 'I was so afraid that I'd lose my job.'

'You're part of the practice, Glenda,' Anna said gruffly, leaning forward and giving the older woman a hug. 'You belong here and we'll work through this together. You'll never lose your job.'

Glenda scrubbed her palm across her face and sniffed loudly. 'Don't be kind to me. It makes it worse. But you're such a lovely girl. And your dad would have been so proud of you.'

'It's going to be OK, Glenda,' Anna said softly. 'We'll work something out. Somehow we'll get you whatever help you need.'

The issue of Glenda and her mother occupied Anna's mind for the next few days, and she managed to do a reasonable job of avoiding Sam. As usual, she ate lunch on the run and in the evening she headed for the beach and jogged along the sand, returning just late enough to avoid the possibility of sharing dinner. She didn't want to sit down opposite Sam again. Didn't want to risk feeling something that she didn't want to feel. *Something complicated.*

All in all, she was doing fine. Life was back to normal.

It was just a shame she couldn't get that kiss out of her mind, she thought crossly as she pushed open the door of the surgery first thing one morning.

It was just because it had been so unexpected, she consoled herself. They'd had a nice evening—she frowned as she remembered it, *an unusually nice evening*—and they'd both just got a bit carried away. Weren't emotions always more intense at night-time? If they kissed during the day they probably wouldn't feel anything at all. Nothing.

When she walked into Reception, Glenda was already at her desk, looking more relaxed than she had in weeks.

'How did it go? I tried to call you last night.' Anna knew Glenda had taken her mother to the hospital the day before but when she'd tried to phone there'd been no answer.

Glenda blushed slightly. 'Actually, after we got back from the hospital, I went for a drink with a friend. I needed to relax and Mum seemed fine so I popped out.'

Anna hid her curiosity, even though she was dying to ask whether the 'friend' was male or female. Privately she hoped it was male. Glenda needed someone to brighten up her life. 'So what did the hospital say?'

'They were really positive and helpful, actually,' Glenda admitted, brushing her hair away from her face. 'And they had lots of amazingly practical suggestions. Like looking for things that trigger her aggressive behaviour. When I talked about it with them, I realised that she gets really, really angry just before she goes to the toilet. So now I know that I need to watch for that and make sure that she gets to the toilet. Who would have thought it could have been brought on by something as simple as that?'

Anna nodded. 'What else?'

'Well, they've got this great day centre where she can go and get involved in all sorts of activities. They do things like art and music therapy. Apparently it gives patients a sense of achievement and that helps to ease some of the frustration.'

'And it means that you can relax, knowing that she's in safe hands.' Anna was relieved that Glenda had been offered some help and support.

Glenda nodded. 'And you were right about them giving me lots of practical tips. They're going to send a nurse round to assess the home, but they've said that it's important to minimise clutter. Apparently that should help to reduce Mum's agitation.'

Anna grinned. 'Hope they never come and look at my house. I invented clutter.'

'And I can vouch for that.' Sam strolled up, smothering a yawn. He looked as though he hadn't been sleeping properly. 'Living with you, Riggs, is a bit like being in a permanent car boot sale. It's a good job your house purchase fell through. You and your belongings never would have fitted into old Jack Lawson's place on the beach. If it didn't already suffer from subsidence, it would have done the minute you moved in. No building could stand the weight of your belongings.'

Anna scowled at him. 'And you're so domesticated and tidy, of course.'

Sam smiled and winked at Glenda. 'At least I can cook.'

'I can cook.' Anna put her hands on her hips and her eyes flashed. How could she have wanted to kiss him? All she wanted to do at the moment was punch him for being so smug and infuriating. 'It's just I don't choose to spend my time slaving over a hot stove for something that vanishes within seconds of being put on the table. It's the ultimate waste of time.'

'What you do to food can't be described as cooking. Is that for me, Glenda?' Sam leaned across the reception desk and picked up his post. 'By the way, we're filming the emergency clinic this morning. And then this afternoon I'm doing a piece to camera on the beach.'

'Will you be wearing your wet suit and carrying a surfboard?' Anna's tone dripped sarcasm and he gave her a solemn look, one that he often used for the camera when he was addressing a serious topic.

'No, I'm doing my caring, responsible doctor bit.' Then he grinned and walked towards his father's consulting room.

Glenda watched him go. 'He's amazing, isn't he? Do you know that he spent the whole of yesterday evening installing gadgets in my house?'

Anna stared at her. 'Gadgets?'

'Yes.' Glenda nodded and ticked them off on her fingers. 'Smoke alarm, some fancy gas thing—and an alarm for Mum. And he shifted some furniture for me. He's incredibly strong.'

Anna inhaled sharply. She didn't want to think about Sam's muscles. It brought back memories of his body pressed hard against hers. *Memories she was trying extremely hard to forget.*

She was still trying not to think about his muscles when Hilda Wakeman hurried in, carrying a large bag.

'Hello, Hilda.' Anna's face brightened. Hilda ran the upmarket delicatessen on the quay and Anna was her most frequent customer. 'How's business?'

'Brisk. I've been up since four-thirty, baking and cooking. It's the only way to keep up with demand. I think tourists eat more than they used to.' Hilda put the bags down. 'Is Dr McKenna around?'

'Just gone into surgery to catch up on some phone calls.' Glenda reached for the phone. 'I'll buzz him for you.'

'No need to bother him. Just wanted to say thank you, that's all.' Hilda gave Anna a rueful smile. 'He did me a good turn yesterday and I always repay a favour.'

It appeared that Sam had done everyone a good turn yesterday, Anna reflected. For a man who professed not to enjoy harbour life, he seemed to have thrown himself back into the community with a commendable amount of dedication.

But it wasn't permanent, she reminded herself.

He was just playing at being a semi-rural GP. He'd be back to the bright lights and the glamour as soon as the summer was over and his father was back.

Sam walked out of his surgery, his face brightening when he saw Hilda. 'My favourite cook!' His eyes narrowed. 'No more problems since yesterday?'

'None.' Hilda smiled warmly. 'Thank goodness you were there.' She turned to Anna. 'Little Nancy, who works for me, cut her finger really badly. Fortunately Sam was passing and brought her up here and did the honours.'

'She needed a couple of stitches. It was a nasty cut. Is she feeling all right today?'

'I've got her working the till and taking it quietly. I did tell her to stay at home but, knowing how busy we are at the moment, she wouldn't hear of it. She's a good girl.' Hilda picked up the bags. 'Now, knowing that you're living with Dr Riggs at the moment, I'm guessing you won't be eating that well, so I've got some things for you here, Dr McKenna, so that you don't have to worry about cooking tonight.'

Anna gritted her teeth. One of the drawbacks of living in a small village was that everyone knew everything about everyone else. Including the fact that she loathed cooking. 'He isn't living *with* me, Hilda—'

'Well, you're sharing a house, which amounts to the same thing,' Hilda said briskly, peering into the bag to remind herself of the contents. 'Marinaded olives, a delicious aubergine salad that the two of you can have as a starter, and—'

'The two of us?' Sam strolled towards her and hooked a finger into the bag. 'Looks fantastic, Hilda. But who are you planning to feed?'

'Well, you and Dr Riggs, of course. Stuck up there in that house on your own and both of you too busy to turn round, let alone cook.' Hilda smacked the back of his hand sharply. 'Don't poke the food. It needs to go straight in the fridge in this heat otherwise you'll be poisoned and blaming me. I've got my reputation to think of.'

Ignoring her stern expression, Sam peered into the bag and sniffed. 'Smells fantastic. I think your reputation as the area's best cook is still intact, Hilda.'

Glenda stood up, her eyes twinkling with amusement. 'Why don't I pop all that in the fridge in the kitchen and you can take it home when you go? Dr Riggs will be delighted. She hates cooking, as you know, Hilda.'

'Of course I know,' Hilda said comfortably. 'It's the reason she stops by almost every night and picks up something for her dinner. But I thought I'd save you the trouble tonight. And I thought I'd make something a bit special by way of a thank you. There's a lovely seafood pie and fresh apple crumble with clotted cream.'

Anna grunted, torn between pleasure at the anticipation of one of Hilda's dinners and irritation at the fact that everyone was discussing her lack of culinary skills so freely. 'I don't know why everyone is so obsessed with the fact that I don't cook. Does a woman always have to cook?'

'Not when they have a deli like mine in the village,' Hilda said calmly, handing the last of the bags to Glenda to store in the fridge. 'And my Geoff popped an excellent bottle of white in the bag, too. A sauvignon blanc, that's his personal favourite. And I added a lovely scented candle. Have a good evening.'

With that she winked at them both and hurried back to her car.

'Scented candle?' Sam stared after her. 'What the hell was that all about? Give me the wine and the food, definitely, but what's with the scented candle?'

Anna scowled and raked her hair out of her eyes. 'You heard. She knows I can't cook and she thinks I'm starving you. Although why I'm supposed to be responsible for the contents of your stomach, goodness knows. And I haven't got a clue about the scented candle. Perhaps it's to keep wasps away.'

'Nothing to do with wasps. She's matchmaking,' Glenda said calmly, fishing in the bag and removing the candle. 'Oh, look—it's one of those special ones set in driftwood. It's so pretty. It'll look lovely on that table on your deck. How romantic.'

She put it carefully back in the bag and Anna felt her colour rise. 'Romantic? Matchmaking?'

Glenda smiled and stowed the bag carefully behind Reception. 'Of course. The whole village is hoping that the two of you will fall in love and set up shop together. It would be a fairy-tale ending.'

There was a pulsing silence.

For a moment Anna stood still, totally speechless. Then her temper exploded. 'Since when did fairy tales come with loud arguments and the threat of physical injury?' She whirled round and glared at Sam. 'Don't just stand there laughing! Say something!'

Sam ran a hand over his face but his blue eyes

gleamed with humour. 'Looks like I don't have to cook dinner tonight.'

Anna all but stamped her foot. 'How can you be so calm? They think you're going to stay, McKenna. Step into your father's place.' She bit her lip. 'They're trying to… They want us to…' She couldn't even bring herself to voice the idea, it was so ridiculous.

'Get together,' Sam finished for her helpfully, his gaze disconcertingly direct. 'They just want a doctor they know. You can't blame them for that. And matchmaking goes on all the time in villages.'

'Between people who like each other, McKenna,' Anna reminded him tartly. 'We don't like each other.'

He looked at her thoughtfully. 'No, that's right. We don't, do we?'

Something in his tone made her remember the kiss and she blushed. 'Well, finally we agree on something. I haven't got time to stand around here all day, talking about village gossip. I've got work to do.'

'Me, too.'

Glenda glanced between them and sighed. 'Well, if the two of you are arguing too much to eat Hilda's food, give me a call and I'll come and eat it.'

'You're seriously going to sit down and eat dinner with the whole harbour watching?'

His eyes flickered along the bay. 'You're paranoid. I don't see anyone showing any interest in us.'

She grunted and swept her hair back from her face.

'That's because you're used to living in London and you automatically assume that no one is interested in you. Here, everyone is interested in you. You should remember that. Somewhere out there someone probably has a telescope fixed on this deck and they're watching our every move. Light that candle and we may as well book the church.'

'Your wrong, actually. In my job it's like being in a goldfish bowl. But, frankly, I don't care who's watching. There's no way I'm wasting this food.' Sam put a loaded plate in the middle of the table. 'You can go and eat baked beans in your bedroom if you prefer. I won't tell anyone.'

Anna stared at the aubergine salad and felt her mouth water. 'You'll never eat all that by yourself.'

'Never underestimate my appetites,' he drawled, a wicked glint in his eyes as he surveyed her. 'And I should probably point out that if you carry on being this jumpy around me, the village is going to be gossiping even more than it is at the moment.'

'I'm not jumpy.'

One dark eyebrow lifted. 'Riggs, you're like a kangaroo. The moment I enter a room, you bounce out of it. This is as good a time as any to ask you why.'

She glared at him. 'Don't flatter yourself it has anything to do with you. I'm a busy woman. Lots to do.'

'If you say so.' With smooth, measured movements he finished laying the table. 'I'm just warning you how it might look from the outside. And don't be embarrassed. I'm avoiding you, too.'

'You are?'

'That's right. It's the only way I can concentrate and get any work done. Now, are you eating or not? The seafood pie is heating in the oven so we need to get started.'

Anna stared at him.

He was having trouble concentrating?

He was thinking about her? Suddenly she felt unsettled and she wasn't used to feeling unsettled. She was used to knowing where her life was going. To being in control. Around Sam McKenna, she didn't feel in control at all.

Her brain told her to leave but her taste buds had other ideas. 'All right, we'll share the meal. But we'll live to regret it. I'm willing to bet that someone is watching.'

'Let them watch.' Sam sprawled in a chair and lifted his beer, his eyes resting on the surf.

'You used to hate all that. The fact that everyone knew everything about you,' she reminded him, picking at an olive. 'It was one of the reasons you couldn't wait to go to London. You wanted to be anonymous.' She laughed as she realised what she'd said. 'Not that you're exactly anonymous, Dr Hotshot.'

His eyes swivelled to hers. 'I'm just a normal, everyday kind of guy.'

'I hate to disillusion you, but you've never been normal, McKenna.' She took another olive, admired its shiny blackness before popping it into her mouth.

'Arrogant, self-assured and wrong about virtually everything. Never normal. These olives are good. What exactly does Hilda do to them?'

'No idea, but they're always sold by lunch-time so it must be something special. How long has my dad been struggling?'

The swift change of subject threw her, just as he'd known it would. 'Most of last winter,' she admitted finally, dropping an olive stone onto her empty plate. 'He had a chest infection in October that he just couldn't throw off. After that he just seemed to slow down. I kept hoping he'd pick up but he never did.'

'Damn.' Sam stretched long legs in front of him. 'I can't believe I didn't notice. He just seemed the same to me.'

Anna stared across the beach. 'That's the strange thing about parents. You see them the way you think they are—the way they've always been—rather than the way they really are. I remember it took me ages to realise how ill Dad was. To me he was just Dad. And then I came home from university one holiday and for a moment I saw him as other people must see him. And I realised he'd aged. And lost weight. And grown old somewhere along the way. I just hadn't noticed.'

She felt a wave of emotion swamp her and blinked several times to clear her vision. No matter how much time passed, she still missed her parents.

'I remember that time. You walked around the whole holiday looking like a ghost.' Sam watched her across the table. 'That was a hard time for you, losing your dad and your mum so close together.'

'Neither of them would have been any good without the other, so it was probably for the best,' Anna said gruffly, turning her attention back to her plate, 'and I got through. Your parents were brilliant.'

'You've always been the daughter they never had.'

Their gazes locked and Anna's eyes narrowed as a thought entered her head. 'McKenna, you don't think— I mean, they wouldn't…'

He didn't pretend to misunderstand her. 'They're as capable of matchmaking as everyone else in the village, so I suppose it's possible.'

She put her fork down with a clatter. 'But they know us so well. They know that we clash, that we drive each other nuts—that we just couldn't—'

'Couldn't we?' He reached for the pepper, a strange light in his eyes as he glanced towards her. 'Just as well they didn't see that kiss the other night.'

Her heart hammered her ribcage. 'We agreed not to talk about that.'

'Your rules, Riggs. I'm willing to talk about it any time you like. And go for a repeat performance.'

Her pulse jumped and she took some sensible breaths. 'That would be ridiculous.'

'Would it? Why?'

'Because we are completely and totally wrong for each other,' she snapped, 'and that kiss was a mistake.'

'You didn't enjoy it?'

'What do you want me to say?' She glared at him.

'That you're good at kissing? Yes, you're good at kissing. Yes, I enjoyed it. But it wasn't real.'

'Felt real enough to me.'

'Look, McKenna...' She took a deep breath and struggled with her patience and the rush of unfamiliar feelings inside her. 'We'd managed to get through a whole evening without killing each other, I'd drunk champagne, which always goes to my head, the atmosphere was gooey, it was dark...' She ladled on the excuses and he studied her carefully.

'You want me to kiss you in daylight when you're sober, just to test that theory?'

'You're being deliberately annoying.' She stood up and picked up the empty plate. 'I'll get the seafood pie.'

Of course she didn't want him to test the theory.

She didn't want him to touch her again.

It was just too confusing.

She didn't like the man. He drove her nuts. Always had done, always would do. And just because he knew how to kiss a woman into a coma, it didn't change that fact.

The situation grew more tense every day.

It seemed that the more she tried to avoid him, the more their paths crossed. And wherever they were, Polly seemed to be filming.

They had a meeting with a group of local teenagers and talked about how they could improve the health provision in the area. It was a lively, stimulating evening and it served to confirm to Anna that

Sam had been right to suggest the idea. A teenage health clinic would work really well as long as they listened carefully to what was needed. The teenagers themselves, led by Katy, brainstormed ideas and decided to design the posters themselves.

'I just love it when someone else does all the work.' Sam leaned back in his chair and smiled at them. 'Just as long as people know that this is an open clinic. No appointments needed. Anyone under the age of eighteen can just turn up and hang out. You can see the doctor, talk to the nurse or just mingle. And every week one of us will give a short talk.'

'Can we talk about confidentiality?' One of the younger girls bit her lip and went pink. 'I mean, what you have to tell our parents and what can just be between us?'

Sam nodded, his expression serious. 'Of course. Good topic. Add that to the list, Katy.'

Katy scribbled away and by the end of the session they'd produced a long list of topics and general ideas for the clinic.

'We'll put a poster up in the surf shop, that's where most of the teenagers hang out,' Katy said, making a few deft strokes with her pen and lifting up her pad. 'What do you think of something like this for the design?'

Anna blinked. 'Katy, it's brilliant.'

Katy flushed. 'I'm doing art at college. I love drawing. I can make it better than this. I'll do it on the computer at home.'

By the time they'd finished, they'd planned their clinic down to the last detail.

'Go on.' Sam turned to her as they locked up at the end of the evening. 'Tell me I was right.'

'It's a good idea,' Anna conceded, dropping the keys into her bag. 'It remains to be seen if it will work.'

'It will work. Katy was really joining in. Are you still seeing her?'

Anna nodded, pausing by her car. 'She keeps a food diary and we talk about it and she's cut down on her exercise. I think she's acknowledging that she has a problem, which is good.'

'Unusual for someone with an eating disorder,' Sam observed, juggling his keys in the palm of his hand.

'Fortunately, I think Katy has only just developed a problem,' Anna said. 'It was a boy that she went out with. Kept telling her she was fat.'

Sam rolled his eyes. 'Teenage boys. Perhaps we ought to do something about body image in our clinic.'

'Good idea.'

He grinned. 'Careful, Riggs. We're agreeing on rather a lot at the moment.'

'Nonsense.' Suddenly flustered, she tugged open her car door and tossed her bag on the seat. The way he was looking at her made her feel hot. Aware of herself. So full of frustrated desire that her whole body felt ready to explode.

She'd never felt like this before. Never wanted a man so badly.

Especially one that she didn't even like. It just didn't make sense.

It was that kiss, she decided crossly, sliding into her car and slamming her car door shut. If they hadn't shared that stupid kiss then none of this would have happened. She could have carried on being irritated by him, finding him infuriating and aggravating. And she could have slept at night.

As it was, she hadn't slept properly for ages and the tension between them was building to almost intolerable levels.

Every time they were in a room together the atmosphere sizzled and thrummed and Anna was reaching screaming pitch.

She'd tried to bury sexual frustration in work, concentrating on her patients, helping Glenda, catching up with all the things that she'd been too busy to do with David ill. But none of it worked.

They carried on for a few more days and in the end Sam took control, grabbing Anna by the arm and hauling her into the nearest consulting room.

He closed the door firmly and pushed her against it, one arm planted either side of her head. 'OK, Riggs, we've tried it your way and it isn't working.'

'What do you mean, it isn't working?'

'You said that if we both ignored it and pretended that it never happened, it would go away.' He stepped closer to her, pressing her against the door. 'It hasn't gone away, Riggs. It's still there.'

She placed her hands on his chest and struggled to breathe.

'I don't know what you mean—' She didn't even finish the sentence before his mouth came down on hers and he showed her exactly what he meant.

The explosion was instant.

Fierce hunger exploded inside her and Anna lifted herself on her toes and pressed herself closer, moaning as he explored her mouth with erotic expertise.

She'd never been kissed like this before.

She'd never felt like this before.

She felt the heat build in her body, felt the powerful throb of his arousal against her and the urgency of his mouth on hers.

Completely forgetting where they were, she gave herself up to sensation. Eyes closed, she breathed in the masculine scent of him, felt the strength and purpose of his hands as he touched her but most of all revelled in the skilled possession of his mouth as he kissed her.

It was only when she felt the cool air brush her exposed breasts that she realised that he'd undone her blouse.

Shocked by how fast things had moved, she placed her hands in the centre of his chest. 'We've got to stop doing this.' She groaned the words against his mouth and he lifted his head just enough to respond.

'Or we could carry on.'

'We can't do that.'

'Why not?' His voice was husky and his eyes

roved over her flushed face, revealing a considerable degree of masculine satisfaction.

'Because sex would complicate things.'

'We're both single people.' He bent his head and kissed her neck, his touch warm and seductive. 'Who are we hurting?'

She couldn't reason or concentrate when he was this close. She just knew it wasn't what she had planned for herself.

She wasn't ready for a relationship. At least, not yet. And when she was ready it wouldn't be with a wickedly dangerous man like Sam McKenna. They clashed. They never agreed on anything. He irritated her beyond belief.

But he knew how to kiss and he had the most incredible hands...

She tried to talk sense into herself and failed, mostly because his mouth was still busy seducing hers. She moaned and kissed him back. Did it really matter if they weren't exactly well matched? If they were totally unsuited in every way except physically? Why shouldn't they just have some fun? As he had rightly pointed out, who would they be hurting?

CHAPTER SEVEN

SAM stood on the beach and tried to concentrate on what he was supposed to be saying.

James, the sound man, was making various adjustments and Polly was talking to the cameraman. In a moment he was going to have to start talking about holiday health and all he could think about was Anna.

He ran a hand over the back of his neck and the make-up girl sprinted forward with her box of tricks.

'Standing in the sun for too long is making you sweat.'

Sam surrendered to her ministrations and chose not to enlighten her. It wasn't the sun that was making him sweat. It was thoughts of Anna. Her fabulous legs. Her amazing hair. The way her mouth and skin tasted. It came as a considerable shock to discover that Anna had the ability to seriously disturb his equilibrium. Who would have thought it?

'OK, Sam, we're ready.' Polly walked towards him. 'We're going to use some shots of families on the beach doing normal things and then we'll have you talking about sun protection. Are you ready?'

Sam nodded. As ready as he'd ever be.

The afternoon passed quickly while they filmed various shots and they were just finishing for the day,

Polly finally satisfied, when there were shouts from the cliffs behind them.

John swung his camera round. 'Someone in trouble up there?'

'Not up there.' Polly caught Sam's arm and pointed. 'Out there.'

He followed her gaze and saw a small rubber dinghy that had floated out past the rocks. There was one little girl in it and she was crying and waving. The sea was rough, the waves crashing around her and threatening to swamp the tiny dinghy. 'Oh, hell, this beach is covered in warnings about the currents and the waves. Why do people ignore them?'

Even as he started sprinting towards the sea, he could hear the screaming, see the sudden surge of people as they sensed drama and danger and moved in to watch.

'Get the people away, Poll,' he yelled, 'and call the coastguard.'

He dragged off his shirt as he ran, trying to identify the family of the little girl in the dinghy. 'Do you know her?' He sprinted past people, barking the question until finally he found the parents at the edge of the waves.

The father was frantically wading into the water towards his daughter.

'I'll get her.' Sam pulled him back and the man gripped his arm hard, panic visible in his eyes as he explained what had happened.

'It's not just her. My teenage son was in that dinghy. He's fallen into the water—he's not that great a swimmer.'

'Stay here.' Sam waded into the water and then turned as someone sprinted up beside him.

It was Anna. Slender and poised in a black swimsuit, her gaze grimly determined. She didn't waste time with words, just handed him a buoyancy aid and kept one for herself. He noticed that she was also carrying a life-jacket.

'Let's go.'

He didn't argue, pleased to have her help. Anna was a first-class swimmer and he knew she had a life-saving certificate.

She dived into the waves with the skill of a dolphin, her strong overarm stroke powering her through the water towards the stricken dinghy. He followed swiftly, overtook her and reached the little girl first.

'He fell in.' The girl was hysterical, clinging to the edges of the tiny inflatable boat, which rocked precariously in the rough sea. It seemed ridiculously insubstantial. 'He was being stupid, playing around, and then he fell in.'

Anna surfaced next to Sam and swam around to the girl, one hand on the dinghy. 'Try not to panic. We'll find your brother. What's your name?'

The girl choked on a sob. 'Lottie—'

'Well, Lottie—' Anna broke off and gave a gasp and a splutter as a wave broke over her head, almost swamping her and the tiny boat. Relieved that she was such a strong swimmer, Sam watched as she surfaced immediately and shook her head clear of the water. 'Lottie, we're going to get you somewhere safe.' Her lashes were clumped together with seawater and she swept a hand across her face to clear her vision. 'I want you to sit still in that boat of yours and hold on very tightly while we work out the best way to do this.'

Her dark hair plastered to her head, as sleek as an otter, she kicked her legs fiercely and looked at Sam.

'This thing is going to capsize,' he said, scraping the water out of his eyes and treading water himself while he marshalled his thoughts. The sea was becoming rougher by the minute and he knew that the dinghy wasn't going to offer protection for long. 'Get a life-jacket on her while I see if I can find her brother.'

She didn't argue with him.

'Lottie, I want you to put your arms in this and then we're going to zip it up.' Anna struggled as another huge wave hit them. She paused for a moment, waited for a lull and then helped the girl into the life-jacket. When she'd finished she turned and looked around her and realised Sam was gone.

For a moment her heart jerked with panic and then she realised that he must have dived down under the water.

Another wave crashed down on her and this time the dinghy was totally submerged. Relieved that she'd got the life-jacket on the girl in time, Anna kicked strongly and held the child above the water, trying to calm her each time a wave swamped them, her eyes flitting around frantically for signs of Sam.

He'd been under too long.

Out of the corner of her eye she saw the lifeboat arrive, but all she cared about now was Sam. Damn, he shouldn't have dived. It was too much of a risk. The waves were too rough, the tide was too strong…

And then he surfaced, right next to her, gasping for air, struggling to keep another body afloat.

'You got him.'

'He must have hit his head on a rock. But he's been under for a while.' Sam's breathing was jerky as he gasped for air. Water clung to his lashes and the rough stubble of his jaw as he carefully held the teenage boy's face above the water. 'We need to get him out of here, fast.'

The lifeboat crew, practised in rescues such as these, swung into action and Anna gladly relinquished the little girl into their capable hands before turning her attention to helping Sam.

'We need to keep him flat—you know that. He has to be lifted out of the water in a prone position or we risk circulatory collapse.'

'I know.'

'And we need to watch his neck.' Sam yelled instructions to the lifeboat crew, who were preparing to lift the teenager out of the water.

Through her watery vision, Anna spotted John Craddock at the helm.

There was a clack-clacking sound overhead and the rescue helicopter arrived.

'Thank goodness,' Anna shouted, gasping as another wave broke over her head. 'They can fly him straight to hospital. Are you OK?'

'Never better.' Sam managed a wry grin. 'Apart from the gallon of seawater I've swallowed.'

Finally the rescue was completed and Sam and Anna swam back to the shore, both of them cold and exhausted.

'Have the parents gone?' Sam accepted a towel gratefully from a bystander and wiped his face.

'Someone gave them a lift to the hospital.' Polly was standing next to him with the rest of the crew. 'Well, I have to say, you two, you know how to give the viewers something exciting to watch. That was amazing.'

Anna twisted her long hair round her hand and squeezed until water dripped onto the sand. 'You were filming that?'

'Every minute.' Polly smiled and shielded her eyes against the sun. 'Not just for our documentary—although for holiday health I think that was a pretty powerful message—but for the news as well.'

Anna rubbed her hand over her face to clear her vision. 'I can't believe you filmed it.'

'It's my job.' Polly handed her another towel. 'Just as this is your job. Sort of.' She pulled a face. 'Actually, I don't think it is your job to plunge into crashing waves and a cold sea to rescue someone who shouldn't have been out in a dinghy anyway. People should think before they act. Now do you see the point of our programme?'

Anna shivered despite the towel and the warmth

of the sun. 'I suppose if it stops someone taking blow-up craft into rough waves, yes.' She rubbed her skin with the towel but her teeth continued to chatter.

'For the record, the two of you were amazing.' Polly glanced at the cameraman. 'We got it all, didn't we? Every adrenaline-pumping minute?'

'Oh, yes.' He grinned and tapped the camera. 'I wasn't missing that. I even got the frantic look on Anna's face when she thought Sam wasn't coming up again.'

Oh, hell.

Anna huddled inside the towel. 'I was just worried about running the practice single-handed,' she muttered, and Polly smiled.

'Of course you were. The funny thing about you two is that you disagree violently on everything that doesn't matter, but when it comes to something important you don't even have to communicate. You just anticipate the other's needs. Just like that time in the surgery with little Lucy. Maybe when you see the footage, you'll see what I mean.'

'Something's making me feel sick, Polly,' Anna said, her teeth still chattering, 'and it's either the seawater I've swallowed or it could possibly be the rubbish you're spouting.'

'Deny it all you like,' Polly said airily, 'but the two of you work well together. And on camera you make magic. This programme is going to be a hit. And you're going to be a hit, Anna. You'd better get yourself an agent.'

She turned away to say something to the sound man and Sam stepped forward with a wicked grin.

'Any time you want to make magic with me, Riggs, just say the word.'

Anna glared at him and opened her mouth to say something sharp, but Polly turned her attention back to them before she could speak.

'Can the two of you explain a little bit about what you were trying to do in that rescue? In relatively simple language, of course.'

Anna smiled helpfully. 'Save someone from drowning?'

Polly ignored her and looked at Sam. 'I thought the two of you could have a conversation about it— you know, something natural but informative.'

He nodded, instantly professional. 'Sure, Polly. Let's just ad lib and see what we get.' He dropped the towel and turned to Anna, water still clinging to his lashes, like some sort of god who had just emerged from the sea. 'Of course, there have been some extraordinary examples of survival after long periods of submersion in ice-cold water—'

'We could experiment if you like.' Anna tilted her head to one side and smiled at him, her wet hair sliding over her bare shoulders. 'I could hold you under ice-cold water and we could see what happens.'

There was a snort of laughter from the sound man.

'Cut!' Polly shook her head and laughed. 'That wasn't exactly what I had in mind, Anna!'

Anna's gaze was locked on Sam's.

Something dangerous gleamed in his eyes. 'On reflection, holding me under ice-cold water isn't a bad idea,' he muttered, taking a step towards her. 'It might be the only solution if we carry on with your plan.'

Aware that the crew was listening, Anna felt her cheeks heat and backed away from him.

'OK, let's try this thoroughly staged and unnatural conversation you want,' she said quickly, suddenly wanting to distract Sam from coming towards her. Had he forgotten that they were being filmed, for goodness' sake? 'Dr McKenna…' She kept her voice brisk and professional. 'It's important to remember that cold can protect lives as well as endanger them.'

This time she played it straight, as they'd requested, talking with Sam about the management of near drowning, using terms that a layman would understand.

Finally Polly was satisfied. 'Fantastic. You two are going to be our star turn. And, Anna, I love your swimming costume.'

Anna stared down at herself in amazement. 'It's just a costume.'

'It looks great.' The sound man scratched the side of his nose and gave her a cheeky grin. 'I think we can guarantee a male audience for this particular series.'

Anna's mouth fell open. 'You're saying that people are going to watch this because they like my swimming costume?'

'No, although that helps. They'll watch because

you're beautiful and full of guts,' Polly said bluntly, 'and because there's enough spark between the two of you to start a forest fire.'

'Oh, not that again,' Anna snapped, scooping her damp hair over one shoulder and deciding that enough was enough. 'If we've finished here, I'm off. I need to warm up after my impromptu dip.'

She sprinted back along the sand towards the house, trying to outrun her feelings. It didn't work.

She slowed to a walk and gave a groan.

No matter how hard she tried, she couldn't stop thinking about Sam. And it was getting worse by the minute.

Damn.

She took the steps that led from the beach to the deck of the house and padded round to the hot tub.

She flicked the switch, slid into the bubbling water with a moan of pleasure and closed her eyes. This was one of her favourite places. She waited for the tension to seep out of her, but this time she couldn't relax. Couldn't get him out of her mind. And when she heard footsteps on the deck, she knew it was him.

Her eyes flew open and she moved in the water. 'I was just getting out.'

'You only just got in.' He was still dressed in his surf shorts and nothing else. He had an amazing body, strong, powerfully built and immensely fit, and he stood there, legs planted firmly apart, totally un-selfconscious.

She, on the other hand, was aware of every male inch of him.

Her throat dried. 'I just wanted to warm up.'

'And how warm are you?' He sat down, swung his legs over the side and slid in next to her, his gaze meshing with hers as he moved in close. 'How warm are you, Riggs?'

She swallowed, trapped by his gaze. 'I'm warming up fast.'

His blue eyes flickered to her mouth. 'Need any help?'

'I think I might,' she managed huskily before his mouth found hers and they both gave in to the greed that had been consuming them both for days.

'Hell, Riggs.' His mouth devoured hers hungrily. 'I love your body.'

'Same here.' She felt their legs tangle, felt his arm haul her close and felt his other hand at her breast. 'Oh, help, we shouldn't do this.'

'Stop saying that.' He groaned the words into her neck. 'We're doing it and that's final.'

'No.' She tilted her head and gasped for air. 'I mean, we shouldn't be doing this here, in public.'

'It's not public.' His tongue tasted her skin. 'This is a private deck. The only way anyone can see is if they're up here with us.'

Her whole body was on fire, her heart leaping in her chest.

'We agreed it was a mistake…'

'We never agree on anything.' His hand cupped her face and his mouth came down on hers again, stifling her cry.

He felt so good. Hard. Strong. Male.

And she wanted him.

She broke away, her breath coming in tiny pants, her fingers digging into his biceps. 'We really ought to discuss this.' She was trying to concentrate but all she could think about was the play of muscle under her fingers and how much she wanted him. 'We shouldn't do this on impulse.' She gasped as his mouth found her throat again. 'We should talk.'

'Talking isn't going to warm either of us up.'

Her eyes closed as she felt the erotic touch of his mouth on hers. She'd thought she'd been kissed before. Dozens of times. But maybe she was wrong because it had never felt like this. No one kissed like Sam McKenna.

She knew that what they were doing wasn't sensible, but it felt too right to even contemplate stopping.

His arm curved around her waist and he pulled her onto his lap. 'Body heat is an important source of warmth in these circumstances, Riggs,' he murmured, his voice deep and unreasonably sexy. 'Important to share what we have.'

Her whole body ached and throbbed and she twisted under the water, bringing herself into closer contact with him, hearing his groan, feeling his immediate response.

'It's time you lost the swimming costume.' His hands skimmed her shoulders, sliding it down, and she gave a strangled moan as she felt his clever, seeking fingers graze her taut nipples.

'McKenna. *Sam!*'

He tugged the costume lower still, his hands sliding over her belly and downwards till she shifted her hips against him, desperate to ease the blinding, greedy ache.

Bringing his mouth back to hers, he kissed her savagely, stoking the fire that flared between them.

It took all her will-power to stop it from going all the way. 'Sam…' She groaned his name, her eyes closed. 'We can't do this. Not here. We should stop now…'

She felt the rise and fall of his chest as he struggled to breathe normally. 'You're probably right. Not here. Are you warmer now? Because that's all I was doing, of course, warming you up.'

She looked at him, her breathing unsteady. 'Just a little warmer. Thanks.'

'My pleasure.'

She was still on his lap, still aware of every masculine inch of him. 'Well… I, er, that was…interesting.'

He ran a hand over his face and made a visible effort to pull himself together. 'It certainly proved a point.'

She could still feel the brush of his hard thigh against hers and her brain was refusing to function. 'What point?'

'That it was nothing to do with the dark, the champagne and the atmosphere.'

She slid her arms back into her costume and moved off his lap. 'We don't like each other, McKenna.'

His eyes followed her every movement. 'We could work on that.'

'We never agree on anything.'

'I'm willing to say yes to you the minute you ask me the right question.'

She stood up, breathlessly aware of his gaze on her body. 'We're going to take a step backwards, McKenna, and try and get a grip on ourselves. We need to stop putting ourselves in the position where this happens. I still think this isn't a good idea.'

It would complicate her life and she didn't need complications.

'Excuse me asking this.' He spread his arms wide along the rim of the hot tub, the muscles in his shoulders bunching. 'But exactly which bit doesn't work for you?'

'The you and I bit.' She flicked her hair away from her face. 'It's just not— Well, it isn't what we do.'

'Why?'

She frowned, but met his gaze head on, never one to avoid an issue just because it was uncomfortable. 'Well, for a start, because it would make things awkward between us.'

'Awkward? What can be more awkward than walking round in a state of permanent arousal, which is what's happening to me at the moment?' The corner of his mouth shifted. 'Riggs, I'm a grown man, not some emotionally stunted teenager. I can make love to you and still have a civilised working relationship, if that's what's bothering you.'

His words had a disturbing effect on her heart rate. 'You're only here for the summer.'

'So?' He shrugged. 'We could have fun. Do you know your problem?'

'I don't have a problem.'

'You plan too much. You need to go with the flow. Live a little. Do something on impulse.'

Impulse.

Anna stared at him. The impulse to dive back into the hot tub with him was almost overwhelming.

She sucked in a breath and pulled herself together. 'It's the ability to reason and think that distinguishes us from animals, McKenna,' she said primly, but there was a definite tremor in her voice and he gave a slow grin that churned up her insides more than ever.

'That must be why you bring out the beast in me.'

'I need to do this my way.'

'Fine. You do whatever you need to do to bring your brain and body in line with mine.' His eyes glittered with serious intent. 'But do it fast, Riggs, before we both burn up.'

Sam stood under a cold shower and wondered if anyone had ever conducted an experiment into the quantity of icy water required to kill a ravenous libido because his was decidedly out of control.

If Anna hadn't stopped him, he would have made love to her in the hot tub and he wouldn't have given a damn if the cameras had been running and the entire village had been watching.

He reached for the shampoo and wondered how long she was going to hold out.

Was she right?

Would it make things awkward between them?

He closed his eyes, let the water rinse the soap from his hair and then reached for a towel, a smile on his face as he contemplated the situation. Things had always been awkward between them. They'd never had a smooth, comfortable relationship. It had always been like walking over rocks in bare feet.

He dried himself, pulled on a pair of clean shorts and stared into the mirror.

Of course, part of him was telling him to run a mile. Anna would be no man's idea of a gentle, compliant partner. She'd be snapping and fighting all the way. He had no doubt that even during sex she'd have an opinion. And she'd probably waste no time in expressing it.

The prospect heated his blood to a dangerous level. The need he felt was so powerful, so all-consuming that he knew it was just a matter of time. It was when, not whether. And he sensed it was the same for her. He doubted that either of them would hold out for long.

'You're both famous.' Glenda made them both a cup of tea the following morning when they appeared for surgery. 'Your rescue has been shown on every news bulletin since last night. Amazing.'

Anna took the tea with a smile of thanks, carefully avoiding Sam's eye. She'd seen the bulletin and winced at the footage of her and Sam. She'd never realised that her black costume was so revealing.

'They'll incorporate a longer version when the programme goes out,' Sam told Glenda, handing her a pile of papers. 'I ran these off the internet for you. Have a read and see what you think. How's your mother doing today?'

'She's so much better.' Glenda settled herself behind her desk and flicked on the computer. 'I've labelled everything in the sitting-room and put the phone next to her, and I followed your idea of sticking my picture next to the speed dial so that she can remember which button to press if she wants me.'

Anna lifted her head. 'You're full of good ideas, Sam.'

'I certainly am.' His eyes locked with hers. 'You ought to try some of them some time.'

She swallowed. Why was it that she was suddenly so aware of every single inch of him? There'd been a time, not that many days before, when all she'd wanted to do when she'd laid eyes on Sam had been to pick a fight. Now, suddenly, she just wanted to strip him naked.

Glenda reached for the keys. 'I'll unlock that front door if you're ready.'

Sam's eyes didn't leave Anna's. 'I'm ready. How about you?'

She knew what he was asking and suddenly she couldn't speak. Aware that Glenda was staring at her curiously, she licked her lips. 'I think I'm probably ready, too.'

Sam's mouth moved into a smile of raw, masculine satisfaction. 'Glad to hear it, Riggs.'

Glenda frowned at them. 'Is something going on that I don't know about?'

'Nothing.' Anna's voice sounded raspy and she cleared her throat and glanced at her watch. 'We need to get going. We've got a busy day and the beach barbecue tonight.'

Glenda nodded, her eyes sparkling. 'I'm certainly going. I've got a girl staying the night to keep an eye on Mum and I intend to enjoy myself.'

Anna grinned. 'And who with, exactly? Would this be the same "friend" you saw the other night?'

Glenda's colour deepened. 'It might be. I presume you're both going?'

Sam suppressed a yawn. 'I'm supposed to be doing a piece to camera about holiday night-life. The perils of enjoying yourself. Too much alcohol and unprotected sex. That type of thing.'

Glenda giggled naughtily. 'I know quite a few people in this village who could star in that.'

Anna gave a reluctant laugh. 'You're both terrible. And, Sam, you should concentrate on the teenagers. You wouldn't believe how many I have in here after parties on the beach. For goodness' sake, talk about safe sex. It's definitely a subject to address in our new clinic.'

Glenda hurried off to open the doors and Sam turned to Anna.

'And when I've finished my piece to camera,' he said softly, 'you and I have some business to sort out, Riggs. And this time we're doing it my way.'

She stared at him, hypnotised by the look in his eyes. 'Your way?'

'Your way hasn't worked and I haven't had an undisturbed night's sleep for weeks.' His eyes dropped to her mouth. 'And it's only fair to warn you that if you're planning to argue then you're going to lose.'

'I wasn't planning to argue.'

'No?' His mouth curved into a sexy smile. 'Now, that is a first.'

Anna spent the entire day in a state of heightened awareness. She went through her surgeries and her calls with only half her mind in action, the other half thinking about Sam and the forthcoming evening.

Why shouldn't they further their relationship? she reasoned.

As he'd rightly pointed out, who were they going

to hurt? They were both consenting adults and neither of them was involved with anyone else. They found each other attractive. It was a relatively simple situation.

Except that it didn't feel simple.

It didn't feel simple at all.

Neither did dressing for the beach barbecue. The problem with being a GP in a small, tight-knit community, Anna reflected as she stared at the dress that she'd laid out on her bed, was that you were always in the spotlight and your behaviour had to be above reproach. She could never risk getting drunk in public or making an exhibition of herself.

Did the outfit she'd chosen classify as making an exhibition of herself?

She fingered the fabric gingerly. She'd bought the dress as a joke. To provoke Sam. But things had moved on and now she had a feeling that she'd be provoking a reaction entirely different from the one she'd originally anticipated.

A womanly smile spread across her face and she lifted the dress.

Impulse.

Wasn't that what Sam had said?

Well, this dress had definitely been an impulse buy, purchased after he'd made that comment about her not being sufficiently 'girly'.

And she was going to wear it.

She was wearing hot pink.

Sam felt his tongue almost fall out of his mouth

as Anna walked out of the house onto the deck. Her silky dark hair was caught up on top of her head, her perfect mouth highly glossed. Her legs were long and lightly tanned and the heels she was wearing looked as though they should come with a health warning.

She paused and angled her head. 'Say something, McKenna.'

He swallowed and dragged his eyes away from her legs. 'You don't wear pink, Riggs.'

'Tonight I'm wearing pink.'

He ran a hand over the back of his neck. 'Is it hot tonight, or is it me?'

She gave a slow smile that made his hormones shriek in protest. 'It's hot. That's why I chose to wear a cool dress.'

'There is nothing cool about that dress, Riggs,' he said hoarsely, licking his lips and wondering how long he was expected to keep his hands to himself. 'This beach barbecue. Is it something you particularly want to go to?'

He was willing her to say no, but she shot him an amused look, her brown eyes teasing. 'It's *the* event of our pitiful social calendar, McKenna. I wouldn't miss it for the world. It's my only chance to go out.'

Which meant that she was going to make him wait.

His eyes were fastened on the dress. It looked simple enough. So why did it cling and hug and skim so cleverly? 'I'm not sure you should be going out dressed like that.'

'Well, I wouldn't normally.' She paused to fiddle with the tiny strap of the dress. 'But someone told me that I should be more impulsive so I thought I'd give it a go. And you have to record a piece to camera, if I recall, all about responsible partying and safe sex.'

Sam ran a hand over his face and tried to think about suitably sober situations. And freezing cold showers. Anything to try and subdue his reactions, which were rapidly spiralling out of control.

'Polly is waiting on the beach for you.' She walked towards the steps, the smooth swing of her hips drawing his eye. 'Let's move.'

Sam swallowed and hoped they were planning to film him from the waist up. Otherwise he was in trouble.

'Cut.' Polly walked over to Sam, ignoring the crowd that was gathering around them. It was dark on the beach, a large bonfire was blazing and the barbecue was sending out the most tempting smells imaginable, and still people just wanted to watch the filming. 'Are you all right? It's not like you to fluff it.'

Sam ran a hand through his hair, his eyes on Anna. 'Must be the audience. I'm finding them distracting.'

Polly glanced at the crowd and then back at him, puzzled. 'You're used to being stared at. Whenever we film in public, you're stared at. I don't see what's different tonight.'

'Don't you?' Sam's voice was soft and Anna felt a shiver of awareness run through her and wondered why no one else could feel the tension between them.

From the moment they'd arrived on the beach

they'd been surrounded by people, Sam by the film crew and herself by local people keen to catch up and enjoy a chat. But even when they'd been separated by others, she'd sensed him watching her every move. Counting the minutes. They both knew exactly what was going to happen later and the anticipation was reaching screaming pitch.

She was starting to wonder how she was going to make it through the evening and, judging from the number of times Sam had already fluffed his piece to camera, his concentration wasn't up to much either.

Polly glanced at the cameraman. 'We've probably got enough—it's an informal setting anyway, so he doesn't have to be word perfect. We just want to give the viewer the impression that they're at a beach party—a bit of scene setting. Have we covered everything?' She checked her notes. 'Drinking, drugs, safe sex—looks about it.' She looked at the sound man. 'Are you happy?'

'Ecstatic,' he said dryly, 'and longing for a drink.'

Polly grinned. 'OK, then, folks, let's join the party.'

Sam undid his microphone and handed it back to the sound man, his eyes never leaving Anna.

She felt her heart kick against her chest as he approached. 'Hi, there.' Her voice sounded croaky, totally unlike her own. 'Are you done?'

His eyes roved over her face. 'Riggs, I haven't even begun.'

Since when had it been so difficult to breathe?

Still, she couldn't resist teasing him. 'You seemed to be having one or two problems remembering your lines, McKenna.'

'My mind was elsewhere.'

Without touching, they feasted on each other, using only their eyes and the power of the mind.

Her whole body was on fire. 'You're staring, McKenna.'

'You chose to wear hot pink.'

It was foreplay, each of them knowing exactly how the encounter would end and, the anticipation heightened the excitement to almost intolerable levels.

'We're supposed to mingle, McKenna.'

His eyes dropped to her mouth. 'Really?'

'It's part of the responsibility of being a local GP,' she said huskily, longing to lift herself on tiptoe so that he could kiss her the way only he knew how. 'You have to chat to everyone.'

'Problem is, Riggs…' his gaze didn't shift from her mouth '…there's only one person here that I'm interested in.'

Heat spread through her pelvis. 'We shouldn't be seen together. It will fuel gossip.'

'I don't give a damn what other people think.'

'Easy for you to say. At the end of the summer you'll be gone and I'll be the one who's still here.'

Finally his eyes lifted back to hers. 'All right. Let's mingle.' Without another word he turned away, leaving her feeling oddly deflated and not understanding the reason. She'd been the one who'd suggested that they mingle. So why was she now disappointed that he was doing just that?

Because she wanted this whole evening to be over. She wanted this thing with Sam to start.

In the distance she saw Glenda arm in arm with one of the crew of the lifeboat and she wondered if this was the 'friend' she'd been talking about. Probably. And she was very pleased for her.

Anna moved among the crowd, chatting, laughing and all the time watching Sam out of the corner of her eye. She watched the way women crowded round him, watched the way they flirted and the way he subtly withdrew from their attentions.

Anna tightened her hand on her glass and felt her heart pound.

She decided that there was nothing quite like the adrenaline rush of knowing that, for tonight at least, Sam McKenna was hers.

He came for her at midnight.

He strolled across the sand, his shirt open at the neck, his feet bare. He looked dangerously handsome and more temptation than a woman should have to resist.

And she had no intention of resisting him.

'We can play this two ways, Riggs,' he said conversationally, coming to a halt just inches away from her. 'We can leave right away and hope we make it back to the house, or I can just throw you down in the sand and have my wicked way with you here. Your choice.'

She caught the glitter in his blue eyes and her breath caught in her throat. 'I've never been particularly into public displays,' she murmured softly and he inclined his head and removed the plastic cup from her hand.

'In that case, we'd better go now. While we still can.' He tossed the cup into the nearest convenient bin and they strolled back along the beach towards the house.

Within minutes the music and laughter had faded into the darkness behind them and all they could hear was the hiss of the sea as it touched the sand.

They walked side by side, both barefoot, the atmosphere choked with the heavy throb of anticipation. Neither of them spoke.

When they finally reached the foot of the steps, Sam paused to let her go first.

She hesitated, suddenly filled with a nervousness that she couldn't explain. 'Sam...'

His gaze locked on hers, his eyes burning. 'I want you. Let's go to bed.'

For a moment she faltered.

Whatever they shared wouldn't last. She knew it couldn't last. They clashed too violently, they both wanted their own way too badly. They were both too strong to be a good match.

But for now...

She swallowed and then turned and sprinted up the stairs, the knowledge that he was right behind her sending her pulse skyward.

They let themselves into the house and locked the

door, and she was just going to suggest that they have a drink first when he took control.

His mouth was firm, possessive and she closed her eyes and gave a whimper of pleasure, acknowledging how much of the evening she'd spent longing for his kiss.

'Much as I love the hot pink dress…' his strong hands slid the straps down her arms '…it's going to have to come off, Riggs.'

The feel of his fingers on her bare flesh made her shiver. 'Maybe we should go upstairs.' Her head tilted back and her eyes closed as he kissed his way down her neck.

'Never make it that far.'

She felt the zip go on her dress and hot pink silk pooled at her feet. 'Sam…'

He swept her up in his arms and carried her to the glass-fronted living room, refusing to let her finish her sentence. 'Let yourself go, Anna.'

And she did.

She felt herself heat and melt under the touch of his hands, for once in her life relishing the fact that someone else was taking charge.

He laid her on the thick rug, his powerful body over hers, his hands peeling away her skimpy underwear with an impatience that made her gasp.

Her fingers fumbled with the buttons of his shirt but her hands were shaking too much to complete the task and she muttered something incoherent and yanked at the fabric, sending buttons flying.

His mouth was greedy on hers and he moved his

shoulders and freed himself of his shirt, his breathing ragged as his hair-roughened chest made contact with the soft mounds of her breasts. The rest of his clothes followed and their bodies tangled and locked as they moved with an erotic desperation driven by a torment of need.

And then he drove himself into her. Hard and fast, he gave them what they both needed, any notion of control abandoned from the moment they'd entered the house. Dazed and desperate, she wrapped her legs around his slick skin and moved with him, wild excitement consuming every inch of her as he hurled her to the outer reaches of pleasure. She cried out and curled her nails into his back, held on and closed her eyes as she hurtled skyward in an orgasm so intense that for a moment she lost all grip on reality.

'Anna…' He said her name harshly, fisted his hand in her hair, and her eyes flew open and locked with his. And then she felt him shudder, saw the sweat sheen on his brow and felt the hot pulse of his own release as his body pumped into hers.

She lay under him without speaking, wishing they could stay like that for ever, locked together, breathless and slick with their own passion.

Eventually he raised himself off her just enough to speak. 'Sorry.' His voice was hoarse. 'I think I forgot the foreplay.'

She chuckled, loving the weight of him on top of her. He had an amazing body. He was an amazing lover. 'I think the last few weeks have been nothing but foreplay.'

'You could have a point.'

'I hope the cameras weren't running, Dr McKenna.' She stretched underneath him, lazy and satisfied as a cat. 'You just gave a very interesting lecture to the general public on the dangers of getting carried away after parties. Of not using contraception.'

He stilled. 'Oops.'

'Yes, oops,' she agreed softly, her hand sliding over his back. 'Don't worry. I'm safe. Let's just hope none of the teenagers out there were watching your performance.'

He gave a lazy grin and touched his mouth to hers, his voice husky. 'Something wrong with my performance, Riggs?'

'I'm not sure.' She was breathless. 'I might need to evaluate it a second time. And maybe a third...'

He lifted his head further still and his lips brushed hers. Her response was instantaneous and she felt his body come alive inside her as the kiss intensified.

'I love your body.' His tongue licked into the corners of her mouth and then he withdrew from her and slid lower, breathing heat and fire over her burning skin, exploring and tasting until his mouth hovered over one nipple.

She felt the warmth of his breath and arched towards him but he held himself slightly away from her, feasting with smouldering eyes, his fingers sliding down the smooth skin of her thigh.

After the frantic, wild lovemaking session that they'd both enjoyed, this time he was taking his time.

'Sam...' She couldn't breathe, needed him so

badly that every feminine part of her ached. 'Sam, please…'

His tongue flickered over her nipple and she cried out, pressing closer, her whole body quivering and shifting beneath his lean, powerful frame. Her hand slid over the bunched muscle of his shoulders and she wondered how it was possible to still want him so desperately when the most intimate part of her body still throbbed from the force of his possession.

It was impossible not to keep touching him as he was touching her, and she slid her fingers through his dark hair, loving the silkiness, the softness of it. The contrast to the hard masculinity of his body. She kissed his neck, his shoulder. Cried out as she felt his fingers touch her intimately.

She didn't understand the hunger inside her, the burning fire that didn't seem to want to be quenched. Her fingers curled round the heat of his arousal and she heard his groan, felt his body shift in response to her touch.

'Are you all right here?' His voice was gruff. 'Do you want to go upstairs?'

She slid one thigh over his. 'I'm not capable of moving.'

'Good point.' He lowered his mouth to hers. 'We'll just stay here, then. You drive me wild, Riggs. Crazy.'

'McKenna.' She slid her other thigh over his and arched against him. 'Can you stop talking and do something about the way I'm feeling?'

His chuckle was low and sexy. 'It will be my pleasure.'

CHAPTER NINE

ANNA beamed at the woman sitting across from her. 'It's so good to see you, Hilda. What can I do for you?'

Hilda looked at her curiously. 'I just wanted to ask you about this bite on my leg. It doesn't seem to want to heal.'

'Then let's take a look at it.' Anna stood up and walked round her desk, her step light. 'How long have you had it?'

'A few weeks. But it's getting worse.' Hilda stuck out the offending limb, allowing Anna to examine the calf. 'You look well, Dr Riggs. A lot more relaxed than when I last saw you.'

'I'm feeling great, Hilda.' Anna frowned at the leg. 'I don't think this is a bite. I think it's probably a flare-up of your eczema. Have you been scratching it?'

'Eczema?' Hilda stared down at her leg in surprise. 'Well, yes, I have been scratching it. It's been driving me mad. I assumed it was a bite.'

'Have you been very stressed?'

'It's the summer,' Hilda reminded her dryly, watching as she walked to the sink and washed her hands, 'it's my busiest time. There's a queue outside my door in the morning when I open and it stays there until I close and my counters are stripped bare of food. It's like exposing yourself to an attack of locusts. I've never known people eat so much.'

Anna laughed and sat back down at her desk. 'Well, I think that the locusts have made your eczema worse.' She tapped the keyboard. 'I'm giving you a prescription for cream to rub in that patch, and make sure you keep up your emollient baths.'

Hilda sighed. 'I'm so tired by the end of the day that if I stepped into a bath I'd probably drown.'

'It will relax you.' Anna handed her the prescription and Hilda pulled a face.

'I daren't relax. If I relax, who's going to cook for tomorrow? I just need to keep this up until the end of the summer. It isn't long now.'

Not long now.

The happiness left Anna like air from a popped balloon.

Once summer ended the tourists would be gone. And so would Sam.

The past two weeks had been idyllic. At work they were very discreet, communicating on a totally professional level, but the moment they stepped through the doors of the house they were lovers. Crazy, wild, self-absorbed lovers. And up until now she'd been so totally caught up in the madness of the present that she hadn't allowed herself to think about the future.

But the future was on her doorstep.

'You and Dr McKenna have done a good job here this summer,' Hilda said, taking the prescription and tucking it safely in her bag. 'Been just what the village needed. It was time for young blood in the practice and Sam's just the man.'

'Sam's just temporary,' Anna said briskly, reaching for some papers on her desk and trying to ignore the sick feeling in the pit of her stomach. 'He was only ever temporary.'

Only somehow, over the past few weeks, she'd allowed herself to forget that. She'd lived so much for the moment that she hadn't realised that tomorrow had arrived.

Hilda looked at her. 'He's a local lad. This is his home and this is where he should be. You know it and I know it.' She sniffed and rose to her feet, her bag clasped in her hand. 'And sooner or later Sam McKenna will work that out, too. He wanted to spread his wings and he's done that. It's time for him to stop messing around. If you want to drop by later, I've got the most delicious seafood lasagne. I'll put a couple of portions aside for you. And a lemon tart.'

'Thanks, Hilda. Without you I would undoubtedly starve.' Anna stood up and walked to the door with her. 'I'll pop by on my way home.'

She watched Hilda go and then closed the door firmly.

In a daze, she walked back to her desk and sank into her chair.

How could it have happened?

How could she have been so stupid?

She'd fallen in love with Sam. Completely and utterly.

And it wasn't supposed to be that way. They didn't like each other. They clashed terribly. They disagreed on everything. They…

She ran a hand over her face and groaned. *They were perfect together.*

So now what?

She stared out of the window, across the harbour to the estuary and the sea beyond. Hilda was wrong about Sam. He wouldn't be staying. Not once the summer was over. They hadn't talked about it yet, but both of them knew he'd be going soon. Back to his life in London.

And she couldn't blame him for that. He'd never pretended that their relationship was anything other than physical. It was her that had broken the rules. Broken the rules by falling in love.

So now what did she do? She obviously couldn't ever tell him, so what did she do? Did she end it?

She watched the boats bobbing in the harbour, the wind catching the flags on the masts, and knew that she couldn't do that.

She wanted to make the most of every minute.

She'd enjoy the relationship until it was time for him to move on.

And then she'd let him go without ever telling him how she really felt.

And spend the rest of her life trying to get over him.

He was going to tell her.

Sam stowed the surfboard in the outhouse and

locked the door. Tonight he was going to tell Anna that he was in love with her.

He was convinced she felt something, too. She had to.

Feeling nervous for the first time in his thirty-two years, he showered and changed and then strolled into the kitchen. It had become their routine. He cooked for both of them, sometimes from scratch, sometimes just reheating a delicacy from Hilda's kitchen.

He opened the fridge and found a seafood lasagne. 'Thank you, Hilda,' he murmured, sliding it into the oven and then grabbing a beer from the fridge.

He could see Anna already sitting on the deck, her slim brown legs stretched in front of her, a medical journal open on her lap. She had a glass in her hand and her mobile phone was on the table in front of her.

He felt something shift inside him.

Who would have thought it?

Who would ever have thought that the two of them would develop this amazing connection?

He walked out onto the deck and bent to kiss her mouth. He couldn't resist it. All day he ached to do just that and had to hold himself in check. He didn't see why he should have to when they were at home.

She pulled away from him, dropped the medical journal and reached for her glass. 'You're late. Problems?'

'Just enjoying the surf.' He smiled and sprawled in a chair next to her. 'How was your day?'

'Fine.' She shot him a bright smile and Sam frowned slightly, sensing that something was wrong. She was different tonight. Brittle.

'Has something happened?'

Her eyes flew to his, startled. 'What could have happened?'

He was now convinced that something had. 'I don't know.' He kept his voice casual. 'It's just that you're a little jumpy.'

Her eyes slid away from his. 'I'm fine. Just hungry, I expect.'

She was lying.

Sam watched her for a minute and then rose to his feet. 'All right—let's eat.' If she was using hunger as an excuse, he'd get rid of that and then see what happened.

He served the lasagne, handed her a bowl of salad and topped up her wine.

'Eat.'

She picked up her fork and poked at the food. 'Thanks. Looks good. Hilda was in today, having trouble with her eczema. All those tourists are stressing her out.' She chattered away, always keeping the subject neutral, always avoiding eye contact.

And she hardly touched her food. She moved it around her plate, shifted its position and worried it with her fork. But hardly any made it to her mouth.

Sam started to eat. 'This is fantastic. I tell you, if she wasn't already married, I'd marry Hilda.' He loaded his fork. 'The woman is a magician in the kitchen.'

Anna put her fork down with a clatter and Sam paused, wondering what he'd said to upset her.

He frowned. If he'd upset her, he wished she'd just yell at him. At least he'd know where he stood then. 'You're not eating. What's wrong?' He reached across the table and took her hand.

She jerked it away and Sam let out a breath. 'Are you tired?'

They'd been up for most of the night making love so he wouldn't blame her if she was tired.

She chewed her lip and for a moment he thought she looked…stricken? He frowned. Why would she look stricken? 'Has something happened? Have you had bad news?'

'A bit.' She gave him a smile but it wasn't very convincing. 'Your dad called me this afternoon.'

'And?'

'And you were right. He's decided to retire. He's going to ring you, obviously, but he said as I was his partner, he owed it to me to tell me first. They're going to spend their winters in Switzerland and their summers here.' She picked up the fork and then gave up the pretence of eating and put it straight down again. 'As I said, you were right.'

Sam struggled with disappointment. For a wild moment he'd kidded himself that she looked so down because she was in love with him and trying to work out how to tell him. Clearly he couldn't have been more wrong. She was worrying about her work. Her future.

Deflated, he suddenly felt angry. He wanted her to

suffer as he was suffering and clearly she wasn't. He scowled. 'You knew that would happen.'

She looked at him, startled, and he realised that his tone had probably been a little too sharp in the circumstances, but he was chewed up inside and she hadn't even *noticed*.

'Now you're the one in the funny mood.' She tilted her head to one side and studied him and he shifted uncomfortably.

Would she see? Was it written all over his face?

He didn't dare risk it. He didn't know if he could hide his feelings because he'd never had those feelings for anyone before, let alone had to hide them.

He stood up. 'I'll get pudding.'

She stared at the heaped plates. 'We haven't finished the lasagne.'

'Do you want more?'

She shook her head. 'No. I don't feel like it. Perhaps it's just too hot to eat.'

'I'll make coffee.'

He clattered around in the kitchen, venting his temper on the plates. She hadn't even mentioned him leaving. It obviously didn't bother her at all.

The irony of the situation wasn't lost on him.

How many times had he had relationships which he'd ended without a second thought, knowing that the woman in question was becoming too involved? And now here he was in that very same situation himself. He was in love with a woman who had no interest in a relationship with him. She was thinking about the practice.

'I've been thinking.' She stood in the doorway, her white strap top showing smooth brown arms and a tempting amount of cleavage. 'Would you help me interview for the new partner?'

He dropped the plate he was holding. 'Sorry. Clumsy.' He stooped and carefully picked up the shattered remains of the plate.

'It's just that you'll be going soon,' she said casually, still leaning against the door-frame, 'and I want to get a new partner as soon as possible.'

Of course she did. Anna the planner.

She couldn't wait to get rid of him.

He dropped the pieces into the bin and looked at her, his face blank of expression. 'If you place the advert, I'll help you interview.'

She smiled brightly. 'Great. We need to choose really carefully. Make sure the person is going to be happy living in such a small community. Probably have to be someone who loves the sea.'

Sam felt as though she'd punched him.

She didn't want him.

Fine.

He'd just have to learn to live without her.

She didn't know what was the matter with Sam but he was permanently in a foul mood.

And she was gutted that he hadn't offered to stay when she'd talked about interviewing a partner.

Which was utterly ridiculous, she told herself firmly, because she'd always known that he wouldn't stay. His life was in London. Why should he change his whole life just because of a little hot sex? She should have known better.

She sifted through the applications, disappointed that there were so many good doctors interested in joining her in the practice. If there'd been no one, Sam would have been forced to stay.

No, he wouldn't, she told herself crossly, he just would have found her another locum.

His new series was due to start filming in London at the end of September and she knew that he and Polly had already had several meetings about the content of the series. There was no question of him staying.

'This guy's perfect. He interviewed the best and he has all the right experience.'

'He'll leave after five minutes.'

She looked at him in exasperation. 'What is going on, McKenna? We've had a really high quality of applicants. Fantastic doctors. And you've rejected the lot of them.'

Sam toyed with his pen, a dangerous look in his eyes. 'This was my father's practice. I care about who takes it over.'

'But you don't care enough to do the job yourself,' Anna snapped, and then caught herself. She'd been trying not to quarrel with him. 'All right. What's wrong with this guy?'

The gleam in Sam's eye intensified. 'I didn't like him.'

'Well, I liked him a lot.'

For some reason that seemed to anger him even more. 'Your judgement is faulty.'

'OK, I've just about had enough of this!' She put her hands on her hips and glared at him. 'What the hell is wrong with you?'

He glared back. 'Nothing's wrong with me.'

'That's rubbish.' Temper blurred her vision. 'Whatever I do, you yell at me! You're crabby and irritable and generally bad-tempered.'

He scowled at her. 'I am not bad-tempered.'

'I haven't heard you laugh for days and we clash on everything.'

'So what's new about that? We've always clashed on everything.'

'Not since—' She broke off and swept her hair away from her face, her colour high. Their physical relationship was something that they just didn't talk about.

'Since we made the stupid mistake of sleeping together? Well, you were right about that.' He gave a crooked smile. 'It changed everything.'

Her heart skipped a beat. 'So is that why you don't come near me any more? Because it was such a stupid mistake?'

To her utter mortification she burst into tears and Sam cursed fluently.

'OK, stop that, Riggs. Don't cry.' He lifted his hands and for a moment she thought he was going to touch her for the first time in days. Then his hands dropped to his sides again and a muscle worked in his jaw. 'I can't stand it when you cry. That's a low trick. It's a girly trick and you don't do girly stuff.'

She didn't need reminding of that.

If she did more 'girly stuff' then he probably wouldn't be leaving.

Anger and frustration burst free inside her. 'I'm crying because I hate you. I hate you, McKenna.' She sniffed loudly and scrubbed the tears away with the back of her hand. 'I really hate you for making me feel this way.'

His hands were still by his sides but she noticed that his fists were clenched. 'What way?'

'Angry.' She blew her nose hard. 'And—and—as if I could strangle you with my bare hands. And sad.' Her eyes filled again. 'You make me sad.'

He was looking at her in horror. 'Sad?'

'Yes, sad. Because what we had was good and it couldn't last.' She blinked and sniffed again. 'Oh, damn. This is all so stupid. It's fine. I'm fine. The sooner you go, the better. At least I get to run this practice in peace, without your input. Your ideas never work anyway, McKenna. You're always wrong.'

'I'm never wrong.' He frowned and raked long fingers through his hair. 'And my ideas always work. Which one didn't work? Name one that didn't work.'

She dropped the tissue in the bin and swallowed, back in control. She could do this. She could watch him walk away and she could carry on her life without him. 'Well, the teenage clinic, for one. We've got the entire village youth congregating here every Friday. It's a nightmare.'

He folded his arms across his chest and looked smug. 'So, in other words, I was right and you were wrong. I said people would come.'

'You were not right. Half of them don't even bother talking to the doctor or the practice nurse. We're not supposed to be running a youth club.'

'But they have the chance to talk to someone if they want to. And don't underestimate the power of peer pressure. If a few of them are talking to the doctor, the others will. Admit it. I was right.'

'They'll stop coming as soon as winter sets in.'

'They won't stop coming.'

She glared at him again. 'Well, you don't care anyway. You won't be here to see it. You'll be back in your fancy television studio, advising people on ingrowing toenails.' Except that wasn't what he did. She knew that now. 'I'm going to ring that guy, that Dr Hampton, and offer him the job.'

'I'll do it.' He held out his hand and took the details from her. 'That way I can co-ordinate dates with him.'

She felt the tears start again and bit them back. 'Fine. Just as long as someone is here to do the work.'

'Fine. I'll arrange it.'

Sam stared at the details of the doctor.

Anna liked him.

The thought made him want to smash his fist into something.

And he was about to offer him the job. Once he picked up that phone, this guy would become a GP in a village practice. He would surf in the evenings and at the weekends, he'd eat Hilda's beautiful seafood dishes and lemon tart and he'd join the lifeboat crew for drinks on the quay. He'd walk the cliffs, run on the sand and sail yachts. But most of all he'd work alongside Anna. They'd make decisions together, develop the practice together, plan for their patients.

Would they sleep together?

Sam's fingers tightened on the pen he was holding and he reached for the phone.

He'd better get it over with.

'There's a trailer for Sam's new series this afternoon. I've set the TV and video in the coffee-room,' Glenda said happily as Anna handed her a pile of forms. 'He and Polly have been thick as thieves all day.'

Anna gritted her teeth.

She shouldn't mind. It shouldn't matter to her. She and Sam were over.

'Have you heard anything from Dr Hampton?' She was surprised that he hadn't been in touch with her. It was all very well for Sam to have confirmed all the details, but surely the man would still want to contact her?

'A letter came this morning.' Glenda handed it over, oddly hesitant.

Anna scanned it, blinked, scanned it again and then her temper exploded. 'Where is he?'

Glenda flinched. 'If you mean Dr McKenna, he's just parked his car and he's walking through the doors as we speak. But, Anna—'

Anna whirled round, lights flashing in her brain as she came face to face with him. 'Of all the miserable, vile, small-minded b—'

'We've got an audience, Riggs,' Sam interrupted her, an answering flash of anger in his blue eyes as he faced her head on. 'You might want to hold onto that temper of yours.'

'I don't care who hears this.' She tossed her hair back, her gaze furious as she waved the letter under his nose. 'You were supposed to offer him the job, McKenna. You were supposed to tell him that he was the one.'

'He wasn't the one.' Sam tried to step past her, a muscle flickering in his jaw. 'I didn't think he was the right person for the job.'

'Well, I did!'

He turned on her. 'I'm well aware of that.' He growled the words like a man goaded to the extremes of his tolerance. 'You made it perfectly clear how much you liked him.'

'And what's wrong with that?' She spread her hands in a gesture of disbelief. 'I was going to work with the guy. I was *supposed* to like him. Or is that what this is all about?' Her hands fell to her sides and she glared at him. 'Is it jealousy, McKenna? Is that's what's wrong?'

They were both breathing rapidly, eyes locked in combat, totally indifferent to their growing audience.

Polly cleared her throat. 'Sam, your new trailer is on air in about two minutes. Why don't we all watch it?'

Sam sucked in a breath, his eyes still on Anna's. 'Fine. Let's watch it.'

Anna had to stop herself from screaming. She didn't want to watch his trailer. She didn't want to see what his plans for the future were because she knew they didn't involve her and that knowledge made her want to cry like a baby.

She stuck her chin in the air. 'Fine. Let's watch the trailer.'

She stalked into the staffroom where Glenda was already glued to the screen. 'Here we go...'

'This autumn, *Medical Matters* moves from London to the seaside, following the trials and tribulations of life in a busy harbour practice...'

The narrator's voice droned on and then there was Sam, standing on the beach, his dark hair blowing in the wind as he talked.

When he'd finished, Glenda pressed the 'pause' button and stared at Anna.

Anna stood in silence.

She opened her mouth to speak and then closed it again.

Sam's eyes were fixed on her face. 'Say something.'

She swallowed. 'You're going to make the programme here?'

Polly grinned. 'It was that or he was going to re-sign, and I'm not about to lose my best medical pre-senter.'

Anna stared at him. 'You were going to resign?' She stared at the TV. 'It said this autumn.'

'The trailer is for you, Riggs,' Sam said roughly. 'We made it just for you. The real series and trailer won't be shown until next summer.'

Her expression was blank. 'Sorry?'

He glared at her in exasperation. 'It's a message from me to you,' he shouted, 'but you're so damn stupid you can't even see it!'

'If you stopped yelling, maybe I'd be able to con-centrate,' Anna yelled, lifting a hand to her chest. Suddenly it was difficult to breathe. 'I don't under-stand.'

'I didn't give the guy the job because I decided that I wanted it myself!' Sam paced the room, his hands thrust in his pockets, his eyes stormy. 'I de-cided that everything he was gaining I was losing, and I discovered that I didn't want to lose it.' He stopped pacing and looked at her. 'I discovered that I wanted it for myself.'

Anna went still. 'What did you want for yourself?'

'The practice.' He ran a hand over the back of his neck and swore softly. 'And you. I wanted you. Which makes me an idiot, I know, because you've made it perfectly obvious that you don't want me.'

He wanted her?

Anna struggled to speak. 'Hold on.' Her voice was

scratchy. 'When did I make it perfectly obvious that I didn't want you? When?'

He shrugged. 'When you started advertising for new partners.'

'I was forced to look for another partner because you were leaving, McKenna!'

'I never said I was leaving.'

'Well, you never said you might stay.' She lifted a shaking hand to her hair and scooped it back. 'And—and you stopped sleeping with me.'

'Because you'd clearly planned your life without me.'

'Because that was how you wanted it!'

They were both shouting, emotions running high, oblivious to the fact that they had an audience. A highly entertained audience. Polly glanced at Glenda.

'Time for us to leave, I think,' she muttered, and Glenda grinned.

'Can we listen at the door?'

They slipped out of the room, unnoticed.

'Why would I have wanted it?' He paced the floor again. 'What we had was amazing. I've never had that with anyone before.'

Her heart jammed in her throat. 'I'm not your sort of woman.'

'What's that supposed to mean?'

'You don't want me. I'm not girly and I can't cook.'

'I don't give a damn whether you can cook.' He frowned, confused. 'I can cook perfectly well myself and if I can't be bothered then Hilda's always standing in the wings. I don't see what your lack of skills in the kitchen has got to do with our relationship.'

'You want a traditional woman. I'm not who you want.'

'Damn it, Riggs! Haven't you heard a single word I've said?' He strode towards her and grabbed her by the arms, shaking her slightly. 'You are exactly who I want. I love you. I want to be with you. I know you don't love me back, but I can still be a decent partner in the practice.'

'You love me?'

His hands dropped. 'That's what I said.'

'Why didn't you say that you loved me before now?'

'Because I'm not some sort of masochist, and you made it perfectly clear that my feelings aren't returned. That I'm not your type—or in your plans.'

Anna shook her head, feeling slightly dizzy. 'They are returned. I love you, too.'

'You stride around here making plans for my replacement while I'm still in your bed, and you—' He broke off and stared at her. 'What did you say? That last thing—what did you say?'

'I said I love you.' She tried hard to breathe normally. 'And if I talked about your replacement, it was only because you never once mentioned the fact that you were tempted to stay on.'

He was still staring. 'I don't think we've been communicating very well.'

'Possibly not.'

'We're probably going to have to work on that.'

'Probably.'

He slid a hand into his pocket. 'This partnership. Are you willing to make it permanent?'

She stared at the box in his hand. 'Is that what I think it is?'

'Yes.' He opened the box and lifted the ring out.

She gasped and covered her mouth with her hand. 'It's stunning.'

He took her hand. 'Will you marry me?'

She blinked back tears as he slid the ring onto her finger. 'If you're willing to risk the fact that I might poison you in the kitchen.'

'You won't be allowed in the kitchen.' His voice was hoarse as he hauled her against him and bent his head to hers. 'There are other rooms in the house that are going to take priority.'

Some considerable time later Anna pulled away, her heart thumping. 'You do realise that your parents are going to be horribly smug about all this,' she muttered against his mouth. 'They'll think it's because of them.'

'I never do anything my parents want,' Sam reminded her, his eyes still half shut as he studied her face. 'If we're together, it's in spite of them.'

'Your mum will be knitting like mad.'

He brushed his mouth against hers. 'Good. Given the number of pregnancies that happen in this village, I'd say that was sensible planning.'

She giggled and kissed him back. 'I love you. Even if you are sometimes wrong about things.'

'I love you, too.' The corner of his mouth lifted

and his eyes gleamed. 'And I'm never wrong about anything.'

'You drive me nuts, McKenna.'

'Always have done, always will do.' And he lowered his mouth to hers.

A MOTHER
BY NATURE

BY

CAROLINE ANDERSON

First published in Great Britain 2000. This edition 2013.
by Mills & Boon, an imprint of Harlequin (UK) Limited,
Eton House, 18-24 Paradise Road, Richmond, Surrey TW9 1SR

© Caroline Anderson 2000

ISBN: 978 0 263 90657 8
ebook ISBN: 978 1 472 01217-3

03-0613

Harlequin (UK) policy is to use papers that are natural, renewable and recyclable products and made from wood grown in sustainable forests. The logging and manufacturing processes conform to the legal environmental regulations of the country of origin.

Printed and bound in Spain
by Blackprint CPI, Barcelona

Caroline Anderson has the mind of a butterfly. She's been a nurse, a secretary, a teacher, run her own soft furnishing business, and now she's settled on writing. She says, 'I was looking for that elusive something. I finally realised it was variety, and now I have it in abundance. Every book brings new horizons and new friends, and in between books I have learned to be a juggler. My teacher husband John and I have two beautiful and talented daughters, Sarah and Hannah, umpteen pets, and several acres of Suffolk that nature tries to reclaim every time we turn our backs!' Caroline also writes for the Mills & Boon® Cherish™ series.

Recent titles by Caroline Anderson:
Mills & Boon® Medical Romance™

THE SECRET IN HIS HEART
FROM CHRISTMAS TO ETERNITY
THE FIANCÉE HE CAN'T FORGET
TEMPTED BY DR DAISY
ST PIRAN'S: THE WEDDING OF THE YEAR*
THE SURGEON'S MIRACLE
*St Piran's Hospital

Mills & Boon® Cherish™
THE VALTIERI BABY
VALTIERI'S BRIDE
THE BABY SWAP MIRACLE
MOTHER OF THE BRIDE

CHAPTER ONE

HE STOOD in the bay window, his eyes scanning the dimly lit street with quiet contentment. It was a pleasant street, the large houses set back from the road and shielded from prying eyes by an avenue of old flowering cherries.

Their branches swayed in the wind, leafless still, the whispered promise of spring barely showing in the brave shoots of daffodils nudging the earth under the garden wall, but the signs were there, and he guessed it would be glorious when the trees blossomed.

A movement in the house opposite caught his attention, and he focused on it. There were lights on downstairs, and he could see people moving about, settling down for the evening.

His house was settled already, silent now except for the running footsteps on the stairs. They ground to a halt by the door.

'Adam? I'm going out now, OK?'

He looked towards the disembodied, slightly accented voice with resignation. 'OK. What time will you be back?' he asked, without any real hope that he would like the answer. He was right. He didn't.

'Late,' she said. 'I'm going to the pub again—maybe meet my new friends. I've got my keys.'

'OK. Goodnight, Helle.'

The front door slammed behind her, echoing through the house and making the windows rattle. Her feet crunched against the gravel of the drive, and she slipped through the gateway and disappeared, swallowed up by the eerie night. Adam dropped his head back against the edge of the window and let out a quiet sigh.

He was tired. It had been a hectic week. The move had taken three days, and he'd spent the next four unpacking and slotting things into their new places while the children had got under his feet and rushed about excitedly and Helle had done the bare minimum. The big Edwardian semi still seemed empty, the huge rooms swallowing up their meagre possessions with ease, but given time he could decorate all the rooms and buy more furniture to fill them.

It was a daunting thought, but there was no hurry, and just for now they were enjoying the novelty of having too much room. After nearly three years of battling for elbow room and falling over toys and clutter, it was wonderful to have the space to spread out.

Skye had her own bedroom for the first time, the boys' room was big enough to have a separate area for each of them, and Helle, their Danish au pair, had a room on the top floor, a huge room with a little shower off it next to the spare bedroom that would double as his study. That gave her privacy, and he had privacy and space of his own in the master bedroom suite at the front—most particularly space.

The size of his bedroom was the only incongruous thing. Like Helle's room above him, it ran across the full width of the front of the house, excluding the bathroom at the end, absurdly big compared to the middle bedroom he'd had at the other house and somehow highlighting his loneliness in a way which that cluttered little room had never done.

He dropped into a chair and closed his eyes, suddenly weary, and wondered how the children and Helle would cope without him tomorrow, his first day in his new job. How would he cope, come to that? It was not only a new job, but his first consultancy, and he felt a little rush of adrenaline at the thought. Nerves?

Absurd, Adam told himself. He was more than capable of doing it, more than ready for the responsibility and the challenge. It was just that with the move to a new area and a new house, a new school for Skye and Danny and a new nursery school for Jaz, there was so much change, so much to deal with.

Someone to share it with would have made it all so much easier, he thought with an inward sigh, but that hadn't been an option. And Helle had been more of a hindrance than a help since they'd moved. She'd been unhappy before, restless and discontented, and now, since they'd moved, she'd seemed permanently attached to the cordless phone, drifting aimlessly around and talking into it in Danish whenever she thought he wasn't listening. Phoning home? Lord alone knows what the phone bill will be, he thought grimly.

He had a feeling his au pair was destined for a fairly imminent departure, which would mean replacing her and settling the new girl in with the children while coping with the new job and trying to sort out the house.

That in itself would be no mean feat. They'd only been able to afford it because it needed to be grabbed by the scruff of the neck and dragged, kicking and screaming, into the next century. The plumbing was ancient and suspect, the heating was intermittent and unreliable, the wiring was safe but woefully inadequate, and there wasn't a single room that didn't need decorating and a new carpet and curtains.

Even on his new consultant's salary he couldn't afford to deal with it all at once, and he certainly couldn't afford to pay anyone to do it for him. Catapulting restlessly out of the chair, he went into the kitchen and poured himself a glass of wine. His eyes scanned the room without the benefit of his earlier rose-tinted spectacles, and the enormity of what he'd taken on swamped him.

It was the little things—the cupboard door that hung at a crazy angle because the top hinge had gone, the worktop that had a hole burned in it next to the cooker, the cracked and broken tiles, the broken sash cord that dangled from the window, taunting him.

How many others were on the point of breaking? What else was wrong that he hadn't noticed or worried about on the building society's huge and extensive survey report? OK, structurally it was sound, but everything he looked at seemed to need some attention. The loo off the hall needed to have its door rehung because it smashed into the basin behind it if you opened it more than halfway, the fireplace in the dining room needed to be opened up and revealed— the list was endless.

Endless, but cosmetic. Nothing time wouldn't cure. Once he'd had time to deal with it, it would be warm and light and a wonderful family home.

One day.

Adam went back to the drawing room, threw another shovel full of coal on the fire, put on a CD and settled down in the chair with his eyes firmly shut against the list of chores awaiting him in that room.

He didn't want to see the crack across the corner of the ceiling, the wallpaper easing off the wall just below it, the chipped paint on the skirting board, the worn and frayed carpet begging to be replaced.

There would be time for that later, once they were settled. In the meantime, he'd relax and try and get himself into the right frame of mind for tomorrow, and try not to think about Helle and the fact that she would probably disturb him coming back in the wee small hours of the night, doubtless utterly wasted after her evening in the pub, and would be hell to get up in the morning in time to get the children ready for school. Which meant he'd have to do it, yet again.

He put it out of his mind. He'd deal with tomorrow when it came. One day at a time, he reminded himself. It had got him through the last two years since Lyn had left. It would get him through the next twenty.

Please, God...

Damn. He was going to be late. His first day in his new job and he was going to be late.

'Daddy, I can't find my shoes...'

'Try under your coat on the floor in the dining room where you threw it last night. Jasper, eat your breakfast, please.'

'Don't like cornflakes.'

'You did yesterday. Danny, have you found your shoes yet?'

A mumble came from the dining room. It could just conceivably have been a yes. Then again...

Adam rammed his hands through his short, dark

hair and stared at the ceiling. Where was Helle? He'd called her three times.

'Do we have to go to school? I hate it there. I want to go back to my old school.'

Adam met Skye's sad blue eyes, old beyond her almost six years, and wished he could hug her and make her better. He'd given up trying. She simply stood and let him hold her, then walked away as soon as he let go. The social worker had said give her time, but it had been nearly three years now, and although she was better, she was still light years from emotional security.

And Lyn walking out on them hadn't helped one damn bit.

'Yes, darling, you do have to go,' he told her gently. 'You know that. I know it's hard at first, but you'll soon settle in and it'll be much better for us here near Grannie and Grandpa. You'll like seeing more of them, won't you?'

She shrugged noncommittally, and he stifled a sigh and went to the bottom of the stairs. 'Helle?' he yelled, and then remembered the neighbours through the party wall. Damn. At least the last house had been detached. Still, the people next door hadn't complained about their new neighbours yet, and the teenage girls had been round already to introduce themselves and offer their services for babysitting.

If Helle didn't get out of bed soon, he might have to take them up on it!

For what seemed like the millionth time, he wondered if he'd been quite mad to continue with the adoption when Lyn had left him. Maybe he should have let the kids go back instead of fighting to keep them. Maybe they would have been better off without him, with someone else instead. Two someones, preferably.

Then Danny wandered out into the hall, tie crooked, shoes untied, hair spiking on top of his head and a grin to gladden the loneliest heart, and he reached out and hugged the boy to his side as they went together back into the kitchen.

'Look—I made you a card at school.'

He handed Adam a crumpled bit of sugar paper with spider writing on it, pencil on dark grey, almost impossible to decipher and yet the message quite clear. 'I love you, Daddy. From Danny.' There was a picture stuck on the front, of a house with a wonky chimney and a red front door just like theirs. Swallowing hard to shift the lump in his throat, he thanked Danny and stuck the card on the front of the fridge with a magnet.

Skye, ever the mother, was coaxing Jasper to eat his now soggy cereal, and she looked up and gave Adam that steady, serious look that made him want to weep for her. 'Is Helle coming?' she asked, and he shook his head.

'I'm going to have to get her up,' he told them. 'I have to leave you guys and go to work, and I can't be late. Not today.'

'Are you scared?' Jasper asked, eyeing him curiously.

'Don't be stupid—course he's not!' Danny said patronisingly.

He sat down. 'Well, maybe a bit,' he confessed. 'Not scared exactly, but it's never easy to meet new people and settle into a new place. It doesn't matter if you're old or young, it's still a bit difficult at first.'

'Even for you?' Danny asked in amazement, gazing up at his hero with eyes like saucers.

He grinned and ruffled the spiky brown hair. 'Even for me, sport.'

'It'll be all right, you'll see,' Skye said seriously, neatly reversing their roles, and he felt a lump in his throat again.

No. Whatever chaos and drama they'd brought to his life, he couldn't imagine that life without them now. They belonged to each other, for better, for worse, and so on. They were a family and, like all families, they had good times and bad times.

Mostly they were good, but if Helle didn't get up soon, he had a feeling that today was going to be a bad one…

Anna was feeling blue. She'd woken that morning wondering what it was all about, and two hours later she was still no nearer the answer. Wake up, get up, eat, go to work, go home, eat, go to bed, wake up—relentless routine, day after day, with nothing to brighten it.

Was she just desperately ungrateful? She had a roof over her head—more than a roof, really, a lovely little house that she enjoyed and was proud of—great friends, and a wonderful job that she wouldn't change for the world—except that this morning, for the first time she could remember, she really, really didn't want to be here.

So what was the matter with her?

Stupid question. Anna knew perfectly well what was wrong with her. She was alone. She was twenty-eight years old, and she was alone, and she didn't want to be. She wanted to be married, and have children—lots of them—one after the other. Children of her own, not other people's little darlings but her own babies, conceived in love, nurtured by her body, raised by her and a man with dark hair and gentle eyes and a slow, sexy smile—a man she'd yet to meet.

Would never meet, she thought in frustration, if her life carried on as it was. Her biological clock was going to grind to a halt before then at this rate.

Oh, damn.

She pushed her chair back and stood up, her eyes automatically scanning the ward, and stopped dead as a jolt of recognition shot through her.

It was him. Dark hair, cut short but still long enough to have that sexy, unruly look that did funny things to her insides. Tallish, but not too tall, his shoulders broad enough to lean on but not wide enough to intimidate, he looked like a man you could rely on.

Her eyes scanned him, taking inventory. Lean hips. Firm chin and beautifully sculptured mouth. Eyebrows a dark slash across his forehead, mobile and expressive. A smile like quicksilver. He'd paused to chat to a child, his hands shoved deep into the pockets of his white coat, and the child was grinning and pointing towards her.

He was good-looking, certainly, but it wasn't really his looks that made him stand out so much as his presence. There was something about him, she thought as he straightened and turned towards her, something immensely strong and powerful and yet kind—endlessly, deeply kind, the sort of enduring kindness that made sacrifices and didn't count the cost.

She'd never seen him before, but her body recognised him, every cell on full alert.

He started towards her with a smile, and their eyes locked, and out of the blue, she thought, At last…!

'Sister Long?' he said, although he knew quite well who she was, if the badge on her tabard was to be believed.

'Anna,' she corrected, looking up at him with startling green eyes, and he felt a shiver of sexual awareness which had lain dormant for so long it was almost shocking. A wisp of dark red hair had escaped from her neat bob and was falling forward over her face, and he had to restrain himself from lifting it with his fingers and tucking it back behind her ear. She smiled and held out her hand, slim and firm and purposeful. 'You must be our new paediatric orthopaedic consultant—Mr Bradbury, isn't it?'

He nodded. 'Adam,' he said, and his voice cracked and he cleared his throat. 'Adam Bradbury. Good to meet you. Have you got time for a chat? My department seem to have organised things so that I'm at a total loose end today, so I thought I'd spend it orienteering.'

She chuckled, a low, sexy chuckle that made his hair stand on end and everything else jump to attention. 'Sure. Come into the kitchen, I'll make coffee.'

He followed her, his eyes involuntarily tracking over the neat waist, the gentle swell of her hips, the womanly sway as she pushed the door out of the way and turned to hold it for him, flashing him a smile with those incredibly expressive eyes.

She spoke, but his body was clamouring so loud he didn't hear her.

'I'm sorry?'

She gave him a quizzical smile. 'I said, tea or coffee?'

'Oh—tea, thank you,' he said, trying to concentrate on something other than her warm, soft mouth. 'It's a bit early for coffee.'

'Well, there's a thing. A fellow tea-drinker. Everyone else dives straight for the coffee.' The smiled softened, lighting up her changeable green eyes and bringing out the gold flecks.

Not green at all, he realised, but blue and gold, fascinating eyes, beautiful eyes.

Bedroom eyes.

Oh, lord.

He stuffed his hands back into his coat pockets and angled them across his body as a shield. He had to work with her. He really, really didn't need the embarrassment of an adolescent reaction!

Anna took him on a guided tour while the kettle boiled. She was glad to get out of the tiny kitchen, to be honest, the current running between them seemed so powerful. Not that he'd really given her any hint that he was interested, but there just seemed to be something that hummed along under the surface.

'We've got twenty-one beds,' she told Adam, walking down the ward towards the orthopaedic section, his area of special interest. 'Six acute medical, six surgical, six orthopaedic and three single or family suites for more critical or noisy or infectious patients. We've got an isolation ward for barrier nursing or immuno-compromised patients—that's another single, but I don't tend to count it. It's the only room that doesn't get stolen for other things.'

'Stolen?' he said with a slow smile.

Anna rolled her eyes. 'Oh, yes, of course—the lines

get blurred and we end up with kids muddled up in the wrong place because of numbers, which drives the bed manager potty and the consultants come to blows over who has which bed for which child.'

His mouth kicked up in a crooked smile of appreciation, and her heart flip-flopped in her chest. Concentrate, she told herself sternly.

'We keep the age groups together if we can—the long-stay older kids are the worst, as you might imagine, and the teenagers in traction are a nightmare.'

'Well, there's a thing,' he murmured. 'You could always put any really difficult kids in the Stryker bed for a little while just to get a taste of real deprivation of liberty.'

'What, like throwing prisoners of war into the cooler? What a fascinating thought…!'

He laughed, and she thought her knees were going to give way. He's probably married with a million children, she chided herself crossly, and told herself to mind her own business.

'Have you moved far?' she asked as they walked down the ward, her insatiable curiosity getting the better of her anyway.

'About a hundred and fifty miles or so. I was in Oxford.'

'Oxford? How lovely. How will you cope with the rural isolation of Audley?' she asked with a laugh, and then her mouth, running on without her permission, added, 'Doesn't your wife mind?'

'She might if I had one, but I don't,' Adam said lightly.

'That must make it easier,' she replied, trying not to smile with delight because he was free, but his next words took the wind right out of her sails.

'Not really,' he told her. 'I've got three children under six and a Danish au pair with attitude, and we've bought a huge Edwardian house that needs every nook and cranny kicked into shape. Easier it's not, but I like a challenge.'

She ground to a halt outside the playroom, and turned towards him, guilt prickling her. 'I'm sorry,' she said sincerely. 'I didn't mean to intrude.'

'You're not intruding,' he said with a gentle smile that reassured her slightly. 'I'm just feeling a little overawed by what I've taken on. How about you? Are you married? Single, widowed, divorced, or other, please specify?'

Anna laughed, relief flooding through her at his light-hearted tone. 'Single,' she replied. Endlessly. Regrettably.

She never found out what he would have said next, because the playroom door flew open and a child came barrelling through it full pelt and nearly knocked her over. Her hand flew out and grabbed him by the shoulder, steadying him, and she looked down into his sparkling, mischievous eyes and shook her head.

'You'll never learn, Karl, will you?'

He grinned. 'Sorry, Sister. I was in a hurry.'

'I noticed. That was how this happened in the first place, wasn't it? Too much of a hurry?' She eyed him thoughtfully. 'You're going to hurt someone with that cast in a minute as well. Do me a favour and go and sit down and do something quiet. You'll be going up to Theatre later this morning, and you really could do with being calm beforehand.'

'Perhaps Karl should be our first experiment with the Stryker bed?' Adam said softly under his breath.

'What a good idea,' Anna murmured, eyeing young Karl thoughtfully.

He looked from one to the other, not sure what they were talking about but obviously edgy. 'What's a—whatever you said sort of bed?' he asked suspiciously.

'You lie in it like the filling in a sandwich, and it turns over from time to time. It's for keeping people with certain conditions like spinal injuries very still.'

'Or settling down overactive youngsters,' Adam added with a smile that belied his words.

'You're winding me up,' Karl said, still not quite sure, and Anna laughed and ruffled his hair.

'You got it. Go and find something quiet to do, there's a good lad, and I'll come and give you your pre-med later.'

He shot off, clearly relieved, and with a smile they headed back towards the kitchen. 'He's got a non-union of the radius after a nasty fracture. They just can't get it to heal, so they're going to sort him out in Theatre this morning and probably pack it and plate it. I'm not sure if they've decided exactly what they're doing.'

'Who's doing it?' he asked.

'Robert Ryder. Have you met him yet?'

Adam shook his head. 'No. Perhaps I'll track him down, see if I can observe. Might be interesting.'

'I'm sure he won't mind, he's very approachable. How about that tea now?' she added as they arrived back at the nursing station by her office. But then the phone rang and it was A and E to say that there was a patient on the way up, a frequent visitor who had suffered yet another serious asthma attack and was now stable but needing observation.

'Can you hang on?' she asked him, explaining the

case briefly to him. 'I really need to see to this child, he's a regular. Or you could help yourself to tea. You're more than welcome.'

'I'll pass. I'll go and meet the rest of the paediatric team about the hospital, and make a nuisance of myself elsewhere. I might go into the orthopaedic theatres and have a nose around, introduce myself to Ryder and see if I can observe Karl's op, as I said.'

She felt a pang of what could only have been regret. 'OK. Maybe next time,' she suggested, and could have kicked herself for sounding like a breathless virgin. Ridiculous. She was too busy to have tea with him anyway! 'Have a good day,' she added with a smile.

'I'm sure I will—and thanks for the guided tour. I'll see you tomorrow, no doubt.'

Anna watched him go out of the corner of her eye as she scanned the ward for the most suitable place to put young Toby Cardew, and she suddenly realised that she was looking forward to the next day for the first time in ages.

Gone were the blues she'd felt that morning, replaced by a shiver of anticipation. Adam was apparently unencumbered by a wife, the fact that he had children already was hardly a turn-off to a paediatric nurse and, anyway, the more the merrier.

You're getting ahead of yourself, she cautioned as she went to sort out a bed for Toby. Just because you think he's attractive and he asked about your marital status, that doesn't mean it will go any further—and, anyway, he might have terrible habits. Why did his wife leave him?

She might have died. Perhaps he's suffering from intractable grief, her alter ego suggested.

Funny. He didn't look like a man suffering from intractable grief. He just looked tired round the eyes, and, if she hadn't been mistaken, he'd been interested in her. She hadn't been mistaken. She knew that look. She'd had plenty of practice at intercepting it over the years.

Too many years, too many times, too many near-misses. The trouble was, the older she got the more likely that the men of her age would be already settled in a permanent relationship—at least, the ones worth having!

Maybe this was one time when she wouldn't have to fend the man off. Maybe this time the advances, when and if they came, would be welcome. Goodness knows, it's about time, she thought.

'Who was *that*?'

Anna looked round at Allie Baker, her staff nurse and second in command, and wagged a finger.

'You've got one of your own,' she told her friend.

Allie grinned. 'I know, and I wouldn't swap him for the world. I just thought whoever that was was rather gorgeous. So who is he?'

'Adam Bradbury, our new paediatric orthopaedic surgeon.'

'I didn't know we had an old one.'

'We haven't,' Anna replied with a smile, checking forms on the clipboard at the end of the vacant bed. 'It's a new post. He's going to be doing developmental problems and post-traumatic reconstruction, that sort of thing, as well as working with the oncologists on bone cancers and the neurologists on spina bifida and so on. I gather he's rather clever.'

Allie grinned. 'And he's got your name on him.'

Anna smiled self-consciously. 'I don't know. I hope so. He's got three kids and no wife.'

'Oh, my God.' Allie looked at her in horror. *'Three kids?'*

Anna shrugged. 'I like kids.'

'You'd have to, working with them all day and going home to them at night. Maybe they're teenagers and nearly off his hands. Maybe they live some of the time with his wife.'

Anna laughed and pushed Allie out of the way gently. 'I'll tell you if I ever get a chance to find out. In the meantime, I've got things to do and you're holding me up. Toby Cardew's coming back.'

Allie rolled her eyes. 'Not again? Whatever this time?'

'I have no idea. This attack was quite severe, I gather. His parents are going potty trying to find the trigger. Their house must be so clean! Mrs Cardew spends hours a day mopping it down.'

'Maybe it's not the house. Maybe it's school, or something on the journey, or a kid he sits next to?'

'They've addressed all that. Maybe one day it will fall into place—it's probably something really obvious that they've overlooked.'

The squeak of the A and E trolley alerted them to the new arrival, and Anna went to greet him. 'Hello again, young man,' she said with a smile of welcome, and patted his hand reassuringly. 'Can't stay away, can you? Must be our wit and charm that keeps you coming back.'

The boy gave a weak grin, and his mother shot Anna a tired, slightly desperate smile. 'Sorry to be a nuisance,' she apologised, but Anna brushed her words aside.

'Don't be silly,' she said briskly. 'That's why we're here, and we're always pleased to see a familiar face. Right, let's have you in bed and make you comfortable, shall we?'

They quickly shifted young Toby across onto the bed and settled him, then left him to rest. Allie made Mrs Cardew a cup of coffee, Anna went to give Karl his pre-med and it only seemed like five minutes before the boy was back from Theatre, his arm cast in a back slab to allow for swelling and with the hand raised.

He wouldn't be running around for a few days at least, Anna thought, and wondered if Adam *had* observed the operation. No doubt she'd find out tomorrow.

A tiny surge of what felt like adrenaline ran through her, and she caught herself looking at her watch and counting the hours until she'd see him again…

CHAPTER TWO

ADAM was due to start the day with a clinic, followed by a ward round to meet the new admissions on whom he'd operate that afternoon. He'd gone back to the ward and checked the notes yesterday evening, and had been foolishly disappointed to find that Anna had gone.

Pity. He'd wanted to tell her about his part in Karl's operation, and discuss what they'd done.

Strictly business, of course. Still, he'd see her today.

That lock of hair that kept falling forward and curving round her cheek was plaguing him. He'd been having fantasies about it all night—which was crazy because he always had fantasies about dark hair spread across his pillow in a fan, and hers was short and red. Dark red, admittedly, but red for all that, and far too short to fan satisfactorily.

Still, he wondered how it would feel sifting through his fingers...

Like silk. It was soft, heavy hair, essentially straight, with just enough bounce to curve under and curl around the pale pearly shell of her ear...

Damn.

He scooped the post off the floor in the lobby and scanned through it, grinding to a halt at the telephone bill. It was the final bill for the old house, and it took his mind off Anna and her attributes very effectively.

He opened it with grim resignation, but even his

wildest expectations were exceeded by its stunning proportions. Helle must truly have spent all day, every day, on the phone to her family and friends in Denmark.

He shook his head in despair, and ran upstairs to her room, rapping loudly on the door. 'Helle? Get up now. I want to talk to you immediately.'

There was a shuffling noise, and the door opened to reveal his hapless young au pair, her hair on end, her eyes blurred with sleep, dragging on a dressing-gown.

'What's the matter?' she asked, looking puzzled.

'This is the matter,' Adam said tightly, brandishing the thing under her nose. 'The telephone bill. It runs into four figures, Helle, and it's not even a complete quarter. I want you downstairs dressed in five minutes, and you'd better have a damn good explanation or you'll be packing your bags and catching the next flight home.'

'Good,' she said miserably, and burst into tears. 'I want to go home. I hate it here.'

You're a sucker, he told himself as he opened his arms and comforted the young woman while she cried. She was little more than a child herself, and it was a lot of responsibility. He should have talked to her more, been kinder to her, instead of expecting so much.

'Come downstairs,' he said more gently, easing her out of his arms. 'We'll have a cup of tea and talk about it before the children get up.'

She nodded and sniffed, scrubbing her nose on the sleeve of her dressing-gown. 'I'll get dressed.'

'Good idea.'

He ran back down, put the kettle on and glanced

at his watch. It was still only six-thirty, and he wondered if Anna was up yet or if she worked nine to five to cover admissions and pre- and post-ops. If she worked shifts and was on an early she'd be on her way there now. If not, she might still be in bed, her hair tangled round her face, her lashes like crescents on her cheeks, her mouth soft with sleep—

'You need a life, Bradbury,' he growled, and banged two mugs down on the worktop just as Helle came into the room.

She hovered apprehensively in the doorway, and he waved her in. 'Come in, sit down, I'm not going to bite you. I just want to know what's going on.'

She sat but, being Helle, she couldn't just sit. She played with the salt, she shredded a paper towel that had been left on the table, tearing it systematically into tiny strips while she waited for the axe to fall.

'Talk to me. Tell me all about it,' Adam said softly, sliding a mug across the battered old pine table, and she looked up, her eyes like huge pools filling yet again.

'I'm just lonely—I want my mum. I'm homesick. I thought it would get better, but then you said we were moving and I had to say goodbye to all my friends, and I thought, how will I cope in a new place?'

A tear fell, splashing on her hand, and she scrubbed it away and went on, 'It was hard before, when my friend Silke was just round the corner. Now it's impossible. I don't know anybody, and the children are at school and there's nothing to do, and I just sit and cry—'

'So you ring your mum.'

She nodded miserably. 'I'm sorry, Adam. I didn't realise it would be so expensive.'

'It's as much as your wages,' he pointed out, not unreasonably.

'But some is you,' she defended with truth, and he shrugged.

'A little. Perhaps the first hundred pounds.'

She swallowed. 'May I see it?'

He handed her the bill—the itemised section that ran to page after page—and she studied it in silence and handed it back.

'Are you going to send me home?'

'Do you want to go? Do you really want to go? Are you so unhappy? I don't want you to be unhappy, Helle. It doesn't help anyone—not you, not me, and certainly not the children.'

She nodded and sniffed. 'I do want to go. I'll miss the children, but I'm so lonely. It wouldn't be so bad if you had a wife, it would be another woman to talk to. It's different—I can't talk to you like I could to a woman.'

Nothing would be so bad if he had a wife, he thought defeatedly, including his own loneliness, but it was out of the question. Lyn's defection had scarred them all, and there was no way he was going there again.

'I'll ask my mum,' Helle went on, miserably shredding another paper towel. 'Maybe she'll pay the phone bill.'

'Never mind the phone bill. Just do me a favour and stay until I can get someone else, Adam, and then I'll forget the bill—OK? Only stay off the damn phone in the daytime, please, until you go home. Deal?'

He wouldn't understand women if he lived to be a

hundred, he thought as Helle burst into tears. He found her an unshredded piece of kitchen roll and watched as she hiccuped to a halt and blotted herself up.

'Deal,' she said finally.

'Good. Now, do you suppose you could get the children up in time for school today, please?'

She nodded. 'I'll wake them now.'

He ate a piece of toast, kissed the children hello and goodbye in one and left for work, his mind on his afternoon list. He had yet to meet the other members of his firm, the registrars and house doctors that were allocated to him in this new speciality that the Audley Memorial had set up.

Most hospitals had one or two consultants who tended to handle the paediatric work. It was unusual to find a post dedicated to it, and he was looking forward to the challenge. He understood they would take referrals from other hospitals within the region once his post was established—it would become the local specialist centre for paediatric orthopaedics, centralising treatment in Suffolk and making it more accessible for patients and their families.

That meant better visiting arrangements, which in turn meant happier patients getting better quicker. He approved of that.

Adam parked his car in the staff car park, then crossed it and palmed the door out of the way and caught himself all but running down the corridor to the ward. Idiot, he thought crossly. She's probably not even there yet—and if she is, she'll be busy.

She was. She was taking report, and he went into the kitchen and put the kettle on and made two mugs of tea. She wouldn't be long.

* * *

'Tea,' he said, thrusting a mug at her, and Anna took it gratefully and drank it too fast, almost scalding her mouth. It was delicious—almost as delicious as him—and nearly as welcome.

'I needed that. How did you know?' she said with a smile as she drained it, and he gave a chuckle and made her another one.

'I wanted to go through the notes of my afternoon list with you,' he said over his shoulder as he stirred the teabag round. 'I think you know some of the patients.'

She nodded. 'Sure. Shall we go into the office?'

'Have you got time?'

She grinned at him. 'One of the nice things about this job is being able to delegate most of it! Come on, I can spare you ten minutes. The notes are in there still.'

She settled down in her chair, her knees propped up on the edge of the desk, her uniform trousers protecting her modesty. 'Tell me about Karl first,' she prompted, trying to concentrate on something other than his long, lean legs stretched out across the floor in her office and the casual way he slouched against her desk.

'Karl? Oh, the lad yesterday. Robert let me assist—it was interesting. We plated it. When we got in there it was quite obvious that the bone had made no attempt to heal. The main reason seemed to be that it had rotated out of alignment, so we had to break the ulna as well to correct the rotation so we could line it all up properly. We plated both just to be on the safe side. It should be a better shape than it was before, anyway, so in a strange way it might have done him a favour. How is he now?'

'Bit groggy. Quieter than yesterday, I gather. I think he had quite a good night. Was it very traumatic to the tissues?'

He shrugged. 'Fairly. I would expect it to be quite sore for a day or two. It was obviously quite a nasty break—I had a look at the earlier plates. It seems likely that he tried to do too much too soon and twisted it out of position inside the cast. By the time it was noticed, it was too late.'

'That's what you get for trying to fix an active young hellion conservatively,' Anna said with a smile. 'They need everything screwed together because they all want a quick fix.'

'Everybody wants a quick fix,' he said with a sigh. 'I think my au pair's going to want a quick fix. I confronted her with the phone bill this morning and she announced she wanted to go home. I bribed her by offering to forget the phone bill if she'd stay until I'd got a replacement.'

'And?'

He shrugged. 'She says she'll stay—for now, at least.'

Anna felt a pang of sympathy. 'Was it horrendous?' she asked, and he rolled his eyes.

'Try four figures.'

Anna's jaw dropped. For the life of her she couldn't conceive of finding time to build up a phone bill that huge, never mind having anyone she wanted to talk to that much!

Well. Maybe that wasn't true—not any more. She could imagine curling up in the evening and having long, cosy chats to this man—

'Let's talk about your afternoon list,' she said,

dragging herself back to earth hastily. 'Who have you got that I know?'

'A baby with congenital club foot? David Chisholm. I think he's been in here. He's about eighteen months.'

Anna thought for a moment. 'David—yes, he has. I remember him. He's had a couple of ops already to let out the short structures on the inside of the legs. He was very bad—worst case I've seen, I think, not that we've had that many. I thought they'd got quite a good result?'

Adam nodded. 'That's right, but he needs another op because he's grown and the feet are turning in again.'

'Aren't they splinting it?'

He nodded again. 'Yes, but it's not keeping up. I'm going to release the tendons again—it's fairly rare, of course, so you don't tend to get that much practice at this sort of thing, but we're learning new ways of dealing with it. Sadly, it's never going to be quite normal, of course, and I haven't met the parents yet so I don't know what their expectations are.'

'High, I think. Most parents' expectations are high. They think we can sort out everything.'

'Well, I'll certainly try my best, but I'm only human,' he said with a wry smile, and her heart hiccuped. Only human's fine by me, she wanted to tell him, but she was being silly again.

One smile! she thought crossly. One smile and you keel over and submit! You'd make a good dog.

Anna tried to pay attention—she really did—but it was hard. In the end she was rescued by the arrival of a new admission, and she went to deal with him and escaped from the intoxicating and mind-bending cosiness of her office. She was busy for the rest of the day, rushed off her feet for most of it, and by the end of it she was feeling ragged.

Then Adam walked onto the ward, still in Theatre scrubs, and her heart did that silly thing all over again and she wanted to kick herself.

'Hi,' he said, his voice soft and low. Shivers ran down her back, and she forced herself to ignore them.

'Hi, yourself,' she said with what she hoped was a friendly smile and not an infatuated drool. 'How was your list?'

'OK. A couple are in SCBU, but you should have the rest. How's little David?'

'Sick and sore, I think. Well, probably more uncomfortable than sore. His mother's with him, but she's pregnant again and she's finding it quite wearing. I keep sending my nurses to rescue her so she can go and have a cup of tea, but she won't let me.'

'Is she staying all night?'.

Anna nodded. 'Yes. She needs to rest, but she won't leave him till he settles.'

'Can I have a quick look?' he asked.

'Sure. He's over here.'

They went over to the baby and his mother and, as Anna had expected, the little boy was propped up against her shoulder, grizzling gently, and she was rubbing his back and making soothing noises. They weren't working.

'Hello, Mrs Chisholm,' Adam said, hunkering down to her level and smiling at her with that special smile. 'How are things?'

'Oh—hello, Doctor. I'm so glad you've come. Not too bad. How was it? Have you been able to do it?'

'It was OK,' he said reassuringly. 'I've managed

to get quite a bit of length on the tendons, so we were able to get his feet into a more normal position in the casts. He'll be a bit miserable for a day or so, but we're giving him plenty of pain relief so he's not really hurting. Once the first few days are over you'll find he's walking much better. May I have a look?'

She held the little boy out, and Adam took him and straightened.

'Hello again, young man. Can I have a look at your feet?' he said softly, his smile gentle. The baby rested sleepily against him with a little whimper, and Adam soothed him automatically before laying him down in the cot.

His movements were sure and practised, Anna thought. You could tell he was a father. His hand brushed the baby's head, smoothing back the damp, ruffled hair that clung to his brow, and quickly he scanned the boy's legs with his eyes.

'I'm checking the colour and warmth of his toes and that the dressings you can see through these windows in the casts aren't showing signs of leaking of the wounds,' he explained. 'Perhaps you could keep an eye on that for us, as you're here. It's possible the legs might swell after a little while, but we'll keep a constant check, and if you notice anything different, perhaps you could tell us.'

She nodded. 'Of course.'

'He looks fine at the moment,' he went on, raising his voice over the baby's unhappy protests. 'I'm pleased. He seems a bit grizzly, though. Perhaps he's not that comfortable. We'll give him something to settle him.'

'I think he needs to sleep,' Mrs Chisholm said, 'but

every time I put him down he cries, and I don't like to disturb the other children.'

'Don't worry about the other children,' Anna hastened to assure her. 'He won't cry for long. He's dead beat. He'll go off in seconds if you can just bear to let him cry.'

'I just feel so mean,' she said, clearly torn.

'Perhaps you should go and get something to eat and leave him quietly alone for a little while and try it,' Adam suggested. 'You might find he drops off if you aren't here to cuddle—it's not worth staying awake then.' The smile robbed his suggestion of any criticism, and she nodded wearily.

'I could murder a cup of tea and a leg stretch, and probably something to eat, actually. I was going to wait until my husband came back and go then, so David wasn't on his own, but are you sure he'll be all right?'

'Of course he'll be all right,' Anna assured her firmly. 'We'll look after him. If he doesn't settle in a minute I'll get someone to cuddle him till you're back, but you've got to look after yourself and the other baby.'

She nodded again. 'OK. Thanks.'

They watched her go, and she was hardly out of the ward before little David stopped grizzling and started to relax into much-needed sleep.

'Peace at last,' Anna said with a soft chuckle, and covered the little boy lightly with his blanket. 'He'll be all right now. Do you still want to give him something?'

Adam shook his head. 'Not if he doesn't need it. I'll write him up for something in case he wakes in the night and is distressed. What are you doing now? Got time to look at my others with me?'

She glanced at the clock on the wall and groaned. 'Not really. Apparently, it's time to go home and I still haven't finished. Do you need me with you to look at your other patients?'

'I wouldn't mind, but it isn't necessary. Anyway I suspect they're all asleep. Are their parents here?'

'Yes, all of them. I'm sure they'd love to see you and ask you about the operations.'

He nodded, pursed his lips for a moment as he, too, glanced at his watch, and then he shrugged. 'I'll go and see them. You don't have to stay, I'm sure I can find my way around.'

'I'll show you where they are and leave you to it. I have to hand over to Allie. Those two beds there,' she told him, pointing, 'and that one in the far corner. OK? Shout if you need help. Allie will sort you out.'

'OK. Thanks. See you tomorrow.'

His smile warmed her. Reluctantly, she dragged herself back to her other tasks, handed over and left the ward with only a handful of backward glances.

She went home, put the kettle on while she changed into jeans and a comfy sweater, and sat down with her feet up and a cup of tea in front of the TV news. It didn't hold her attention. It couldn't even begin to compete with that sexy smile and the smoky green eyes that were beginning to haunt her every waking moment.

What made him so different? Nothing obvious. Over the years she'd been out with several men, most of them very pleasant, most of them perfectly nice.

Nice. Pleasant.

She didn't *want* 'nice' and 'pleasant'. She wanted

someone who made her blood sing, whose touch would reduce her to putty, whose eyes could turn her heart inside out and melt her into a puddle at his feet.

They hadn't all been nice, of course. There had been Jim—he'd been charming and utterly faithless. She'd had her fingers burned by him and had been much more circumspect after that. Not that she'd ever been in the slightest bit promiscuous, but everyone seemed to imagine that if you dated them more than twice at the outside you were destined for bed.

Anna didn't work like that. It had to be right, and it had only been right very rarely. Just recently—like in the last three years or so—it hadn't been right at all.

'You're turning into a desperate old maid,' she said in disgust. 'One smile from a halfway presentable man and you're there waiting with your tongue hanging out. That's so sad.'

She smacked her mug down, stood up and went through into the kitchen. The fridge revealed very little of any interest, and the freezer was worse.

'Great,' she said in disgust. 'I have to go shopping. Marvellous.'

She slammed the freezer door, stuffed her feet into her old trainers and pulled on her tatty but snuggly duffle-coat. She wasn't going to see anyone. She didn't need to dress up.

She drove to the nearest supermarket, picked up a little trolley and started wandering randomly up and down the aisles. Nothing appealed. Well, nothing healthy. She glanced into the trolley next to her, wondering what other people ate that might be more interesting than the usual things that she bought, and she sighed.

Fish fingers, low-fat oven chips, frozen veg, chicken legs, rice—about as inspired as hers, except that this trolley actually had something in it.

Three loaves of bread, lots of tuna and ham and salad ingredients, little cakes—lots of convenience foods, really, she thought. Busy household. Working mother, probably. Poor woman—

'Anna?'

She looked up, startled, and found Adam looking at her curiously.

'Hi,' she said weakly.

'Hi. Thought it was you. Is there something wrong with my trolley?'

'Your— No, of course not! I didn't know it was yours. I was looking in it for inspiration, actually.'

He gave a wry snort of laughter. 'I should give it a miss, in that case. I buy what the kids will eat, which sometimes seems like utter rubbish. It's the au pair's job, of course, but she's having the evening off, so it's down to me to buy the junk food today.'

'It doesn't look too bad. At least you're going for the low-fat options.'

'Ever the conscientious father,' he said with a fleeting smile. 'Which reminds me, they're running riot in the next aisle. I must go.'

She watched him disappear round the end of the aisle and, because she was only human and curiosity was part of human nature, she found herself drifting after him. They'd vanished, but she soon found them.

He was lifting a little boy off the top of the bread display unit, smiling apologetically at a disapproving member of staff and throwing a packet into the trolley with one hand while he clamped the protesting child to his side with the other.

'No, if you can't behave then you'll have to stay here with me where I can keep an eye on you.'

'I'll look after him,' a little girl promised, and Adam put the boy down. 'Stay right next to me,' she told him sternly, and he nodded and slipped his hand into hers.

Big sister, Anna thought with a gentle smile.

'Daddy, can we have supper here, please?'

The middle one, Anna thought, looking at the little face shining up at him with obvious devotion. What a lovely family. A huge lump formed in her throat, and she was just about to slide round the corner of the aisle and find a little privacy to get herself under control when Adam turned and saw her.

'Um—yes, sure,' he said distractedly, and smiled at her. She wondered if he knew he'd just been conned, and had to hide her own smile of amusement behind a smile of greeting. 'My brood,' he said, waving at them. 'Skye, Danny, Jasper, this is Miss Long. I work with her.'

'Anna,' she corrected, and directed her smile to the children. 'Hi. Are you making sure he buys all the right things?'

'No, they're making sure I buy all the *wrong* things,' he said with a laugh.

'We're going to have supper here,' Danny told her. 'Do you ever do that?'

'I have done,' she said, willing Adam to ask her to join them. He didn't need to. Danny did it.

'You could have supper with us—couldn't she, Daddy?' He swivelled his head round, leaning over backwards and nearly toppling into the bread.

Adam reached out and steadied him, and gave Anna a helpless look. 'If you'd like to—you're more than welcome to join us, if you can stand it. It'll probably be egg, beans and chips if they get their way.'

Thank you, God! 'Egg, beans and chips sounds
good,' she said with a bright smile. 'If you mean it.'

'Of course I mean it,' he said, his eyes softening.
'You're more than welcome. Are you all done?'

'Yes,' she lied. To hell with doing the shopping.
She'd get the rest another time. This was much more
interesting!

They went through the checkout, parked their trolleys and joined the queue, and Danny chatted ingenuously all the way through the selection procedure
and most of the way through the meal. He was a
sweet, open child with spiky, untidy hair the same
dark brown as his father's, and a direct blue gaze that
cut straight to her heart.

Jasper was similar—smaller and quieter, or perhaps
simply overwhelmed by his big brother, hanging on
his sister's every word.

And Skye—Skye was different. She had soft,
lustrous brown hair, not quite as dark as the others,
and the same penetrating blue eyes, but there the similarities ended.

Her eyes were distrustful. That was the difference,
Anna decided. Skye was guarded, she hardly spoke
except to Jaz, and she was politely distant with Anna.

That was fine. She didn't need the instant trust of
every child in the world, but she sensed that Skye's
reticence hurt Adam, and for some reason she didn't
want to go into that hurt her, too.

There was only one awkward moment, when she
wondered if she really ought to have been there. Skye
looked at Adam and said softly, 'Is Anna your girlfriend?'

He looked startled for a second, then shook his head. 'No. We work together. She's a nurse.'

Skye glanced at her consideringly, then went back to her meal without another word, leaving Anna thoughtful. It hadn't sounded, from her tone of voice, as if a girlfriend was something Skye wanted Adam to have. Because she felt threatened? Because she was jealous? Or because he had a constant stream of them and Skye didn't like it?

The table was crowded, and Anna was more than ever aware of Adam's long legs tangling with hers every time he moved. Finally the children were finished, and he met her eyes over the litter of dirty plates and cups of fizzy drinks and smiled distractedly.

'We have to get back. We've got frozen food in the trolley—or we did have. I expect it's all thawed by now.'

She nodded, conscious of a silly little spurt of disappointment. Of course he had to go—Jasper was yawning, Skye was bored and uneasy, and they couldn't possibly sit there all night. She conjured a bright smile. 'Yes, you'd better get back. Thank you so much for asking me to join you. I enjoyed it.'

He gave a disbelieving snort of laughter. 'You're too polite. Come on, kids, on your pins, let's make a move.'

She followed him out of the shop, looking like the Pied Piper with the children trailing behind him raggedly. Jasper kept wanting to look at things, and had to be dragged screaming past the little rocket ride just outside the door, with its coaxing invitation, 'Come on, climb aboard and we'll head for the skies!'

'I want to have a go!' Jasper sobbed, and Adam

scooped him up into his arms and hugged him, walking resolutely away.

'It's too late. You can have a go next time. It's too cold to hang about waiting, and we can't do everything in one night.'

'Don't want to do everything! Want to go in the rocket!'

'Jasper, Daddy said no,' Skye told him firmly, and the screaming subsided to an unhappy sobbing. They paused at the edge of the car park, and Adam rolled his eyes at Anna in mock despair.

'I'll see you tomorrow,' she said, and he nodded, hesitated a moment and then spoke as if on impulse.

'You could come back for coffee—if you could stand the chaos of bedtime and a house that needs cleaning and decorating from attic to cellar.'

A slow smile spread over her face. She could stand anything if it meant spending time with him and his family and getting to know him better. 'I should think I'll cope with that,' she said softly.

'Follow me,' he said.

Oh, yes, she thought. I'll follow you. I'll follow you to the ends of the earth if you ask me to. Just say the word.

Then she caught the look on Skye's face, and wondered why the little girl was so unhappy about her presence. She needed to know more about the situation, and perhaps this was one way to find out.

CHAPTER THREE

'OH, IT'S gorgeous!'

Adam looked mildly disbelieving, but Anna shook her head at him and laughed, gazing around, enraptured, at the lovely, welcoming hallway with its high ceilings and gleaming mahogany handrail. 'It is! It's truly wonderful—oh, it's going to be so lovely. It just feels—I don't know, *right*.'

'That's what I felt. It's why I bought it,' Adam said with a smile, but then the smile grew wry. 'Emphasis on "going to be", though. If and when I ever get the time and the money—not to mention the energy. Right, kids, upstairs and get yourselves ready for bed, please. It's way past your bedtime. I'll be up in five minutes.'

They ran up, and Adam seized several of the shopping bags from the hall floor and headed towards the back of the house. Anna picked up a couple more and followed him.

'You'll do it—don't be so defeatist. It's early days—heavens, most people wouldn't even have unpacked yet!'

'I haven't, not entirely. The dining room's still stacked up with boxes, but they're mainly books destined for shelves that don't yet exist and the dining room doesn't really matter. We don't exactly dine in style.'

'Shame on you,' Anna teased, then cocked her head on one side. 'Can I help?'

'Please—put the kettle on. I just want to put the frozen stuff away and check the kids, then we'll sit down for a bit of peace and quiet.'

She looked around at the kitchen. It was lovely, but it needed help. The units were awful, but they were easily replaced, and if the doorway from the breakfast area could be moved to the other side of the chimney breast, then the table could sit by the window and that would be much better.

The house looked, from the little she'd seen, as if it had been 'modernised' in the fifties, and it certainly needed some sympathetic restoration, but the potential was huge. Her curiosity was running riot. What was the rest of the house like?

'Right, that's that lot. How's the kettle?'

'Not boiled,' she told him. 'Can I have a guided tour?'

His face fell comically. 'Oh, lord,' he groaned, rolling his eyes in obvious embarrassment. 'I hate to think what a mess it is, and Helle's rooms will be chaos gone mad.'

'I'm not looking at the mess—I'm looking at the house, at the potential,' she coaxed, her avid curiosity unwilling to remain unsatisfied. 'If you really, really mind I'll let you say no, but I'd love to see it if you can bring yourself to let me.'

He hovered, just for a second, then squared his shoulders. 'Oh, what the heck, come on, then. Just don't say I didn't warn you,' he grumbled, and she laughed softly.

'I promise.'

'You can give me some advice. Skye's bedroom is first on the list, and I don't know what to do.'

'Ask her,' Anna said promptly, cautious of

becoming involved. 'It's her room—she's more than old enough to have ideas.'

'If only she would share them,' he murmured. 'Come on, then, let's get this over with.'

Anna went up the stairs after him and followed him straight down the landing and into Skye's bedroom. It was above the kitchen and overlooked the back garden, heavily shadowed now in the dark but fascinating to Anna for all that. She'd glimpsed it from the kitchen and itched to explore it in daylight. Her own garden was tiny, and she'd always thought she'd love a bigger garden. She tried not to envy him.

Skye was sitting on the bed, still fully dressed, colouring in a book. She glanced up and then looked away, dismissing them.

'I'm showing Anna the house,' Adam told her. 'Is it OK to come in?'

She shrugged.

'I'm sorry, it's an awful cheek—Skye, do you mind?' Anna asked, wary of stepping on clearly sensitive little toes.

She shrugged again, noncommitally, and carried on colouring. Anna looked around. It was desperately in need of love and attention, but it was bigger than Anna's sitting room, and way bigger than her bedrooms had ever been. There was a pretty little fireplace against one wall, cast iron and delicately patterned inset tiles, and Anna would have given her eye teeth for it as a child. As an adult, in fact!

'What a wonderful room—it's huge,' she said with genuine awe. 'My bedroom at home is much smaller!'

'Before, I had to share with the boys,' Skye said, clearly impressed that her room was bigger than

Anna's. 'Well, after she went. First I had the little room, but then the au pairs had it.'

Au pairs? As in, lots of them? Of course, they didn't come for long, Anna thought, and wondered if 'she' was their mother. Inevitably. And she'd gone somewhere. Where? It was suddenly a minefield, and she picked her way through it with enormous care.

'Do you know what you want to do with it now you've got such a lovely room?' Anna asked her. 'It's all yours—it must be wonderful, I should think, to be able to choose.'

Skye shrugged. 'Don't know.' She seemed to withdraw into herself then, as if too much attention was focused on her, and Anna gave a slight smile and moved further away, giving her room.

'I'm sure you'll have lots of fun deciding. I always think that's the best bit.' She turned towards Adam and pushed him gently towards the door. 'Come on, let's leave her in peace. I want to see the rest. What's next?'

He showed her the loo and bathroom, both in need of tidying up and probably refitting in a more sympathetic style than the ugly suite that was there. Still, it worked, she supposed, except for the dripping tap, although an Edwardian original would have been more attractive.

'I'm going to refit it when I get time,' he told her. 'I thought I might rearrange it to fit a loo in here as well—it seems silly not to have one in the bathroom, and there's tons of room.'

'Can you do plumbing?' she asked, impressed, and he laughed.

'Me? I'm an orthopaedic surgeon, don't forget. I'm

a dab hand with a saw and a screwdriver, and I'm good at plugging vascular leaks, too.'

'Hmm. Let's just hope your pipes heal,' she said with a smile, and he chuckled.

'They won't need to. You wait, it'll be perfect. Come and see the rest.'

He took her into the boys' room, and they were much more welcoming and extrovert than Skye had been. She was shown their toys, and how each of them had their own space in a corner of the even bigger room, and they bounced around and generally didn't look ready for bed.

'Your teacher's going to complain about you being too tired in the morning, Danny,' Adam threatened mildly, but he didn't seem to be worried. 'Come on, into your pyjamas, wash your faces and clean your teeth, boys, please,' he said with more firmness, and they grumbled off to the bathroom, leaving Adam and Anna to finish the house tour.

'I don't think we should look at Helle's rooms while she's out,' Adam said thoughtfully, pausing at the foot of the attic stairs. 'It doesn't seem right.' He hesitated just a fraction, then shot her a crooked little smile. 'That just leaves mine.'

He opened the door behind him, walked in and groaned softly. Anna went up on tiptoe and peered over his shoulder.

'So you didn't make the bed—so what?' she said, and nudged him gently through the doorway. He moved out of her way, letting her see the full extent of the room, and it took her breath away.

It was lovely. Well, no, it was a mess. The walls needed papering, the curtains were ghastly, the carpet was in shreds and the colour scheme seemed to have been put together by a committee. Mentally, she painted it a soft, pale ivory cream. White, but not white. Restful. Tranquil.

Neutral carpet—jute, perhaps? Off-white curtains, soft and diaphanous, drifting in the warm spring breeze. Pale ivory bedlinen, a duvet like a cloud of thistledown—and Adam, reaching out for her.

She realised she was staring at the bed, picturing him in it, picturing *them* in it. Together. The crumpled sheets and tumbled quilt sprang into focus, and she could see the imprint of his head on one of the pillows. Her breath jammed in her throat and she looked round a little wildly.

A door caught her eye. 'What's in there?' she asked, desperate for something else to think about— anything else except that rumpled, evocative bed!

'The shower room.'

'May I?' Anna crossed to it without waiting for his permission, opened the door and found herself in a narrow little room, functional but tired. She turned and smacked straight into his chest, her hands flying up to act as buffers.

They landed lightly on Adam's ribcage, splayed out over the broad expanse of bone and muscle that her fingers itched to explore, and with a tiny sigh she stepped back and dropped her hands. 'Sorry,' she murmured.

She glanced up at him, and her eyes locked with his. They were burning, dark and smoky, and sending a thousand conflicting messages.

'Anna?' he said softly.

She could never work out afterwards which one of them moved first, but somehow they ended up together, her hands pillowed lightly on his chest again, his hands coming up to frame her face with gentle, reverent fingers that drew her closer.

His mouth hovered for an instant, then he closed his eyes and lowered his head that last, tiny distance.

Heat. So much heat, so carefully controlled. His lips were soft, feather-light, coaxing and promising, and Anna felt need rip through her like a tidal wave. Her fingers curled, clinging to him, bunching his sweater in both hands and hanging on for dear life.

Of their own accord her lips parted, and with a soft sigh he traced the moist inner edge of her mouth with his tongue.

It wasn't enough. Holding his sweater wasn't enough. She dropped it, sliding her arms up and locking them behind his head, drawing him down closer. Her body arched against his, and with a ragged sigh he wrapped his arms around her, cupping her bottom and lifting her against the cradle of his thighs.

'Anna,' he groaned, and his mouth took hers, finally given free rein.

It was glorious. She lost touch with everything except the feel of his body hard and needy against hers, as needy as her own, aching and longing and desperate.

Then abruptly, without warning, Adam lifted his head and released her, backing away. His eyes were tortured, the hard planes of his cheeks drawn taut with emotion.

'The children,' he muttered unsteadily, and she became dimly aware of the boys screaming and Skye reasoning with them.

What had they been thinking about? 'You'd better go and sort them out,' she said in a voice that didn't quite seem to belong to her.

He rammed his hands in his pockets and stepped back further, tipping his head back and dragging in lungfuls of air. 'I'm sorry,' he grated, and, turning on his heel, he went out, leaving her alone to gather the shreds of her composure around her.

She turned slowly, looking at herself in the mirror over the basin. The light was unforgiving, showing clearly her lips, slightly bruised and swollen with passion, her eyes clouded and confused, her skin flushed where his stubble had scraped her.

She looked definitively kissed, she thought, and the tiny bubble of hysterical laughter broke as a strangled sob. She splashed cold water on her face, blotted it dry with a towel that was still damp—from his shower?

The thought did nothing for her composure.

She went back into the bedroom and looked around, and suddenly the bleak emptiness of it struck her like a blow. There was the bed, a simple, ordinary divan with a velvet headboard, a chest of drawers that had seen better days but which with attention could be lovely, a lightweight chair that had a shirt abandoned on it, one sleeve trailing on the floor. And, apart from the fitted cupboards each side of the delicate tiled fireplace, that was it.

It was a huge room, and it had a bed, a chair and a chest. No pictures, no lamps, no *pair* of chairs, no his and hers dressing-gowns dropped across the foot of the bed—just the bare essentials for a lonely man struggling to do the best for his family.

She felt tears welling up to blind her, and dragged in a deep breath to stem them before she made a fool of herself.

Just in the nick of time. Adam put his head round

the door and gave her an apologetic smile. 'You OK?' he asked in a gruff undertone.

Anna nodded. 'Yes—thanks. Do you need a hand?'

He shook his head. 'They're all done. I'm going to make some coffee, or would you rather have tea?'

She smiled. 'Tea, please. I'll come down.'

Odd, how one kiss could make so much difference. He hadn't known what to say to her, and she left just as soon as she'd drunk the tea. He didn't kiss her goodnight—well, a light brush of his lips over her forehead, all he dared to do for fear of losing control.

She'd awakened a raging demon in him that screamed for fulfilment, and he needed time to wrestle it back under control before he dared to touch her again.

He should never have asked her back for coffee. It had been a foolish thing to do, too risky in the raw emotional state he was in. Asking for trouble.

He went up to his room, uncaring that Helle was still out and would probably wake him yet again on the way in. It seemed unlikely that he would be asleep.

As he opened the door, he was hit like a sledge-hammer by the image of Anna standing there, her arms wrapped tightly round her slender body, her eyes shimmering with tears. He'd wanted to kiss them away, to lay her down on the bed behind her and love her till all her tears were dry and she slept peacefully in his arms.

The longing ache nearly undid him. He sagged against the wall, his head dropped back, eyes sight-less. All he could see was her mouth, soft and ripe, just before he'd kissed her. He'd felt the soft press of her breasts pillowed against him, and his hands had itched to know them, to feel the heavy fullness of them in his palms, to lower his head and take them in turn into his mouth and suckle her…

He turned and slammed his fist against the wall in empty frustration. Why here? Why in this room, where nothing would distract him from the memory of her pliant, willing body arching against him?

He groaned and threw off his clothes, showered—hot water, because he knew it would take the melt waters of the Arctic to make any difference—and crawled into his unmade bed, dragging the quilt up round his shoulders against the cold and burrowing down into the pillows, trying to escape.

He couldn't. The image was too powerful, too fresh, too necessary to his starving body for him to let it go.

So he lay there, thinking of Anna, and even the incessant clamouring of his body couldn't drown out the empty ache in his heart—an ache that he was suddenly very afraid only she would be able to fill.

He needed her. In so very many ways, he needed her, but the children came first. They had to.

For the thousandth time he wondered if he'd done the right thing by them in keeping them, but after nearly a year, how could he have let them go? Almost all of Jasper's life at the time? The baby hadn't known anyone else, and Danny had never been more than a couple of feet from him while he'd been awake. Even Skye, terribly wounded by the death of their mother and then Lyn's defection, had needed him, perhaps in her way even more than the others.

The last two years had been hard, but they'd got through them together and they were on the mend, all of them. He just had to be there for them, see them through.

So he had needs, too. Tough. He couldn't let that alter his course, let it hurt the children, not in any way. They were too precious and vulnerable and utterly dependent on him.

But the loneliness ate at him, and when Helle's noisy return woke him in the night his pillow was damp...

Anna contemplated skiving off.

She thought about it long and hard as she got ready for the day, but in the end she sighed, put on her coat and went to work, as she'd known she would.

Anyway, she wanted to see Adam—sort of. She wasn't sure. There'd been a lingering tension about him as they'd sat in the kitchen for their drinks. Significantly, he hadn't even suggested going into the sitting room, and she'd felt he'd wanted her out of the way, so the moment her tea had been downed she'd left.

He'd kissed her on the forehead, a light touch, too brief and yet with a curious lingering, as if he'd wanted more—much more.

Maybe too much more.

Whatever. Anna parked at the hospital, went in and shed her coat in her locker, pulled a clean, colourful tabard on over her uniform and pinned on her watch and badge.

'Just in case I forget who I am,' she often joked, but today she thought it was quite likely. It would serve to remind her that she was a work colleague, a single woman, not his wife, not Mrs Adam Bradbury.

'Anna Bradbury,' she found herself saying, testing

it, and could have thumped her head against the nearest wall. 'Leave it alone,' she growled at herself, and looked up to find Allie eyeing her with curiosity.

'You OK?' she asked doubtfully.

'I'm fine. How are you? How are the wedding plans?'

Allie pulled a wry face. 'Oh, advancing, I suppose. Mark wants to get married now in a register office, my mother wants to have the full works and palaver for her baby girl—you know how it is.'

'Yes—and your mother will win,' Anna said drily, trying not to think about marrying Adam and what sort of wedding she'd choose.

Two days, she told herself fiercely. That's all you've known him, two days. How can you even *think* about it?

Then she looked up and saw him striding onto the ward, and he smiled at her as if she was the best thing he'd seen all week, and she thought, *That's how I can think about it.*

'Hi,' he murmured once he was in earshot.

'Hi,' she replied. Her voice was catching and early-morning soft, and she felt like a lovesick fool. Still, it was wonderful to be this close to him again after—what, less than twelve hours?

You're losing it, she told herself silently.

Allie had vanished, leaving them alone in a void that pulsed with emotional and sexual tension. Adam's eyes searched hers, then with a sigh his lids slid shut briefly and he turned away. 'Um—about last night.'

Oh, hell. 'I know. It was a one-off, it didn't mean anything, forget it—is that what you're going to say?'

His smile was wry, his eyes softening with humour. 'Actually, no. I was going to ask why you ran away.'

Anna felt her brow pleat in a puzzled frown. 'I thought you wanted me to go?'

'No.' He shook his head. 'Well—I don't know. I don't know what I wanted.'

I do, she thought. I know exactly what you wanted, because I wanted it, too, and I just bet you didn't sleep a wink more than I did.

'I'm sorry I misunderstood. I'll make up for it when I've got a moment, but now I have to go and take report from the night sister. I'll catch up with you later.'

'OK. I'm busy, anyway. We'll grab a cup of tea later in the day, perhaps.' His smile curled round her heart, warming her, and she took it with her into the office, unaware of its tender reflection on her own face.

'Morning,' she said brightly. 'How's it been?'

The night nurse, Angela Davis, rolled her eyes. 'OK, if you like mayhem. You look happy.'

'I do?' How odd, Anna thought. I feel confused, not happy. Excited and scared and puzzled all at once. 'So, what's been happening?'

'All sorts. Karl Fisher's been in a lot of pain and he's been crying in the night. I got him written up for some stronger analgesia, but he's still suffering. All he can say is ''I thought it was going to be better'', which just makes you feel dreadful. Still, the hand looks good and sensory and motor response in it are fine, so it's just post-op pain and nothing more sinister, I'm sure. It might be an idea to get Robert Ryder or Adam Bradbury to look at him—I'm not sure who he belongs to now.'

'Neither am I,' Anna agreed. 'I'll ask Adam in a minute. He's about, I think. Anyone else been a problem? Any admissions?'

'Toby Cardew—asthma attack.'

'But he's only just gone home!' Anna exclaimed in horror. 'What triggered it—any idea?'

'None. They were muttering something about anxiety—seems like it's the only thing left.'

'I should think it is,' Anna agreed. 'They've checked all the obvious allergens and some of the less obvious, and eliminated just about everything else.'

'Quite. All that's left is exercise, and he was in bed, sleeping, anxiety, which seems possible, and meteorological changes, like humidity, for example, but as he was inside and had been for some time it seems unlikely. Whatever, he's back, he's stable now just about, but he was bad.'

Anna nodded. 'I'll go and see him—is Mum with him?'

'Yes, she's been here all night. Dad's at home with the others.'

'Fine. Anyone else?'

'Oh, yes. An appendix. Andrew Reed, aged eight— he's been to Theatre and was on the point of rupture when they opened him up, apparently. And Tim Scully, a nasty greenstick fracture of the radius and ulna—child fell out of the top bunk. First night in a new bed. Typical, isn't it? They said he was so excited about the bed he couldn't wait to get in it, and then, of course, he needed the loo during the night because he hadn't remembered to go in the excitement, and he fell getting onto the ladder, apparently.'

'Has he gone to Theatre?'

'No—he's all prepped and ready, and they've

called Adam Bradbury in to look at him. I think he's going to operate this morning. That's why Bradbury's on the ward, I think you'll find.'

And Anna had thought it had been because of her. How silly. She felt a huge wave of disappointment, and suppressed it. He had a job to do, and so did she. It wasn't just some surreal tearoom, or a film set. They finished going through the other patients, and she took the keys and the responsibility for the ward from Angela, and went to see if Adam was still about.

He was—talking to the parents of Tim Scully, the young lad who had fallen off his bunk bed, so while he finished she went to see Toby, their asthmatic. He was in a bed in a side room, propped up on the bed table, his arms folded and leaning forward on a pillow, still struggling for breath despite all the medication.

His nostrils were flaring with each inspiration, and his whole body seemed to be involved in each breath out, and she quietly went through some breathing exercises with him, trying to relax him and shift some of the mucus that was obviously blocking all his bronchial tubes.

He did manage to cough and shift some of the thickened mucus, and after that he seemed a little better. He sank back against the raised end of the bed, propped almost upright, and she tucked the bedclothes round him and left him to rest. His mother looked exhausted, and Anna took her hand and squeezed it.

'Cup of tea?' she offered, and Mrs Cardew nodded gratefully.

'Thanks. It's been another of those nights.'

'I'm sure. Why don't you try and have a nap if he goes off? It would do you good.'

She nodded. Anna found Pearl, their kind-hearted orderly, and asked her to make Mrs Cardew tea, then tracked Adam down just as he was leaving the ward.

'Hi. Can you have a look at Karl before you go?' she asked. 'He's been suffering in the night.'

'Sure.' He turned and retraced his footsteps and she fell in beside him. 'Any idea what's wrong?' he asked.

'Post-op pain. No neuro or vascular problems obvious, apparently, just pain.'

'Might be the cast.'

'They thought it was all right.'

He nodded, and stopped beside Karl's bed. 'Hello, young man. I gather you've been uncomfortable in the night.'

Karl nodded miserably. 'It really, really hurts,' he said unhappily. Adam examined the arm gently, turning it this way and that, feeling the fingers for warmth, testing the reflexes.

'Can you feel that?' he asked a few times, moving from place to place, and Karl nodded.

'Is the pain in the bone? Or is it the skin and muscles that hurt?'

'I don't know. It just hurts,' he said, and started to cry.

Adam laid a gentle hand on his shoulder and squeezed it comfortingly. 'OK. I'll give you something for the pain, then I want you to have an X-ray and see if we can find out a reason for it, and I think we'll have the cast off and look inside it in case it's too tight or your arm's just too bruised to sit inside it. You could have it in a sort of soft padded cradle beside you, but you'd have to lie very, very still for a day or two. We'll see. Let's try the painkillers and the picture first.'

He stood up and picked up the chart, scribbling down a prescription in the bold, jagged writing that was becoming familiar to Anna. 'Here—can you give him this, please, and set up the X-ray? I suppose I need to sign something to authorise that.'

His grin was infectious. 'Oh, yes,' Anna said with an answering smile. 'Of course. You have to sign for a cup of tea in this place.'

'Put me down for one later. I'll be ready for it. I'm going to do Tim's arm now. He's all prepped and ready, I gather?'

'So Angela said. What are you going to do?'

'Open reduction and internal fixation. There's no way you can get a satisfactory result with anything less. It's a heck of a fracture for such a little fall, but I think he caught it in the ladder, between the ladder and the bed, and he's quite a hefty lad. No matter, I can fix it.'

He found himself thinking of Anna as he straightened up the drastically bent and damaged bones and screwed plates onto them to hold them in place. She'd seemed pleased enough to see him, if the light in her eyes was anything to go by.

It was hard to pretend enthusiasm to that extent, he thought, turning the screw that brought the radius neatly into alignment. It didn't need to be drawn together because the bone was still connected, just badly bent, exactly like a young, green stick—hence the term greenstick fracture. He tackled the ulna, thinking still of Anna's eyes and the softness of her mouth when she'd smiled at him.

The rest of the surgical team were gossiping about someone he didn't know, and he ignored them, working steadily, thinking about the children and Helle and how he was going to get a replacement for her.

Not only how he would get a replacement, but how he would *keep* the replacement. Au pairs seemed to have a very short shelf life, and the departure of each one brought trauma and loss to the children's lives.

It was unsatisfactory for them from an emotional point of view, but he supposed it at least kept the attachments they formed fixed firmly on him, and not on the carers. That was good, because he, God willing, was going nowhere.

He straightened up, turned the limb back and forth to examine the position, checked the warmth and colour of the fingers and closed the incision, satisfied that he'd reduced the fracture to the best of his ability and that it would heal fast and well.

That was all he could do. He pulled off his mask, smiled at the team and thanked them, snapped off his gloves and dropped them in the bin with his hat and gown.

Tea with Anna, he thought, and headed back to the ward.

CHAPTER FOUR

It WAS the weekend. Apart from a brief cup of tea when he'd come back to the ward to talk to Tim's parents about his operation, Anna hadn't seen Adam all day. He'd been in Outpatients doing a clinic, and he hadn't reappeared.

Karl's X-rays had been sent down to him in Outpatients, and he'd sent back instructions for the cast to be removed and for the boy's arm to be rested in a padded gutter support until the following day, when it would be put in an open cast if the pain improved and the swelling of the soft tissues subsided. Apparently, when he'd been coming round from the anaesthetic he'd flung his arm against the cot-sides of the stretcher. It was possible that the cast had become slightly bent then, before it had quite hardened, and that even such very slight pressure had been enough to make Karl miserable.

Once it was removed he seemed much more comfortable, and fell asleep immediately, a sure sign that he'd had a difficult night. Tim was still largely out of it after his operation, and Andrew Reed, who'd been admitted in the night with acute appendicitis, was improving hourly.

And now it was the weekend, and she was off, by a miracle, and it stretched ahead of her emptily. The chances of bumping into Adam at the supermarket again were so slight as to be not worth considering, and, short of going round there and ringing his doorbell, she couldn't think of any way she could see him until Monday.

What on earth was she supposed to do to fill the time? She couldn't bring herself to do any of the things she normally did. They seemed so empty somehow, so fruitless.

She wondered what Adam would be doing, and if the children were looking forward to having him to themselves. Danny would be, she thought with certainty, and probably little Jaz, but Skye—Skye was a strange one, a poor, lonely little girl, very self-contained and withdrawn.

Worryingly so. In many ways, Anna thought, she probably needed her father more than the others.

Curiosity teased her again. She found herself wondering about their mother—his wife, in fact. When had she left, and why? Had she gone willingly, or had their divorce been acrimonious and bitter?

Did he still love her? That thought was oddly painful to contemplate.

She found herself remembering the kiss, going over those few brief moments in her mind for the hundredth time. Would it happen again? Oh, lord, she hoped so.

The television failed to hold her attention, and finally, at only a quarter to ten, she gave up on the evening, had a quick shower and went to bed. She had hardly put her head on the pillow when the phone rang beside her, and she propped herself up on her elbow and picked up the receiver, a little glimmer of hope edging into her heart. He didn't have her number, but...

'Hello?'

'Anna? It's Adam.'

He stopped, and she had the oddest feeling that he didn't quite know what to say. Funny, she felt the same. She said hello again, hoping she didn't sound inane and wondering if the smile on her face was obvious in her voice, and afraid that it probably was. 'How are you?' she asked, her finger winding absently into the curling flex.

'I'm fine. Look, Anna, I'm sorry to ring you at home so late—I had to do some sleuthing to get your number. I hope you don't mind.'

'Of course I don't mind.' She sat up straighter, concerned by the note in his voice, and pulled her finger free. 'Adam, is something wrong?'

He sighed, and she could visualise him stabbing his hands distractedly through that dark, silky hair. 'No, not...wrong, exactly. It's just...Helle's gone to London for the weekend, I'm supposed to be on call and the kids are with my parents just up the road. I just...'

He sighed again, and then went on, his voice soft and gruff and intimate, 'I just wanted to talk to you. The house seemed awfully empty and, well, I thought it might be nice to see you, but it's too late, really, so I thought I'd phone. Have a chat.'

He ran out of words again, and Anna pushed the quilt off her legs and swung them over the side of the bed, sitting up. 'It's not too late,' she said gently. 'Either to phone or to come round, if you want to.'

'It's after ten.'

'That doesn't matter. Do you want to come here, or do you want me to come to you?'

'I'll come to you—it seems only fair as it's my idea. It's freezing outside. I can bring my bleeper. Where are you? How do I find you?'

She gave him concise directions, ran a mental eye over the house and groaned inwardly. She could usefully have spent the last three hours doing housework instead of moping about him.

Oh, damn. There was no time to choose clothes. She pulled on her jeans and a clean jumper, pulled them off again, puffed a little cloud of perfume in the air and walked through it, then dragged the clothes back on and ran downstairs, banging cushions and tidying the kitchen rapidly.

It would take him ten minutes, tops, and she'd already been more than five.

She turned off the centre light, put on the lamps each end of the sofa, lit the fat church candles on the dresser and went to put the kettle on. She only had tea or coffee to offer him, no wine or spirits or anything like that, not even beer, but he was driving so perhaps it was just as well.

The doorbell rang, cutting off her stream of panic, and she paused for a second, drew a steadying breath, ran her hands down her jeans in case the palms were clammy and went to the door, swinging it open with a welcoming smile.

He looked wonderful. He was untidy, his hair rumpled, the poloneck of his sweater rolled over crookedly, but his eyes would have put the Olympic torch to shame and his mouth...

She drew him in, went up on tiptoe and kissed it, just lightly, just once, but it was enough. He dropped something that landed with a soft thud, and then she was in his arms and his mouth was on hers and she could stop fantasising about his kiss because it was happening again and it was real, more real than she thought she could bear.

Then he lifted his head, gave her a crooked smile and bent and picked up the thing he'd dropped. 'Here, for you. Sorry, the corner's bent but I don't suppose it matters. I got, um, distracted.'

Chocolates. Sinful, decadent chocolates, not just ordinary ones but deep, dark continental liqueur chocolates with a zillion calories each. 'How on earth did you know?' she said with a laugh, and looked up into his wonderfully expressive eyes and forgot to breathe again for a moment.

'I didn't—I just guessed,' Adam confessed gruffly. 'I would have brought wine, but I'm driving and I thought the chocolates would be a nice compromise.'

'Thank you.' Anna went up on tiptoe and kissed him again, then took his arm and drew him into her living room. 'Sit down, I'll get you a drink. Tea or coffee? It's all I've got, I'm afraid, unless you want water or fruit juice?'

'Coffee'll be fine. Let me help you make it.'

'Oh, the kitchen's a mess—'

He laughed softly, cutting her off. 'Fair's fair. You saw my house at its absolute worst yesterday.'

'But I've got no excuse,' she protested.

Hmm. He was just as stubborn as her, obviously, because he turned her round, put his hands on her shoulders and propelled her gently back out into the hall and down to the kitchen.

'It looks fine—what are you talking about?' he said from right behind her, his breath puffing softly against her nape. She had a crazy urge to lean back, just a tiny little bit, and bend her head, and let his lips stroke a trail of fire over her skin...

As if she'd willed it, she felt his lips against her hair, his touch like the brush of an angel's wing, so light yet with so much power. Her eyes drifted shut and she stood motionless as his hands eased her back against him, so she could feel the heat of his body through her thin sweater, warming her.

His lips moved lower, caressing the sensitive skin of her nape, hot and slow and unbelievably erotic. His tongue traced a pattern on the skin, then he blew, just softly, and she felt the touch of ice over the fire.

'You're beautiful,' he murmured, and his voice was husky with promise.

Her breath jammed in her throat. Make love to me, she thought. Don't stop. Take me to heaven. Please…

He let her go, stepping just out of reach and leaving her abandoned in a sea of emotion so powerful she thought she'd drown. 'Coffee?' he said softly, and she moved then, like an automaton, taking mugs from the cupboard, finding the coffee, a spoon, sugar.

'Do you want sugar in your coffee?' she asked, realising she'd never made it for him. She'd hardly done anything for him. She'd known him three days!

Just three short days, and yet she knew he was more important to her than anyone else she'd ever met. OK, it was hasty, it was foolish and impulsive and precipitate and all the other things that her mother would have warned her about, but it was also *right*.

She turned to give him his coffee, and found him watching her with a strangely intense expression. He took the mug from her and put it down.

'No, I don't want sugar. I want to make love to you, but it's too soon,' he said gruffly. His honesty rocked her, and brought tears to her eyes.

'No, it's not,' she said, with a matching honesty. 'It's not too soon—not for us. I feel as if I've been waiting for you for years.'

For a moment Adam said nothing, then the breath left him in a rush and he closed his eyes. When he opened them again the heat in them consumed Anna. He held out his hand, and wordlessly she went to him, placing her hand in his and leading him upstairs to her bedroom.

In the doorway, she hesitated. 'It's a mess,' she said softly, and he gave a strangled laugh.

'Do you really think I care?' He turned her, his eyes searching hers, and she knew he could see only her. 'Oh, Anna,' he whispered, and drew her into his arms. His mouth found hers, and his kiss was tender. 'I didn't come here for this,' he murmured gruffly. 'That's not why I rang you—'

'Shh. It's all right, I know.' She lifted her hand, her fingertips searching his face, stroking the line of his cheekbone, the muscle jumping in his jaw, rubbing lightly backwards against the rasp of stubble, somehow so erotic against her skin. Her hand slid round to cradle his nape and draw him down to her again. 'Make love to me,' she murmured. 'Please. Now. I need you.'

His eyes flared and darkened, and with a ragged groan he sought her mouth and took it. Fire seemed to rip through her, and her legs buckled and gave way.

He caught her against him, lifting her and setting her down gently in the middle of her tumbled bed. He undressed her slowly, his fingers shaking, and she could see from the harsh rise and fall of his chest how aroused he was, just how much effort it took to hold on to his control.

'You are so lovely,' he whispered unsteadily. His eyes tracked over her, then locked with hers, and the raw hunger in them found an echo in her heart. 'Anna, I need you.'

'I know. It's OK.' She knelt up in the middle of the bed and seized the hem of his sweater, dragging it over his head with a total lack of ceremony. Her patience, such as it was, was at an end, and she needed him now, needed to hold him, to touch him, to be part of him. Nothing else mattered, and no other thought entered her head.

She stripped him, her breath jamming in her chest at the sight of his body, lean and muscled and so, so ready. She touched him with trembling hands, feeling the hot satin of his skin under her palms, the shudder as she skimmed her fingers over him, learning him, treasuring him with her touch.

'Anna,' he whispered, his breath jagged, his control in tatters. Good. That was what she wanted. She didn't want technique, she didn't want skill, she wanted him. Just him. Nothing more, nothing less.

'Yes,' she answered, and drew him down into her arms...

Boneless.

She was curled into his side, her head cradled on his chest and one knee wedged between his thighs. They were just about as close as they could get, and about as drained. Gradually Anna's senses returned, her breathing slowed, her heart settled to a steady rhythm. Adam's was beating just under her ear, slow and strangely comforting.

She didn't move. She couldn't move. She just lay there, like an abandoned doll, sprawled against him and listening to his heartbeat. She felt his hand on her back, gliding slowly over the skin, caressing her absently. She gave a soft sigh of contentment, and he turned his head, pressing his lips to her forehead.

'OK?'

'How can you even ask that?' she mumbled, too slaked to move her mouth properly.

A low chuckle rumbled through his chest, and he hugged her closer, pulling the covers over her and tucking them round her shoulders. 'It was pretty spectacular, wasn't it?'

Something niggled at her—something important—but she couldn't think what it was or deal with it. She closed her eyes, squirmed a little closer to him and sighed again. Biology was a very clever thing, she thought idly, and then remembered what it was that was niggling her.

Oh, damn.

Her finger outlined a pattern on his chest. 'Um...did I miss something, or did we just forget to use anything?' she asked quietly.

He went still, his hand on her back coming to rest where it was, his breathing suspended for a second. Then he moved again, his hand resuming its gentle rhythm against her spine. 'No, you didn't miss anything, Anna, but it's OK. You aren't going to catch anything from me.'

'Catch anything?' she repeated, puzzled. She wasn't thinking about catching so much as falling.

'The last woman I slept with was my wife, over three years ago,' he confessed. 'You're safe.'

Three years? No wonder he'd been so responsive to her touch! And her to his, of course. Between them they'd stacked up a lot of years of abstinence. Small surprise that their lovemaking had packed such a punch.

'I was more worried about getting pregnant,' she explained. 'I'm not on the Pill.'

Again Adam went still, and then he spoke, his voice flat and expressionless. 'There's no need. When I said you're safe, I meant it in every sense. I can't get you pregnant, Anna. I'm sterile.'

Shock held her motionless for several seconds, then her breath left her as if her lungs had been punctured.

Sterile?

Adam, sterile? Adam, who had three children, couldn't get her pregnant?

'But you've got three children,' Anna said in confusion. 'How come…?'

'They're adopted.'

'Oh.' What else was there to say? She dragged in a deep breath, and let it out in a shaky gust. 'Are you sure?'

'That they're adopted? Absolutely,' he said, a thread of humourless laughter in his voice.

'No—I meant—that you can't have children,' she said, hardly able to say the words. There was a huge, empty void opening up inside her, and she was desperate to stop it spreading because she knew it would consume her. She wanted his child—*needed* his child.

'Yes, I'm sure,' he said quietly after a moment, and she could hear the pain in his voice. She put her own pain on one side and concentrated on his. She could deal with hers later. This was important.

'What happened?' she asked gently. 'Do you know?'

'I had mumps when I was twenty-five. I was really ill with it—I'd never had it and we visited my wife's sister. Her children went down with it just after we'd left them and, of course, I'd picked it up. I developed severe orchitis as a complication, and then a few months afterwards when we decided to start a family, nothing happened.'

'So you had a test.'

'Yes. They found very few healthy sperm. Low motility, that sort of thing. Lyn was gutted. We tried everything—crazy positions, centrifugal spinning to concentrate the sperm, syringes—all sorts. We didn't make love for years. We had sex—carefully orchestrated sex timed to coincide with her ovulation, not a single sperm wasted on frivolous entertainment, and month after month we failed. We couldn't go down the IVF or ICSI route, because the treatment didn't agree with her, so that was that.'

Anna swallowed the tears that were hovering in her throat and threatening to choke her. 'So you decided to adopt.'

'Yes. We decided to adopt. We went through all the screening procedures with all their intrusive and highly personal investigations, and shortly before we were approved we were given some catalogues of children—the kids nobody wanted. They're called ''Children Who Wait'', and there is simply page after page of tragedy. They're mostly families, because they're the hardest to home. Nobody wants a family group. They want a baby. We were looking for a baby, just one, and then we saw my three and I just fell for them. I knew they were right.'

'What did Lyn think?'

He shrugged. 'I don't know. At the time she agreed to try, but she never seemed too wholehearted—it was always me. I should have listened to her, I suppose. She had reservations for good reasons. I had none. I knew we could give those children a good home.'

'How old were they?' Anna asked, trying to picture the sorry little family.

'Skye was three, Danny not quite two and Jaz was a little baby. Their mother was dead, a drugs overdose, and there was no father figure in evidence. It was a cut-and-dried adoption with no strings—it should have been easy. Instead, it drove us apart, although I didn't realise it at the time. I was too taken up with the children to see the signs, and we were in the process of finalising the adoption when Lyn left me.'

Even now, after all this time, Anna could hear the hurt in his voice. There was more to the story, she could tell, but not even she could have guessed the full extent of the hurt Lyn had inflicted on them.

'Was it very bitter?' she asked gently.

'Bitter?' Adam dragged in a deep breath and let it go on a harsh gust of laughter. 'You could say that. She went off with my best friend,' he said rawly. 'They'd been having an affair for months. She was pregnant.'

Her eyes closed to keep out the horror of his words, but they swirled round in her head, shocking in their simplicity. 'Oh, Adam,' she said brokenly, and slid her arms round him to hold him close. 'I'm so, so sorry.'

His grip tightened. 'It's OK. I got over it. I continued with the adoption, with the reluctant blessing of Social Services, and we struggled through and we're coming out of it now. Danny was all right, more or less, but Jasper was lost without Lyn and Skye was devastated.'

'I can imagine that,' Anna said sadly. 'Poor little girl.'

'She was. She'd just started to come out of herself and thaw with us, and she was right back to square one. Worse, really, because her mother had died and been taken from her. Lyn had *chosen* to leave. That was harder to take. Skye was very, very hurt, and very difficult, and she still is.'

'And you? Were you very hurt?'

He nodded slowly. 'At the time. Betrayed more than anything else. I could understand about the baby. I knew how important it was to her—she used to say she had a biological ache to carry a child. I understood that. I had a biological ache to be a father, to see my wife swell with my child, to hold my baby in my arms. I love children. I really, really wanted a child of my own, but it couldn't happen for me.'

He broke off and took a steadying breath. 'I'm sorry, it still gets to me,' he said roughly.

'That's OK,' she murmured soothingly, her soft heart aching for him. 'Take your time, I'm not going anywhere.'

She thought he'd ground to a halt, but then after a moment Adam continued his heartbreaking story.

'I offered to let her go. When we found out it was me, I offered to divorce her if that was what she wanted. She said it wasn't. We went through the infertility programme, and again I asked her, before we started the adoption proceedings. She said no. She said no, and yet, once the children were there, living with us, and they'd been with us nearly a year—then, of all times, she turned round and said she wanted to go and that she was carrying someone else's child.

'I can't forgive her for that—for what she did to those poor, vulnerable little children—and I can't forgive my closest, oldest friend for being a part of it—

for lying to me, for listening to me unburden myself and pretending to sympathise, and then, when my back was turned, for sleeping with my wife. I nearly killed the bastard for that.'

Anna said nothing. There was nothing to say, nothing she could add that wouldn't sound trite or insincere.

'I'm sorry,' he went on after a moment. 'I don't talk about it very often, and it still gets to me.'

'Do you ever see them?'

'No. I can't forgive them for what they did to the children, and it would be hypocritical to have anything to do with them. Anyway, I'm not a sucker for punishment.' He turned his head and kissed her gently. 'I'm sorry, Anna. This all got rather heavy. I didn't mean to unload on you like that, but you may as well know the whole story.'

'Don't apologise,' she murmured. 'I've been wondering why she left. Now I know.' Knew more than she'd ever wanted to know.

Adam shifted slightly, turning towards her, and trailed a feathery kiss across her brow. 'Anyway, it's nothing to do with us,' he said softly. 'It's all gone. Finished.' He kissed her again, over her eyes, down the line of her jaw, in the soft hollow of her throat. 'Forget about it now. Let me make love to you again.'

Forget about it. Just like that, as if it was so easy.

But he was right. She would forget it now, and concentrate on him, and this moment, and then later, when she was alone, she'd deal with it.

His mouth was tracing a line of fire over her shoulder and down her arm, then back again to claim her lips. The fire spread through her body, and she arched against him, suddenly desperate to hold him close.

. And then in the distance they heard his bleeper, and with a muttered curse he rolled away from her and grabbed his underwear.

'Don't move,' he instructed, and ran downstairs. She heard his voice on the phone, and then a moment later his footsteps on the stairs.

'I have to go in,' he said gruffly. 'Stay there. I'll ring you if it's going to be brief. Otherwise I'll see you tomorrow. OK?'

She nodded. 'OK.' She nearly told him to come back anyway, at whatever time, but then she thought better of it. She needed to be alone. She had a lot of thinking to do.

He tugged his sweater over his head, turned the roll-neck down and bent to kiss her goodbye.

'I'll see you later. Think of me.'

As if she could do anything else, with her body still humming from his loving and her heart in shock.

She waited till the door closed behind him, then got up and put on her dressing-gown and went downstairs. The candles were still burning, mellow pools of golden light flickering against the wall. She turned off the side lamps and curled up, opening the chocolates. They'd been going to share them over coffee, but the coffee was sitting, cold, on the side in the kitchen and he was gone.

Adam's words stayed with her, though, echoing in her head like a death knell. 'I'm sterile. I can't get you pregnant. *I'm sterile—sterile—sterile...*'

Anna swallowed, but the tears fell anyway, dripping off her chin and splashing heavily on her hands. She was grieving, she realised dimly—grieving for Adam and for the children he would never have, and for Lyn, denied her husband's child, and for herself, for the fledgling dreams that had been trampled in the dust.

The phone rang, and she answered it, gulping down the tears.

It was Adam. 'It's going to be a long night,' he said apologetically. 'Don't wait up. I'll ring you tomorrow. Save me some of the chocolates.'

'OK,' she promised, trying to inject a cheerful note into her voice. 'See you tomorrow.'

She hung up just before the sob broke, and, curling up in the corner of the settee, she finally gave in to the tears.

CHAPTER FIVE

IT WAS a long and tragic night. Adam struggled to save the legs of a young woman involved in a car accident, while another team lost the battle for her fiancé's life in the next theatre.

He had to amputate one leg in the end, because he was unable to restore the circulation, and the other would be permanently disfigured and might well prove too difficult to treat successfully.

He did his best—he always did his best, but sometimes it just wasn't good enough, and it grieved him. She was twenty-two, a lovely girl poised on the brink of the rest of her life, and suddenly that life had been trashed by an act of fate.

And he wasn't even supposed to be operating on her! He'd come in to see a child with a pelvic fracture which hadn't need surgery in the end, and he'd been asked to stay to help because the orthopaedic team were at full stretch with a succession of RTAs.

So there he was, with a beautiful young woman needing his help and no way of undoing the damage that had been done, and he thought of Anna at home and her beautiful legs and how devastating it would be for her, and he felt gutted.

It was five o'clock in the morning before he finished, and he talked to the woman's devastated parents until nearly six. Then he showered and dressed before leaving the hospital, his thoughts still with Anna.

It was hideously early—too early to go round there—but he found himself headed in that direction anyway. He just needed to see Anna, to hold her, to be with her. It had been such a bloody night, and he needed her warmth and gentleness.

He rang the doorbell, and after a moment she appeared, looking sleepy and rumpled and pleased to see him.

'I'm sorry. I know I said I'd ring, but I just wanted to see you.'

She looked at him searchingly, understanding in her eyes. 'Bad night?'

He nodded. He didn't want to go into details. He wanted to leave it behind, to take her in his arms and finish what he'd started.

'Any chocolates left?'

She smiled guiltily. 'A few. They're in here—I fell asleep on the settee.'

He followed her into the sitting room, lit only by the two candles which had burned almost down to the end. One was spluttering, the other not far behind.

'Coffee?' she offered, and he smiled wearily.

'I've got a distinct feeling of *déjà vu*,' he said with a chuckle. 'Perhaps I'd better have tea. Might be safer.'

'Stay here. Eat the chocolates.'

'I will.' He sank wearily into a chair and helped himself. Cognac and chocolate on an empty stomach and no sleep was a lousy combination. He tried the Grand Marnier instead, and then Drambuie. No better. What he needed was sleep.

Anna came back, a tray in her hands with two gently steaming mugs, a milk jug and a pot of tea.

'For refills,' she explained, and he gave a tired smile. 'Why don't we take it upstairs to bed with the chocolates?' he suggested.

It was a good idea—at least, in theory. In practice it was too comfortable. He drank the first mug of tea, ate one more chocolate and then fell asleep with Anna snuggled up against his chest, waiting for the next mug of tea to cool.

By the time they woke it was stone cold, the sun was streaming in through a crack in the curtains and he was due at his parents' for lunch in less than an hour. He stared at his watch in disbelief, dropped his head back on the pillows and sighed.

'What's wrong?' Anna asked sleepily, raising her head from his chest to look down into his eyes.

'Nothing,' Adam said. He lifted a hand to brush her hair back off her face so he could see her better. She looked wonderful—soft and warm and creased with sleep. 'Nothing,' he repeated more softly, and felt a great wave of tenderness sweep over him. 'I have to go soon, but not yet. Not before I make love to you.'

He lifted himself up on one elbow, rolling her onto her back so he could touch her and see her. Her dressing gown was gaping slightly, and he eased the sides apart, his breath catching at the sight of her pale, slender body. He blew a thin stream of air over her nipples and they peaked for him, bringing a smile to his face.

'You're lovely,' he said softly, and, bending his head, he kissed her.

Anna felt as if she was on an emotional roller-coaster. On the one hand, she'd had the best and most wonderful weekend of her life. On the other hand, under-lying it was a deep sadness, a coming to terms with all that could never be.

How bittersweet, she thought, that when she finally met the man of her dreams, he had one fatal flaw—he couldn't make the rest of her dreams come true. Of course, he had children, three lovely children who had already captured her heart, but it wasn't the same as having a baby of her own.

If she stayed with Adam, if their love grew, she would never have a child of her own, would never know the joy of carrying a growing baby inside her, of suckling it at her breast, or witnessing the first tooth, the first step, the first word. It had been her expectation, as it was every woman's expectation, that one day she'd marry and have children. Yet, if she married Adam—and it was far too soon to be thinking about that yet—that expectation would never come to fruition.

And yet, even after just one weekend, the prospect of not being with him was unthinkable. But would their love grow? Was it just lust, a mutual physical craving, an itch that needed scratching, or was it something deeper, more lasting, something that could stand the test of time?

Be patient, she told herself. Give it time to reveal itself.

But patience wasn't her strong point, and coupled with a lack of sleep it did nothing for her temper.

'I thought you'd just had a weekend off?' Allie said cheerfully, looking disgustingly happy for that time of the morning.

'I have,' Anna told her with a wry smile. 'I'm sorry. Am I being a grump?'

'Only slightly drastically. Anything to do with our gorgeous new consultant?' she added in a soft sing-song voice that had colour rushing to Anna's cheeks. Allie's eyes widened.

'Good grief!' she exclaimed in a stage whisper. 'What on earth were you two up to? I've never, *ever* seen you blush!'

'Allie, shut up,' Anna growled suppressively. 'I don't want the world to know.'

Allie cocked her head on one side and grinned. 'So there is something to know, then?'

What was it in her face that gave her away? Whatever it was, Allie's eyes softened and she pulled an apologetic face. 'I'm sorry. I'm being nosy—not that you did any such thing when I first started going out with Mark...'

'That was fair game—you'd known him for five years! I've only just met Adam.'

'No,' Allie corrected her, 'I'd known him briefly *five years ago*. That's different—and, anyway, so what? When it's right, it's right. I knew when I was eighteen that Mark was right for me.'

Anna put down the notes she was checking and gave Allie a wry smile. 'Funny, isn't it? I took one look at him, and I thought Adam was right for me. Now I'm even more sure, but—' She broke off, unable to tell Allie the personal things Adam had revealed to her.

'But?'

She shrugged. 'Allie, I can't—'

'Is it his kids? Is the ex-wife a pain?'

'It's complicated,' Anna said evasively. 'I can't explain. He told me things that I can't discuss with you, Allie.'

'He's not still married?' Allie asked, horrified, and Anna shook her head.

'No. Nothing like that. Forget it. It doesn't matter.'

And it didn't, she told herself again a few minutes later when Adam came on to the ward. It didn't matter at all, not compared to the joy of being with him and the love they could share.

What an astonishing discovery...

It was a difficult day. Adam was in and out of the ward—mostly out, because he was operating that morning—but when he was there and he saw Anna, it was as if the sun had come out.

He told Karl Fisher he could go home with a new cast on now that his pain had subsided, and little David Chisholm with his club foot operation had been discharged over the weekend. Tim Scully's greenstick fracture was settling down, and he, too, was going home with a closed cast—and with strict instructions to sleep in the bottom bunk until he was more mobile!

Anna offered Adam a cup of tea before he went up to Theatre, but he didn't have time. Today's list was short but complicated, and he wanted to get on with it. His patients were prepped, he'd seen their parents and gone over the cases again, and now he wanted to get started.

His first case was a fourteen-year-old girl with one leg seven centimetres shorter than the other. It had been fractured across the lower growth plate of her femur when she was eight and had stopped growing, and now she was having an operation to elongate it. This involved cutting through the thigh bone, putting an external support on the bone and turning a key every day just a fraction. As the bone tried to heal, so the gap would increase again and the bone would have to grow a little more to fill it.

And thus, if all went well, the leg would become at least nearly as long as the other one, if not the same length.

Bones, though, were easy. It was the muscles and nerves that caused more of a problem, and sometimes the pain of stretching them proved too much and treatment had to stop. Because of this, his patient had been doing lots of stretching exercises to her short leg to encourage the tissues to give in advance so that it was less of a shock to them. Hopefully, it would provide enough leeway to make a useful improvement.

Adam saw her in the anteroom, just before her anaesthetic, and smiled at her encouragingly. 'Hello again, Kate. All right?'

She nodded a little nervously. 'Bit scared.'

'I'm sure. Don't worry, I'll look after you. It'll be a bit rough for a day or two, but I'm sure it will be worth it.'

He winked at her mother, who was hovering distractedly by her side and trying to be brave, and she smiled back. She was near to tears, poor woman. 'Don't worry,' he told her as Kate slipped quietly into anaesthesia. 'She'll be all right. I'll come and see you as soon as we've finished.'

It was straightforward, to his relief. He exposed the bone, making a staggered cut through it so that as it extended, the ends would still overlap, giving greater support than a straight cut through the shaft would have done. He closed the wound, attached the external fixator with the help of the X-ray machine to make sure that the alignment of the bone was good, and got her out of Theatre in a shorter time than he'd anticipated.

That was good, because the next case would be long and difficult and he was impatient to start it.

A young lad with scoliosis had been referred to him for correction of the lateral curvature of his spine. It was quite severe, and with earlier intervention could have been helped considerably, but his ribs were twisting and consequently his chest was being compromised.

And now he had to be straightened, in a two-part operation over the next few weeks. Today was the first part, and he would have a rod wired to his spine all through the length of the twisted part, and by tightening up the wires the bones could be slowly persuaded into line.

He would need fixed halo-pelvic traction afterwards to help keep the spine straight, and gradually the curve would surrender and could be straightened further in a subsequent operation.

It was tricky, and it could result in paralysis if it went wrong. Nevertheless, such complex spinal surgery was his speciality and what Adam loved to do, because it made such a difference to the mental and physical well-being of the children he treated. Success wasn't guaranteed, though, and that kept a nice professional edge on the proceedings and added challenge.

Adam liked a challenge, and as he opened young Damian George's spine his focus became absolute. He forgot Anna, he forgot the children—he forgot everything except the bones and muscles under his hands, and the child in his care.

* * *

Damian had been gone for hours, Anna realised. It was three o'clock, and she was due to go off duty, but she hung on, wondering how Damian was doing and cherishing a foolish hope that Adam would come onto the ward to see him.

She was in the kitchen, making a cup of tea, when he appeared behind her, coming up close and cupping his hands over her shoulders. His fingers squeezed gently in greeting.

'Hi,' he murmured softly.

She gave in to the urge to sink back against him for a moment, and dropped her head back against his chest. 'Hi. How did it go?'

'Long and slow,' he said wearily. 'It was worse than it looked on the X-rays. I had to trim and prune quite a lot to get the result I wanted—hopefully, it'll pull straighter now. His ribs were pretty messy. Still, they should work better now, they're actually free to float, or they will be.'

'Is he here?'

'No, he's still in Recovery. He took quite a hammering under the anaesthetic. I just came to see my favourite nurse. Is that tea for me?'

She smiled and turned so she was facing him, with hardly the thickness of a piece of paper between them. 'It can be. What's it worth?'

He chuckled, his eyes glittering with intent, just as the door opened.

'That's enough of that—break it up. What's going on in here?'

Anna chuckled and slid sideways out of Adam's reach. 'Wouldn't you like to know? Hello, Josh. Good holiday?'

'Wonderful.' He buzzed her cheek with a kiss and gave Adam a thoughtful look. 'Missed me?'

'Not so as you'd notice. It's actually been quite peaceful. I don't believe you two have met—Josh, this is Adam Bradbury, the new orthopaedic consultant in paeds. Adam, meet Josh Lancaster, one of our consultant paediatricians. I thought you were due back for this morning?' she added curiously to Josh.

'We were. Plane was delayed—we landed at Heathrow at six this morning, and I came straight here. I've been in a clinic, trying to catch up, and Lissa's taken the children home to put them to bed. No doubt they'll be up all night.'

'No doubt,' Anna said with a laugh. 'Got time for tea?'

'I'll make time. So, Adam, what do you think of the Audley Memorial?'

'Well, the nursing staff are very obliging,' he said with a slow, lazy smile, and Anna turned quickly away before Josh could catch the laughing look in her eye.

She was too slow. His curiosity aroused, he hung around, so there was no opportunity for an intimate chat with Adam. They talked about the hospital, and where Adam had been before, and then Adam put his mug in the sink, kissed her on the cheek and said softly, 'I have to go and see Damian. I'll ring you tonight.'

That's blown it, she thought, and she wasn't wrong. Josh gave her a long, thoughtful look and arched a brow enquiringly.

'What?' she said crisply.

He threw up his hands. 'Nothing.'

'It's not nothing. I know you, Josh. If you've got

a problem, spit it out.' She turned to wash up Adam's mug, her back to him.

He was harder to deter than that. He picked up a teatowel and the mug, and moved to stand beside her, his back to the worktop, just in her line of sight. Patiently he wiped the mug, and Anna gave in first.

'Well?'

He lifted his shoulders. 'All a bit quick, isn't it?' he murmured. 'He only arrived on Wednesday. Here we are, the following Monday, and he's kissing you goodbye on the ward. It just seems a bit—I don't know—hasty.'

She dropped the cloth into the sink and turned slowly to face him, furious.

'Do you have a problem with that?' she asked tightly.

He shrugged again. 'A bit too much, too soon, perhaps?' he offered, and she slammed her mug into the sink, sloshing water over the edge onto the floor.

'How dare you?' she said icily. 'Who the hell appointed you my big brother anyway? And besides, you can talk! What about you and Lissa? The second night, wasn't it?'

He coloured and looked away. 'OK. Point made.'

'Bloody good job, too. Don't interfere, Josh. It's none of your damn business.'

He sighed. 'I'm sorry. I was just worrying about you, Anna. You've been getting broody. I've watched you with the kids, and you're—I don't know. You're desperate for a relationship, and I'd hate to see you rush into an affair with someone just to get pregnant.'

'Is that right?' she asked, snatching the teatowel from him and wiping out her mug with a vicious twist. 'Well, let me tell you something, buster,' she went on, pain welling up inside her. 'There's no way it's going to happen, because he can't get me pregnant, so you can save your breath!'

And spinning round, she put the mug and towel down on the worktop, put her face in her hands and howled.

'Oh, Anna.' His voice was soft, contrite, and he turned her against his chest and rocked her gently while she cried. 'Anna, I'm sorry,' he murmured. 'I had no idea.'

'Of course you had no idea!' she said crossly, pushing away from him and fumbling for a tissue in her pocket.

'Here.'

He handed her a piece of kitchen roll, and she blew her nose and wiped her eyes and glared at him again. 'Look at me, I'm a mess. I've got a kid coming back from Recovery I want to settle before I go off duty, and I look as if I've been through the wringer.'

'You needed that,' he told her gently. 'When did you find out?'

'Friday night.' She sniffed loudly and glared at him. 'And I didn't need it! For your information I've been doing it all weekend, every time Adam was out of sight! I thought I'd got over it, put it in perspective.'

He shook his head slowly. 'Anna, I'm so sorry. I suppose it's too late to tell you to leave well alone?'

She scrubbed her nose on her tissue again and pulled a face. 'What do you think?'

'I think you've given him your heart, you poor, silly girl, and I just hope he knows what a treasure he's holding in his hands.'

Damn him. It set her off again, and she got through

another two sheets of kitchen roll before she managed to pull herself together. 'How do I look?' she asked him, and he gave a wry, apologetic smile.

'Like hell.'

'Thought so.' She splashed cold water on her face, rummaged in her pocket for her rescue kit, put on a streak of lipstick and dabbed some concealer on her lower lids. 'Better?' she asked, shoving them back in her pocket.

'You've done that before?'

She smiled ruefully. 'Only every time I lose a child. Right, I have to go and settle Damian.' She went to the door, then paused, her hand on the knob. 'Josh, what I said about Adam…'

'It won't go anywhere. You know that.'

She smiled again. 'Thanks. You're a love. I'm sorry I bit your head off.'

'My pleasure,' he said with a wry chuckle. 'Any time.'

She went out into the ward and found Adam with Damian and his parents in the side ward near the nursing station. The boy was in the Stryker frame that was used for spinal cases, so that he could be turned regularly without damaging him.

He had an aluminium halo attached to his skull, and it was fixed to rods leading to another set of screws in his pelvis, holding his spine in traction. It looked far worse than it felt, but because of the pain of the spinal surgery he was attached to a syringe driver delivering painkillers in a steady, measured dose.

It would be a long, slow process to correct the spinal deformity and allow the newly remodelled bones to heal, and in the meantime he was going to be bad-tempered and tearful.

Anna had seen it all before, and knew it would present quite a nursing challenge. He was in a side room now for peace and quiet, with a nurse to special him, but once he was feeling better he would go out into the ward to provide him with some entertainment and diversions.

And that was when their real problems would start.

Adam looked up and smiled at her, then looked away, then looked back again, his eyes narrowing slightly as he scanned her face.

Oops. She hadn't got away with it. Trust him to notice. He'd spent the weekend studying her every feature. She might have realised he'd be impossible to fool.

'Sister Long,' he said quietly. 'Come and join us. You've met Mr and Mrs George, haven't you?'

'Yes, of course. How are you?' she asked the parents. 'Can I get you anything? You must have had a very trying day.'

Damian's mother smiled wanly. 'It's just so draining, waiting.'

'I know. Well, I'm going off duty now, but if you want anything, ask any of the nursing staff and they'll sort it out. Jenny will be keeping an eye on him and reporting back to Mr Bradbury, and she'll be in here with you all the time until she goes off duty at nine. There will be another nurse on for the night, and I'll be back on at seven. If there's anything you want to know, just ask one of us. OK?'

She left them with a smile, and retrieved her coat from the locker room and headed off the ward.

'Anna!'

She stopped, waiting while Adam caught up with her, and looked up into his searching eyes. 'Hi. Sorry, I thought you were busy.'

'I am. Are you all right?'

She gave him a sad smile. 'Yes, Adam, I'm all right. I'm just tired. I'm going home to bed.'

'Can I ring you? I don't want to wake you.'

'I don't mind,' she said softly. 'I don't suppose you can come round?'

He shook his head. 'Well, not until much later—about ten, and it's too late.'

'It is really,' she said reluctantly. 'You could, though, if you wanted to.'

'I'll see.' He moved away from her, back towards the ward. 'Later. Take care.'

She smiled and watched him go, then turned and made her way out of the hospital. She'd miss him if he didn't come round, but perhaps it would be better if he didn't. As Josh had said, it was too much, too soon, and she maybe needed time to come to terms with it all.

Adam got as far as his car, then thought better of it. Be rational, he told himself. You can't spend every minute of every night with her, and then work all day. It's just silly.

He locked the car again and trudged back inside, hung up his coat, poured a small glass of Scotch and went up to his room. There he kicked off his shoes, settled himself on the bed and picked up the phone.

'Hi,' he said in answer to her hello. 'Are you all right?'

'Mmm. I was asleep. It's lovely to hear your voice.'

'Are you in bed?' he asked, and felt the longing ache begin.

'Mmm. I miss you. It seems odd without you here now.'

He closed his eyes and groaned softly. 'Anna, don't,' he murmured. 'I was coming over.'

'You should have.'

'No. We need sleep. Anyway, I've got a drink now, I can't drive.'

'Oh.' Was it his imagination, or did she sound disappointed?

'Are you really OK?' he asked again, still concerned about her. He was sure she'd been crying, but he couldn't imagine why. Surely she and Josh—

'You and Josh,' he said abruptly. 'You don't have a thing going, do you?'

Her laughter nearly cut through his eardrum. 'Josh? Are you kidding? He's got a gorgeous wife he'd kill for, and two beautiful little children, a boy and a girl. There's no way he'd look at another woman.'

'What about you?' he asked, trying to keep the acid burn of jealousy in check.

She hesitated for a moment, and when she spoke there was a note of reproach in her voice that made him ashamed. 'What about me, Adam? Didn't the weekend convince you? I don't have a thing going with anyone—only you.'

'I'm sorry. I didn't mean to sound like that. I just wondered... You seemed upset after you talked to him. I didn't know why.'

She sighed softly, and he wished he'd gone round there, that they were having this conversation face to face, so he could read her beautiful expressive eyes.

'I just got upset—he asked about you. He thinks

it's too sudden. He behaves like a big brother with us all. It's nothing. You learn to ignore it after a while.'

Big brother? He had an overwhelming urge to push Josh Lancaster's teeth down his interfering throat. How *dare* he presume to tell Anna off for her relationship with him?

'Hey, stop it, I can feel you getting angry,' Anna said in gentle reproach. 'He means well. He's very kind.'

Adam didn't want to talk about him any more. He didn't want to talk, full stop. He wanted to hold her, and touch her, and watch her fall apart under his hands. He looked at the untouched Scotch in the glass, and wondered if he had any self-control at all.

Then he heard Jaz cry out in his sleep, and with a sigh he picked up the glass and drained it.

That would fix it. He couldn't go to her now. He didn't ever drink and drive, not after what he'd seen in A and E. 'I have to go,' he said reluctantly. 'Jasper's crying, he needs me. I'll see you tomorrow. Sleep well.'

'You, too. Hope he's all right.'

'He'll be fine. 'Night, Anna. Take care.'

He put the phone down very carefully, swung his legs over the edge of the bed and padded softly next door. Danny was asleep in his bed behind the door, and Jasper was sitting up on the far side, knuckling his eyes and sobbing quietly.

'It's all right, Jaz, I'm here,' he murmured reassuringly. Scooping the little lad up, he sat on his bed and cradled him against his chest.

'Had a dream,' Jaz hiccuped unhappily. 'I was f'ightened.'

'It's all gone now,' Adam assured him. 'You're safe now, I've got you.'

And if I'd gone to Anna, I wouldn't have been here for him, and Helle wouldn't have heard him over her music.

Suddenly his burning desire to be with Anna was extinguished, replaced by the need to nurture and care for his children, and shelter them from the fears and perils of their hitherto insecure little lives.

'It's all right,' he said again, rocking him until the little body relaxed against him and was still. Then he slid Jaz under the covers, tucked him up and went to bed, trying not to think of Anna and how big and empty his kingsize bed felt after sharing her much smaller one all weekend.

He couldn't abandon his responsibilities, and he didn't want to. What he wanted, what he needed, was a retreat, somewhere he could run to and hide when it all got too much. An oasis of calm and warmth and tenderness, a place to go to recharge his batteries and refill his soul.

He thought of Anna and her gentleness, and her peace seemed to steal over him.

'Goodnight, my love,' he whispered softly. 'Sleep tight.'

Two miles away, Anna lay in bed with her hands wrapped around a scarf Adam had left there. It was soft and cosy, and it carried the faint tang of his aftershave. She cradled it under her chin, and thought of him, and ached for him. She felt his presence with her somehow, almost as if he was thinking of her. Was he in bed already? Hers seemed awfully empty without him. Empty and cold.

Goodnight, my love. Sleep tight.

She snuggled the scarf closer, inhaling deeply and focusing on him in his huge bed in that enormous, empty bedroom.

'Goodnight, my love,' she whispered in the silent room. 'Sleep tight. See you tomorrow.'

She seemed to feel his arms around her, holding her, his warmth stealing over her, and within moments she was asleep.

CHAPTER SIX

'DAMIAN, we're going to turn you,' Anna said gently. 'All right?'

'No-o-o,' the boy protested, his voice barely audible. 'Please, no.'

'Sorry, sweetheart. I'll give you a bit more pain relief, OK?'

'Does it hurt him very much?' his mother asked, looking troubled.

'Probably a bit,' Anna told her as she overrode the syringe driver and gave him a little more of the drug. 'It's also quite scary. When I was training we had to lie in it and be turned so we knew what it was like, and it's a bit unnerving. It squashes you a bit with both halves on and, although you're pretty stable inside it, you do feel a bit vulnerable. I can quite understand why he doesn't like it, but he'd hate being turned any other way much, much more, believe me.'

Anna and Jenny clipped the other half of the revolving bed-frame on top of him, fastened it securely so that he was firmly sandwiched between the layers, and then turned it over, so that he went from his back to his front, with his face cradled in a special cut-out.

He whimpered as they turned it, but it had to be done, and once the upper piece of frame was removed they soon made him comfortable again.

Anna left the dressing until Adam arrived. She was sure he'd be in early to check up on Damian and Kate before going to his clinic, and she was right. He appeared shortly before eight, and she left Allie taking report and joined him just outside Damian's room.

Adam gave her a brief but intimate smile of greeting and moved a little further away from the door so they were no longer in earshot. 'Morning. How's my favourite nurse today?' he murmured.

'Busy—how are you?'

'Ditto. I've got a clinic in a minute. How's he been in the night?'

'All right, I think. He hates being turned over.'

'I'm sure he does. I expect it hurts. Use the override on the syringe driver a few minutes before to give him a bit of extra pain relief,' he suggested.

'We do. It still hurts.'

'Hmm. Well, there's nothing else we can do, he's on the most we can really give him. It'll get better. Today will be the worst, I expect. Can I have a look at the wound?'

'Sure. I've got the trolley ready. I was waiting for you.'

'Thanks.' His smile warmed her down to her toes, and she knew it was nothing to do with Damian and everything to do with their conversation last night. 'Anna?'

She paused on the threshold of the room.

'I missed you last night,' he said, so softly she could hardly hear him.

'Ditto,' she replied just as softly. 'It was a long night.'

'What time do you have lunch?'

She laughed under her breath. 'If and when I can get away, usually. Why don't you ring me when you're free?'

'Good idea. Right, let's see how Damian's getting on.'

'Are you OK?'

Anna looked up from her paperwork to see Josh leaning over the top of the work station, his arms propped on the high, narrow counter.

She gave him a forgiving smile. 'Yes, I'm fine, thanks.'

'I hear interesting things about your Mr Bradbury,' he murmured. 'I gather he's pretty top-flight.'

'So I'm told.' It didn't surprise her. She imagined he was the sort of man who was good at everything he did, and if his love-making was anything to go by, he was a stickler for detail.

'Robert Ryder was impressed. He assisted with a case on Friday night, apparently, and saved a leg anyone else would have given up on. Apparently, the young woman is doing well, despite having lost the other leg and her fiancé in the crash.'

So that was what he'd been doing. She'd wondered what it had been that had put that haunted look in his eyes. 'I don't know how anybody can bear to do orthopaedics,' she said with a shudder. 'The trauma side is so messy.'

'A and E is what gets me. You get the lot. I really, really don't like blood.' He grinned. 'So what have you got for me?'

'Oh, hundreds of new admissions,' she teased. The phone rang, and she scooped it up.

'Children's ward, Sister Long speaking. Can I help you?'

'Lunch?'

She glanced at her watch. 'Can you give me five minutes?'

'Sure. I'll meet you in the Gallery.'

'OK.'

She cradled the phone and looked up at Josh. 'Right. Allie will show you your new cases. There are only two. One's got some kind of flu that won't shift and is turning into what looks like pneumonia, the other looks like diabetes.'

'Thanks. I'll go and see them. You go and have lunch with your maestro.'

She coloured. 'What makes you think—?'

'Don't bother,' he said with a lazy grin. 'It's written all over your face in letters ten feet high.'

'My face isn't that big.'

'Your smile is.'

She laughed and stood up. 'Are you going to watch my every movement?'

'No—actually, I'm hoping to sell you tickets for the Valentine Ball on Saturday night. It's a fundraiser for the children's facilities in the department. You have a moral duty to support it. We've got a couple of spaces on our table—why don't you join us?'

'I'll ask him,' she promised, her heart thumping at the thought of spending the evening dancing with Adam. 'I'll let you know.'

She all but ran through the hospital, and found him sitting at a table in the Gallery coffee-shop. It was the nearest to the paediatric ward, and served snacks and drinks. Hardly lunching out, but it was quick, and that was all she had time for.

Adam stood up and came towards her, ushering her to the counter. 'You took six minutes,' he said in mock reproof, and she glanced at her watch.

'Did I?'

He laughed. 'I have no idea. It just seemed like a long time. What are you going to eat?'

She shrugged. 'I don't know. A sandwich?'

'Good idea.'

They took their selection out of the chiller, added mugs of coffee to the tray and he paid for it and led her back to the table where he'd been sitting.

'I'm starving,' she confessed, biting into her sandwich enthusiastically.

'Must be all that activity at the weekend,' he teased gently, and she felt herself colour a little.

'It seems a long time ago,' she said wistfully, picking out a prawn.

'Too long. What are you doing tonight?'

She looked up into his eyes, and read the unmistakable invitation in them. 'Waiting up for you?' she suggested, and he gave a crooked, sexy smile that made her heart flutter.

'Sounds good.'

'This weekend,' she said, trying not to drown in his eyes, 'there's a Valentine Ball in aid of the hospital children's facilities. Josh asked if we wanted to join their table. I said I'd ask you.'

He looked thoughtful. 'A Valentine Ball? I haven't danced for years. Have you got strong shoes?'

She chuckled. 'No—little strappy, open-toed ones—and I warn you, I love dancing, so you'd better be good at it.'

'I'll do,' he confessed, and searched her eyes. 'Fancy it?'

She nodded. 'I do, actually. I haven't been to a ball for ages, and I love to party.'

'OK, Cinderella,' he said with a lazy, sexy smile,

'you shall go to the ball. Just don't turn into a pumpkin at midnight.'

'That was the coach,' she laughed, and he grinned.

'So it was. My mistake. What time tonight?'

Tonight. Her heart slammed against her ribs. 'Whenever. What time can you make it?'

He shrugged. 'Depends on the kids. I can't stay long. Last night Jasper woke up crying and needed a cuddle—I'd hate to think I wasn't there for him.'

'What does he do when you're at work?'

'He cries, I suppose,' Adam said heavily. 'I don't know. I try not to think about it.'

'They need a mother,' she said, her heart aching at the thought of Jasper lying crying in his bed, all alone. 'Poor little loves.'

'No,' he said with quiet certainty, and a chill ran over her. 'No, Anna, they don't need a mother, and I don't need a wife. Don't start thinking along those lines, please. I need you, yes—God knows I need you—but not as a wife. Not as a mother for my children. Been there, done that. It was a disaster. No, our relationship's going nowhere, Anna, except where it is—a beautiful little oasis of calm and tranquillity in the midst of my chaotic existence. I'm sorry if that's not what you see for us, but it's all I can give you— all I can ask of you. I'm sorry.'

She dropped her eyes, unwilling to let him see the pain she knew must be all too obvious in them. You're wrong! she wanted to shout. Of course you need a wife!

But perhaps he didn't. Perhaps he was right. She sat there, chasing bubbles in her coffee with the spoon, and swallowed the hurt before she made a complete ass of herself.

'Anna?' His voice was kind, and he placed gentle fingers under her chin and tilted her head so he could see into her tear-filled eyes. 'Damn,' he said softly, and brushed a tear away with his thumb. 'Oh, sweetheart, don't cry. I didn't say I don't need you. I do—probably more than you can imagine.'

He glanced around, sighed and dropped his hand. 'We can't talk about this here. I'll come round tonight—*may* I come round tonight?'

She closed her eyes and looked away. 'I don't know. Yes, of course you can come round.' She gave a tremulous sigh and met his eyes again. 'Of course you can. I'll see you later.'

She stood up and brushed the crumbs off her tabard, then without another word she left him there, went into the nearest ladies' loo and shut herself in, flushing it to drown out the sobs that wouldn't be suppressed.

Give him time, she told herself, blowing her nose and scrubbing tears from her cheeks. Give him time.

She washed her face, patted it dry, dug in her pocket for her rescue kit and went back to the ward, patched up and ready to go.

'Hell, again?' Josh said, cornering her in the kitchen. 'What now?'

'He doesn't need a wife.'

Josh smiled. 'Good. He's thinking about it.'

'No. I said his children need a mother. *I'm* thinking about it, not him. He put me right.'

Josh let out his breath on a harsh sigh. 'So you won't be joining us for the ball, then?'

His bleeper squawked, and he went into the office to use the phone. He came back a moment later, a wry smile on his face. 'Curious. That was Adam—he asked if I'd got the ball tickets. He'd like to buy two. Apparently, he's under the illusion that you'll still go with him.'

Her humourless little laugh was cut off in its prime. 'Oh, I will—he's right. I can't refuse him anything. I love him, Josh, and he needs me. That's the long and the short of it. I love him, and I'll take any crumbs he throws me—and that's all he can spare. Crumbs…' Her voice cracked on the word, and she bit her lip and turned away.

'Hey, hey, don't be so pessimistic,' Josh said encouragingly. 'Lots of people fight shy of commitment, especially if they've been burned before. If he says he needs you, Anna, he'll relent in the end. Take my word for it. You hang in there and make yourself indispensable to him. He'll come round. Lissa did. You just have to wait him out. Withhold privileges or something,' he suggested, laughter in his voice.

'I can't be so calculated,' she protested. 'And anyway, I need him, too.' She let out a soft sigh. 'I know I'm going to get hurt, whatever happens, but I can't walk away.'

'I'm sorry,' he said gently, and laid a kindly hand on her arm. 'Look, if you need a shoulder to cry on, you know where we are, any time, day or night. Just come round. Lissa's there most of the day, and we're always in in the evening. You know you're welcome.'

She dredged up a smile. 'Thanks, Josh. You're a good friend.'

'Any time.'

She went out into the ward and found Allie, and her friend shot her a searching look.

'Don't ask,' she warned. 'Please.'

'Oh, Anna! Come on, you need to be busy,' she

said briskly. 'Damian needs turning—want to give me a hand? And then we need to check the dressing on Kate's leg.'

Together they turned Damian again and made him comfortable, and then went to see Kate, who was just starting the leg-lengthening procedure.

She was in a little pain, but she seemed relieved that the operation was over and the real business of stretching out the short leg could begin. Adam had showed her how to turn the key, and how far, and she would be doing it herself, an important part of the process.

The wounds looked clean and healthy, and Anna was impressed at the neatness of the incision and the almost invisible stitching. It would heal beautifully, she realised. Just another of Adam's many skills.

Then she checked the little girl with pneumonia and made sure she was comfortable and breathing as well as she could. She was being monitored frequently, and her vital signs had been improving over the last hour or so that she had been in.

'Dr Lancaster's ever so kind, isn't he?' the child's mother said, and Anna agreed.

He was kind. Kind and thoughtful, and he'd moved heaven and earth to convince Lissa to marry him when she'd been expecting their first child. When he talked about patience, he was at least talking from a standpoint of personal experience. Perhaps he was right.

And perhaps pigs flew.

The doorbell rang at a quarter to ten, and Anna opened it to find Adam there, flowers in his hand and regret in his eyes. 'Can I come in?'

'Of course you can. I said that.'

He put the flowers down, and drew her into his arms. 'I'm sorry I hurt you,' he murmured. 'I just didn't want you building up unrealistic dreams. I'm sorry if I was too late.'

You were too late the moment I first saw you, Anna thought, and hugged him gently back. 'Don't be silly. Do you want a drink?'

He shook his head. 'No. I just want you.'

Without a word she turned and led the way upstairs.

It was strange, the rest of that week. She was looking forward to the ball, but she was too busy to think about it much, and Saturday was rushing up like an express train.

'Have you got a dress?' Allie asked on Friday, and she nodded.

'A strappy cream thing—it's quite slinky and it's split all the way up to wherever, but it suits me and I own it and I don't have time to go shopping.'

Allie laughed and shook her head. 'You ought to spoil yourself. Don't you want to impress him?'

Pain stabbed her. 'I don't think a dress will do it,' she said drily. 'Come and give me a hand with Damian. I want to move him out into the ward. He's bored and fractious, and I think he might be better with something to look at and someone to talk to. We'll need to do something ingenious with mirrors so he can see the television, but I'm sure we can cheer him up.'

They were just moving him into his new position when her senses went on red alert. She lifted her head, and Adam was standing in the entrance to the ward, watching her. He was too far away for her to see his expression, but she had known he was there. How strange, and yet not strange at all. She felt she knew everything about him. Why would she not know when he was near?

He came towards her, every step echoing her heart-beat, and a fleeting smile quirked his lips. 'Hello, all. Hi, Damian. How are things?'

'Boring,' the boy said.

'We're moving him so there's more to see and do,' Anna explained. 'We're going to rig up mirrors so he can see round the ward, and watch the television and so on.'

'That should make things better for you, Damian. Good—' He turned to Anna. 'Could I have a word, Sister, please?'

'Of course.' She left Damian in Allie's capable hands and followed Adam into the vacated side room. 'What is it?'

'Apart from the fact that I just wanted to see you?' he said with a wry smile. 'I've got a six-year-old child with osteogenesis imperfecta who's just moved into the area recently and is supposedly coming in for correction of bowing and multiple fractures of both femurs. She's very small—tiny for her age, no bigger than a toddler—and she's very frail. She's got a pigeon chest and scoliosis, and very limited limb growth. I don't know what I can do for her, I suspect not a lot, but she's fallen and broken her arm and leg this morning and she's coming up in a minute.'

'Are you going to pin and plate her?'

He shrugged. 'I don't know. I can't decide. I have to say I'm not very hopeful. I think she's too fragile to treat except very conservatively, and I'm wary of going in and doing more damage. There's nothing to screw anything to, it's all too fragile, and really I don't know how she's survived so far. I've never seen such brittle bones.

'It's a collagen problem, of course, and the brittle bones are just a symptom, so I think we might try to treat the collagen deficiency long term, but for now we might have to put her in a very lightweight cast so, please, make sure the nursing staff know how fragile she is.'

'I will,' Anna promised, wondering how they would manage her. 'She'll need a Propad mattress and sheepskin. I'll see to that. She'll need a cot as well, I think—I don't want to risk her falling out of bed. We'd better pad the bars. Is her mother coming with her?'

'Yes. She's the one that's got her through so far, so I would use her whenever possible. She's used to handling her and they have a system, apparently. I have to say, I think we might lose her. She's really brave apparently, but, of course, every fracture hurts as much as another, and just because it happens to her all the time that doesn't mean it isn't painful.'

Adam sighed and ran his hands through his hair. 'I thought I had some time this afternoon to catch up on my paperwork, but it doesn't look like it now. She's come to the top of the list in a major way, but I don't think I'll do a lot before Monday. I'll come and see her once you've got her settled and I'll decide then. I'll go and have another look at the pictures and see what I think. I might ring an old colleague.'

He was just leaving the room when he turned back. 'Still all right for tomorrow?'

'I am—what about you?'

He closed his eyes and grunted with laughter. 'Helle can't babysit. She's going to London again. My parents have said they'll come and stay—that means I'll get the third degree if I stay out after midnight.'

'Really?'

He laughed again. 'Maybe. I don't know. I haven't tried. Knowing my mother, she'd be delighted to know there was a woman in my life. She's insatiably curious as it is. She knows I'm taking someone to the ball, she just doesn't know who—and she certainly doesn't know we're having an affair. She'd be over the moon. She thinks I'm a recluse.'

No, just a lonely, generous man who'd given his heart to his children and sworn to protect them no matter what the cost.

'We'll just have to go home early, then,' Anna said with a smile, and his eyes darkened fractionally.

'Promises, promises,' he murmured, and walked away, whistling softly.

'You look stunning.'

Anna laughed and stroked Adam's satin lapel. 'You don't look so bad yourself. I like the bow-tie—very professional.'

'And it's real,' he told her smugly. 'None of your elasticated nonsense.'

He helped her into her coat, dropped a quick, hard kiss on her lips and then had to wait while she wiped the lipstick off his mouth with a tissue.

'Why did you do that?' he asked. 'I thought I'd set a trend.'

'Very fetching. It's not your colour. You'd look better in plum.'

'I'll bear it in mind.'

It was only a short drive to the hotel where the ball was being held, and it was moments before they'd handed over their coats and were inside, surrounded by red roses, silver hearts and romantic music.

'St Valentine, eat your heart out,' Adam said softly in her ear. 'Right, where are the others? Do we need to meet up with them?'

'Over there—I can see Josh waving. They're all there.' And, please, she thought, don't let Josh grill him about his intentions or let on that he knows anything. Anything at all!

He didn't. He stood up to greet them, and said, 'I expect you know most of us. This is my wife, Lissa, and Sarah Jordan, Matt's wife, from A and E, and you know Matt and Mark and Allie already. We're still waiting for Nick and Ronnie Sarazin—they might be late. One of the children was ill, apparently. Now, can I get you two a drink? I'm just going up to the bar.'

The meal was wonderful, and as they lingered over coffee the master of ceremonies called for everyone's attention, thanked them for supporting the cause and ordered them to dance. The band struck up, and Adam turned to Anna with a challenging smile.

'You wanted to party,' he said slowly. 'Let's party.'

She returned his smile, stood up and took his hand. 'Excuse us, folks. We're here to dance.'

She followed him onto the empty floor and went into his arms. It was a pacy number, with a heavy beat, and he slotted one thigh between hers, laid a guiding hand on the small of her back and led her in an intricate series of swoops and swirls that left her laughing and breathless and everyone clapping.

It was followed by another, and another, with everyone joining in, and then the band slowed down and he locked his arms behind her back and smiled down at her. 'Enjoying yourself?' he asked.

'Absolutely. You're an exhibitionist,' she said in amazement, and he laughed. 'And a liar,' she added. 'You didn't tread on my toes once!'

'Ah. I asked if you had strong shoes—I didn't say I was going to tread on you! You're pretty special, you know that? You didn't miss a single beat.'

'Nor did you. I'm stunned. So many men have two left feet.'

'Ah, well, you know what they say about good dancers.'

She tried to stifle a smile. 'If you're fishing for compliments on your technique in other areas, you can fish,' she teased.

'You're a hard woman.'

'I wouldn't want you to get a swollen head.'

'No danger of that. I'm sure you wouldn't allow it for a moment.' He drew her closer and sighed in her ear. 'You smell good,' he murmured.

'So do you. I could breathe you in all night.'

'Not a chance. I think Josh is back with our drinks, and I'm gasping after that lot,' he said, and eased away from her with reluctance. 'Shall we go back to the table?'

'We ought to, or they'll complain that we're being antisocial.'

Needless to say, they were teased about the dancing.

'Very sexy,' Lissa said, eyeing them with interest.

'Tell me, were you actually screwed together, or was that just an illusion?'

'Lissa!' Josh exclaimed, and everyone laughed aloud.

'Just an illusion,' Adam assured her with a smile.

'I just wondered if, being an orthopaedic surgeon, you could lend a whole new meaning to the term "joined at the hip".' She turned to her husband and eyed him speculatively. 'Josh, can you dance like that?'

'Not in public,' he said reprovingly, and Anna laughed, still on a high from the best dance she'd had in years.

'You're just a stuffed shirt. Your wife wants to dance, Josh, take her up on it. You might not get a better offer all night.'

'Later. I need to get a bit more tanked up before I make an ass of myself.'

They all laughed, and the conversation settled down and became more general. Adam was asked about his house, and he told them about the general state of it and the vast amount of decorating that needed to be done.

'You ought to have a stripping party,' Lissa suggested. 'They're always lots of fun.'

Everyone laughed, and Adam shook his head. 'I'd worry about your wife, if I were you, Josh,' he said with a chuckle. 'I think you've got your hands full there.'

'Wallpaper,' Lissa said firmly, trying not to laugh. 'You get everyone round and hire wallpaper strippers and get loads of food in and, Bob's your uncle, it's all stripped. Fun. We'll come.'

'You haven't been invited yet,' Josh reminded her, and she rolled her eyes.

'I'll have you know I'm a dab hand with a wallpaper stripper,' she said proudly.

'I'll think about it,' Adam promised. 'And now, if you'll excuse us, I'm going to take Anna back to the dance floor and find out what else she can do.'

'This I have to see,' Mark said with a chuckle. 'You've been hiding your light under a bushel, Anna.'

'You've all had your chance,' she reminded them. 'It's not my fault you didn't know a good thing when you saw it.'

'Stop flirting with them, they're all taken,' Adam said, towing her to her feet. 'Come on, woman, I want your body. The night's awasting.'

It couldn't get any better, she thought, but she was wrong. They danced together, they danced apart, they danced around each other, they jived, they tangoed, they waltzed, and then finally, with the last and most romantic number to wind up a valentine ball, they stood almost still and swayed against each other.

Anna thought she'd never been so in tune with anyone or so aware of them in her life. She rested her head on Adam's shoulder, her arms round his waist under his jacket, and wished the evening didn't have to come to an end.

Finally, though, it was time to go, and they said goodnight to the others and walked back to the car, his arm slung round her shoulders, their hips bumping with every stride. It was a cold, crisp night, but they were warm from the dancing and still running on adrenaline, so they hardly noticed.

He parked outside her house and cut the engine, then took the keys from her and opened her front door, closing it behind them and drawing her back into his arms.

'Where were we?' he asked gruffly, and slid her coat over her shoulders. His own followed it to the floor, then he kicked off his shoes, shucked off his jacket, tugged the bow-tie loose and slid the cuff-links free.

Anna turned and walked towards the stairs, kicking off her shoes as she went, and he followed her, catching her by the ankle and placing a kiss in the centre of her foot.

She laughed and pulled it away, turning round and watching as he stripped off his shirt and dropped it on the hall floor. The trousers followed, and the socks, leaving him in nothing but wholly inadequate briefs. She backed up the stairs, trapped by the fever in his eyes, and went into the bedroom.

She'd set the scene tonight, placing candles on the chest of drawers, putting fresh linen on the bed, his flowers in a vase on the dressing table. It probably gave away too much, but she didn't care. She was no good at hiding things, she never had been, and he might as well know the truth.

She lit the candles, and while she stooped over them, Adam bent and laid his lips against the bare, heated skin of her shoulders. 'You're beautiful,' he murmured, sliding down the zip on her dress and easing the fine spaghetti straps off the shoulders.

It puddled round her ankles, leaving her dressed in nothing more than a pair of slinky tights, and he slid his hands round from behind her and cupped her breasts, their reflection in the mirror pearly in the candlelight.

'Beautiful,' he said again, and turned her into his

arms. His kiss was tender, slow and lazy, belying the heat that raged between them.

Or maybe not. A shudder ran through him, and he lifted his head and looked deep into her eyes, his own filled with fire.

'I want you,' he said, his voice uneven. 'Make love with me, Anna. I need you.'

Adam's honesty tore through her, and her arms wrapped around him and held him close to her heart. His head dropped against her shoulder, his lips pressed firmly against the soft skin of her throat, and he stood there for several seconds without moving. Then he lifted his head and gave her a crooked little smile.

'We've got a dance to finish,' he murmured, and peeled the gossamer tights away. He lifted her and laid her in the middle of the bed, and then he kissed her, every inch of her, his touch gentle and reverent, until she wanted to weep with longing.

Finally, when she thought she'd die without him, he moved over her, his body trembling under her hands, and then he hesitated, poised over her, their eyes locked.

'I love you,' he said softly, and then her body welcomed him, and she knew she could never love anyone more than she loved this man...

CHAPTER SEVEN

'I HAVE to go.'

Anna opened her eyes and looked up into Adam's sombre face. His eyes were troubled. 'I know,' she murmured.

'I'm sorry. You know I'd stay if I could.'

She nodded. 'It's all right, I do understand.'

He kissed her, then levered himself up and swung his legs over the side of the bed.

She watched him as he stood up and walked to the door, retrieving his briefs on the way. 'I have no idea where my clothes are,' he said with a wry grin.

'Just follow the trail,' she suggested, and blew him a kiss.

A few minutes later he reappeared, dressed, and came and sat on the edge of the bed. 'I think I've found everything,' he said. His eyes were still shadowed with regret. His head descended slowly, blocking out the mellow, golden glow of the candles, and his mouth touched hers. 'I'll see you on Monday morning. Look after yourself.'

'You, too.'

He ran lightly down the stairs, and then a moment later she heard the front door closing, then the sound of his car starting outside in the street. She looked at the bedside clock. It was three-fifteen. They'd been home less than two hours.

She told herself she was being greedy, wanting more of him, but she missed him already. She lay down with her head where his had rested on the pillow and breathed deeply, inhaling the faint scent of his aftershave and something more individual, something just Adam.

Her arms felt empty, but her heart was full. He loved her. He'd said so. That must surely be progress?

She curled up on her side, tugging the quilt round her to keep her warm, and eventually she fell asleep.

When she woke, the candles had burned right down, and the sun was shining through the crack in the curtains. She looked at her watch. Nine-thirty. Only six hours' sleep, and yet she felt wonderful. She threw off the quilt, pulled on her robe and went downstairs, picking up the trail of discarded clothing as she went.

Her toe hit something, and she looked down to see a small leather wallet on the floor. Adam's. She bent and picked it up, hefting it in her hand. He'd need it today—he might go and fill the car up with petrol and then realise he didn't have it, or spend hours searching for it.

She'd take it round. It was no trouble, and it was a good excuse to see him again. She took a cup of tea with her to the bath, drank it while she soaked in the lovely hot water and then washed and dressed in record time.

She left the house by ten, and arrived at Adam's shortly afterwards. His car was the only one on the drive, so she turned in there and pulled up beside it. His parents must have gone. Good. She didn't need an inquisition this morning, and she was sure he didn't either.

She hoped he was up. She tipped her head back and looked at the windows, and saw his curtains open.

Good. She didn't want to wake him if they were all still asleep, but she didn't think it was likely. Children woke up revoltingly early, on the whole.

She rang the doorbell, listening to it echoing down the hall, and a moment later the door swung open to reveal an elegant, grey-haired woman in her sixties. His mother. It must be. Oh, yipes. She thought they'd gone, as the car wasn't there. She'd just assumed—

'Can I help you, dear?' the woman asked, and she conjured up a smile.

'Yes. Is Adam in?'

'He is—he's in the garden with the children, building a bonfire. Hold on, I'll get him.'

She was about to turn away when Anna stopped her. 'It's all right—I've got his wallet. He dropped it in my house last night. Perhaps you could just give it to him?'

The woman searched her face slowly, then smiled. 'You must be Anna—come in, dear. Give it to him yourself, I'm sure he'll be pleased to see you. I've just made a big pot of tea, actually. Perhaps you'll join us, or are you a coffee person?'

Anna found herself in the kitchen, clutching a couple of mugs and being ushered toward the table. 'Sit down, I'll get him. Adam? Adam, it's for you. Anna.'

He came in, and did a mild double take. 'Hi—I thought you were on the phone.'

'You dropped your wallet,' she said, suddenly feeling guilty for allowing his mother to talk her into staying. 'In the hall. I thought you'd want it. Your mother gave me a cup of tea.'

'I can imagine,' he said drily, and gave a wry grin. 'Thanks for bringing my wallet round. It was good of you. I would have missed it later.'

Adam hooked a chair out with his foot and sat down, cradling the mug in his hands. 'I was just telling my father about Lissa's stripping party,' he said, not looking at all worried that she was there, ensconced uninvited in his breakfast room. 'Do you think anyone would come?'

'Oh, yes,' Anna said instantly. 'I'm sure they would, just out of curiosity. It's a sort of alternative house-warming, isn't it?'

He laughed. 'I suppose so—very alternative. I hardly know most of these people, though. Why would they bother?'

'Because they're nice? Because they like doing things to help and to make people welcome? Because they'll do anything for a free meal? When were you thinking of?'

He gave a short laugh. 'I wasn't, really. It sounds like bedlam. I'm not sure I can stand more than one room at a time in chaos.'

Anna looked round her and raised an eyebrow. 'Nothing on the walls is better than what's there now—but you might need a crack-filling party to follow it!'

'Don't.'

His mother entered the room behind him, trying hard to look casual and failing dismally. 'Biscuit, anyone?'

'No, thanks, I've only just had breakfast. Anna?'

'I'd love one. I sort of forgot breakfast today.' In my haste to get here. Oh, dear.

'I'll get them. More tea, Anna? Adam, do you want a top-up, darling?'

'No, thanks,' they said together, and their eyes locked and they smiled.

'Stay for lunch,' he said impulsively, and so she did, and they planned the stripping party, and finished building the bonfire, and before they knew what was going on it was night-time and she had to go.

'Thank you for today,' she said as he saw her off at the door. They were in the porch, in the space between the inner and outer doors, and although the doors had stained glass in them, the light in the porch wasn't on and so they had an element of privacy.

'It's been a pleasure,' he said, and, as if he couldn't help himself, he lowered his head and kissed her. It was only a brief kiss, but there was enough heat bottled up in it to keep her warm all the way home.

What had he been thinking about, asking Anna for lunch? She'd stayed all day, and it had been torture. He'd wanted to hold her, and touch her, and his mother's eagle eyes had missed nothing.

Neither had the children's, and in the bath after she'd gone the boys were grilling him.

'She's nice—why can't she come and live with us instead of Helle?'

'Yes, why can't she? I don't like Helle.'

'Yes, you do, Jasper,' Adam said firmly, taking a flannel and scrubbing it over his grubby little hands.

'I don't. She's not as nice as Anna.'

Adam had to agree privately, but it didn't make his life any easier. 'She's got a job,' he told them, going back to the original issue while he lathered. 'She can't come and work for us.'

'She could just stay.'

'She's got a house.'

'We've got a house. I bet her house isn't as big as our house.'

No, Adam thought, but it's warm and cosy and it's a peaceful haven compared to this. He lifted Jasper out of the bath, wrapped him in a towel and gave Danny a helping hand out.

'You could ask her,' Danny persisted. 'I bet you haven't asked her.'

'No, I haven't and, what's more, I'm not going to. Helle's going anyway, remember, and we're getting another au pair. She's coming soon.'

Not soon enough, though. Helle was starting to drive him mad. She often failed to come back after the weekend—like this weekend, for instance. She would probably turn up at eight tomorrow morning, after he wanted to be at the hospital, and it would be a logistical nightmare.

He'd probably have to take the children round to his parents and leave them to drop them at school— which meant getting them up early, getting their snacks organised, finding all the things for their school bags. It was hell, and all because Helle couldn't be bothered to come back when she was supposed to.

'Skye?' he called, sticking his head out of the bathroom door. 'Your turn, darling.'

'Coming.'

He pulled Jasper's pyjama top on over his head, cleaned his teeth, trundled him into the loo next door for a last visit and returned to Danny who was just rinsing out the toothpaste. 'What about your hair? Want me to rub it dry?'

He stood in front of Adam obediently, allowing him to towel it. Then, when it was dry enough for the night, he looked Adam straight in the eye and said, without warning, 'I think you should ask her.'

'Me, too,' Jasper said, pulling up his pyjama trousers as he reappeared.

'Ask who what?' Skye said, coming into the overcrowded bathroom behind Jasper.

'Nothing. Come on, boys, let Skye have her bath in peace.'

He bundled them out of the room, went back in five minutes later and washed Skye's hair for her, then helped her dry it and combed it carefully through.

A mother's job, he thought sadly, and swallowed the lump that came out of nowhere. Damn Lyn. Damn her, damn David, damn both of them.

'Ouch!'

'Sorry, darling,' he said, instantly contrite. He had to stop himself from hugging her automatically, and instead stroked her head where he'd tugged a tangle. 'I wasn't concentrating.' He finished her hair more carefully, then rinsed round the bath and hung up the damp towels while Skye cleaned her teeth.

Ten minutes later they were all kissed and settled, and he poured himself a much-needed glass of wine and sat down in front of the television.

It couldn't hold his attention. All he could think about was Anna, and how she'd danced with him last night, and that he'd told her he loved her.

He hadn't meant to do that. He'd meant to keep it to himself, but he'd fouled up. She'd looked so lovely, her face delicately flushed with passion, her eyes soft, her touch so tender—it had cut through his defences, and dragged the truth from him. She'd deserved the truth, and he'd given it to her, but she deserved more than that.

She deserved the follow-up, the next course, the icing on the cake, and he couldn't give her that.

No matter how much he might long to.

Little Emily Parker was the worst case of brittle bone disease Anna had ever seen. She'd been immobilised in casts over the weekend, but now Adam was going to try and pin her leg. If successful, he would straighten and pin the other one by cutting the bone into little pieces, rearranging them in a straight line and putting a pin through them. 'Like stringing beads on a knitting needle,' he explained to them.

'Will it be better then?' Emily asked in her curiously flat voice. She was deaf as well, from the damage to the little bones in her inner ear, and it just compounded her problems.

'I hope so,' Adam told her honestly. 'I'll do my best, and I'm good at what I do, but I can still only do what I can. I will try for you, though. I think the arm would be better in a cast, though, for now. I don't want to do too much to you at once.'

'Thank you,' her mother said. She sounded weary. No wonder, Anna thought. Emily had spent most of her six years in hospital for one thing or another, and her mother had been with her for most of it.

She and Adam left Emily's cot, and went back into the office. 'Are you OK?' she asked him, looking into his tired eyes. 'You look a bit harassed this morning.'

'Helle didn't come back from her weekend. She's back now—I just got her on the phone. I gave her hell. I expect she'll have packed and gone by the time I get home. Oh, well. So be it. I must contact a nanny agency. The au pair people are taking for ever and I need some cover.'

'What about the girls next door? Can they help out?' Anna suggested.

'Well, they can babysit occasionally, but not much more than that. I have to do something permanent—it's no good going on like this. Helle's just not reliable enough, and neither was the last one.'

He looked at his watch and sighed. 'I suppose I ought to go and scrub and start my list. I've got the two-year-old with spina bifida for closure of the spinal tract, and little Emily, and the two fractures that have come in overnight that need my attention. I'll see you later—are you in tonight?'

She would have cancelled almost anything. As it was, there was nothing to cancel. 'Yes, I'm free,' she told him. 'Come round, if you've still got an au pair.'

He snorted softly. 'On second thoughts, don't hold your breath. I might ring you instead.'

He did, to tell her that Helle had still been there when he'd got home, but was only going to work the week.

'What about the phone bill?' Anna asked, knowing how soft he was. 'Are you going to hold her to that?'

'I don't suppose so,' he admitted. 'It was an attempt to persuade her to stay for a while, but it's not been very effective. I've tried an agency, but they can't do anything before next week at the earliest.'

'If I can help at all, just ask me,' Anna offered, but he didn't take her up on it. Still, the offer had been made. 'How was the op on Emily?' she asked. 'I had to leave before you came back to the ward.'

'OK. Not as bad as I thought. I did both legs, and I left her arm in a cast. I just hope the ends of the bone are strong enough to stand the strain. That's the danger, of course. Still, there's only so much I can do. The spinal tract case was easier than I thought, but one of the fractures was a monster. You'll meet him tomorrow—he'll be with us for a while. How was Damian today?'

'Bored,' she said with a smile that he must have heard in her voice. 'I've got a girl in on work experience who wants to be a doctor—I'm going to get her to entertain him and find ways of making his life more interesting. It should help her make up her mind one way or the other.'

Adam chuckled, a low, sexy sound that unsettled her, and she shifted her position on the bed and wished he was there with her.

They talked for nearly another hour, saying nothing much, just enjoying the sound of each other's voices, and then finally he sighed. 'I have to go. I can hear one of the boys up. I'll see you tomorrow. Think of me while you curl up all alone in your bed.'

Hah! As if she needed telling! She lay back against the pillows and sighed softly. Give him time, she said to herself for the millionth time. He'll come round. Josh said so.

Josh was an expert in persuasion. He'd moved his caravan onto Lissa's drive and camped outside her house when she'd been pregnant with their first baby. Eventually she'd surrendered. Maybe Adam would give in, too, if she waited long enough.

'Whose idea was this?' Adam asked himself, standing in the middle of the hall while his house was systematically stripped from floor to ceiling. The boys' room, Skye's room and the sitting room were all on the agenda, and the party seemed to have divided into three camps.

There were the sober, serious types, mostly talking shop and arguing about surgical techniques. They seemed to be in the sitting room, and from his position in the hall Adam began to wonder just how serious they were. They certainly weren't all that sober as the party wore on, and he hardly dared go in there.

Upstairs, the women had split up and taken some of the children each. The boys seemed to be in the boys' room, and the girls in Skye's. Anna was with Skye, and Allie was in there keeping her company and helping. Lissa and Sarah were in the boys' room, and they had by far the hardest job, Adam could tell.

He stuck his head round the door and winced. All the boys' things were piled in the middle of the room, and all round the sides the wallpaper was yielding to their endeavours—except that they were all short, and so the paper was only off on the bottom half.

'I thought you were good at this?' he said to Lissa with a grin.

'I am—I'm wonderful! Look behind the door.'

He looked, and found the wall clear. 'Fantastic!' he murmured. 'I'm amazed. So much order out of so much chaos!'

'Of course. Ben, stop that, please! Sorry, he's getting a bit hyper.'

'Maybe it's time for a break,' Adam suggested, mindful of the ordered-in pizza keeping hot in the oven. Afterwards, he was to wonder about his choice of words, but at the time it seemed logical.

'Right, everyone, downstairs,' Lissa ordered, and they whooped and skidded towards the door.

'Hey, steady, chaps,' Adam said, but he was ignored. Pizza was way up the list, long before listening to adults.

There was a crush, of course, and Ben and Danny got in a race. It probably would have been fine if Ben hadn't slipped on a bit of sticky paper on his shoe at the top of the stairs, but he did, and in horror they watched as he tumbled over and fell headlong. Then, suddenly, halfway down there was a cracking noise and he halted abruptly and screamed.

They all froze, and then Lissa's hands flew to her face and she started to shake. 'Oh, my God,' she whispered, and Adam pushed past her.

'It's OK, Ben,' he said, and went carefully down to the boy's level. Ben's arm was through the banisters and, needless to say, it was broken. He was sobbing now, and behind him Adam heard the sitting-room door open.

'What is it?'

'Ben—he's fallen downstairs and hurt his arm. He's all right, aren't you, sport? Let's get you out of here. Josh, can you give me a hand?'

'Sure. OK, little one, don't worry, Daddy's here.' He looked at Adam, his face ashen. 'What do you want me to do?'

'Just lift him up a little so I can get the arm through. He's broken the spindle—I can probably bend it out of the way. That might help.'

Seconds later the sobbing child was free, and Lissa was rushing down the stairs with tears in her eyes. 'Are you all right, darling? I'm here. Don't worry, it's all right.'

'It's a classic greenstick,' Adam said quietly. 'It'll need pulling out under anaesthetic and plastering, and I think he'll be fine. Can you feel all your fingers, Ben? Wiggle them for me.'

He wiggled them and nodded tearfully. 'It hurts.'

'I'm sure it does, Ben. I'm sorry. Well, you're going to have to go to hospital and be sorted out. Think you can cope with that?'

He nodded, and Adam looked up the stairs at Anna, who was holding Jasper by the hand. Damn Helle for leaving so suddenly, he thought. Still, she'd offered… 'Anna, I hate to do this to you, but could you watch them for me until I get back? Give everyone pizza and ice cream, and then—'

'Don't worry, we'll manage,' Anna said. 'You take Ben, and we'll sort out the rest.'

Well, they'd done it. They'd given everyone pizza, and then while the children ate ice cream and watched television in the breakfast room, the women organised a clear-up, gathering up bin bags of paper and mopping down floors, and the men moved the furniture back into position.

Matt and Sarah took their children home, and Allie and Mark left once they were sure everything was cleared up.

'Right, how about you three? Shall we see what your rooms look like?' Anna suggested.

'Messy,' Skye said heavily. 'I thought it would make it nice.'

'It will be nice,' Anna assured her. 'We've taken off most of the paper—a little bit longer and all the rest will be off, then you can have what you want on the walls. Have you decided?'

'No.'

A dismissal? Anna thought so, but it was hard to tell. Sometimes she wondered if Skye didn't dare express an opinion in case it was the wrong one. Was she so desperate for approval that she'd daren't hold a different view to anyone else?

Poor little mite, she thought.

'Still, at least the bed's made. Boys, what about your beds? Are they ready to get into?'

'Dunno.'

She followed them in and found their room similarly restored. Someone had been busy while she'd sat with the youngsters in the kitchen. She helped them change, wash and clean their teeth. Then she sent them to the loo and tucked them all up in bed.

Skye turned away when she went to kiss her, but Anna kissed her anyway, because she knew the child needed spontaneous displays of affection. 'Sleep tight, poppet,' she said, and turned her light down.

'Not too dark!' Skye said in alarm, and Anna turned it up again.

'OK?'

'Thanks. 'Night, Anna.'

'Goodnight, Skye. Sleep well—and well done. You've worked very hard today.'

She went downstairs, past the spot where poor little Ben Lancaster had caught his arm, and into the kitchen. It, too, was clear now, and there was nothing to do but sit and wait.

She went into the sitting room, bare and damp and smelling of wallpaper paste and soggy lime plaster, and dropped into the nearest chair. She was bushed, but even so she tried to stay awake for Adam coming home.

He might be hours. She knew that, and wondered if she wouldn't do better to go to bed, but she didn't want to—not in his house, with his children there. It wouldn't seem right. She moved to the sofa, pulled a throw off the back of it over herself and snuggled down with a cushion. She'd be fine like this until he got back…

Adam was exhausted. He'd been on the go all day, and just when he'd thought he was winding down he ended up in Theatre with little Ben Lancaster.

It was a straightforward enough break, and it didn't really take very long, but even so he'd been gone some three hours by the time he admitted defeat and plated it for a good result. It was trying to rotate, so he'd had little choice, but now he was wiped out and he just wanted to crawl into bed and sleep.

With Anna.

He let himself into his house, and found Anna in the sitting room under the throw. She should have gone up to bed, he thought, and then wondered where. In the au pair's room, without any bed linen? Or the spare room, where he'd slept last weekend when his parents had stayed?

Or his bed.

What a tempting thought.

Oh, lord, he thought, it's getting too cosy. She's here all the time—all day last Sunday, all day today, now tonight—it was getting too close, too much. The children were beginning to be a pain about her, especially Danny, and he didn't know what to do about it except keep her away.

He woke her with a kiss, like a princess in a fairytale, and, like a fairytale princess, she opened her eyes and looked at him and smiled.

'Hi. How is he?'

'Plated and in for a couple of days. It was a bit nasty. He'll be fine. I'm sorry to be so long.'

'It's all right. You look shattered. I'll get out of your hair now.' She stood up, picked up her coat and bag, which were by the door, and went up on tiptoe to kiss him goodnight.

'See you tomorrow,' she promised.

'I might get a babysitter.'

'Do that. Not your mother. Her eyes are too sharp.'

Adam chuckled, kissed her again, more thoroughly this time, and thanked her for looking after the party.

Then he watched her go, watched her walk out to her car and get in it and drive away, and wondered how he could be so perverse.

He'd wanted her to go, hadn't he? So why, then, was he so irrationally disappointed when she did?

CHAPTER EIGHT

ANNA was on duty on the Sunday morning after Adam's party, and the first person she saw when she went in was Josh, sitting by Ben's bed and reading to him.

She went over to them and greeted them with a smile. 'Morning, all. How are things? How are you feeling, Ben?'

'It hurts,' he said fretfully.

Anna felt the tips of his fingers sticking out of the end of the cast. They were warm, not hot, and they wriggled when she touched them. Good.

His arm was in a special sling attached to the bed, the hand supported upright to minimise swelling, but it meant he couldn't fidget very easily and that was hard for a little boy, especially such an active one as Ben.

'He's all right,' Josh told her. 'He had a bit of a restless night. I stayed with him—Lissa's at home with Katie, stressing out. I've rung her a couple of times, but she doesn't believe he hasn't succumbed to the anaesthetic, I don't think.'

Anna smiled understandingly. 'Why don't you tell her to come in? She'll feel happier when she's seen him.'

'She's on her way. She wants to see the post-op X-rays—ah, here she is. Ben, Mummy's here.'

Anna turned to greet Lissa, and in the distance, just

coming onto the ward, she saw Adam with his three children in tow.

'It's a party,' she said with a smile, and waved at him.

The children waved back, all except Skye who looked around her worriedly and moved a step closer to Adam. Anna went over to them, leaving Lissa and Katie to talk to Ben and Josh in peace.

'Hi,' she said softly. 'Is this a social call, or are you working?'

'Bit of both. I thought I'd check up on him—how is he? I was a bit concerned about his circulation.'

'Seems good,' she told him. 'His fingers are nice and warm, and they're wriggling from time to time when he gets bored.'

'All the time, then, I should think, if Danny's anything to go by, eh, sport?'

'Is he going to be all right?' Skye asked, her eyes like saucers, studying the sling doubtfully.

'Yes,' Adam told her gently. 'He just needs time for the bones to join together again, then he'll have the little metal bits out that are holding them together at the moment, and he'll be as good as new.'

'Metal bits?' Danny asked, avidly interested.

Adam looked at Anna. 'Can we have the plates?'

'Sure.' She fetched the X-rays from the file trolley, and Adam snapped them into the light box on the wall near Ben's bed. 'Can you see, Ben? That's your arm, and here are the bones, and these white things are the little metal plates that hold the break together, and these little things are the screws. They'll come out in about four weeks, when you're better, and then you'll just have a cast on for the rest of the time.'

'Can I see the first ones again?' Josh asked, and Adam snapped the initial plates up onto the screen.

'Ow,' Lissa said under her breath, and Adam nodded.

'Ow, indeed. You can see why I had to operate—there's a distinct rotation here where he left his arm behind in the banisters and tried to keep on moving. In too much of a hurry for your pizza, weren't you, Ben? Never mind, I expect you can have some as soon as you get home.'

'Which will be when?' Josh asked.

Adam shrugged and pulled a thoughtful face. 'Couple of days? I'd like to get the swelling right down and get a proper cast on it, then he can get back to normal for a while.'

'He was lucky it wasn't a little further down towards his hand,' Josh said pensively, studying the plates. 'It would have hit the epiphysis and that would have been drastic.'

'What's the epiffy-thing?' Ben asked, looking from one to the other.

'The growth plate. There's a special place on each bone where it does its growing, and if you break it there it can stop growing properly. That doesn't matter when you're big, but when you're little it can be more of a problem,' Adam explained.

''Cos you'd end up with one short arm,' Danny said, his mind working visibly.

'That's right. There's a girl in here at the moment who did that to her leg, and it didn't grow, and now we're trying to make her leg grow longer with a special operation.'

'Did you do the operation?' Skye asked, speaking for the first time.

'Yes.'

'What's Jaz looking at?' Danny asked, and they looked round to see the little boy squatting under Damian, peering up through the cut-out in the Stryker bed at his face.

'That's Damian. He has to lie in a special bed at the moment. He gets very bored. I expect he'll be pleased to have someone to talk to. I take it the locks are all on it?'

'Oh, yes,' Anna assured him with a laugh. 'There's no way he can spin it round and dump Damian on the floor. Nevertheless, I think we might get him out from under it. Jaz, come here, sweetheart.'

He said goodbye to Damian, and came running over, throwing himself at Anna. She scooped him up into her arms with a laugh, swung him round and settled him on her hip, then looked up to see a steely expression on Adam's face.

'I'd better take these kids out of here,' he said tightly. 'Jasper, come on.'

Anna put him down and watched them as they left the ward, puzzled by their abrupt departure.

'Was it something I said?'

'God knows,' Josh murmured, moving to stand beside her. 'That man moves in mysterious ways. I think he panicked.'

'Panicked?'

'You're getting too close, Anna—hang in there. You're getting to him.'

'Oh, lord.' She tugged at her tabard, looked at her watch and straightened. 'Um, I have to go and get on. I've got to take report and get on with the day. I'll see you later.'

Too close, she thought, trying to ignore the hurt

Adam's abrupt departure had caused. How can I be too close? I love them, I love him, he loves me—how can we all *possibly* be too close?

Adam didn't come round that night, and she didn't see him until Monday afternoon, because she was on a late and he was in Theatre. He came round to do his post-op checks, though, looking harassed, and she confronted him.

'I thought you were coming round last night,' she said, trying not to sound accusing.

'I was—I'm sorry I didn't get to you, but Danny was sick and I didn't think it was fair to leave him with the babysitter.'

'You could have phoned.'

He nodded. 'I know. I'm sorry. I thought I'd finish stripping the sitting room and the night just got away from me. I didn't want to ring you at midnight.'

'I wouldn't have minded. I had a lie-in this morning.'

'Lucky you,' he said with a rueful smile. 'I didn't. The new nanny started today. I think she's going to be a disaster. I'd come round tonight but I need to be there. As if that wasn't bad enough, it's half-term week this week, and the kids are going to be at home all the time with her and I don't see it working.'

'Why don't I come to you?'

'No. I don't think that's a good idea. Not with the kids in the house. I might slide out if I can get away for a minute, but it will be a flying visit.'

Crumbs, Anna thought sadly. That's all he can spare—just the crumbs from his life.

He arrived at ten past ten, and his eyes showed the signs of his domestic strain.

'Problems?'

'Like you wouldn't believe,' he said, going into her arms with a sigh of relief. 'I'm sorry, this really is going to be a flying visit, but I just needed to see you, get a bit of sanity in my life.'

He eased away and tilted her chin, looking down into her eyes. He looks so unhappy and torn, Anna thought, and lifted a hand to caress his cheek. The stubble was rough against her palm, curiously erotic. She drew his head down for a kiss, and he took her mouth hungrily.

'How long can you stay?' she asked, and he laughed softly against her mouth.

'Long enough,' he murmured, and kissed her again.

He lied. It wasn't long enough. For ever wouldn't be long enough to give him all the love she had to give.

Ben made good progress, and went home on Tuesday morning, to his parents' relief. Lissa had found it very difficult to juggle Katie and Ben, and Josh had found it impossibly hard to see his patients and ignore Ben's pleas for attention every time he'd gone past his line of vision. They'd had to move Ben so that he hadn't been able to see his father so easily, and then Ben had got upset because Josh had been out of sight.

When Lissa took Ben home, Josh kissed him goodbye and watched them go with a sigh of relief.

'Thank God for that—now I can get on with my work without feeling guilty,' he said to Anna with a smile. He searched her face and the smile faded. 'How are things?'

She shrugged. 'Much the same. I don't know how long I can go on like this, Josh. I feel like a hamster in a cage, and he gets me out when he wants to play with me.'

'I think that's a bit harsh,' Josh said gently. 'He does have problems, Anna. Those kids need a lot of time and attention. Skye, especially, needs a lot of one-to-one.'

'She needs a mother,' Anna said tightly.

'She's had two already. Perhaps what she needs is just what Adam's giving her—stability and security. I hate to say it, but I wonder if I was wrong. I don't think it's right for Adam, but it might well be right for the children, and perhaps he's just about strong enough to do it—to make that sacrifice for the kids. In which case, Anna, you're going to get very badly hurt.'

'I know,' she said softly, her voice rough with tears. 'I don't agree about Skye, but I think you're right about Adam, and I think he's capable of hurting both of us if he feels it's what he has to do. Only time will tell.'

The phone rang, and she excused herself to answer it, then snapped into action. 'OK. Thank you. We'll start getting ready. We've got a few beds—not many. I'll see if I can mobilise a few discharges or cancel any operations. Thanks for letting me know.'

She looked up at Josh. 'A school bus has overturned. There are lots of orthopaedic injuries and some head injuries. They'll be coming in to A and E shortly. Can you clear any of your patients?'

He ran an eye over the ward. 'I don't know. You might want to contact Adam, see if he's got anyone that can go. I'll have a flick through the notes and think about it.'

She rang Adam in the outpatients clinic, and he

groaned. 'I've got a full clinic this morning—I'll have to leave them and go over to A and E to assess the kids as they come in. Damn. And that means I'll be home late, and the new nanny has to leave at six.'

'Do you want me to go round there?'

'No—I'll contact my mother. If I can't get hold of her, I might ask you. Thanks. As for the beds, I haven't got anyone I can transfer or discharge—unless we send Kate home. She's getting on all right with her leg and it's healed well. I was sending her home tomorrow, but she could go today. Go and talk to her mother, see what she says.'

'OK. I'll speak to you later.'

She found Allie, started her off on shuffling patients to get the spare beds all grouped together, and found Mrs Funnell and Kate. 'We've got a problem,' she told them. 'We need all the beds we can lay our hands on, and Mr Bradbury was going to suggest that Kate went home tomorrow. He thinks, in fact, she could go home today, if you feel you can cope and you're ready for it. Of course, you can always ring up or come in for advice. How do you feel?'

'I'd love to go home,' Kate confessed. 'I'm so bored in here. I want to go back to school.'

'Well, that might be a bit quick but you should be able to manage at home all right, I think. Do you need to ring anyone?'

'My car's here,' Mrs Funnell said. 'I can take her straight away.'

'Well, I think Mr Bradbury will come up and see you first—oh, here he is now.'

Their eyes met and they shared a brief but intimate smile. 'Kate's keen,' she said, and he grinned at the girl.

'How did I guess?' Adam looked at her leg, and nodded. 'You'll be fine,' he told her. 'Go home and enjoy yourself. Not too much weight-bearing, and you'll have to come back every day for physio, but you should be all right now. I'm sorry to hustle you, but I don't think you mind too much, do you?'

Kate grinned. 'Absolutely not. It's brilliant.'

He chuckled, winked at Anna as he turned away and then strode off, presumably to A and E. The phone rang again, and Anna left another nurse sorting out Kate's discharge notes and went to get the phone.

'Right,' she said, gathering them all together. 'First one's coming into A and E now. Make sure every-thing else that needs doing gets done. I'll deal with the new admissions. Allie, I want you to take over the running of the rest of the ward for now, please. Make sure nothing falls down the cracks. I don't want drugs forgotten and treatment neglected just because we're going to be rushed off our feet. And don't for-get to smile at the children. They'll be scared, they'll be hurting. Their parents will be panic-stricken. Be calm and be kind, and keep your eyes open for any-thing that's been missed. Right, off you go.'

Adam went into A and E, looked around and found a cluster of doctors around Patrick Haddon, one of the A and E consultants. 'Right, we've got three or-thopaedic teams on standby, including Adam Bradbury— Hello, Adam, come and join us. You know Robert Ryder, don't you, and his registrar David Patterson? You'll be the three teams. I want you to work together on the orthopaedic cases, prior-itising and allocating them to your teams according to your areas of expertise. I know we've got one pelvic fracture coming in, and possibly others. There may be spinal injuries. Neuro are standing by for those, but I gather your Stryker bed is in use at the moment, Adam?'

'Yes, it is, but he's virtually ready to come off it. I could free it if it was absolutely necessary.'

'OK. We'll see. Lots of arms and legs, I expect. That's normal. There are internal injuries, of course— Nick, you're in charge of those. I want everyone triaged, stabilised, X-rayed and sorted as fast as possible—just don't miss anything in your hurry. Right, I can hear a siren—I think we're in business.'

It was chaotic, but they were so busy there wasn't time to notice. The pelvic fracture was nasty and needed external fixation, and Adam, scanning the plates of the other children who had been processed, decided he ought to take the pelvis. He was just about to pull the plates off the light box when he noticed a tiny, almost invisible little line across one of the vertebrae.

'I want another view of this,' he said to the radiographer. 'Very, very carefully. It looks like a very unstable fracture. Don't shuffle him about.'

'OK. What view do you want?'

'Lateral, please—and oblique. Might pick up more.'

He was right. It was a fracture through the vertebral body of the fourth lumbar vertebra, and the lateral view showed a segment of bone poised to slice into the spinal cord.

'That will need fixing,' he said to Robert Ryder. 'I want a CT scan before I do anything, and he needs to stay on the spinal board. He'll need blood cross-matched. Those pelvic fractures will be bleeding heavily into the tissues.'

'You'll have to fight the neuros for the scanner. They've got a couple of head injuries.'

'We can wait for them. I need to do a couple of others first, I think. He's not that urgent, he's just critical. What else have we got?'

They scanned through the notes, went round and saw the injuries at first hand and then they started in earnest.

Adam's first case was a nasty fracture of the hand and arm, and he worked for two hours to restore the circulation and realign the bones to his satisfaction. That case was followed by his pelvic and spinal fracture patient. After studying the CT scan, he decided how to tackle the vertebral body and went in carefully through the abdomen, meaning to tackle the bone from in front of the cord.

'Pressure's crashing,' the anaesthetist warned. 'Have you got a bleed there?'

'I reckon. Whoops,' he said as they opened the abdomen. 'I think we have a major leak. Can we have four units in here fast, please? This kid's going to bleed to death. Where the hell is it coming from? Can I have some more suction? Thank you.'

It was a race against time, but finally he found the leak, a vessel that had been ruptured by the end of one of the pelvic bones. Once it was stopped, they could begin to work on the patient again, and Adam focused on him and forgot about everything else.

There was no time to worry about the patients that were waiting, or the nanny his children hated, or whether his mother would get the answerphone message.

* * *

Anna stayed on after the end of her shift, checking head injury cases every few minutes for change in status, monitoring possible internal injuries, providing post-op care to the minor orthopaedic cases that came back from Theatre.

She gathered that there was a boy with a spinal fracture that Adam was fixing, who also had a severely broken pelvis. She wondered how on earth they were going to nurse him, and then Adam appeared, rubbing his eyes and flexing his shoulders.

'You look bushed.'

'I am bushed—what are you still doing here?'

'Helping out. They're rushed off their feet, I could hardly go. Have you spoken to your mother yet?'

'No—I'm going to do that now. I'll ring home and see if there's been blood-letting. What have you got for me, or are they still down in A and E?'

'Two fractures—an arm and a leg. Displaced fracture of the olecranon, and a femur. Simple fracture.'

'Brilliant,' he said, rolling his eyes. 'I hate elbows. OK. I'll do the femur first. Keep the elbow still and give pain relief—is it written up?'

'I believe so. She's crying.'

'I'm sure she is. If I'd yanked off the end of my funny bone, I reckon I'd be crying.'

He disappeared into the office and came out a minute later looking ragged. 'My mother's there. The nanny's gone. She's sacked her. She smacked Jasper this morning because he was crying. Mum's reported her to the agency. What the hell do I do now?'

'Your femur and your elbow. Your mother is quite capable. Don't worry.'

'And what about tomorrow?'

'Bring them in. They can sit here and watch telly

and do drawings and play with the others. It won't be a problem. Go and operate.'

Adam flashed her a weary smile and headed off towards the corridor. Anna carried on with her post-op and pre-op care, checking drips, calming parents, and it was hours before the ward settled to something approaching normality.

She went home, ate a sandwich in the bath and crawled into bed. She was just dropping off to sleep when the phone rang, and she stretched out an arm and grabbed the receiver.

'Hello?'

'Hi.'

Her heart did its usual jig, and a smile curved her lips. She settled down with a contented sigh. 'Hi. How was it all in the end? Done your elbow to your satisfaction?'

'Yup. Done it all. I'm home, finally.'

'How are the kids?'

'Asleep. I'm going to ring the agency in the morning and give them hell. I've bribed my parents to stay until the weekend, but they go to Florida on Tuesday. That gives me not quite a week to sort something out.' He sighed. 'Do you know, I can quite see why women don't make it up the career ladder. It would be so much easier if I were self-employed or had a less pressured job.'

She could have told him the answer, but he didn't want to hear it, and she was sick of throwing herself against that particular brick wall. 'Have a bath and go to bed,' she told him.

'I'm in the bath,' Adam said. 'With the cordless phone and a glass of wine. Bliss.'

'I'm in bed,' she said softly.

She heard his indrawn breath, and smiled.

'Did I wake you?'

'Not really. I don't mind, anyway. It's nice to talk to you.'

'I wish I was there with you,' he said softly. 'I could do with a hug.'

'Only a hug?' she asked, and he gave a low chuckle.

'OK. I confess.'

'I wish you were here, too,' she admitted. 'I never used to mind sleeping alone.'

'Close your eyes and pretend I'm there.' Her lids drifted shut, powerless to resist, and he carried on talking, driving her crazy with his soft, hypnotic voice. 'Imagine I'm touching you, running my hands over you, feeling your skin burn against my palms. Imagine my body—'

'Adam?'

There was a startled grunt, followed by a splash and a muttered curse.

Anna's eyes flew open, and she started to laugh. 'Is that your mother?'

'Yes—I'm on the phone,' he said through the door.

'Oh. Right. I've made tea.'

'Thanks.'

She heard the footsteps retreating, and the sound of his muffled laughter. 'I could kill her. I nearly dropped the phone in the bath.'

'She's lovely.'

'She's everywhere.' He sighed, and lowered his voice. 'I want you.'

She swallowed. 'I know. Why don't you sneak out? Tell her you need to buy milk or something, or you need a walk.'

'I could tell her I need to come and see you. She'd love it. She hasn't stopped talking about you since the day after the ball.'

'So why don't you?' she asked softly, but she knew he wouldn't.

He gave a quiet sigh, and for a moment he was silent. When he spoke, she could tell he was back to reality, back to his responsibilities and duties. 'No. I'll see you tomorrow. Are you on early?'

'No, I'm on a late.'

'Fancy a wake-up call?'

'Adam!'

'What? Oh, damn. Yes, Mum, I'm coming!' He sighed again and gave a lazy, sexy chuckle. 'I wish. I'll see you tomorrow. Sleep tight.'

'What on earth?'

Anna slid her legs over the side of the bed, grabbed her dressing-gown and ran downstairs, shoving her hair out of her eyes with one hand as she fumbled for the door.

'Breakfast,' Adam said, pushing the door shut and pulling her into his arms.

She laughed and looked up at him through bleary eyes. 'You're crazy. I was asleep—it's only half past six!'

'I'm sorry.' He cupped her chin, his thumb absently caressing her cheek. 'I missed you last night. That phone conversation did nothing for my sleep patterns.'

'I'm sure. I had some pretty colourful dreams myself.' She ran her tongue over her teeth and pulled a face. 'I need five minutes in the bathroom. Put the kettle on, there's a love.'

She ran upstairs, showered rapidly and cleaned her teeth, then came out to find Adam naked in her bed with a tray of fresh, steaming tea and a plate of chocolate-filled croissants on his lap.

He patted the mattress beside him. 'Breakfast in bed,' he said with a slow smile, and her heart thumped.

'Sounds good.'

'It will be,' he promised, and moved the tray out of the way. 'You can eat later. That's dessert.'

Anna had a silly smile on her face all day. Adam had only been there an hour, but it had been the most wonderful hour of her life to date. The memory carried her through a difficult shift, with every bed full and many of their little patients in quite critical condition.

The boy with the fractured spine and pelvis was being nursed flat in a bed with a special mattress, because he couldn't be turned due to the external fixator on his pelvis. He was catheterised because of bruising to his bladder nerves, and his legs were tingly and funny, he said, but all in all he'd escaped lightly.

Adam had been to see them all and was satisfied with their progress. He was wonderful with the parents, Anna thought, watching him in action. He explained just enough, so that they didn't feel patronised and yet understood what he'd had to do and why.

It was a skill a lot of doctors didn't have, Anna knew, but it didn't surprise her that Adam had it. He seemed to have a natural ability to communicate, and a real empathy for the parents.

Little Emily Parker with her brittle bone disease

was the only one he was really concerned about, and yet she was making progress. It was just slower than he'd hoped, and he was concerned about her chest.

'It's very compromised,' he murmured. 'Those ribs are a very funny shape. There's no way she can be getting any real movement through them, so all her breathing's abdominal.'

'The prognosis is pretty awful, isn't it?' Anna said thoughtfully.

'I would say she's on a knife edge,' Adam admitted. 'I don't know what will get her in the end—a cough, probably. She'll end up with fluid on her lungs and drown. Just keep her away from anyone with a cold.'

It wasn't possible. On Thursday she started coughing, and on Friday morning, when Anna went in, her bed was empty.

'Where's Emily gone?' she asked the night sister, a dreadful suspicion forming in her mind.

'Ah. We lost her at three o'clock this morning. She got pneumonia. Her lungs filled, and then she arrested. Adam tried to resuscitate her but he couldn't get her back. He was gutted.'

Anna sat down with a bump. 'Oh, damn,' she said heavily. She thought of the gutsy little girl with her terribly deformed bones, and her dedicated mother who had spent most of the past six years protecting the fragile child from the world. And now she was gone, wiped out, taken by some trivial and inconsequential cold.

'It was inevitable,' the night sister said pragmatically. 'It was bound to happen, Anna.'

'I know,' she said, but that didn't stop it getting to her. After she'd taken report, she went into the kitchen, howled, blew her nose, washed her face and got out her rescue kit. That was where Adam found her, dabbing concealer under her eyes. She looked at him in the mirror then put it down and turned and took him in her arms.

'I'm sorry, love,' Anna said tenderly, and he hugged her hard. She could feel the tension in him, feel the pain still looking for a way out.

'Come and see me tonight,' she said, and he nodded.

'I will.' He moved out of her arms and slumped against the edge of the worktop with a harsh sigh. 'How many patients have I lost? How many times have I gone through this process? You'd think I'd get used to it.'

'I'm glad you haven't. I think it makes you a better doctor.'

Adam gave her a crooked smile. 'I don't know about that, but I think it makes me a better parent. I went home and stood in Skye's room and looked at her, and wondered how I'd feel if it had been her. They were the same sort of age—Emily was a little older, although you would never have known that from looking at her.'

He looked down at his hands, hands that had failed, and sighed again. 'I know it had to happen, I know it was a blessing in disguise, I know she'd suffered terribly in her life and was lucky to have survived so long. It still hurts.'

'I know. Want to borrow my lipstick? It works for me.'

He laughed softly and hugged her again. 'You're a treasure. I'll see you tonight, if not before. I might even come clean with my mother and spend the evening with you. How would that be?'

'Lovely,' she said, and wondered what it was really like to be a hamster in a cage and be taken out occasionally for the odd run around before being put back again.

She stopped her train of thought there. Adam was stressed enough, torn in all directions, and it wouldn't help at all if she was sulking because he couldn't tear himself into even more bits. He needed her. That was all that mattered at the moment.

He needed her, and she loved him. There was nothing more to say.

CHAPTER NINE

ADAM took Anna to a quiet country pub, where they sat in the corner by a log fire, and he dropped his head back against the wall and sighed. He was tired—tired, and sad, and worried about the children.

'What a day,' he mumbled.

'How are the kids?' she asked, zooming in on his main concern with her usual accuracy.

He shut his eyes and groaned. 'Don't. I still don't have a nanny sorted out. I rang the agency and told them what I thought of them, so that takes care of them as a source of child care.'

'Oops. Bit firm, were you?'

He met her eyes and dredged up a laugh. 'Just a bit. Put it like this, I don't think they're in any doubt about my feelings. Then I tried the au pair agency again and they've promised me someone, but they can't do anything for at least a fortnight, and my parents are going to Florida in three days' time.'

He picked up his beermat and shredded it absently. 'What do I do, Anna?' he asked with studied calm. 'Do I give up work?'

'Don't be silly!' she exclaimed. 'You can't—you're too valuable. What would your patients do without you? Your gifts are too great to be wasted, Adam. You have to work.'

Strange, how her words warmed him and made him feel better. Some things, though, couldn't be made better. 'I lost Emily,' he said.

'You didn't lose her, Adam,' she pointed out gently. 'She was already lost when she was born. Taking responsibility for that is assuming too much. You simply aren't that omnipotent. Leave that sort of thing with God, where it belongs.'

'I could be a carpenter,' he suggested, and Anna had a feeling he was only half joking.

'I doubt if you're good enough. Wood doesn't heal.'

He suppressed a smile. 'Are you insinuating that my carpentry skills aren't up to scratch?' he said indignantly. 'Damn cheek.'

'I'm sure they're wonderful. It doesn't help your problem, though. You need a solution in three days,' she reminded him, 'and carpentry isn't it.'

Adam sighed and rammed a hand through his hair, leaving it rumpled. 'So what do you suggest?' he asked. 'The hospital crèche is too crowded to take them and, anyway, they need to get to and from school. Besides, that doesn't solve the problem of what I do at night when I'm on call. I need live-in help. I can't get the kids up in the middle of the night and bring them with me every time.'

'I could stay with you,' she suggested.

He was tempted—very tempted—but not because it solved anything. 'How does that help?' he asked sceptically. 'You go to work as well.'

'And they're at school. I work from seven to three by choice. That means if they come to work with you at eight or thereabouts, they could get a taxi to school from the hospital, and I could pick them up at the end of the day. You could get home whenever you get home, I'll be there at night when you're on call, and there'd be the added bonus that we'd see each other every evening.'

They would indeed. He looked at her thoughtfully. 'You really mean it, don't you?' he said in quiet amazement. 'You'd do it.'

She rolled her eyes. 'Well, of course I mean it! Why would I not?'

Adam searched her eyes for an age, then looked away, shaking his head. He could get addicted to her presence, and so could the kids. 'No. It's not a good idea.'

'Have you got a better one?'

'No,' he told her honestly. 'No, I haven't.' He thought of the children growing dependent on her, and asked himself how much difference two short weeks could make. Surely they wouldn't get addicted that fast? 'It's only very temporary, I suppose,' he said thoughtfully. 'Just until the new au pair comes in a fortnight.'

'Was that a yes?' Anna asked.

He shrugged. 'I don't see I've got a choice,' he said heavily. He knew he wasn't being very gracious, but the thought of Anna there all the time was so tempting he thought it was clouding his judgement, and he was busy looking for the pitfalls. 'It's not ideal, but it solves nearly every problem. Can you switch your rota for the next two weeks so you're on earlies?'

She laughed softly. 'I can do what I like with the darned rota. It's my responsibility. I devise it. Certainly I can change it.'

'I might have to take you up on your offer, then,' he said with a smile, and she held out her hand.

'Done,' she said, as he shook it, and he felt a huge burden lifting off his shoulders.

Whatever the drawbacks, however foolish it might be, at least he would know his children were safe, and that had to be the most important thing.

He lifted her hand to his lips and kissed her palm. 'You're a wonderful woman, do you know that?' he said quietly, and soft colour brushed her cheeks.

'I just want to be able to get my hands on you day and night,' Anna said, laughing dismissively, and he thought of the nights, when the children were asleep, and the hot rush of desire nearly choked him.

Adam swallowed hard and picked up his glass, draining it. 'Another one?' he asked. 'Or do you want to wait and have wine with our meal?'

'You're driving.'

'I'm always driving. I don't need to drink. What about you?'

'Neither do I. Spring water would be fine, thanks.'

She handed him her glass and smiled up at him, and he wondered how he was going to survive having her at home.

No. That would be easy. The hard bit would be letting her go, and it suddenly dawned on him that he might have made a dreadful mistake.

Anna moved in on Sunday evening, to the children's great delight and excitement. She brought with her only the clothes that she'd need and the food left in the fridge, because her house was only a mile or so away and she could pop back for anything else, so 'moving in' was a bit of an exaggeration, but the children thought it was great fun.

They helped carry her case and bag up to the attic,

and Skye put her wash things out in the shower room while Jasper passed her the underwear from her little bag and Danny struggled to put her blouses on hangers.

She gave him a hand once the underwear had been put away in the chest of drawers, and then there was a knock on the door and Adam appeared with a tray of tea, juice and biscuits. The children swooped on them instantly.

'I thought refreshments might be in order, but you'll need to be quick,' he said, and she met his eyes over the children's heads and smiled.

'Thanks. Forget the biscuits, but I'm gasping for a cup of tea.' He handed her a mug and she cupped her hands round it, sipping gratefully. 'Mmm. Wonderful. Just what I needed.' She looked around her and sighed softly. 'This is a lovely room. I'm going to like staying here,' she said in contentment.

'Have you got everything you need?'

Everything, she thought. Him, the children...

'I'm sure I have. If not I can ask, can't I, kids? You'll help me.'

'You've got loo paper and soap—I checked,' Skye told her soberly.

'Thank you, darling. That's kind.'

'I helped Daddy make the bed,' Danny said proudly. 'He gave you his quilt cover!'

Adam laughed a little awkwardly. 'It's the only one without rips, I think. Our washing line at the other house was a bit near the fence, and there was a nail sticking out of it that used to catch the clothes. I keep meaning to go shopping, but I suppose I might as well wait and get something that goes with whatever we do to the rooms.'

'That makes sense.'

Anna smoothed her hand lightly over the fabric. His quilt cover. That would destroy any chance she might have had to sleep! 'It's very kind of you to be so considerate,' she said, rather touched that all of them seemed to have gone to so much trouble over her visit.

'I polished the table,' Jasper said in satisfaction. 'See.'

She did. She saw shiny places, and places with dust on, and little fingerprints all over most of it. 'It's lovely,' she said with a lump in her throat. 'Thank you, Jaz. Thank you, all of you.'

'Right, you lot, downstairs and get ready for bed. I'll come down and see you in a minute.'

They trailed off, grumbling gently, and Adam pushed the door to and sat down sideways on the bed next to her, one knee hitched up. 'Are you sure you've got all you need?' he asked again, and she nodded.

'Sure. Do you want me to get the children ready for bed now?'

He looked faintly startled. 'Good grief, no!'

'No? So what do you want me for?' she asked curiously, and he gave a strangled laugh.

'Apart from the obvious?'

Warm colour slid up her throat and touched her cheeks, and he leant forward and brushed her lips with his.

'Apart from the obvious,' she echoed, her heart pattering in her chest.

He shrugged. 'Just the end of the day, like we said. If you just pick them up from school and bring them home and make sure they're safe, that's all I need. I don't expect you to do anything except act as a safety net. You might want to cook the odd meal, but even that I'm not bothered about.'

Adam reached out a hand and cupped her cheek, and she turned her face into his hand and kissed it lingeringly.

'It's good to have you here,' he said gruffly. 'Thank you, Anna. It's a huge weight off my mind. The children's safety and happiness are so important to me— I feel so responsible for them.'

'I know you do. Does anyone ever tell you what a good father you are to your children?'

He looked away, a wry and slightly self-conscious smile quirking his lips. 'Not often, but it's not why I do it, so I don't need the accolades. I just do my best. Sometimes it's not enough, but most of the time we get by.'

'They're lucky to have you.'

His mouth tightened. 'Not as lucky as they thought they were going to be. It's difficult sometimes, being alone, but it beats being held to ransom.'

He stood up and retrieved the tray from the floor, gathered up the mugs and glasses and headed for the door. 'I'll see you later. Come on down when you're ready for some company.'

It was odd, Anna thought, watching the empty doorway. She didn't know where she stood with him while she was in this role. Normally she would have gone downstairs and made herself at home with him, but tonight she felt a little shy and awkward, as if she should be staying in her room like the hired help.

It was absurd. She knew it was absurd, and yet she felt as if she didn't belong, and she realised why Helle had been homesick. It would be so easy to feel you had to stay up here out of his way.

'Anna, what time do you want to eat?'

She went out onto the landing and hung over the banisters. Adam was standing at the top of the first flight of stairs, looking up at her, and she felt suddenly silly for her reticence. Of course he expected her to join him!

'Whenever,' she said. 'Do you want me to cook it?'

He shook his head. 'I was going to get a take-away. I've fed the children—I thought we could have a Chinese or Indian.'

'Sounds good.'

Blow the unpacking, she thought. A few pairs of trousers and jeans weren't going to come to any harm. She ran downstairs in her socks and joined him in the kitchen.

'Have a look at the menu,' he said, and they haggled over what they wanted and then later stole each other's choices anyway. And then it was time for bed and suddenly she really *didn't* know what he expected of her.

With the children in the house, she felt it would hardly be appropriate as their relationship stood for her to sleep openly with him. On the other hand, she wasn't sure if sneaking around and being deceitful was actually any better.

'I'll see you to your door,' he said in an undertone as she paused at the bottom of the attic stairs. His mouth tipped in a sexy smile. 'It's only courteous.'

'Of course,' she agreed with an answering smile, and tiptoed up so as to not disturb the children.

Once up there, he ushered her into her room, closed

the door and leant back against it, drawing her into his arms.

'I've been wanting to kiss you for hours,' he confessed, and, threading his hands through her hair, he scattered kisses over her brow and lids and cheekbones, over the plane of her jaw, down over the sensitive skin of her throat.

'Adam,' she whispered urgently, and he lifted his head and found her mouth, answering her plea. Her hands settled on his chest, feeling the solid warmth of his body so near—

'Daddy?'

He dragged his mouth from hers, his breathing ragged. 'Yes, darling,' he called through the door. 'I'm upstairs. I'm coming down now.' He kissed Anna again, just briefly, and gave a rueful wink. 'Sleep well, sweetheart. I'll see you in the morning.'

He went out, closing the door softly behind him, and she went to bed alone but happy. Adam was near, very near, and he seemed to be mellowing.

For the first time since he'd told her they were going nowhere, she felt a glimmer of hope. Cherishing it, she fell asleep and didn't wake until he called her in the morning.

That Monday Adam took Damian back down to Theatre and completed the surgery to his spine that would hold it in the final position, and then he removed the halo from his skull and the lower half of the frame from his pelvis.

Damian was now as straight as he could be made, and he needed mobilisation and physiotherapy to get him back onto his feet. Adam wondered how much taller he would be. Typically, it was a couple of centimetres, but Damian had been more distorted than most and the gain might be more.

Whatever, he was sure the boy would appreciate having his mobility restored and being shot of the restrictive Stryker bed and halo traction. He'd be able to turn his head, and look around, and sit, and walk with help—a great change from the immobility of the last three weeks.

His bed was next to that of Richard Lewis, the boy with the fractured pelvis and spine, who had regained sensation rapidly following the accident and would make a complete recovery.

In the meantime, Richard had to lie still, and Damian could spend some time with him and entertain him. Adam was sure Anna would find a way of bringing them together usefully.

She was wonderful with the kids, Adam thought. She managed them all so well—the sick, the crotchety, the bored. She kept them cheerful, yet disciplined and under control. She was a natural with them, and with his own, and he thought again that she would be the most wonderful mother.

The thought brought a pain he'd thought he'd forgotten, with an intensity he didn't remember.

He wanted to see her swollen with his child.

It took his breath away, the pain. He dragged in some air, and tipped his head back, rolling his shoulders and flexing them.

'You all right, Adam?' the anaesthetist asked.

'Yes—just a bit stiff. I need to move around for a minute. Perhaps you could close?' he said to his registrar, and, stripping off his gloves, he left the operating room and went out into the corridor, resting his head back against the cool wall and closing his eyes.

Damn. He'd thought he was over it, thought he'd come to terms with it, and in many ways he had, but there was something basic and primitive in him that needed to pass on his genes. He understood, he could rationalise it to death, but it didn't make it any easier.

He wanted to give Anna a child, and he couldn't.

And because he couldn't, she'd leave him. Maybe not now, maybe not for years, but she was only twenty-eight. What about when she was thirty-eight? When the sands of time had run away for another ten years, what then? Would she feel the pressure of that last trickle of sand in the egg-timer?

When had she become so important to him? When had he allowed her so close that she'd sneaked up inside him and become a part of him?

Two weeks, he told himself. In two weeks the new au pair would come, and Anna would move out. And then, Adam told himself, he'd stop seeing her. Stop going round to her house and making love to her in her beautiful candle-lit bedroom, stop flirting with her and teasing her and kissing her every chance he got.

It was unfair to her to trap her, to use her, to keep her on a string for his own benefit, no matter how much he needed her. He had to sever the link, cut her off, let her go for her own sake. He had to be cruel to be kind.

He swallowed the lump in his throat, and shrugged away from the wall. His registrar wasn't good enough to sew up Damian's incision. It had been reopened, and it was harder to make a neat job under those circumstances. He owed it to Damian to do the best job he could.

He scrubbed again, donned new gown and gloves and went back into the operating room.

*   *   *

Adam was busy that week with emergencies, and so Anna hardly saw Adam on the ward. Damian was mobile at last, and loving every minute of it, and although he was still in a certain amount of pain, the freedom more than made up for it.

Richard, the boy with the spinal and pelvic injuries, was the same age, and they struck up a friendship which Anna encouraged. Adam, on one of his flying visits to the ward, remarked on it to her.

'It's good for Damian, too,' Anna said thoughtfully. 'He was entertained by the others when he was trapped, and I think he realises it's a chance to give back some of what was given to him. Hopefully he won't get bored before Richard's a bit more mobile.'

'Mmm. I want to keep him pretty still for a while longer. That spinal fracture was pretty unstable and I know I've wired it together, but it may not be adequate if he does too much too soon. It does need time to heal. We'll give him another week and then I'll get it scanned again and see how much it's healed. That's one thing about kids—they do heal incredibly fast.'

'How's Ben Lancaster, by the way?' she asked. 'Have you seen him again?'

'Yes, Lissa brought him in yesterday to have the stitches out and a new cast. It's looking good. He'll have the plates out in another couple of weeks and he'll be fine. I'm pleased. The arm's nice and straight, which is a miracle when you think how bent and twisted it was when he fell. I must mend that banister, by the way. Remind me to glue it tonight.'

'Write it on your hand,' she suggested with a smile, and he laughed.

'That'll look good in my clinic! I'll just rely on

your wonderful memory,' he said, and then checked his watch and sighed. 'I have to go, talking of clinics. I've had a couple of patients added onto the beginning of the list that I thought I should see urgently. One's a knee following a ski injury. The GP's written "IDK" on the letter. I'm not sure if that means "internal destruction of the knee" or "I don't know"—could be either!

'The other's a baby with bilateral CDH. I may have to operate on her hips pretty soon, if the letter from her new GP is anything to go by. Apparently, it's been missed until now, and speed is of the essence with these congenital dislocations.'

'Will you do both cases tomorrow?' Anna asked, and he shrugged.

'I don't know. How are we for beds? Most of the school bus kids have gone—have we got any capacity? I've got three others booked already.'

She ran a mental eye over the ward, thinking of the tonsils, grommets and appendectomies that would be going home. 'A little. An extra two would fit, if we don't have a rash of emergencies. It might change by tomorrow, of course.'

'I'll check. I'll book them provisionally if I think they need it. The ski knee will be quick, I suspect, probably an arthroscopy. The baby might take longer. I'll keep you posted.'

After Adam had gone she checked the list of patients again to make sure she'd got beds available, and when he rang from the clinic at ten to three she confirmed that, emergencies permitting, they would have room for his extra two cases.

'Good. I've told them I'll ring them in the morning if I can't do it. They're coming in at eight, starved and ready to prep—I thought that was better than having them overnight unnecessarily, just in case we need the beds for something else. Are you going home now?'

'Shortly. Don't worry, I haven't forgotten the children.'

She heard his low chuckle. 'Sorry. It's hard to stop worrying. Old habits die hard.'

'Like old soldiers. Relax, Adam, it's all under control. We'll see you later.'

Anna hung up the phone, handed over the keys to Allie and left. As she drove to Jasper's nursery school, she found herself humming softly. It was just what she needed. Previously, when she'd gone off duty, the rest of the day had seemed to hang on her hands sometimes.

Now it was full, and not only full but fulfilling. She realised she was having a ball. The children were wonderful, and she was having more fun with them than she could have imagined. The boys were warm and spontaneous and cuddly, and even Skye was starting to mellow.

Life was better than it had been for years. Possibly better than ever.

'Anna, could you help me do my bedroom?' Skye asked on Wednesday after school, when Adam was still at work.

'Of course. What do you want to do?'

'Finish the walls—the paper's all half-off and I want to make it tidy and nice. Daddy's done the sitting room—it's all ready now for the wallpaper, he says, but it looks much better. I know we can't stick on the paper, but can we make it clean like that?'

'Of course,' Anna agreed, and they spent the next couple of evenings scraping damp wallpaper while the boys played around underfoot and shot each other with mock guns made of cardboard tubes.

And by Friday night, it was filled and sanded and ready for painting or papering.

'I want it all pretty cream and pink,' Skye told her. 'Daddy says it can be painted, but I want it all swirly.'

'We can do swirly with paint,' Anna said confidently, and demonstrated some ragging and sponging techniques for Skye.

'Like that,' Skye said about the colourwashing. 'In pink and cream.'

And so on Saturday afternoon, when Adam came home from the hospital, Anna was up a ladder with Skye below her on the lower part of the wall, and they were painting.

'Good grief,' he said faintly, hesitating, dumbstruck, in the doorway.

'Hi,' Anna said, brushing a strand of paint-streaked hair out of her eyes. 'I hope you don't mind—Skye asked if I could give her a hand, so we're having a go at colourwashing.'

'So I can see,' he said, bemused. 'Um, want a hand? I'll change.'

'Thanks.'

He was back in a minute or two, dressed in scruffy jeans with a rip in the knee and dribbles of paint all over them, and Anna realised he was no stranger to decorating. 'I'll start the woodwork,' he said, and, picking up a piece of discarded sandpaper, he moved in on the window.

It took the whole weekend, but by Sunday night Skye was back in her bedroom and it looked lovely.

'All you need now is a new carpet and some curtains,' Adam told her. 'You'll have to choose them next weekend—and then, I suppose, we should tackle the boys' room.'

'We', Anna thought, and wondered if that included her. She thought so, and felt warm inside.

'What about your room?' she asked as they went downstairs when the children were settled. 'Are you going to do anything with that?'

'Not yet,' he said with a weary laugh. 'Not until the sitting room and kitchen and hallway are sorted out, and the boys' room is finished, and I've refitted both bathrooms.'

'Not this week, then,' she said with a smile, and he laughed again, hugging her to his side.

'No, not this week. Thanks for helping Skye. You're a star.'

'My pleasure.'

He pushed the kitchen door shut, turned her into his arms and kissed her hungrily. 'I miss you,' he said gruffly after a long, lingering moment, resting his forehead against hers. 'We never seem to get any private time any more.'

'We could go to my house—we could ask one of the girls next door to babysit,' she suggested.

His eyes darkened, and he kissed her again. 'You're full of good ideas,' he murmured, and then they heard Skye's footsteps overhead and he straightened and moved away from her, going to the bottom of the stairs and looking up. 'Are you all right, Skye?'

Her voice drifted down from upstairs. 'Just going to the loo,' she said, and he came back and sighed.

'I'll get a babysitter,' he said with a chuckle. 'This is trashing my nerves.'

Of course, if they weren't trying to pretend that there was nothing between them, Anna thought later, there wouldn't be a problem. If the children came into the room and found them in each other's arms, it wouldn't matter. It wouldn't matter if they were married—it would be expected.

She looked at the shower cubicle in her own bathroom, and sighed. She wanted a bath. She just fancied lying down and having a long, hot soak.

Surely Adam wouldn't mind? She changed into her dressing-gown and went downstairs, washbag and towel in hand. He was just coming out of Skye's bedroom, and she asked if it was all right.

'Of course it's all right. I was just thinking the same thing. You go first, I'll follow you. I'll have your water—the tank's not that efficient and the kids have already had a bath. Give me a knock when you've finished.'

Anna nodded and went into the bathroom, filled the bath with steaming water and soaked for as long as she felt was fair. It felt wonderful, but Adam was waiting, and after all it was his bath. She washed quickly, dried herself, wound her hair into a turban and went along to his room, tapping softly on the door.

He opened it instantly and came out, a tender smile on his face. 'You're all wet,' he murmured, and brushed a little trickle away from her throat with his thumb. It dragged slightly against her skin, astonishingly erotic, and he bent his head and took her mouth in a searing, mind-blowing kiss that left her shaken to her foundations.

'Dear God, I want you,' he said unsteadily, and his eyes seemed to scorch her already heated skin. They tracked to the neck of her dressing-gown, which had fallen open to reveal the soft swell of her breasts, and his lids grew heavy with desire. 'I'll come to you later,' he promised in a charged undertone. 'After midnight, when the children are really asleep.'

'OK.' She backed away, her eyes locked with his, then turned and ran lightly up the stairs to her room, need pouring through her. The waiting was agonising. It was hours before she heard his footsteps on her landing, and then he slid into bed beside her, his body hot and taut and needy.

There were no preliminaries. They weren't necessary. She reached for him and took him in her arms, and he moved over her and entered her with one swift, desperate thrust. She wrapped her arms around him tighter, clinging to him as he drove them both over the brink.

'I love you,' he said rawly, as if the words were torn from him without permission, and then his body shuddered against hers, and his arms tightened convulsively as if he were trying to hold her close against him for ever.

The tears she'd held in check spilled over, and she laid a tender, fervent kiss against his stubbled cheek. 'I love you,' she whispered, and his mouth found hers in a kiss that seemed full of desperation.

He said her name almost soundlessly, reverently, and then, with one last, lingering kiss, he left her.

Anna lay without moving, her emotions raw. What had happened? Something was different, some element of desperation and despair. A terrible foreboding filled her, a deep fear that something had changed or was about to change, and that she was going to lose Adam.

You're getting paranoid, she told herself crossly. Nothing's changed.

And yet, if that was so, why had their emotions been so intense—and why, when he'd said her name, had it sounded like a prayer?

CHAPTER TEN

ANNA wasn't wrong. Something *had* changed. After that night Adam didn't come to her again, neither did he take up her suggestion that they should get a babysitter and take some time out at her house.

In itself that didn't matter. She didn't miss their love-making so much as the closeness it brought, and that was missing in other parts of their lives as well.

Gone were the fleeting touches, the stolen kisses in the pantry, the little pats on the bottom as she passed him on the landing. Instead, she caught the occasional brooding look, and sometimes she surprised a look of sadness in his eyes.

He's going to end it, she thought. He's just waiting until the new au pair comes, and he's going to end it.

She felt sick at the thought, and so she buried herself in her work, helped the children with their homework, started on the decorating in the boys' room and fell into bed exhausted each night.

Adam was out later and later, going back to the hospital at every opportunity, and even Danny noticed it.

'Why is Daddy so busy?' he asked on Thursday evening. He was pushing pasta shapes around his plate, and Anna looked at him closely.

Poor little love, she thought. They're all so fragile, so emotionally vulnerable. Every last little nuance of

Adam's moods affected them, and they were leaning on her more and more for support.

That was fine—unless Adam *did* intend to end their relationship, in which case how would they cope?

She vowed to take it up with him that night, to tackle him about it and ask him if that was what he intended. She had to know. The waiting was killing her.

And then the phone rang, and the woman from the au pair agency asked to speak to him.

'I'm sorry, he's at work. Can I take a message?'

'Oh, if you would,' the woman said, sounding relieved. 'It's just that the au pair we promised him has broken her leg, skiing, and she won't be able to come for at least six weeks, and I don't have another replacement, not at this time of the year. I'm so sorry. Could you ask him to come back to me if he wants to discuss it further?'

'Sure,' Anna agreed, and cradled the phone.

'Who was it?' Skye asked.

'The au pair agency. Your new au pair's broken her leg and she can't come on Sunday.'

'Yippee!' Danny yelled, leaping up from the table and sending his pasta shapes flying. 'We get to keep you!'

He threw himself at Anna, and she caught him, hugging him automatically.

'We'll see,' she said cautiously. 'I'll have to talk to your father about it.'

'Talk to his father about what?' Adam said from behind her.

'The au pair's not coming, Anna said so, and she's going to stay instead,' Danny said, totally altering the slant on it.

She met Adam's steely eyes frankly. 'It wasn't quite like that,' she began, but he cut her off.

'Really? Perhaps you'd care to explain how it was, then. Children, up to bed, please.'

'But we haven't had pudding!' Jasper said indignantly.

'Take a yoghurt up with you. I want to talk to Anna.'

They trailed off, and she turned to face him, her anger boiling out of control. 'What the hell was all that about?' she demanded in a furious undertone.

'I might ask you the same thing. I come in and my son tells me you've cancelled the au pair and you're staying on in her place—'

'She's broken her leg.'

'So we'll have a different one.'

'There isn't one.'

'How convenient.'

She stepped back, shocked. 'You really think I'd do that? Cancel your au pair and tell the children I'm staying, without discussing it with you?' She wheeled round, too angry with him to stand there, and he came after her, grabbing her arm and turning her to face him.

'Anna, stop. What are you doing?'

'Packing,' she said crisply. 'Let go of my arm.'

'No. You can't go.'

'Watch me.'

'Dammit, talk to me!'

'Why? So you can misinterpret everything I say? Go to hell, Adam.'

He released her. 'You're too late,' he said softly. 'I'm already there.' He turned away. 'For what it's worth, I'm sorry. I didn't mean to jump down your throat. It's just that I'm finding this situation between us more and more difficult, and I was looking forward to getting back to normal.'

Without me, she thought, and her heart nearly stalled.

'We need to talk about this,' she said, but his bleeper went, and moments later he left the house, looking relieved.

Saved by the bell, she thought bitterly, and then the children crept down the stairs, looking ashen.

'Is he angry with us?' Skye asked tensely.

'No, darlings, of course he's not. He's just disappointed that the au pair can't come.'

'He didn't sound dis'pointed,' Danny commented with characteristic bluntness. 'He sounded cross.'

'He's tired,' Anna said, making excuses for him when actually she wanted to string him up and hang him out to dry. 'He'll be all right later. He's working very hard.'

She gave them their pudding, bathed them and put them to bed, then cleared up the kitchen. She'd cooked for herself and Adam, but she had no idea what time he'd be home and, anyway, she wasn't hungry.

She watched television in the sitting room for a while, then checked the children and went up to her room, sitting in the dark and waiting for him. At ten-thirty the phone rang, and she ran down to answer it in his bedroom.

'Anna, it's me. I'm in Theatre. I've had an emergency, and it's going to take longer than I thought. Don't wait up for me, I could be hours. I'll see you tomorrow.'

In fact, he didn't make it home at all, and she took

the children in to the hospital with her at seven next morning.

'Go and find something to do in the playroom,' she told them, and went to speak to the night sister. 'Seen Adam?' she asked.

'Yes, a little while ago. He's in ICU. He's been in Theatre all night, he looks like death warmed up. I told him to go home to bed, but he says he can't. He's got a fracture clinic.'

'Thanks,' she said, and went to find the children. They were happy with the toys, so she left them to it and took over the ward and started on the morning routine.

The taxi driver came as usual and took the children off. Unusually, Jasper was clingy.

'You'll have a lovely time at school,' Anna assured him comfortingly. 'And, anyway, it's Friday. It's the weekend tomorrow—we'll do something nice to-gether, all right?'

'Promise?'

'I promise,' she said fervently, and hoped that Adam did nothing to make her break it.

Adam appeared at eight-thirty for a quick ward round, and he looked awful. Her natural sympathy came to the fore, and she remembered his words the night before when she'd told him to go to hell. 'I'm already there,' he'd said, and today he looked it.

'Why don't you get your registrar to do your frac-ture clinic so you can rest?' she suggested.

'He already is. We're both doing it. He's no better than me—we were both up all night.'

'I'm sorry.'

He sighed and met her eyes, and his were red-rimmed and bloodshot. 'How are my patients?' he asked wearily.

'All right. Damian's thriving—still in a little pain but much better. Richard's moving better for the physio—I'll get the notes and come round with you, if you like.'

'I can manage,' he said. Taking the notes from her, he went and spoke to each of his patients in turn, checking the charts on the end of the beds, talking to them, making notes.

'Thanks,' he said when he'd finished, handing back the notes. 'And if you get a minute, could you contact the employment agencies and see if you can get a nanny for the evenings next week?'

'We need to talk about this,' she said firmly, but he shook his head.

'There's nothing to say. I can't go on with this. My parents are back on Monday night, they can cover some of the time—perhaps the nights. I just need someone for after school.'

'So get your secretary to ring,' Anna snapped.

'Fine, I will. I just thought you might like to do it as you know what's expected.'

'Or what's needed? They aren't quite the same thing, Adam, as you well know.'

His jaw tensed, and he turned away. 'I can't handle this. I'll see you later.'

'No, you damn well won't,' she said tightly in an undertone. 'One minute you tell me you love me, the next minute you won't talk to me and you're telling me to find a replacement au pair. What the hell is going on?'

He looked back into her eyes, and his face was

etched with lines of pain. 'Don't, Anna. Don't make it harder.'

'Make what harder? Are you telling me it's over? Because, if so, I think you might at least have the decency to do it in private!'

She spun on her heel and walked off, almost running into the treatment room and busying herself with sorting and tidying the sterile supplies. Hot tears spilled over her cheeks, and she dashed them away angrily.

She never cried! She absolutely never cried, at least not about men, and now this man seemed hell bent on tearing her heart into little pieces.

'We'll talk tonight,' he said from the doorway. 'After the children are asleep.'

'Don't force yourself,' she said, her voice clogged with tears.

'Dammit, Anna—'

'Don't ''dammit'' me,' she said, spinning round and not caring if he saw the tears welling in her eyes and dripping off her chin. 'I'm not a toy, Adam. You can't just pick me up for your amusement and then drop me because it ceases to be convenient.'

'Anna, that's not what it is.'

'What is it, then?'

He sighed and ran his hands through his hair. 'I'll talk to you tonight. I'll come home as soon as I can, OK?'

She nodded, sniffed and turned away. 'Fine.'

He went out, and the swing door swooshed shut behind him, leaving her feeling more alone than she'd ever felt in her life.

Adam felt sick. He was torn, so torn. His children needed stability. They needed something to rely on.

He couldn't let them get attached to every woman he had an affair with, and he would have to be blind not to see how attached they were to Anna.

Not that having affairs was something he did often. She was the first woman since Lyn, and the thought of touching any other woman after Anna was too painful to consider...

He pushed the thought aside and got out of the car, locking it and walking up the path with dread in his heart. He needed her, and yet he didn't see how he could juggle things so he was living two lives and doing either of them justice. He had to get her out of the house, but could they go back to how they were before? Would it be enough?

God knows. Sometimes he felt he needed her more than he needed air, or water, or sleep...

He went in and found Anna in the kitchen, sitting at the table with a cup of tea. She looked awful. She'd been crying, and her eyes were red-rimmed and swollen.

Adam felt like the worst bastard in the world, but he had no choice. He had to protect his children.

He sat down opposite her. 'Anna, I'm sorry,' he said quietly, his voice rough with emotion.

She met his eyes. 'I thought you said you loved me?' she said in a voice overflowing with tears. 'I thought you cared?'

'I do care.' He sighed heavily. 'I *do* love you.'

'Then what's this all about, Adam? I'm not trying to steal your kids' affection, or come between you, or anything like that.'

'I know. I just can't let them get too close to you, Anna.'

'Why not? They get close to the au pairs, and they leave, and they get close to teachers at school, and go on to the next class, and they make friends and then move, and have to learn to deal with it. Why am I any different? What makes me so special that I'm not allowed near them? Am I an undesirable influence or something?'

'Of course you're not,' he protested helplessly. 'Don't be silly.'

'So why? Why, Adam? I love you. You love me. How can that be wrong?'

He closed his ears to her persuasion. He couldn't let her talk him round. It was too important.

'It's not wrong,' he told her quietly. 'I just have to keep my priorities right, and that's going to hurt us both—I know that.' He swallowed hard, trying hard to shift the lump in his throat. 'You have to leave here. I can't go on like this, wanting you, loving you, knowing it's going to end.'

'So are we going back to the way we were? With you coming round whenever you can spare a minute from your hectic schedule to fit in a bit of sexual recreation?'

'That's not how it is.'

'Isn't it? Sometimes it feels like it. But I've got no choice. You know that. I can't turn you away. You need me, and I need you. I don't agree with you, but they aren't my children, so I'll respect your feelings even though I don't think you're right.

'Just do me one small favour,' Anna went on in a voice filled with pain. 'Don't pretend that what's between us is less than it is. Don't turn our love into a secretive, hole-in-the-corner affair. Keep it separate from your life with the children, by all means, but don't pretend I don't exist. I won't be treated like something you're ashamed of.'

'I'm not ashamed of you, or what we have between us,' he told her honestly. 'Do you want to know the truth? I wish I'd never met you. I was happy before, and now I want things I can't have, and I'm ruining your life. I can't give you children, or happy ever after, and you deserve all that and more. I can't give it to you, and I can't keep you hanging on in limbo— we can't go back to how we were.'

She stared at him in silence for a while, then sighed unevenly. 'So that's it, is it? It's all over? Can you just tell me why, Adam? That's all I want. I just want to know why.'

He chased a crumb around on the tabletop. 'You don't know what it was like with Lyn,' he said quietly. 'Every time she had a period, my life was hell. She cried, she ranted, she accused me of cheating her. We tried everything. Nothing worked. Then she seemed to come to terms with it. She told me she was happy to adopt, but all the time it was festering inside her, destroying her.'

He looked up into Anna's wounded eyes. 'It would destroy you, too. Maybe not at first, but eventually. The need to have a child would tear you apart—'

'No.'

'Yes. Trust me, I know. Every time I look at you I hurt because I can't give you a child. It's basic biology, Anna. Survival of the species. Continuation of the human race. It's fundamental and powerful, and unbelievably destructive—and it'll destroy you as surely as it destroyed Lyn.'

'No,' she said firmly. 'It won't, because I'm not like Lyn. I don't want to have just any child. I want to have *your* child. I want to conceive it, and carry it, and give birth to it, and raise it. And I can't. I know that. It hurts, God, yes, it hurts, but it's nothing compared to the thought of losing you.'

Adam's heart contracted at the pain in her carefully controlled voice. He wanted to stop her, to tell her it was all right—but it wasn't.

'Anyway,' she went on, quietly reasoning with him, 'you can give me a child. You can give me three—three beautiful children who I love more than I can say. And they love me, Adam, and they need me.'

'They'll get over you.'

'No. No, they won't. They need me. Skye, especially, needs me. She needs a mother, Adam, and I want to be that mother. She's so scared to love, so afraid it'll be taken away from her again. You can't take me away from her, Adam, I won't let you. She won't survive it.'

'I have to,' he said rawly. 'I can't trust anyone but myself, Anna. I know how I feel.'

'And do you know how *they* feel?' she interrupted. 'Do you know how sad and confused they've been this week while you've been out at the hospital, burying yourself in unnecessary work? They think you're angry with them, Adam.'

Guilt hit him like a sledgehammer. All week he'd been avoiding Anna, trying to distance himself from her so that the break would be less painful, and all he'd done had been to drive the children into her arms—exactly what he'd been striving to avoid.

'I'll talk to them,' he said. 'Explain.' Though God knows how I'll explain, he thought numbly.

His bleeper squawked, and he sighed raggedly and

stood up, reaching for the phone. He spoke to the hospital, then hung up.

'I'm needed in A and E—multiple trauma, child of ten. I'll be back when I can.'

He headed down the hall, grabbing his coat off the end of the banisters. Anna was behind him.

'I'll wait up,' she said. 'We need to finish this conversation.'

'It's finished,' he told her firmly. 'I'm sorry, Anna—more sorry than I can say, but I can't let it go on. I know you believe what you're saying, but I've heard it all before. It won't work. I want you out of our lives, no matter how painful it will be at first.'

'Well, I'll let you tell the children,' she said, her voice clogged with tears again, 'because I can't.'

'I'll tell them,' he said heavily. 'I'll tell them tomorrow.'

'No. Tomorrow I promised Jasper we'd do something. I can't break my promise.'

'I'm afraid you'll have to. I'm sorry. I have to go.'

He went out, closing the door softly behind him. As he got into the car, he could see Anna still standing in the hall, motionless. I'm sorry, my darling, he said silently. I'm sorry...

Anna stood there for a long time, unable to move, unable to breathe. She heard Adam's car start, then the lights swept across the front of the house as he turned and drove away.

She heard a creak on the stairs behind her and turned, her eyes dimly taking in a little figure standing halfway up, near the banister Adam hadn't yet got round to mending.

'Are you going?' Skye asked in a terrified whisper.

She nodded, swallowing hard. 'Yes. Not now, but tomorrow. I'm sorry. He's going to get another nanny for you—'

'But I want you. I love you.'

'Oh, Skye.'

The tears wouldn't be held in check, and she ran to catch the little girl as she flew down the stairs into her arms. 'Darling, I'm sorry. It's just—'

What? What was it? Nothing just. Unjust, perhaps. How could she explain a father's complex motivation to his tiny, terrified child? 'Skye, I love you, too, my darling, but sometimes things don't work out the way we want them to. But we'll still be together sometimes, I promise. You can still see me.'

'How?' Skye asked in a choked little voice.

'You can come and visit me, if your father will let you, and you can phone me and write to me, and I'll write to you, all of you, and I—I only live round the corner, Skye. When you're older you can cycle round to see me, if you still want to, and we can go shopping together and do girl stuff, OK?'

'But you won't be here to tuck me up at night, and au pairs aren't the same. You're like my mum—she used to tuck me up, and then she died, and Lyn did it, and then she went, and now you're going, too.'

'Shh, sweetheart,' Anna whispered, biting back her sobs. 'I'll still be here for you, I promise. I'm not going anywhere. I just won't be living here any more, but I won't be far away, and I'm not going to forget you—I couldn't forget you. Never. I promise.'

'I want you to stay,' Skye said, and sobbed uncontrollably. Her heart almost breaking, Anna scooped her up in her arms and carried the little girl to her room, settling her down on the bed in the crook of her arm.

'Skye, we can't always have what we want, but sometimes things work out for the best. I have a job to do, and I can't really be here all the time. But if I hadn't stayed we wouldn't have become such good friends, would we? And so it's good that I've stayed. I know you're sad I'm going, and I'm sad I'm going, but we'll still be friends. Do you understand?'

'Sort of,' Skye said with a sniff. 'I was sad when my hamster died, but Daddy said think how lucky I was that I had him and he was such a nice hamster. I suppose it's like that, really.'

'Just like that,' Anna said, aching. 'Now, why don't you get into bed and I'll read you a story—all right?'

'OK. And then you can tuck me up.'

'OK.' Anna picked up a book. 'How about this one?'

'Mmm.'

'Right. ''Once upon a time there was a big fat caterpillar...'''

'We lost him. Sorry to get you out under false pretences. He arrested before we could stabilise him.'

Adam nodded. 'OK. I'll go home. Thanks, Ryan.'

He went back out to his car and sat for a moment, dreading the coming confrontation with Anna.

She wasn't going to back down without another fight, he was sure, and every word she spoke was like an arrow in his heart. It all made so much sense, if only he could dare to trust her—dare to believe in her.

'Oh, damn,' he muttered, and turned the key, starting the engine. He had to get it over with, no matter how painful. He had to let her move on, give her a chance.

She'd find love with someone else—someone who could give her the child he knew she needed.

'Hell.' He pulled over and blinked hard, pressing his fist to his mouth. This was going to be so hard to do, but he had to do it for her sake.

He dragged in a deep breath, looked over his shoulder and pulled out into the light evening traffic. He wondered if she'd still be standing there in the hall. He half expected to find her there when he came in, but she wasn't.

He closed the door softly and leant back against it, steadying himself. Give me strength, he prayed silently. Help me do the right thing.

He could hear her voice coming from upstairs, and he kicked off his shoes, stripped off his tie and hung his jacket over the banisters, then walked quietly up the stairs. He'd wait for her. She was with Skye, reading a story, and he sat on the top step and listened to her voice. It was enough to send him to sleep. He was so tired—so tired and sad and full of despair. How would they cope without her?

'"And the caterpillar had turned into a beautiful butterfly." There. Isn't that nice?'

'Thank you.'

'My pleasure, darling.'

'Tuck me up.'

'OK. There. All right now?'

'You will see me?'

See her? Adam's brows pleated in a puzzled frown.

'Of course I'll see you. I promised you, Skye.'

'And you'll write to me?'

Oh, lord. Skye knew. How? Had she overheard?

He listened, agonised, to the rest of the painful exchange.

'Yes, I'll write to you, if Daddy will let me, and you can phone me any time you like, all right? I'll always be there for you, Skye, I promise.'

'I love you, Anna.'

'Oh, Skye, I love you, too, darling. Come on, don't cry any more. It'll be all right. Your new nanny will be nice, and your granny and grandpa will be back soon and you can see them.'

'And you'll see me?'

'Yes. I will see you. I promise. Now, go to sleep, darling, or you'll be too tired tomorrow.'

Tears choked Adam. Slowly, soundlessly, he stood and turned towards Skye's door, just in time to see Anna emerge.

She walked through the door, wrapped her arms around her waist and sagged against the wall, tears streaming down her cheeks.

He was a fool—a stupid, deluded fool. Anna was nothing like Lyn. Lyn had never cried for anyone except herself. Anna was breaking her heart because a little girl loved her, and he was tearing them apart. Tearing them all apart, because he was afraid to trust her, to believe in her, to give them all a chance.

'Anna?'

She looked up, her eyes stricken, and he held out his hand.

'Come—talk to me.'

She came, but she didn't take his hand. She kept her arms wrapped round her body, holding herself together as she followed him down the stairs to the sitting room.

He closed the door firmly behind them and turned to her.

'I'm sorry, I was wrong,' he said unevenly. 'I should have trusted you to know your own feelings. I should have had more faith in you. Just now, hearing you talk to Skye—you're right. She loves you, she needs you, and I think you need her, too. And as sure as God made little green apples, I need you, my love.'

'So what happens now?' Anna said, her voice raw with unshed tears. 'Do I stay as the nanny, or do I go back to being the mistress, or what, Adam?'

'Neither. I swore I'd never marry again, but...I love you. You mean more to me than I can begin to understand. You're my life.'

'You say that, but you were going to send me away, Adam,' she said with her usual logic. 'How can I believe you? What if you change your mind again?'

'I won't,' he promised. 'I was only doing it for the children. I thought it was the right thing to do, and I was wrong. I don't even know if in the end I would have been strong enough to let you go.'

He searched her eyes for any sign of forgiveness, but they were expressionless, shimmering with tears. He forced himself to go on. 'I love you. I need you in my life. Marry me, Anna—please? Be my wife. Be their mother. I know I can't give you the child you want, and that will haunt me to the end of my days, but I can give you more love than you'll ever know what to do with. Please?'

He closed his eyes, unable to bear the suspense, and he felt the soft touch of her hand against his face, brushing away the tears. 'Oh, Adam,' she said gently. 'Of course I'll marry you. I love you. I love you all.'

Adam's arms wrapped round her, crushing her

against his chest, and a ragged sob rose in his throat. 'I thought I'd lost you. I thought I'd said too much— that you couldn't forgive me.'

'There was nothing to forgive. You did it all for love.' She tipped her head back and looked up at him, and he brushed the tears from her cheeks with gentle fingers.

'I can't believe I've found you. I've been waiting for you all my life, and I didn't dare to believe in you. I'm such a fool.'

'No, you're just wary,' she said gently. 'It'll be all right, Adam. You'll see. It'll be all right because we've got each other, and that's all that matters. Just dare to believe, my darling. It's all there, waiting for you. You just have to believe in it.'

He took her mouth in a tender, reverent kiss. Sweet relief coursed through him, leaving him trembling in her arms.

And then a little voice behind whispered, 'So are you going to stay?'

Anna turned, and Adam saw Skye standing in the doorway, her eyes filled with a hope she didn't dare trust. Adam knew exactly how she felt.

'Yes,' he said firmly. 'Yes, she's going to stay. She's going to stay for ever.'

He reached out his arms, and gathered Skye and Anna into his embrace. This was real. This was love. This, he could believe in...

Have Your Say

**You've just finished your book.
So what did you think?**

We'd love to hear your thoughts on our
'Have your say' online panel
www.millsandboon.co.uk/haveyoursay

- Easy to use
- Short questionnaire
- Chance to win Mills & Boon® goodies

*Visit us
Online*
Tell us what you thought of this book now at
www.millsandboon.co.uk/haveyoursay

YOUR_SAY

&
What will you treat yourself to next?

& HISTORICAL
Ignite your imagination,
step into the past…
6 new stories every month

INTRIGUE…
Breathtaking romantic suspense
Up to 8 new stories every month

Medical Romance™
Captivating medical drama –
with heart
6 new stories every month

MODERN™
International affairs,
seduction & passion guaranteed
9 new stories every month

n o c t u r n e™
Deliciously wicked
paranormal romance
Up to 4 new stories every month

RIVA™
Live life to the full –
give in to temptation
3 new stories every month available
exclusively via our Book Club

You can also buy Mills & Boon eBooks at
www.millsandboon.co.uk
Visit us Online
M&B/WORLD2

Mills & Boon® Online

Discover more romance at
www.millsandboon.co.uk

- **FREE** online reads
- **Books** up to one month before shops
- **Browse our books** before you buy

...and much more!

For exclusive competitions and instant updates:

Like us on **facebook.com/millsandboon**

Follow us on **twitter.com/millsandboon**

Join us on **community.millsandboon.co.uk**

Visit us Online
Sign up for our FREE eNewsletter at
www.millsandboon.co.uk

WEB/M&B/RTL5